A HEART DIVIDED

BATTLES OF DESTINY

A HEART DIVIDED

AL LACY

A HEART DIVIDED

© 1993 by Lew A. Lacy

published by Multnomah Books
a part of the Questar publishing family

Edited by Rodney L. Morris
Cover design by David Uttley
Cover illustration by Phil Boatwright

International Standard Book Number: 0-88070-591-4

Printed in the United States of America.

For information:
Questar Publishers, Inc.
Post Office Box 1720
Sisters, Oregon 97759

93 94 95 96 97 98 99 00 01 02 — 10 9 8 7 6 5 4 3 2 1

To my beloved parents, Charlie and Patty O'Brien Lacy:

It was you, Pop, who first put a Western book in my hands...Zane Grey's *Wildfire*. In my formative years, you encouraged me to read and appreciate good literature about the Old West. This developed as you hoped it would. I soon learned to love and value America's heritage, and eventually began to write Western and historical novels.

And precious Mama...thank you for believing in me, and for the unfailing love and encouragement you showed me over the years. You have a vital part, too, in every novel I write. When at the beginning I faced the seeming insurmountable challenge of producing great numbers of books, it was your sage words that impelled me to take on the task. You've told people many times, "From a very small child, Al always was good at making up stories!"

PREFACE

★

While studying American history in high school I was struck with a strange fascination for the Civil War. That fascination grew stronger when I studied it again in college, especially since the bulk of my college education was obtained in southeastern Tennessee, where Southerners old and young are still fighting the Civil War (at least in conversation).

Known also as the War of the Sixties, the Great Rebellion, the War Between the States, the War for the Union, Mr. Lincoln's War, the War for Separation, the Second War of Independence, the Lost Cause, the Last Gentlemen's War, the War against Slavery, the Yankees' Invasion, the War for Abolition, the War of Secession, the War of Southern Planters, the War against Northern Aggression, the Confederate War, the Union War, the War for Southern Freedom, the War of the North and South, and the Brothers' War, the compelling four-year conflict has continued to enthrall me until at last I have become a full-fledged Civil War buff.

My personal library is quite extensive, and among literally hundreds of volumes are dozens of books on the Civil War. My enchantment with this dynamic period in American history has lured me to many of the sites where the battles took place.

I have stood on the long rampart of Lookout Mountain at Chattanooga, which overlooks the site where the Army of the Cumberland clashed in a bloody battle with the Army of the Tennessee on Chicamauga Creek. My feet have carried me across the grounds of Fort Oglethorpe, Georgia, where the early morning dew still rests on the rusty old cannons and the pyramids of cannonballs that stand beside them.

I have often been in the Rich Mountain area of West Virginia, and have explored the meadows and forests that make up the battle-fields of Gettysburg, Chancellorsville, and Fredericksburg. I have walked the narrow streets of Harper's Ferry where troop and supply trains met along the Potomac River—a strategic town that once held a Union arsenal—and I have stood on the very ground at Winchester, Virginia, where General Stonewall Jackson launched his campaign across the Shenandoah Valley. I have watched the vagrant winds toy with the tall grass on the slopes of the Bull Run battlefield, and I have seen sunlight dance on the surface of Antietam Creek, on whose banks was fought the bloodiest one-day battle of the war.

One of my most exciting moments was when I stood on the porch of the restored Wilmer McLean house in Appomattox Court House, Virginia, and viewed the very room where on Sunday, April 9, 1865, General Robert E. Lee signed the documents of surrender before General Ulysses S. Grant, bringing the bloody conflict to an end.

Not all historians agree on every detail of the war. I have long been a subscriber to the *Civil War Times Illustrated* magazine. In almost every issue, there are letters to the editor that take exception to a story or article in a previous issue. Some readers are unhappy that a writer has made a "mistake" on a date, military leader, type of weapons used in a particular battle, number of men killed in a certain battle, and so on. In researching some of these complaints, I have found that both the writer and the person sending the letter have solid basis for their arguments.

The same thing could happen in this series on Battles of Destiny, so I ask for some tolerance from my readers. I will do my best to be accurate on all historical points, but if you find a discrepancy, please save yourself the price of a postage stamp and understand that these things happen. I remind you that the books in this series are *novels* based on history, not historical textbooks.

The series is written for the simple pleasure and enjoyment of my readers. If the stories thrill you, excite you, stir your emotions, and give you a better appreciation for America's great heritage, my extensive research, diligent probing of my imagination, and long hours at the word processor will be worth it.

PROLOGUE

✦

When the first Confederate shell arched through the predawn sky and exploded behind the walls of Fort Sumter on April 12, 1861, it touched off one of the greatest points of crisis in the history of America. Not only did the War Between the States quickly develop into a bloody conflict between two societies with opposite views on slavery, but it moved inexorably toward something almost unthinkable—a tragic clash between families. Brothers fighting brothers, even fathers fighting sons.

In the century between the end of the Napoleonic Wars and the commencement of World War I, the most catastrophic military conflict fought anywhere was the American Civil War. Some historians have alluded to the Civil War as a combination of "The Last Medieval War and the First Modern War." I agree. As the first modern war, it ominously foreshadowed the horrors of warfare that have followed in the twentieth century.

The Civil War introduced trench warfare, propaganda, warfare of psychological attrition, aerial observation, naval blockade, economic warfare, iron-clad ships, and the Gatling gun, as well as the horrible impeding influence of filthy, disease-ridden, prisoner-of-war camps.

Compulsory enlistment for military service was also put into use for the first time in American history during the four-year war between the North and the South. Both sides began using conscription when the War was two years old. Prior to that, and even after conscription was adopted, both armies had problems with teenage boys lying about their age in order to get in the fight. Both the North and the South had set the youngest age limit at eighteen, but often the deceitful youths were accepted because they looked to be old enough.

The Civil War brought about many other firsts. It was the first war to have photographers taking pictures on the battlefield. It was the first war to employ repeating rifles, and to use railroad artillery, naval torpedoes, flame throwers, land mines, electrically exploded bombs, telescopic sights for rifles, fixed ammunition, the wigwag signal code, and periscopes for fighting in the trenches. During the Civil War, the bugle call, "Taps" was first played, the first naval camouflage was invented, and the Congressional Medal of Honor was first introduced.

With all of its firsts in modern warfare and the hatred that raged between the North and the South, the Civil War cost more American lives in the four years from Sumter to Appomattox than the two World Wars, Korea, Vietnam, and Desert Storm *combined.* The carnage that took place between April 1861 and April 1865 was appalling. Of the three million men who saw action afloat and ashore—Union and Confederate—more than a million were casualties. Well over 600,000 lost their lives as a direct result of battlefield combat (including those who were wounded, then died of infections and various diseases contracted because of their wounds). Another 400,000 were wounded, but lived to tell of the horrors of the war. Many of them were blinded, and a great number lost limbs. Some could not tell of the war's horror because they lost their minds.

This virtual caldron of blood was spread wider than the casual follower of the Civil War realizes. According to government authorities, there were some 95 major battles, 310 minor battles, and over 6,000 skirmishes, some of which the soldiers themselves called "squabbles" or "dust-ups." If a man died in a "dust-up" he was just as dead as if he had been killed in a major battle. The bulk of the fighting took place on Southern land. However, a few battles were fought on Union soil, including two of the bloodiest—Gettysburg and Antietam. Blood was shed in land-fighting as far north as Vermont, and as far west as the Pacific coast. California saw 6 skirmishes, Oregon 4, and 19 occurred in New Mexico Territory. There were other skirmishes in the territories of Washington, Utah, and Idaho.

The fighting in Vermont was a result of Confederate raiders striking the town of St. Albans. Other Rebel raiders shed blood in Illinois, Minnesota, and New York. The southernmost fighting happened between Union and Confederate forces on a blood-soaked sandy beach in Florida known today as Cape Canaveral.

The story I am about to tell you begins on the Gulf of Mexico, just off the Florida coast at Pensacola, some six hundred miles northwest of that beach. Before we get into the story, it is important that I point out a few things about the naval part of the Civil War.

At the very beginning of the War—only days after the Union flag was lowered in surrender at Fort Sumter—President Abraham Lincoln formally ordered a blockade of the entire coast of the Confederacy, from Chesapeake Bay, whose waters lapped the shoreline of Virginia, all the way to the southernmost tip of Texas. Lincoln knew that if the North was going to win the War, it had to take control of a dozen major ports and some two hundred minor ports and inlets.

The reason was two-fold. If the Union could block the ports and inlets, it could prevent the Confederacy from receiving supplies, weapons, and ammunition from foreign sympathizers. On the other hand, by seizing the ports and inlets, the Federals would be able to float in their own troops, weapons, ammunition, supplies, mules, and horses that were necessary to conquer the Confederacy.

Lincoln's call for a Union blockade of the entire Confederate coast was a tall order. At the beginning of the War, the Federal government possessed some ninety warships, but fifty of these were sailing vessels that had been used a generation before, and were now obsolete. Of the forty steam-driven ships, half were docked at foreign harbors, and it would take time to get them back into home waters.

Ready for immediate service were five steam frigates, five first-class screw sloops, four flat-bedded steam-driven barges, a half-dozen tugboats, and a few small assorted harbor craft. With this small navy, the Federals were commanded by President Lincoln to blockade and control over thirty-five hundred miles of Confederate coast line. They had, also, to control such rivers as the Mississippi and the Tennessee, not to mention the extensive sounds along the Atlantic coast.

When the War began, the South had no navy at all. Realizing that their long coast line was vulnerable, they began improvising immediately, but they faced a gigantic handicap. Their supply source was very limited.

As the War progressed and the rival armies fought back and forth on land, the balance of power was slowly but steadily tilting in favor of the North. On the Atlantic Ocean, in the Gulf of Mexico, in the coastal sounds, and up and down the inland rivers, the Union's growing naval power was making itself felt.

In the minds of the Federals, there were three ports on the Gulf Coast that must be conquered first: New Orleans (the Confederacy's largest city) Pensacola and Mobile. These cities were railroad ports. Once they were in Union hands, the Yankees would concentrate on capturing the railroads so they could float their barges from the North, around Florida's southern tip into the Gulf of Mexico, and dock them at each of the three cities. The railroad would provide the best means of transporting reinforcements, weapons, ammunition, supplies, mules, and horses inland.

In December 1861, the Union navy was rapidly bolstering its strength with both men and ships. At that time, the U.S. Navy Department in Washington appointed veteran Rear Admiral David G. Farragut as Flag Officer of the newly formed Western Gulf Blockading Squadron. By spring, the squadron had a sufficient amount of gun boats to begin their assault and blockade.

Aboard the flagship *Hartford*, Farragut led his strong fleet into the mouth of the Mississippi River and opened a prolonged bombardment of Forts Jackson and St. Philip, which guarded the approach to New Orleans. The mortar boats blasted the forts for a week, then in the predawn darkness on April 24, 1862, Farragut's ships went steaming up the river toward New Orleans. The commanders of both forts had run up white flags.

By the end of the day on April 25, New Orleans had surrendered, and was taken over by Union troops. Control of the mouth of the mighty Mississippi was now in Federal hands.

Admiral Farragut's fleet had sustained some damage in taking New Orleans, and found it necessary to lay up in dock while repairs were made. Early in May, the *Hartford* led the fleet into the Gulf of Mexico and steamed eastward toward Pensacola.

Just off the Pensacola coast was Fort Pickens, a Confederate stronghold. The troops who manned the fort fought hard, but were no match for Farragut's gun boats. On May 10, Fort Pickens and the city of Pensacola surrendered to Farragut and his men. Quickly, Union troops were brought in under the command of Major General Frederick Steele. While occupying the fort and the city, Steele's forces also went to work to capture the railroad.

With the fall of New Orleans and the conquest of Pensacola— along with several more minor ports—Mobile Bay assumed a position of primary importance to the Confederacy. It was the only large inlet still under Southern control.

Fully aware of that, Admiral Farragut set his sights to bowl his fleet through the mouth of the bay and attack Mobile as soon as he could muster more gun boats. The attack was delayed, however, because Farragut and his squadron were held to Mississippi River duty by the demands of the Vicksburg, Mississippi, and Port Hudson, Louisiana, campaigns. After the successful capture of Port Hudson in July of 1863, the sixty-two-year-old Farragut was physically worn out. He left his command and sailed to New York for a rest.

The U.S. Navy Department was reluctant to make an attempt at entering Mobile Bay without Farragut's leadership. They let him rest until January of 1864, then ordered him back to the Gulf with orders to move on Mobile and capture it. Upon returning to his post and studying the situation, Farragut told the Navy Department he could not capture and occupy Mobile without the aid and support of land forces. Such a campaign would take time to prepare.

Navy Department officials contacted the Senate Military Committee, asking for army help in setting up and carrying out the Mobile campaign. The Committee, by permission of President Lincoln, ordered Major General E.R.S. Canby, commander of the Military Division of West Mississippi, to provide the land forces Admiral Farragut needed.

Despite constant drains on his manpower from the Virginia theater, Canby managed to make fifty-five hundred men available for the task. They were the Union Army of the Cumberland's Fourth Corps, under the command of Major General Gordon Granger.

Farragut and Granger met aboard the *Hartford* off the coast of Louisiana in mid-February and made their plans. Mobile Bay was guarded at its mouth by two bastions of strength: Fort Morgan, a pentagonal work on the western tip of Mobile Point, and Fort Gaines on the east side of the two thousand-yard-wide channel at the entrance to the bay on Dauphine Island.

The plan was for a simultaneous attack on the forts by land and naval forces. Granger's men would move in from the Gulf on small rafts and "hit the beach" at Dauphine Island. They were to capture Fort Gaines while Farragut's navy pounded the stronger Fort Morgan with their big guns. Once the forts were out of commission, the admiral's fleet would steam up the thirty-mile length of Mobile Bay to the city.

Granger and his men would follow, and be there to help Farragut capture Mobile. When it was done, the last major Confederate port would be in Union hands. The time of the attack was set for daybreak on August 5. Both men agreed that it would take that long to be fully prepared for the battle.

In the meantime, through Confederate spies, word was sent to Major General Dabney H. Maury, commander of Rebel forces at Montgomery, Alabama, that three large, flat-topped, steam-driven Union barges had left a New Jersey harbor on May 30, on their way south. Their destination was Pensacola. The Yankees now had control of the railroad from Pensacola north, some fifty miles. This put them ten miles into Alabama, just south of the town of Brewton.

The Union barges were laden with fifty army mules and a hundred cavalry horses to replace those that had been killed in inland battles further north in Alabama. The plan was to put the animals ashore at Pensacola, place them in railroad cars built for hauling stock, and take them the fifty miles into Alabama. From there, they would herd them to Union strongholds farther upstate.

The barges had been seen rounding the southern tip of Florida on June 11, and according to Confederate intelligence were due to dock at Pensacola before sunrise on June 17. Determined to keep the much-needed Union animals from being put ashore, General Maury sent the ninety-four men of B Company, First Alabama Battalion Sharpshooters to thwart the landing.

CHAPTER ONE

⋆

The full moon was clear-edged and pure against the deep blackness of the night. Its silver beams danced on the rippling surface of the Gulf of Mexico.

Captain Ryan McGraw and his ninety-three men of B Company, First Alabama Battalion Sharpshooters, were huddled on the beach a hundred and fifty yards east of the Pensacola inlet where Fort Pickens stood in silent repose. It galled McGraw and his men that the Confederate fort was in the hands of Major General Frederick Steele and some two hundred Yankee soldiers.

Careful to keep themselves in the deep shadows of the towering palm trees that clustered heavily along the beach, the Sharpshooters watched two sentries patrolling atop the fort's wall. McGraw was studying the clouds being driven by gentle winds from the west. He hoped more clouds would come. The task he and his men faced would be much less dangerous if the moon's brilliance was subdued.

"All right, men," McGraw said in a low voice, "it's midnight. We'll let those clouds cover the moon, then put the plan into action. We've got to have the rafts in position before those barges show up."

Every man knew his job. Captain McGraw would take twenty men who would belly down on three makeshift rafts and paddle their way out into the gulf at a southeasterly angle until they were far enough south to observe the trio of Yankee barges coming up from Florida's southern tip. The plan was for each raft bearing seven Sharpshooters to slip quietly up behind the barges. There were reportedly five crewman on each barge.

McGraw figured the rafts should be able to get close enough to gun down the crewmen before they were spotted. Once the Yankees were disposed of, the Sharpshooters would board the barges, turn them due south, secure the rudders to hold that direction, and give them full steam. They would move back onto the rafts and head for a designated spot on shore.

Docked at the wharf some fifty yards from the fort were five boats that would easily hold twenty men apiece. As soon as McGraw and his raft team had shoved off, ten Sharpshooters were to move stealthily to the wharf, loose the boats, and row them as fast as possible to where the others waited in the shadows of the palm trees on the beach. They would all climb in the boats and row up the shoreline to pick up the raft crews and make their escape east along the beach. Once they could get safely back on land, they would beeline for Montgomery.

If the Yankee sentries on the fort walls spotted the ten Rebels who were after the boats, the rest of them were to open fire and give them cover. Once the boats were gone, General Steele and his men would have no way to go after the barges. They would hear the gunfire out on the gulf when McGraw and his men took out the crewmen, but they would be helpless to do anything about it.

None of the men in McGraw's outfit liked the idea of leaving the helpless horses and mules adrift in the broad gulf, but there was no choice. If the Union army in Alabama received the animals, more Rebel soldiers would die. It made the distasteful task easier when they realized it was better to sacrifice Union animals than Confederate men.

Knowing they had a full moon to deal with, Captain McGraw and his men had replaced their gray uniforms with dark clothing.

They had also plastered their faces and the backs of their necks with mud.

Captain Ryan McGraw had placed his right-hand man and best friend, Lieutenant Judd Rawlings, in charge of the men who would stay ashore. Rawlings was twenty-three years of age, and like the rest of the Sharpshooters, well-seasoned in battle after nearly three years of fighting Yankees. He stood six feet in height on a lanky frame, but was wiry and tough. He had dark-brown hair with a handlebar mustache to match. Born and raised in Tupelo, Mississippi, he spoke slowly with a heavy drawl.

Among those men with McGraw were Sergeants Hap Hazzard and Noah Cloud. Hazzard was twenty-four, stood six-feet-one, and weighed a solid two hundred and thirty pounds. He had carrot-red hair and the temper to go with it, yet the big, tough, iron-jawed Rebel from Huntsville, Alabama, was the clown of B Company's Sharpshooters. Cloud was twenty-three, exactly the same height as Hazzard, and outweighed him a mere seven pounds. From Soddy Daisy, Tennessee, he was tough and fearless, always loving a good fight. He and Hap had become close friends, though a stranger would not believe it, for they often argued heatedly and sometimes settled their arguments with fisticuffs.

Captain Ryan McGraw, leader of the now-famous B Company Sharpshooters, was twenty-eight years old, aggressive, resourceful, and tough as pig-iron. He stood six-feet-three inches in height on a muscular frame of two hundred and ten pounds. He had thick, sand-colored hair, with medium-length sideburns, a heavy but neatly trimmed mustache, and pale-blue eyes.

As a private in the First Alabama Battalion late in 1861, McGraw had been chosen by General Dabney Maury to form the Sharpshooters unit because he had proven himself a capable fighter who could readily teach others. Upon receiving the assignment, he had been promoted to sergeant. Growing up in Hattiesburg, Mississippi, he had learned the use of both musket and revolver at the hands of his father. He could "shoot the eye out of a squirrel" with either weapon.

Ryan's father, Thomas McGraw, was a land developer in Hattiesburg, and had become quite wealthy. From the time Ryan was a mere lad, the family had a Japanese gardener, who over the years taught Ryan martial arts. By the time he was in his late teens, he was an expert and could kill a man with his bare hands if forced to do so.

By the spring of 1862, McGraw had developed his unit into a crack outfit of fighters, and had proven himself invaluable to the Confederate cause. He was promoted to lieutenant in May of that year. After leading his men in many battles and skirmishes for the next four months, and distinguishing himself under enemy fire, he was promoted to captain by a direct order from General Robert E. Lee. Known best as "McGraw's Sharpshooters," the unit had become an infamous thorn in the flesh for the North.

Each man in McGraw's Sharpshooters was highly skilled with rifle and revolver. He was also deadly in hand-to-hand combat, having been instructed in martial arts by his leader. McGraw had trained them well and whipped them into the Confederate army's toughest fighting unit. They were a close-knit, roughneck, battle-hungry bunch.

Periodically, as men in the unit were killed in battle or wounded too severely to remain in uniform, McGraw was given new recruits to train and toughen up. If a man did not immediately submit to the captain's hard discipline, he was mustered out of the unit. There was no room for men who did not fit in. They must function smoothly as a unit. Any man who rebelled against McGraw's leadership was looked upon as if he were as much an enemy as a blue-bellied Yankee.

McGraw possessed that rare ability, not learned from books, to control those fiery, turbulent spirits, and to attach them to himself with unbreakable cords. In him they recognized not only the courageous, able leader, but also the commanding officer who would not hesitate to correct a man who made a mistake, or to lay his life down for that man if called on to do it.

Captain McGraw understood the men under his command—their strong points, their weak points, and the limits of their capabilities. Though he expected his men to fight with courage and valor, he never asked a man to do more than he was able. Neither would McGraw ever ask a man to do something he would not do himself, nor would he ever expect a man to risk his life in a situation that McGraw himself would avoid. The tough leader of B Company Sharpshooters was a practical man of action, with a dauntless, fiery soul and a heart that put his men first and himself last whether in combat or out of it. He was also a God-fearing man who was not ashamed to be known as a Bible reader and a man of prayer.

When the clouds overhead had fully covered the moon, McGraw led his twenty men into the cool waters of the gulf, carrying the rafts. In the bleak stillness of the silver night, a solitary gull wailed a haunted cry from somewhere in the shadows of the palm trees.

When the men were thigh-deep in the water, they crawled onto the flat wooden surfaces of the crude vessels and began rowing southeast. Each man was equipped with two holstered six-shot .44 caliber Colt Dragoon revolvers, a long-bladed knife sheathed on his belt, and a .44 caliber Henry repeating rifle, holding sixteen cartridges.

The rapid-firing rifles were first produced in 1862 by Benjamin T. Henry and sold only to the Union. In early 1863, however, the Confederates in Virginia had managed to capture a Federal supply train. In one of the cars was a load of Henrys, along with plenty of ammunition. General Dabney Maury was able to secure enough of them to amply supply McGraw's Sharpshooters.

While the rafts moved swiftly over the relatively calm gulf waters, McGraw glanced skyward. The clouds that covered the moon would soon drift away, but there was a huge bank of them rolling in from the west.

The captain's raft was between the other two, which were no more than six feet away. Speaking to the entire team, he said, "We'll be back in full moonlight in a few minutes, men, but it looks like we've got good cover on the way."

On shore, Lieutenant Judd Rawlings gathered nine men with him, each armed like the men on the rafts. Reminding those who remained beneath the palm trees to keep an eye on the sentries, he led the nine toward the wharf, keeping to the shadows as much as possible. Rawlings was glad for the cloud cover.

Reaching the edge of the trees where they would have to scurry to the wharf in the open, Rawlings halted his men and looked toward the sky. Estimating that they would have seven or eight minutes before the moon was exposed again, he eyed the vague silhouettes of the two sentries on the wall and whispered, "Okay, men. Keep low and run like rabbits!"

Within a minute, the lieutenant and his men were flattened in the boats. There was no commotion on the fort walls. They sighed with relief, knowing the sentries had not seen them. Releasing the boats from the dock, the Sharpshooters rowed them stealthily away from the shore. They were halfway to their comrades who waited beneath the palm trees when the moon shone down in full strength. Looking back at the fort walls, they expected to hear shouting and gun shots, but all was still. At the moment, no sentries were even in sight.

The huge cloud bank was nearing the moon as Captain McGraw and his raft team bobbed quietly on the gulf. It was nearly 2:00 A.M. It appeared that the moon would be covered for the rest of the night.

McGraw had placed Hazzard and Cloud on the other two rafts as leaders. Sitting next to the captain was Private Curt Dobbs, who was looking back across the three miles of water toward the shore. In the brilliant moonlight, he could see the five boats moving slowly eastward a few yards off the beach.

"Captain," said Dobbs, "I wonder if them Yankee sentries are asleep. You'd think they'd have seen Lieutenant Rawlings and the others."

Before McGraw could reply, Hap Hazzard's deep bass voice inserted, "It ain't that the Yankees are asleep, Curt. It's just that

Rawlings and those boys are good at what they do. When you've been trained by our illustrious captain, here, you're a tactical expert."

"Amen," piped up Noah Cloud, whose eyes were fixed on the eastern edge of the gulf. "If General Lee wants to win this war, he oughtta let Cap'n McGraw train *all* the Confederate troops. He's the best—"

Cloud stopped because of what he saw in the distance. "Cap'n," he breathed, rising to his knees and pointing eastward. "The barges are comin'."

Every eye was instantly fixed on the three oblong shapes in the silver light. McGraw looked above and said, "This is working out perfectly. The moon will be covered in another few minutes. Small as we are, the barge crews won't be able to see us at all. I'd say they're about two miles off shore, so we're in good shape. Let's start moving north slowly. The rate they're going, we'll be in the correct position to sneak in behind them when they reach this longitude."

A little over an hour had passed when, under the thick cloud cover, the Sharpshooters on the rafts waited for the barges to come between them and the shore. Peering through the darkness, they could make out that the barges were about thirty-five feet wide and sixty feet long. Specially constructed wooden railings lined the edges of the flat decks to keep the animals from falling off.

At the rear of each barge was a small elevated pilot's cabin. Directly below the cabin was the big steam engine. A paddle wheel the width of the barge churned water at the stern. The wooden railings ran across the deck in front of the cabin and engine, giving the crew some room to move about on either side.

The barges were running abreast of each other, and as they floated past the rafts, the Sharpshooters could tell that the fifty mules were together on the vessel closest to them. The other two barges carried the cavalry horses. The sounds of mules and horses carried clearly on the night air.

McGraw assigned Hazzard's raft to take the nearest barge, Cloud's was to attack the next one, and the captain's would go for the one closest to the shore. As they rowed hard in the wake of the paddle wheels, the Sharpshooters were not concerned about being heard. The rumble of the steam engines, the slap and grinding of the paddle wheels, and the noise of the one hundred and fifty beasts would drown out any sounds made by the men on the rafts.

The barges were about four miles from Fort Pickens and had begun to angle toward shore when the three rafts were lined up behind them. In the gloom, the Sharpshooters could make out three men on each deck, which told them that there were two in each cabin. Captain McGraw was to fire the first shot as a signal for the others to cut loose.

The men on the rafts found it relatively easy to keep up with the heavily laden, slow-moving vessels. When they were within twenty yards, McGraw drew a bead on one of the crew and squeezed the trigger. The Yankee was standing next to the cabin when the bullet hit him. He buckled and fell as Confederate rifles opened fire in a deadly salvo. Surprised crewmen were toppling to the deck. One on the center barge took a slug, staggered a few steps, then fell into the gulf.

McGraw saw one of the men in the cabin of the barge ahead of him stick his head out the window, then duck inside quickly. McGraw drew a bead on the window and waited. Seconds later, the man was at the window, aiming a rifle. McGraw's gun barked and the Yankee fell forward, dropping his weapon to the deck.

While Confederate Henrys continued to blast away at the men on the barges, Hazzard saw one of them hop over the wooden railing and disappear among the frightened mules. The other four crewmen were down. Telling his men to row up to the barge, Hazzard laid his rifle down and made ready to jump from the raft to the slow-moving vessel. Bending low for leverage, he sprang from the raft onto the barge's deck. Pulling out one of his Dragoon .44s, he made a quick check on the four Yankees, and found they were all dead.

The mules were braying and jostling about on the deck, their eyes bulging with fear, as Hazzard leaped the railing and dropped down among them. He caught sight of a dark uniform threading through the animals. The Yankee was heading for the bow.

Shoving his way forward, the big Sharpshooter raised his head and heard the report of a pistol a split second before its lead bullet whizzed past his ear. A second shot followed just as he ducked down.

The mules shrieked in panic, wheeling about and clashing with each other. The barge was rocking dangerously. Hazzard bent low and worked his way among the terrified animals in the direction of the Yankee. His gun was cocked and ready. Suddenly the shifting, wheeling mules parted, giving Hazzard a full view of his enemy. The Yankee was in a half-crouch at the front rail, bringing up his revolver. The big redhead ducked and fired, but his aim was spoiled by the swaying deck. The Yankee's bullet hissed past Hazzard and buried itself in the rump of a mule.

At the same time, another mule directly in front of the Yankee whirled about and knocked the revolver from his hand. It sailed over the rail and dropped into the gulf. Hap heard the wounded mule dig deck and hit the wooden railing behind him as he holstered his gun and headed for the weaponless man. The mule hit the railing full-force, shattering it, and plunged into the dark water.

When Hap approached him, the Yankee swore at him and swung a roundhouse haymaker. Hap batted the fist aside and chopped him with a solid blow. The Yankee staggered back against the rail. In the dim light, Hazzard could make out the man's terror-stricken features. He was going to die, and he knew it. Hazzard moved in close and locked his powerful hands on the man's head. One vicious twist, a snap, and the body went limp, falling to the deck.

The barge slowed. Hap wheeled about and saw one of the Sharpshooters from his raft in the cabin. The throttle had been eased back, and the flat-decked vessel was coming to a halt. In the deep water, the wounded mule was threshing about and bobbing below the surface. Hap pulled his revolver, cocked it, and took aim. When the mule surfaced, the Dragoon roared, and the mule went limp.

The gunfire had stopped at the other two barges. Glancing toward them, Hap saw Noah Cloud and the men with him tossing bodies into the gulf. On the other barge, Captain McGraw and his men were doing the same thing. Hazzard bent over and tossed overboard the man he had just killed.

While the engines of the barges were idling, McGraw called out above the noise of the animals and said, "All right, men. Fire up the boilers. Let's get these things turned around and headed out to sea. We've got an appointment on shore with our pals."

Major General Frederick Steele was fast asleep in his quarters at Fort Pickens when the door burst open and Colonel Arthur Benton rushed in. Shaking the general, Benton cried, "General Steele! Wake up!"

Steele moaned groggily, opened dull eyes, and stared up at Benton, who was outlined against the doorway. Someone outside the door was holding a lantern. Rubbing his eyes, the general mumbled, "What is it, Colonel?"

"The Rebels are attacking our barges, sir!" exclaimed Benton.

Steele shook his head to clear the cobwebs. "You mean the barges that are due in with our horses and mules?"

"Yes, sir! If you listen, you can hear it now!"

As the general worked his heavy body to a sitting position, the distant sound of gunfire met his ears. Cursing, he stood and shuffled to his clothes, which hung on a rack. As he struggled to get into his pants, he growled, "Those aren't big guns. Sound like rifles to me. Can't be Rebel ships."

"No, sir," said Benton. "I estimate they're about three to four miles out on the gulf, and I think the stinking Rebs are using our boats to attack the barges."

"*Our* boats?" gusted the general, snapping his suspenders over his shoulders.

"Yes, sir. All five of them are gone. They must have—"

"*Gone?*" boomed Steele. "How did they get in close enough to steal our boats? Sentries go to sleep on duty?"

"No, sir. We...uh...we had a slight mix-up, sir."

"Mix-up! What do you mean?" rasped the general, sitting down to pull on his boots.

"The Rebs must've come in and taken the boats at the changing of the guard. When the two sentries on duty over the midnight hour were ready to go off duty at twelve-thirty, their replacements hadn't shown up. They expected them any minute, so they came inside."

"They *what?*" roared the general. "You mean they left their post before their replacements had reported in?"

"Yes, sir."

"Who are they?"

"Jenkins and Galloway, sir."

Slipping into his coat, Steele grunted, "Jenkins and Galloway are to report to me right after breakfast."

"Yes, sir."

"So whose fault is it that there were no replacements?"

"Well, sir, like I said, there was a slight mix-up. As you know, Lieutenant Madsen is in charge of sentries. It seems he thought he had told Sergeant O'Toole to assign sentry duty for that shift because he was tied up with other things. But O'Toole says Madsen never did any such thing. So we—"

"Are there sentries on the walls *now?*"

"Yes, sir."

Bowling through the door with the colonel on his heels, Steele said, "Madsen and O'Toole are to report to me right after breakfast, also."

Walking stiffly, Steele made his way outside the fort, where he found about eighty men standing in a group, looking southeastward through the gloom. The gunfire had stopped. The three barges could barely be seen, but the sound of braying mules and neighing horses could be heard.

Colonel Arthur Benton drew up beside Steele and said, "The Rebs will probably go ashore with the animals somewhere, sir. Shall I round up a unit of men and head up the beach?"

"Forget it," mumbled the general. "I doubt that's what they'll do. They don't need the animals. I'm sure they've made this move simply to keep us from getting them. They're not dumb enough to—"

Steele stopped midsentence when the sound of steam engines being given full throttle met his ears. He waited silently, cocking his head and listening. Presently he said, "Colonel, they're moving away. If I was a betting man, I'd bet they're going to aim the barges seaward and let them go."

"Sounds like something Rebels would do, sir," agreed Benton.

CHAPTER TWO

✭

Federal forces had been unable to take control of the Confederate railroad any farther north than Brewton, Alabama, ten miles above the Florida state line. Major General Dabney H. Maury, who commanded the Confederate Army in Alabama, had successfully blocked the Yankees from gaining more track with a stubborn artillery battery that had dug in where the tracks crossed a bridge over a deep gully a mile and a half south of Brewton. The Yankees were held at bay and were waiting for reinforcements before they attempted to overpower Maury's artillery.

Captain Ryan McGraw and his Sharpshooters had left Montgomery on a military train early on the morning of June 13. Their horses rode in cars built for carrying stock. When the train stopped in Brewton, the horses were unloaded, and the Sharpshooters rode to a large farm just east of town, owned by widow Mabel Griffin.

One of McGraw's Sharpshooters was Corporal Luther Mangus, who had grown up in Brewton and had worked for Mrs. Griffin's late husband as a farm hand when in his teens. When plans were being made by General Maury and Captain McGraw for the Sharpshooters to thwart the landing of the horses and mules at Pensacola, Corporal Mangus had suggested that since they couldn't go by rail any farther south than Brewton, they contact Mrs. Griffin. She would supply them with materials to build the rafts they needed, and a team and wagon to carry the rafts to the Florida coast.

Maury and McGraw liked the idea. Contact was made by telegraph, and Mrs. Griffin, a Southerner to the core, said she would be more than happy to supply whatever they needed. Since her husband's death in January, she had hired a middle-aged man named Ben Rice as farm foreman. Rice and her teenage son, Johnny Ray, would help the Sharpshooters build the rafts.

At midafternoon on June 13, McGraw and his men rode onto the Griffin place and were welcomed by Mabel, her son, and the foreman. The rafts were quickly constructed with husky logs and flat boards, and by midmorning on June 14, the Sharpshooters were ready to head for Pensacola. Johnny Ray Griffin, eager to have a part in the war against the Yankees, volunteered to go along and drive the wagon.

His mother objected that he was too young to be doing any such thing. The boy argued that even though he was only fifteen, he was tall for his age and looked older. He could handle the job.

Captain McGraw saw the fear in Mrs. Griffin's eyes and told Johnny Ray the job would be too dangerous. He could not take the responsibility of allowing him to drive the wagon even if his mother would allow it. Mabel gave the captain an appreciative grin.

With Johnny Ray looking on enviously, the Sharpshooters had moved off the farm and headed south. Corporal Luther Mangus drove the wagon, leaving his horse in the Griffin barnyard.

They reached the Florida coast in the early afternoon on June 15, and stashed the horses and the wagon in a heavily wooded area three miles east of Fort Pickens near the western tip of Santa Rosa Island. After dark, they carried the rafts to the beach and waited for the right time to head out onto the gulf to intercept the barges.

On the morning of June 17, Johnny Ray Griffin helped the farm's four male slaves do the chores, then went into the house for breakfast. The aroma of bacon and biscuits met his nostrils as he entered the kitchen from the back porch.

Ben Rice was just sitting down at the table, and Mabel was pouring him a steaming cup of coffee. Looking up, she smiled at her tall, slender son and said, "Get your hands washed, Johnny Ray. We're about ready to eat."

While the youth scrubbed his hands at the wash basin next to the cupboard, he said, "Ma, since I got my weeds cut yesterday, is it all right if I go squirrel huntin' this mornin'?"

Mabel looked at Ben, and Johnny Ray saw it. He knew it was Ben's responsibility to keep him busy, and on the farm it was an easy thing to do. Preempting what Ben might come up with on the spur of the moment, he said, "Squirrel would sure taste good for supper, wouldn't it, Ben?"

The foreman smiled and said to Mabel, "I think squirrel would taste good for supper."

Mabel set the coffee pot on the stove. "I declare. A woman hasn't got a chance when she's outnumbered by the men around her house!"

Johnny laughed and sat down at the table. His hazel eyes shined as he said, "You'll be glad I went huntin', Ma. You like squirrel, too."

Placing crackling bacon on a plate and setting it on the table, the widow smiled at her son and kidded him. "Well, I do, but first you've got to hit the squirrels when you shoot at them."

Johnny Ray laughed. "Ma, you know I never miss!"

"Never?" she chuckled, turning back to the stove.

The youth's face tinted slightly. "Well...I don't miss very often."

Ben spoke up. "I've noticed you drill them squirrels pretty accurately, boy. How do you do it?"

Raising his hands and making like he was sighting down the barrel of his rifle, Johnny Ray replied, "I just pretend they're Yankee soldiers, Ben. Makes it real easy to hit 'em."

Mabel placed a platter of hot biscuits on the table and eased onto her chair. "Johnny," she said levelly, "I don't like the Yankees any more than you do, but it bothers me to hear my fifteen-year-old son talking so casually about killing them."

"They're our enemies, Ma," Johnny Ray said defensively. "If I was three years older so's I was of enlistment age, I'd already be out there on a battlefield somewhere shootin' blue-bellies by the dozen." He paused a few seconds, then added, "When I turn eighteen, I want to join up with McGraw's Sharpshooters!"

Mabel's face went rigid. Through tight lips, she said, "I hope by the time you're eighteen, this horrible war will be over." Tears filmed her eyes. "I don't want you out there on a battlefield, son. I want you right here on the farm, safe and secure."

"But Ma, lots of mother's sons are out there fightin' so's the war can end. If I could go fight right now, I'd do my part to end it by killin' lots of Yankees!"

Mabel wiped away the tears with the back of her hand and said, "No more talk about killing Yankees, Johnny Ray. Now it's time to thank the Lord for the food. I want you to pray."

Young Griffin bowed his head and gave thanks for the food God had provided, and was eagerly talking about his squirrel hunt as soon as he said, "Amen."

When breakfast was over, Johnny Ray went to his room and loaded his Springfield musket. Replacing the ramrod in position beneath the barrel, he strapped on his ammunition kit, clapped the battered straw hat on his head, and returned to the kitchen. He kissed his mother's cheek and received the "be careful" routine that mothers always recite. Telling her he would be back with a dozen or so squirrels on a string by noon, he left the house.

Ben was just coming out of the wood shed as the youth passed by on his way to the hunt. Ben had an armload of wood he was taking to Mabel for the cookstove.

Johnny Ray smiled and said, "Set your mouth for some scrumptious squirrel, Ben. I'll be back with plenty, later."

"Hold up, boy. I need to talk to you before you go."

The bright-eyed youth halted and smiled. "Yes, sir?"

Moving close to him, Ben said, "Johnny Ray, I know I'm not your pa...and I'm not tryin' to be...but I think you need a little fatherly advice."

"About what, Ben?"

"Well...it's the war talk. Seems the war is just about all you talk about any more. I understand how you feel. I'm a true Southerner myself. But mothers have a real tender spot in their hearts when it comes to their boys goin' off to war. I don't know if you've ever thought about it, son, but when a woman brings a child into this world, she has to go right up to the very edge of death to do it. This makes her offspring mighty precious to her. So...when you talk about wantin' to go off to the war and kill Yankees, you're cuttin' awful close to that tender spot. Do you know what I'm sayin'?"

Johnny Ray was quiet for a moment. Then he answered, "Yes, sir. I know what you're sayin'. And I wouldn't hurt Ma's heart for nothin' in this world. But there's somethin' I need to make you understand, Ben. The main reason I wish I could go and fight Yankees is because I want to stop 'em before they get to my mother's door. I've heard what those stinkin' blue-bellies do to Southern women...and I ain't never gonna let 'em get close to Ma. I want to get this war over so's what Yankees ain't dead will be sent hightailin' it back north where they belong. I don't want anything bad ever happenin' to her."

Ben smiled. "I'm glad you want to protect her, son. Only thing I'm sayin' is, don't talk about the war and wantin' to fight in it in front of your ma, okay?"

"I got the message, Ben. She won't hear it from my lips any more. But if the war's still on when I turn eighteen, I'm joinin' up. Wouldn't be right for me to sit back and let other fellas my age go off and fight, would it?"

"Of course not, son. I'm just prayin' this thing'll be over soon, and all the mothers' sons—Confederates and Yankees—can go home."

"Me, too," grinned the youth. Moving away, he said over his shoulder, "See you about noon."

Johnny Ray made his way across the fields and through the woods, keeping an eye open for squirrels, both in the trees and on the ground. He spotted a couple of them as he walked, but both were too far away. He didn't want to waist rifle balls or gun powder. He came to a creek that rambled over the countryside, lined with trees and brush, and he knew that squirrels liked to play there. Many times he had bagged a number of them along the creek, which was some two miles south and west of his house.

At that time of the year, the creek ran three feet deep at a width of about twenty feet. Johnny Ray came to a familiar spot where there was a break in the heavy brush that lined the creek, and slipped between the branches. The bank was steep, so he sat down and scooted toward the water's edge.

Suddenly he heard voices. Somewhere nearby, some men were talking. Leaning out over the water to see past the brush, he looked downstream. About sixty feet away, he could see booted feet and dark-blue trousers at a clearing on the bank.

Dark-blue trousers!

Yankee soldiers? Possibly. The gully where the Yankees and the Confederate artillery were at a standoff at the railroad bridge wasn't but a mile or so from the creek. Maybe the blue-bellies were on some sort of scouting mission.

Swallowing hard, young Griffin worked his way up the bank through the brush the same way he had gone down. When he reached the top of the bank, he carefully rose to his feet and moved slowly toward the men in blue. He could hear them talking as he crept nearer, keeping close to the heavy stand of brush.

Reaching another break in the thick foliage, Johnny Ray found his assumption to be correct. Three Union soldiers—a corporal and two privates—were seated on the creek bank, chatting. There were no horses around, so Johnny Ray knew they had come on foot. His heart pounded like a triphammer as he heard them discussing their mission. They were to scout out the area and see if there was a safe way to bring troops around behind the artillery battery dug in near the railroad bridge. They had decided to take a short break before moving on.

Johnny knew what he had to do. As a loyal Southern boy, he must capture these blue-bellies and take them home. Captain Ryan McGraw and his Sharpshooters would be returning soon. Johnny Ray would turn them over to Captain McGraw.

A thought passed through the youth's mind: Maybe I shouldn't try this. It's plenty dangerous. No one would expect a mere fifteen-year-old boy to attempt to capture three enemy soldiers. He wouldn't be blamed at all if he reported seeing them but had not tried to take them prisoner.

Johnny Ray bit down hard on his lower lip and shook his head. No! he thought. It's my duty! And besides, when I take them in as prisoners, it will show everybody that I am old enough to be a soldier!

Licking his lips, the determined youth switched the musket from hand to hand as he wiped sweat from his palms. Easing the hammer back to firing position as quietly as possible, he kept his eyes on the Yankees. Their voices and the rippling sound of the creek had prevented them from hearing the dry, clicking sound. Assessing the situation, he saw that the Yankees wore no sidearms or knives. Each had a Henry repeating rifle beside him on the bank.

Johnny Ray looked around to make sure there were no other Yankee soldiers near. Seeing no sign of anyone, he took a deep breath and squared himself with the path that led down to the water's edge. The soldiers were facing the creek with their backs toward him. Just as the determined youth started to move, one of the privates turned his head. He was looking back into the brush along the creek, but Johnny Ray feared he might be in the Yankee's peripheral vision.

He froze on the spot. To move would draw the man's attention. He felt a faint pins-and-needles sensation along his spine.

Suddenly a thrush fluttered out of the thicket and took flight. The other soldiers laughed at their comrade as they watched the bird fly away. The corporal said, "What's the matter, George? You spooked? You thought some Rebel was sneaking in on us, didn't you?"

George laughed it off, saying he was just smart for being cautious.

The other private chuckled, "Sometimes a fella can become too cautious, George. You know...get to where he jumps at everything that moves."

George mumbled something as he picked up a stone and threw it into the creek. Johnny Ray knew it was time to make his move. Gripping the musket in ready position, he headed down the steep bank.

The Yankees heard him coming and jerked their heads around. Johnny Ray was still within the edges of the brush above them as he stopped and shouted with a squeak in his voice, "Hold it right there!"

The Yankees sat within a dozen feet of him, their faces registering their surprise.

"On your feet!" snapped the farm boy, waving the muzzle of his musket threateningly.

Corporal Leonard Halsey slowly moved his hand toward the rifle next to him as he spoke sternly, "You'd best put that gun down, kid. You're dealing with well-trained soldiers, here. By the looks of you, I assume you're from some farm nearby. Go on home. You've got no business throwing a gun on us."

Johnny Ray ground out the words, "You dirty Yankees are trespassin' on South'n land. That makes it my business." Noting that Halsey's hand was nearing the rifle, he rasped, "Touch that gun and you'll die!"

The corporal pulled his hand away and slowly stood up. Privates George Calkins and Eddie Smith followed suit.

"Now look, kid," Halsey said levelly, "your fooling around like this is gonna get you killed."

"I'm not foolin' around!" spat the youth. "I'm takin' you as my prisoners. Captain Ryan McGraw will see to it that you go to the prison camp up by Montgomery. All right, now...I want you two privates to throw your rifles in the creek, one at a time."

Smith looked at his partners and said with a paper-thin laugh, "This local yokel really thinks we're gonna do what he says."

"You first!" Johnny Ray snarled at Smith. "Toss your rifle in the creek!"

"Sonny," spoke up Corporal Halsey, "you're not thinking too clearly. That old musket can only fire once. You shoot one of us, the other two will get you. We'll kill you for sure."

"Maybe you're not thinking too clearly, either, Corporal," countered Johnny Ray. "If I shoot one of you, I'll shoot to kill. Are you willin' to be the one to die, so your two yahoos can finish me off?"

While Halsey glared at him, young Griffin fixed Smith with steely eyes and hissed, "I told you to throw your rifle in the creek."

Jutting his jaw angrily, Smith growled, "We're gonna kill you, kid."

"Where do you get that 'we' stuff?" asked Johnny Ray. "If you make the first move toward me, you'll be dead." The youth's stomach was fluttering, but he kept up his tough stance. "Now, either throw your gun in the creek as I told you, or come after me."

Smith glanced at his companions. They could offer no help. Cursing under his breath, he picked up his Henry by the tip of the barrel and threw it in the stream.

Johnny Ray's muzzle swung on George Calkins and he commanded, "You next."

Calkins reluctantly followed Smith's example. When the rifle splashed in the water, young Griffin said to Halsey, "Now, Corporal, I want you to pick up your gun very carefully, keeping the muzzle aimed at the ground, and lever a cartridge into the chamber. Then I want you to hand it to me butt first."

"Kid," Halsey breathed hotly, "before this is over, you're gonna be dead."

"Just do as I tell you," retorted Johnny Ray, "or you're the one who'll be dead."

The corporal bent over and picked up his Henry, thinking there had to be a way out of this predicament. It would be bad enough to become a prisoner of the Confederates, but what shame he and his two comrades would face when it got out that they had been captured by a lone farm kid. Careful to keep the rifle's muzzle pointed groundward, he worked the lever. The cartridge slid into the chamber, and the hammer was cocked.

Holding the musket in his right hand with the butt braced against his hip and the muzzle pointed dead-center on Halsey's chest, Johnny Ray extended his left hand and said, "Gently, Corporal. Place it gently in my hand. If you make any kind of a quick move, this musket will go off."

When it was done, Halsey took a step back and grunted, "You said Captain Ryan McGraw would see to it that we go to the prison camp at Montgomery. Are you talking about *the* Ryan McGraw of McGraw's Sharpshooters?"

"The same. Now I'm going to back up the bank, here, and I want the three of you to follow me, single file. Anybody makes a questionable move, he dies."

When young Griffin had them on level ground, he made them walk side by side in front of him with their hands cupped behind their necks.

As they moved across a grassy field, Halsey asked, "So where's McGraw and his Sharpshooters camped out?"

"You'll find out," replied Johnny Ray, not wanting to tell them that the Sharpshooters had been on an assignment in Florida.

The three Yankee soldiers looked at each other with concern. Hoping that the rustling of their feet in the grass would drown out his whisper, Calkins said, "Len, we gotta do something. Once this hayseed turns us over to McGraw, we're done for. I don't want to spend the rest of the war in that stinking Rebel prison camp!"

"Well, I don't either," whispered Halsey, "but what can we do? I know about these Southern farm boys. They learn to handle a gun as soon as they can pick one up. If we'd tried to take him back there by the creek, one of us would be dead."

"So what do we do, now?" whispered Smith. "We've got to get away from this hick before he takes us into McGraw's camp."

Johnny Ray's voice cut the air. "You Yankees think us hayseed hicks are deaf, do you? I'm warnin' you...try any tricks on me, and I'll kill you."

"You're just a kid," countered Halsey over his shoulder. "You shouldn't be putting a gun on someone and threatening to kill them."

"You kill Rebels, don't you?" pressed young Griffin. "Then what's wrong with a Rebel killin' you?"

"We're soldiers," argued Calkins. "Soldiers are supposed to kill the enemy. That's what war's all about."

"I am a soldier, too!" snapped Johnny Ray.

"You're lying!" Smith said. "You aren't old enough to be a soldier. And besides...where's your uniform?"

"Don't need a uniform to be a soldier."

"Then what proof have you got that you're a soldier?"

"I've got three prisoners of war. Isn't that proof enough? Only soldiers take other soldiers prisoners of war, don't they?"

When no answer came, Johnny Ray said, "You Yankees would rather it was a soldier who captured you than a hayseed Southern farm kid, right?"

The men in blue exchanged despairing glances. It was going to be embarrassing when the day came that their fellow-soldiers learned of their capture by a mere boy.

Looking past his prisoners, Johnny Ray could see the uneven roof-lines of the house, barn, and outbuildings on the Griffin farm in the distance. "Not much farther, now, enemy soldiers," he said advisedly. "You're doin' fine. Just don't get any cute ideas between here and there. By now I would've bagged me a dozen squirrels. I haven't fired a gun all day. It's so unnatural for me. So don't do anything to tempt me to pull one of these triggers."

Mabel Griffin was in her sewing room at the rear of the house when she heard the old grandfather clock in the hall chime ten.

Blending with the last few chimes was Ben's excited voice, coming from the yard. "Mabel! Mabel!"

Laying her sewing down, Mabel went to the window and looked around the yard for the foreman. When she saw him, he was near the tool shed, looking toward the south pasture. The day was warm, and the sewing room window was wide open. Sticking her head out, she called, "What is it, Ben?"

"It's Johnny Ray! He's comin' in."

"A bit early, I might say," laughed Mabel. "Does he have a string of squirrels?"

"Nope, but he's got somethin' else. You ain't gonna believe it!"

"Well, what is it?"

"You'd better come back and look for yourself."

A half-minute later, Mabel stepped off the back porch and hurried to where Ben was standing. Grinning from ear to ear, he pointed toward the pasture and said, "Look!"

Mabel's jaw slacked and a gasp escaped her lips as she saw the three Yankee soldiers with their hands clasped behind their necks, followed by young Johnny Ray, holding two rifles on them. They were about thirty yards from where she stood, moving past a cluster of apple trees.

Ben chuckled, "What do you make o' that, Mabel? That boy of yours has done got hisself three Yankee prisoners!"

"You what?" exclaimed Captain Ryan McGraw, looking toward the Griffin barn, throwing his leg over the saddle.

Corporal Luther Mangus drew the wagon to a halt as the rest of the Sharpshooters dismounted. Mabel and Ben stood beside Johnny Ray at the back porch of the farm house, smiling proudly.

The bright-eyed youth stepped close to McGraw and repeated what he had said a moment earlier. "I captured three Yankee soldiers, sir, and we got 'em tied up in the barn."

Mangus climbed down from the Griffin wagon, eyes wide, and said, "Johnny Ray, did I hear you right? You captured three Yankee soldiers?"

"Yep," grinned the youth. "I told 'em I'd be turnin' 'em over to Captain McGraw and the Sharpshooters. They ain't terribly happy about it, but it's about to happen, anyhow."

"How did this come about, kid?" queried Hap Hazzard, who stood next to his friend Noah Cloud.

All the Sharpshooters gathered in a tight circle and listened as Johnny Ray told how he had stumbled onto the Yankees at the creek and caught them off guard. There was a round of laughter, then Captain McGraw said, "Well, let's get a gander at these Yankees."

Johnny Ray and Ben led McGraw and Lieutenant Rawlings to the barn. Inside, Leonard Halsey, George Calkins, and Eddie Smith were bound hand and foot, and tied together around one of the thick posts that supported the barn roof. Stepping through the wide door and viewing the prisoners by the light of the setting sun, the captain smiled and said, "Good afternoon, gentlemen. I'm Captain Ryan McGraw."

At sunrise the next morning, Mabel, Ben, and Johnny Ray stood at the rear of the house and watched the sullen-faced prisoners being placed on army horses with their hands tied behind their backs. They would ride double with three of the Sharpshooters.

Captain McGraw laid a hand on Johnny Ray's slender shoulder and said, "You did real good, son. We're all proud of you. General Maury is going to be proud of you, too. I wouldn't be surprised if you got a letter from him."

"Do you suppose since I captured those blue-bellies, General Maury would put in a good word for me to the army so's they'd let me join up?"

Shaking his head slowly, McGraw replied, "The general wouldn't do that, Johnny Ray. There's a reason the army has an age limit for recruits. You did real good in taking these prisoners, but there's a whole lot more to soldiering than that. You'll just have to wait till you turn eighteen before you can enlist."

Johnny Ray's features showed disappointment. Nodding, he said, "I understand, Captain McGraw. It's just that...well, I want to do my part to help win the war."

"You did a big part yesterday, son," smiled McGraw. "Now, your ma needs you here. You take care of her...and be all the help to Ben that you can."

"Yes, sir," said Johnny Ray.

Mother, son, and foreman stood together and watched the Sharpshooters ride away. When they were almost out of sight, Captain McGraw turned and waved. Mabel, Ben, and Johnny Ray waved back. Sergeant Hap Hazzard, who rode beside McGraw, said, "Cap'n, that there is one fine boy."

"You can say that again," grinned McGraw.

CHAPTER THREE

✶

M ajor General Dabney H. Maury was standing in the door of his tent conversing with one of the camp's lieutenants when Captain Ryan McGraw and his Sharpshooters came riding in. The long column of riders caught his attention instantly. Confederate soldiers all over the camp stopped what they were doing to stare at the Sharpshooters and their Yankee prisoners.

Maury, who was nearing sixty and walked with a limp from a wound sustained in the Mexican War, moved toward the column with Lieutenant Foster Twite tagging along.

Raising a hand for the Sharpshooters to halt, McGraw drew rein, saluted Maury, and slid from the saddle. The general eyed the three blue-uniformed prisoners and said, "How'd it go, Captain?"

"As planned, sir," replied McGraw. "I'll give you a full report in your tent at your convenience."

"All right," nodded the silver-haired general. "Since it's almost one o'clock, most of the men have already eaten, but a few are still in line over at the cook shack. I'll let you eat lunch with your men, then you can come to the tent. Lets' say...about two o'clock."

"Fine, sir."

Looking at the prisoners, Maury said, "I see you captured some."

McGraw grinned. "*We* didn't, sir, but a fifteen-year-old farm boy did."

"Maybe we need to recruit this boy."

McGraw chuckled, "That's exactly what the kid wants, sir. I'll tell you about the capture when I make my report."

"Good enough," replied Maury. Then turning to Foster Twite, he said, "Lieutenant, take charge of the prisoners and remove them to the prison camp."

Captain McGraw dismissed his men, telling them to corral their animals and head for the lunch line. Telling the general he would see him at two, he turned toward his own horse.

"Oh, Captain," spoke up Maury, "your seven new men arrived yesterday."

"Good. They seem to be Sharpshooter material?"

"They shoot like it. Be up to you to toughen them up."

"Well, given a little time, I can do that if they're made out of the right stuff."

"I think they are, but the time you have to work on them is going to be very short."

"Another mission?"

"Mm-hmm. A big one. I'll tell you all about it at two o'clock. In the meantime, if you want to meet your new men, they're settled in at the spot designated for your unit."

The Montgomery army camp was situated a half-mile north of the town. It covered some twenty acres of open meadows and wooded areas, the meadows making up about two-thirds of the camp. The horses were kept in the woods where it was easy to confine them in a rope corral. A small brook ran through the camp, threading its way through the woods and providing water for the animals. The Sharpshooters had their tents pitched close to the brook a few yards from the edge of the woods.

As Captain McGraw led his horse toward the corral, he thought of the seven men he had lost in two skirmishes some twenty-five miles east of Montgomery. It always hurt him deeply to see his men killed. General Robert E. Lee had ordered that B Company First Alabama Sharpshooters always be maintained at an even hundred men plus their captain. It was up to General Maury to see that it was done.

The Sharpshooters deposited their animals in the corral and headed for the lunch line. McGraw put his horse among them, then headed to where his new men were waiting to meet him.

The captain shook hands with each man, and asked where he was from and how much combat experience he had. He told them he would begin their training as soon as his meeting with General Maury was over, then excused himself to go have lunch with his men.

At precisely 2:00 P.M., McGraw approached the door of General Maury's tent. The flap was open, and Maury looked up from his battered old desk and said, "Come in, Captain."

McGraw entered and sat on a straight-backed chair, facing the desk. Maury listened intently as the captain gave his report, telling how the Sharpshooters had overcome the Union barge crews, sent them to watery graves, and headed the barges out to sea at full throttle. He commended McGraw and his men for a job well done, saying the loss of the horses and mules would greatly cripple the Union cavalry and army in Alabama.

McGraw then explained to his commander how Mabel Griffin had aided them by donating materials to build the rafts and loaning them her team and wagon so they could get them to the coast. He also told Maury about young Johnny Ray single-handedly capturing the three Union soldiers.

Laughing, the general said how ashamed the three Yankees must be to have been taken by a mere boy. He would send a letter of appreciation to Mrs. Griffin for her help, and a letter of commendation to the boy for his courage and monumental accomplishment.

Taking a deep breath and letting it out slowly, General Maury leaned forward, picked up a folder from his desk, and said, "The big mission I mentioned to you earlier has been ordered by General Lee. These are the orders. You have exactly one week to whip those new recruits into shape. I'm shipping your unit to Fort Morgan at Mobile Bay on the twenty-sixth."

McGraw's mouth pulled tight. "Mobile Bay, eh? Farragut?"

Nodding, Maury said, "In person. He's building up a fleet of gunboats off the coast, south of the bay. We knew it had to come. Old 'fair-guts' has Vicksburg, Port Hudson, New Orleans, and Pensacola as feathers in his cap. If he can capture the bay and the city of Mobile, he'll have us completely blockaded, and he knows it. Mobile will be his biggest prize."

McGraw lifted his hat, sleeved sweat from his brow, and said, "He's not only thinking of blockade from the sea, but he also remembers how Mobile figured in the Stones River and Chicamauga campaigns."

Maury nodded, recalling that prior to the Battle of Stones River and, later, the Battle of Chicamauga, great numbers of Confederate troops and guns had been shifted from Mississippi to Tennessee to fight in those campaigns. The only way the Rebel warriors could get to Tennessee in time to meet the Union forces was to travel by rail from Jackson, Mississippi, to Mobile. From Mobile, they went north to Selma, where they railroaded east to Atlanta. From Atlanta, they rode the rails northward into Tennessee. If Admiral Farragut could take Mobile, that vital link could never be used again.

"You're right about that," Maury said solemnly. "There's another reason, too."

"Sherman's proposed move on Atlanta?"

"You hit the nail on the head. As you know, then, Sherman is expected to launch a drive for Atlanta some time next spring. Mobile will once again be vital, since our army in Georgia would have to receive its supplies from Mobile. The only other seacoast link for our Georgia forces is Charleston, and it is under threat at this time, too. It is of utmost importance, Captain, that we hold Mobile. General Lee wants you and your men to join forces with General Page and his one hundred and twenty men at Fort Morgan. We must not let Mobile Bay fall into enemy hands."

"What about Fort Gaines, General?" asked McGraw. "How many men are there?"

"I'm not sure. I think about fifty. There aren't as many guns in Fort Gaines. From what I understand, though, General Page is doing something to force the Union's ships closer to Fort Morgan. It has some very big guns."

"Doing something like what?"

"Well, from what I know about it, he's driving wooden pilings into the bottom of the bay from Dauphin Island, where Gaines stands, toward the other side of the bay's mouth...and he's also planning to drop torpedoes into the water between the pilings and Fort Morgan."

"Torpedoes? Pardon me, sir, I haven't been around naval warfare before. What are torpedoes?"

Maury smiled. "They're a new device for sinking ships. You're aware that our Brigadier General Gabriel Rains has developed what he calls 'land mines' for use on the battlefield."

"Yes, sir. A wicked device, but quite ingenious. I haven't seen them, yet, but I hear they'll blow a man to bits if he steps on one."

"For sure," nodded Maury. "Well, General Rains has come up with a 'sea mine.' It works on the same order, only it blows holes in the hulls of ships. He calls it a torpedo. He has invented two kinds, and I understand that General Page is going to use both of them in Mobile Bay."

"How do they work?"

"The first one General Rains came up with was simply a beer keg filled with gunpowder. Numerous little tubes project from the sides of the keg. The tubes contain fulminate, which upon contact with a ship's hull will explode. That sets off the powder in the keg. It'll blow a big hole in a hurry. The beer keg kind are anchored to the bottom of the bay—or whatever body of water you are attempting to protect—with thin rope lines. The wood of the keg makes it quite buoyant, so the torpedo rises to the surface. They're tied so they are just a bit under the surface, and hard to see. Deadly, I'll tell you."

"Sounds like it."

"The other kind are metal cones, usually tin. They simply float on the surface, but it's impossible to dodge them, even if you see them. The cones are filled with powder and attached to the ends of a tin cylinder filled with air, which gives it buoyancy. The charges in the cones are detonated by a spring mechanism connected to a trigger wire. One bump by a ship, the trigger sets off an internal spark. Makes quite an explosion, I understand."

"That'll give Admiral Farragut something to think about."

"I'd say so. There's something else for him to think about, too. Our new ram, the *Tennessee*."

"I've heard about it, sir. Must be some kind of ship."

"She's considered the strongest and most powerful iron-clad ever put afloat. As you know, I was down at Mobile a few weeks ago. The *Tennessee* was moving about just off shore. Formidable thing. Looks like a giant turtle. Her sides are covered with iron plates six inches thick, thoroughly riveted together."

"I've heard it's a floating fort."

"That's putting it mildly. Her biggest guns are the Brooke cannons. Has six of them. They fire a solid shot weighing a hundred and ten pounds."

"Whew! Farragut probably knows about her. Wonder what he's thinking."

"I'd like to know that myself," chuckled Maury.

McGraw shifted positions on the hard chair and asked, "How many vessels does Farragut have off shore from Mobile Bay, sir?"

"At the moment, about fourteen, but there are more on the way. I figure he won't attempt to move in until he's built up quite a fleet. So far, he has nothing to match the *Tennessee*, but there could be something in the making."

"What about land forces, sir? Are we bolstering up for what may come in behind Mobile?"

"General Lee and I are working on that right now. He wants you and your Sharpshooters down there by June twenty-seventh...twenty-eighth at the latest. So I've made arrangements for a special train to take you to Mobile on the twenty-sixth."

"All right, sir," said McGraw, rising to his feet and rubbing his left shoulder. "I'll have my new recruits as ready as possible by then. The rest of my men, as usual, will be eager to get to Fort Morgan when they learn that there's going to be a fight."

Maury stood and eyed the captain massaging his shoulder. "Still bothered with that?" he asked.

"A little. I'm not too sure it will ever be the same, sir. But that's war, isn't it? I guess nobody's ever the same after being in battle."

Limping around the desk, General Maury replied, "You're right about that. I'll sure never be the same. This leg gives me a lot of trouble." Extending his hand, he said, "You're a good officer, McGraw. I appreciate your excellent work. General Page is plenty glad to know you're coming down there, I'll tell you that."

"Thank you, sir," McGraw responded with a half-smile, meeting Maury's grip. Clearing his throat nervously, he said, "Well, I guess Mrs. McGraw's son better get busy and whip his new men into shape." With that, he turned, passed through the tent door, and headed to where his Sharpshooters were camped.

Darkness had fallen on Sunday, June 26, 1864, when McGraw's Sharpshooters assembled at the Montgomery depot. They had left their horses in the camp, knowing their duties at Mobile Bay would not call for riding. Four supply wagons stood by, waiting for the train to pull in from the railroad yards. McGraw made sure his unit was well-equipped with weapons and ammunition.

It had rained for an hour just before sundown, and the air was warm and humid. Captain McGraw stood on the platform with Lieutenant Rawlings, discussing the situation at Mobile Bay. Lanterns on poles cast their dim light along the platform. The same subject was on the lips of the rest of the men, who were eager to do their part to withstand the impending Union aggression.

Finally, they heard the engine's deep chugging sound and turned to see a cloud of smoke belching from the stack. The big engine rolled to a halt, its firebox glowing in the inky night. Two men climbed down from the cab, and McGraw and Rawlings recognized them both. Engineer Charlie Coggins and fireman Lou Andreasen had taken the Sharpshooters and their horses to Brewton on their Pensacola mission several days before. Coggins greeted the two officers, then said, "Captain McGraw, we're pulling three coaches behind the coal car. Your men can unload the wagons into coach number three. Won't leave much room in that car, but coaches one and two will hold about fifty men apiece."

"That'll be fine, Charlie," grinned McGraw. "Lieutenant Rawlings and I will ride in the rear coach. The rest of them can divide up between the other two."

McGraw ordered the men to load the supplies in the third car, then explained the situation to Sergeants Hap Hazzard and Noah Cloud. Hazzard would be the leader in coach number one, and Cloud in number two. If the train was attacked by Union forces, the Sharpshooters were to retaliate quickly.

Twenty minutes later, the big engine hissed steam and belched smoke and they were underway. General Lee had put great stock in McGraw's Sharpshooters, depending on them to strengthen the forces at Fort Morgan. In explaining their mission to his men, Captain

McGraw had relayed Lee's message as it had come to General Maury: *The fort must stand at all costs.* Neither the city of Mobile nor the strategic bay can be allowed to fall into Union hands. The results of the battle there would greatly affect the outcome of the War.

Captain McGraw sat pensively next to a window in the third coach, watching the burning cinders from the engine filtering against the dark night like fireflies. Lieutenant Rawlings sat next to him, writing a letter by the light of the overhead lanterns. He had slid a keg of gunpowder between his knees and was using its lid as a table.

After a while, McGraw pulled his attention from the window, looked at his friend, and said, "Another letter to your pa?"

"Yeah, he's been awfully lonesome since Ma died. I know Sis and her family are there, but he needs to hear from his soldier-boy son, too."

"I'm sure that's true. I hope you can get a letter through to Tupelo."

"All I can do is try. I don't know if any of my letters have been getting to him. The way we've moved around, there's no way Pa or Sis can get a letter back to me. I just hope they've gotten mine."

McGraw looked back out the window. The steady rocking of the coach and the rhythmic click of the wheels was almost hypnotic. Moments later, he was startled as Judd's voice interrupted his sleepy state.

"I bet I know who you're thinking about!"

Ryan straightened on the seat, yawned, and said, "Wrong, ol' buddy. Not this time. I've come to the place that I won't let myself dwell on her any more. No use torturing Mrs. McGraw's only son. She's probably fallen for some other patient and married him by now."

Rawlings shrugged. "Maybe...then maybe not."

"I'll probably never know, anyhow. It's best that way. She deserves someone better than me."

The lieutenant licked the envelope and sealed it. Giving his friend a mock-scowl, he said, "What're you talking about, Ryan? There's nobody better than you."

McGraw chuckled hollowly. "If you could talk face-to-face with the Lord in heaven about that, He could fill you in on that subject."

"Look," pressed Rawlings, "you need to quit punishing yourself for something that wasn't your fault."

"Maybe if I'd been a better husband, Tori wouldn't have—"

"Oh, yes she would! From all you've told me about her, no matter how good a husband you'd been, she'd have run out on you. Some women are just that type, and Victoria is one of them."

"She didn't seem to be when we first met and married."

"So she changed. Sometimes people do that. You can't lash yourself for what happened. You're still young. When this war's over, you need to find yourself the right gal, marry her, and have a happy life. You deserve it."

There's only one gal that I want, thought McGraw, *but I can never have her. She was kind and warm to me, but there was nothing to indicate she felt anything more than friendship. However, I'll never forget that sweet kiss she planted on my cheek when she said, "Maybe someday we will meet again."*

Judd used his foot to slide the powder keg back across the aisle, then placed the sealed letter to his father in his small valise, telling himself he would mail it in the morning at Mobile. Stretching his arms, he yawned and said, "Well, Cap'n McGraw, I think I'll saw a few logs."

"Yeah, me too," Ryan said, yawning.

Rawlings lifted his lanky frame off the seat and doused all the lanterns but one. He lowered the flame on it, then sat down, stretched out his legs, crossing them at the ankles, and tipped his hat over his face. "G'night, boss," he mumbled.

"G'night, lowly subject," said McGraw.

The lieutenant chuckled and was snoring in less than a minute.

Ryan looked out the window. With the single lantern burning low, he could see the world outside. The clouds were breaking up, and there was pale moonlight showing through. A thin mist from the earlier rain was creeping over the Alabama countryside, spreading itself over the fields and through the woods like a blanket of cobwebs. *Eerie*, thought Ryan, then drifted off to sleep.

As the Confederate troop train cut its swath through the misty night, engineer Charlie Coggins sat in the cab with his head out the window, watching the track ahead by the light of the huge headlamp. Fireman Lou Andreasen finished shoveling a new batch of coal into the firebox and was just closing the iron door when he saw one of the Sharpshooters moving along the catwalk on the coal car. Andreasen had noticed his muscular body and carrot-red hair before.

Smiling as he entered the rear of the cab, Hap Hazzard said, "Evenin'."

"Evenin'," echoed the fireman above the thunder of the engine. "Somethin' I can do for you?"

"Naw. I just couldn't sleep. Thought I'd come and see how this bucket o' bolts works."

Andreasen grinned and glanced over his shoulder at the engineer, who was not yet aware of Hazzard's presence. "Don't let Charlie hear you call it that," he chuckled. "This engine is his baby."

Extending his hand, the fireman said, "I'm Lou Andreasen."

Hazzard shook his hand. "I'm Sergeant Hap Hazzard."

"I've noticed you before," smiled Andreasen. "You were on the train when we took the Sharpshooters down to Brewton. Hear you boys sent some Yankees into the gulf as fish food on that mission."

"You might say that," grinned Hap.

"You think it's gonna be a real battle when ol' 'fair-guts' comes tootin' into Mobile Bay, Sergeant?"

"It'll be a hot one, I figure."

Charlie Coggins turned around on his window-side seat and smiled, then looked past both men at another husky figure moving along the catwalk. Noah Cloud stepped into the cab, looked hard at Hazzard, and said, "I came into your coach to kiss you goodnight, and you weren't there."

"I'd rather be kissed by a suck-egg mule than you!" Hazzard growled.

Cloud laughed. "I was only joshin'! I wouldn't kiss you, and neither would a suck-egg mule!"

While Coggins looked on with a wide grin, Andreasen said, "I see you two are good friends."

"*Friends?*" chortled Cloud. "Hah! Ol' carrot-head here is just one notch from bein' a Yankee!"

Hazzard's ruddy face went beet-red. "A *Yankee?* Why, I oughtta throw you off the train right here and let the night-crawlers eat you!"

"Hmpf-f-f!" snorted Cloud. "Maybe you oughtta, but you ain't man enough!"

Hazzard jutted his jaw and started for him. Thinking they were serious, Andreasen leaped between them, saying, "Wait a minute, you two! There's no reason for violence, here. You men are on the same side!"

Both sergeants broke into hearty laughs, each throwing an arm around the fireman's shoulder.

"You're okay, pal," said Hazzard. "Sorry to have scared you. We go on like this most of the time."

"Most of the time?" asked the fireman, eyes wide.

"Yep," put in Cloud, "unless we're fightin' Yankees."

"Otherwise we'd go crazy," said Hazzard.

Cloud turned to Coggins and asked what time they would get into Mobile. The engineer pulled out his pocket watch and angled it toward the light from a small window in the iron door of the firebox. "Well, it's 1:15, now. We'll be comin' up on the Sepulga River in another forty to forty-five minutes. Mobile's another three hours after we cross the Sepulga, so we'll pull into Mobile just about five o'clock. It'll be dawn about the same time."

Hazzard and Cloud decided to look the cab over, showing interest in every detail. Coggins, delighted to show off his engine, took the time to explain how everything worked, while keeping an eye on the track ahead.

When Coggins had finished educating the sergeants on the engine, Andreasen said, "Will you gentlemen excuse me? I've got to shovel some more coal. Got to keep the boiler hot."

"We've got to get back to our men," said Hazzard. "Thanks for the hospitality." Cloud followed the big redhead along the catwalk on the coal car.

Captain McGraw was jolted from a deep sleep when the train suddenly braked. By the dim light of the lantern, he saw Judd Rawlings rolling in the aisle where he had been thrown from his seat.

Leaping to his feet and shaking his head to clear the cobwebs, McGraw stepped over his lieutenant and bolted through the door. Entering the next coach, he found the men tossed about from the sudden stop. Noah Cloud was picking himself up off the floor. Dashing past him, McGraw said, "Something's wrong, Sergeant! Get these men awake and alert. Be ready for anything!"

Charging into the next car, he found the same thing, only Hap Hazzard was about to open the front door.

"You stay in here!" shouted the captain. "Get the men awake and alert. Be ready for anything! I'll see what's going on."

"Yes, sir," nodded Hazzard, opening the door and stepping aside to make room for McGraw to pass.

When the captain was darting along the side of the coal car on the catwalk, he saw immediately why Coggins had stopped the train.

The Sepulga River lay before them in the moonlight, but the trestle that supported the bridge over the river was ablaze.

Coggins was hanging out one side of the cab, and Andreasen the other. They both eyed McGraw as he drew up. Coggins said, "Looks like the Yankees set fire to the bridge, Captain! Sorry to make the stop so sudden, but we were on a curve and you can't see the bridge till you're almost on it."

McGraw's attention was fixed on the burning trestle. It was afire on both sides of the river, but the flames had not yet joined in the middle. The river was about seventy feet wide where the bridge crossed, and both banks were sloped so that the bridge that spanned it was about a hundred and twenty feet long.

"What do you think, Captain?" asked Coggins. "Should we try to cross it?"

"Better get inside the cab," said McGraw. "Could be the Yankees are waiting out there in the brush to snipe at us."

As engineer, fireman, and McGraw moved inside the cab, Lieutenant Rawlings came off the catwalk, eyes wide as he noted the blazing bridge. "Yankees!" he gasped.

"No doubt," replied the captain, "but I'm wondering if setting the bridge afire wasn't just a random thing. Since they've been unable to capture and control this line between Montgomery and Mobile, about all they can do is try tearing up track or burning bridges. The latter is by far the easiest. This train was on nobody's schedule. There's no way the blue-bellies could have known it was coming. At this point we can't be sure, but if it *was* a random thing, they won't be hanging around to shoot at us."

"I hope that's the case," breathed Rawlings.

Turning to the engineer, McGraw said, "Charlie, you asked if we should try to cross the bridge."

"Yes, sir. My thought was that maybe it hasn't been burning long enough to weaken the superstructure. The flames are almost up to the top, but they climb pretty fast on wood like that. There's a good chance we can still get the train across."

"I was thinking the same thing myself." Looking back at Rawlings, McGraw said, "Lieutenant, we've got to get this unit and our supplies to Fort Morgan. I realize to move the train onto the bridge is taking a chance, but I've got to risk it. Since there's a possibility that the superstructure could collapse, I want you to take the men and walk across the bridge right now. They'll need to be alert in case there *are* snipers waiting."

"Yes, sir," nodded Rawlings, "but I think you should let us surround you for protection as we cross."

"I won't be with you. I'll be here in the engine."

"But you said yourself that the bridge could collapse," argued the lieutenant.

"That's right, Captain," interjected Coggins. "It's gonna be plenty dangerous aboard this train when it's on the bridge. If it collapses, it's about ninety feet down to the water. Not much chance of surviving that kind of fall."

"Exactly," said McGraw. "That's why you and Lou are going to walk across with my men. Yours truly will take the train over. You can show me how to handle the throttle and the brake."

The old man opened his mouth to argue, but McGraw cut him off. "There'll be no discussion on it, Charlie. While Lieutenant Rawlings is getting the men off the train, you can give me instructions." To Rawlings, he said, "Go, man! The flames are climbing to the trestle!"

Within three minutes the Sharpshooters were assembled on the ground beside the train. Coggins and Andreasen reluctantly left the cab and joined them. Smoke from the blazing trestle was billowing skyward.

Rawlings stepped up beside the cab and said, "Captain, I think you should let me run it across."

Flanking him were Hazzard and Cloud. Both asked to take the captain's place, but McGraw quickly commanded all three to move the men onto the bridge and get across.

Waiting in the cab, Captain McGraw watched his one hundred Sharpshooters bend low, rifles ready, and hasten onto the bridge. The crackling flames below gave off ample light so that he could watch them all the way across. Keeping the engineer and the fireman tight amongst them, the Confederate soldiers trotted across the bridge, coughing from the smoke clouds that rose from below.

McGraw was relieved that no shots came from out of the dark to pick them off. When the last man was safe on the other side, Lieutenant Rawlings took off his hat and waved it, signaling the captain. The Sharpshooters huddled together and looked across the river, concerned for the safety of their leader.

The flames were now licking close to the track bed on top of the bridge. Soon the rails would be red hot. Ryan McGraw released the brake, shoved his hat to the back of his head, and laid his hand on the throttle. Easing it forward, he felt the big engine move beneath his feet. The couplings between the cars creaked, and the train moved toward the blazing structure that spanned the river.

Sweat clung to McGraw's forehead, and his lips were a tense, straight line.

CHAPTER FOUR

✦

Moving slowly, the big engine rolled onto the burning trestle. Captain Mc Graw could see flames now leaping up around the edges of the bridge and licking through the cross-bars beneath the tracks.

Smoke was filling the cab. He cupped one hand over his mouth and gripped the throttle with the other. His eyes smarted from the smoke and teared up. Heat waves seemed to surround the cab. Blinking to clear his vision, McGraw coughed and leaned out the window, looking for his men. The Sharpshooters were standing together in the firelight, but with the heat waves and the smoke, he could barely make them out.

The massive superstructure moaned and swayed slightly as it bore the full weight of the train. Fear swept over McGraw and sent icy streamers all the way to his joints and marrow. His heart was pounding his ribs.

The captain gritted his teeth and willed a veil of calm to settle over him. The engine was moving, but it seemed to be inching forward at a snail's pace. He wanted to give it more throttle, but Charlie had cautioned him not to give it too much steam at once. It could cause the huge steel wheels to spin, which would jar the weakened framework of the trestle.

McGraw knew it should take less than two minutes to get the train across the bridge, but the seconds seemed like hours. He sleeved sweat from his face and felt a cold trickle down his back.

The ravenous flames were eating away at the wooden superstructure, and the roaring of the fire made the whole experience seem like a wild dream. Suddenly the bridge began to sway dangerously. Giant timbers were cracking beneath him like rifle shots...and Ryan McGraw knew it was no dream.

He couldn't see them through the smoke at all now, but McGraw could hear his men shouting frantically for him to hurry. His nerves were stretched taut, and he was aware of pain in his left shoulder as he urged the throttle forward ever so slightly, hoping to gain more speed without jarring the bridge.

The locomotive picked up speed, but still it seemed to be crawling. McGraw wiped smarting tears from his eyes as he continued to lean out the window and look for the end of the bridge. The smoke cleared briefly, and he caught a vague picture of the Sharpshooters bunched up beside the track, shouting that the bridge was about to go. A few more hour-long seconds passed and finally the engine was on solid ground, followed by the four cars.

McGraw cut the throttle and applied the brakes. The steel wheels shot sparks in every direction. When the train ground to a halt, McGraw could hear the Sharpshooters whooping and sending up a cheer. His knees felt watery. He leaned against the side of the cab, heaved a sigh and said, "Thank you, Lord."

Hap Hazzard was first in the cab, with Judd Rawlings, Noah Cloud, Charlie Coggins, and Lou Andreasen on his heels. The big red-head laid a steadying hand on McGraw's shoulder and said, "Nice job, Cap'n! You drove like a professional engineer, but I hope you don't ever have to do it again."

"I'll let you do it next time, Hap. One of those trips is enough for a lifetime."

Just then, the gigantic superstructure gave a death moan and the blackened trestle cracked and popped, giving way to the flames. It buckled, sending out a horrendous splitting sound, and collapsed with a mighty roar. Hundreds of timbers sailed downward like flaming torches, hissing and sending up billows of steam as they plunged into the deep waters of the Sepulga.

The Sharpshooters stood in silence until the last section of the bridge had come apart and dropped into the dark waters below, then their captain said, "All right, men, all aboard! In spite of Yankee skullduggery, this train's going to Mobile. Let's go!"

There was an exultant shout, and the rugged men of B Company piled back into their coaches. Captain McGraw and Lieutenant Rawlings returned to the supply car, and soon the train was rolling south once again.

As McGraw and Rawlings sat side by side in their "private" car, the lieutenant said, "I don't mean to be mushy or anything, but I'm sure glad you got across."

McGraw looked at him and grinned. "Thanks, ol' buddy."

After a few seconds, Rawlings asked, "While you were on the bridge, did you think of a little southern honey-blonde?"

McGraw eyed him levelly in the dim light. "You writing a book?"

Rawlings grinned. "No, but I was just wondering. Sometimes when a fella thinks his number might be up, his mind goes to the person who means the most to him."

The captain chuckled evilly. "It did. I thought of you!" As he spoke, McGraw rubbed his left shoulder.

"Aw, go on!" chortled Rawlings. Then noting what the captain was doing, he asked, "That shoulder still bothering you?"

"Yeah. It's been giving me some pain lately. I think I was pretty tense up there on that bridge. I'm sure my nerves and muscles were stretched plenty tight."

"I can understand that. Tell you what. Why don't I move to another seat and let you have this one all to yourself? That way you can at least lie down on your back...and I can do the same thing. Maybe we can get a little shut-eye if we're lying down. Okay?"

"Sure. It's worth a try."

When the lieutenant was on the seat in front of him, McGraw stretched out with his head next to the coach's side and his feet touching the floor in the aisle. He lay with his arms folded across his chest, listening to the steady clicking of the wheels beneath him. When he closed his eyes, one image after another raced across the screen of his mind.

The image that repeated itself over and over was that of a beautiful face surrounded by honey-blonde curls. Judd Rawlings's question kept echoing through his head: "While you were on the bridge, did you think of a little southern honey-blonde?"

Sleep fled from Ryan McGraw. His heart ached for Dixie Quade, and all he could do was think about how they met. His mind flashed back to that cloudy day in November of 1862. It was cold and bleak. He and his Sharpshooters were in a battle near the southern tip of Guntersville Lake in northeastern Alabama. Under intense fire by Yankee infantrymen, they were pinned down in a heavily wooded ravine.

Muskets rattled and rifles roared in the ravine. Blue-white smoke filled the cold air, and Rebel yells and Yankee shouts made the heavens shake.

Captain McGraw was hunkered in a thick patch of brush on the ravine's steep west bank, firing his revolver at Yankee soldiers on the ridge of the east side. Next to him was a frightened Rebel soldier, eighteen-year-old Bobby Brinson, who was not part of the B Company

Sharpshooters. Brinson had been in a bloody battle in the woods an hour earlier, and had seen his best friend killed right next to him. The friend's blood had sprayed Bobby's face and uniform. The shock had been so great that young Brinson wandered from the scene of the battle, moving across a field as if in a sleepwalk.

There had been heavy fighting the entire morning all over the Guntersville Lake area with two units of Alabama artillery facing off against the invading Northern army, and First, Fourth, and Sixth Alabama Infantries shooting it out with the Yankees in open fields and in the woods.

Just before noon, Colonel Derrick Pendleton of First Alabama Infantry had ordered McGraw to maneuver his men across an open field to the ravine and work their way behind a Yankee artillery battery. They were to get in close enough to pick off the artillerymen from a stand of trees nearby. It was while the Sharpshooters were working their way across the field that they spotted the young Rebel soldier moving aimlessly ahead of them. Without a word to his men, McGraw zigzagged toward Brinson in a dead-heat run and took him down with a flying tackle. McGraw was able to get him into the relative safety of the ravine, where he found it necessary to slap him to bring him out of his daze.

After a few moments, Bobby came to himself and began weeping as he told the Sharpshooters of his friend being hit with flying shrapnel from an exploding cannonball. Surprised to find himself with McGraw and his men, young Brinson told them he belonged to the Fourth Alabama Infantry. The captain then told him to stay with the Sharpshooters until they could get him back with his unit.

Keeping Brinson close to his side, McGraw led his men through the deep, winding hollow. When they were drawing close to the Union artillery unit they were to wipe out, they were suddenly attacked from both ridges by Yankee infantrymen, shooting from the heavy brush.

The Sharpshooters scattered and dived into the thickets on the steep banks of the ravine. McGraw saw young Brinson go stiff and freeze in his tracks. Snatching him by the collar, he dragged him into the brush. He noticed two of his men go down and winced at the sight of it.

As McGraw fired his revolver at the enemy across the ravine, Brinson knelt beside him, terrified. He hugged himself and trembled all over. His earlier experience had shaken him severely. While reloading, McGraw said above the noise of the gunfire, "Bobby, it'll be okay, son! We'll make it out of here! Just hold on!" Teeth chattering with fear, Bobby looked up at him and nodded shakily.

There were B Company men strung out in the brush on both sides of their captain on the west bank. The ravine was a bedlam of noise and shouts. On the opposite bank, a few Yankees were already dead. Some were on the ground and others were sprawled atop the brush along the crest of the ridge, the thick branches supporting the dead weight of their bodies. Directly below them, nestled in the thickets, Sharpshooters were shooting at Yankees on the west ridge above McGraw and the Rebels who fought from that side.

Suddenly a massive rush of blue uniforms swarmed along the west ridge. Muskets popped like firecrackers and bullets thwacked brush all around. Sharpshooters fired repeatedly from the east bank at the swarm of Yankees. Ryan McGraw pivoted and blasted away at the enemy soldiers above him, killing two before they could back away over the crest of the ridge to reload their muskets.

A third appeared directly above him, raised his musket and fired. McGraw felt the heat of the bullet as it hummed past his right ear. His own gun spit fire, and the Yankee came tumbling down the bank, rattling brush. Bobby Brinson looked up, and the dead man snagged to a stop in the bushes just above him.

McGraw heard Bobby eject a blood-curdling scream, but he was busy blasting away at another Yankee on the ridge above him. When the man-in-blue went down dead, McGraw turned to check on Bobby, but he was gone. Then, from the corner of his eye, he saw the young Rebel groping his way through the brush at the base of the bank. Just as he turned to shout at him, Bobby broke free of the entanglement and began staggering across the bottom of the ravine in mindless terror. Bullets were hissing and plowing dirt all around him.

"Bobby!" bellowed the captain. "Get back here!"

There was no response. The terrified youth continued tottering in the open, disoriented. Holstering his gun, McGraw plunged down the steep bank with ragged branches clawing at him. When he touched bottom, he bent low and dashed toward the reeling youth as fast as he could. He was within twenty feet of him when a bullet tore through Bobby's right leg, dropping him like a rock.

At the same instant Bobby went down, McGraw's chest seemed to explode high up on the left side. The powerful impact of the slug spun him around and it felt like the ground flew up and hit him in the back. The breath was knocked out of him, and his left arm and shoulder were numb.

Bullets continued to chew earth around him as he sucked hard for air and tried to get up. The ravine was filled with smoky, acrid air, and made him cough. With effort, he rolled to his knees and looked about for young Brinson. When he spotted him several feet away, Bobby was writhing in pain, clutching his bleeding leg.

McGraw had no thought for his own safety. The frightened young soldier was hurt and in danger of being killed. He had to get Bobby back into the brush. From somewhere, a strong shout rose above the thunderous din of battle. McGraw was sure it was Hazzard's voice.

Walking on his knees to Bobby, McGraw loomed over him and gasped, "C'mon, kid. I'm going to carry you out of here."

Bobby blinked and said through gritted teeth, "You're hurt, Captain!"

"My legs are okay," breathed McGraw, extending his good arm. "Let me get you on my shoulder. Hurry!"

The captain heard Hazzard shout again as he struggled to get Bobby on his shoulder. When the weight was fully on him, he took a deep breath, willed the strength into his legs, and stood up. With the wounded young soldier draped over him, McGraw headed toward the west side of the draw.

He was aware of numerous shouts amid the gunfire as he staggered beneath the weight. His men were cheering him on. As he drew near the brush, he caught a glimpse of Hazzard's ruddy face through the smoke, and Jim Henry Hankins beside him. He was within five steps of Hazzard and Hankins when he felt the raw quiver of his knees beneath him. In spite of the hot lead hitting all around, Hap was almost to him when his legs gave way under Bobby's weight. As young Brinson was lifted off him, McGraw cried, "Hap, get back into the brush!"

McGraw's head was swimming, and his own voice sounded distant and unfamiliar to his ears. He was aware of Hankins kneeling beside him when a whirling black vortex seemed to be sucking him down into a dark abyss. The gunfire began to fade away as it echoed off the walls of the abyss that was swallowing him. Then all was black...and silent.

Captain Ryan McGraw had no idea how much time had elapsed since he had passed out, but it made no difference. There was sharp pain pulsating in his left shoulder, and he was aware of a rocking sensation, accompanied by hard jolts against his back. Brilliant light assaulted his eyelids. Seconds later, the brilliance subsided. Slowly he opened his eyes and looked directly above him. He was in a moving wagon, but could see no other person. Looming over him were tree tops silhouetted against patches of blue sky, and periodically he caught a glimpse of the sun.

McGraw tried in vain to find his voice. What had happened? He couldn't remember. Who was transporting him in the wagon, and where were they taking him? Why couldn't he see anyone?

Determined to find out who was driving the wagon, McGraw tried to roll into another position. The movement shot a fiery bolt of pain through his left shoulder, and the whirling vortex was back. It took only seconds to swallow him again.

Captain McGraw had the sensation of being thrust upward dizzily and felt light against the lids of his eyes once again. He lay still, without opening them, hoping his head would stop spinning. Vaguely he recalled coming to briefly in the back of the wagon, and remembered the sharp pain in his left shoulder. This time, he felt no pain anywhere. His mouth and throat were dry. He released a tiny groan and ran his tongue over equally dry lips.

He heard footsteps, accompanied by the sound of a woman's skirt when she walks. Suddenly he was aware that someone was standing over him. A soft, sweet voice said, "Captain McGraw. Captain McGraw."

His dizziness was fading. Ryan opened his eyes, blinked a few times, and tried to focus on the object that hovered over him. It was a dull blur.

The soft voice spoke again. "Captain McGraw, can you hear me?"

Ryan's tongue was dry as sand in the hot sun, but he forced himself to answer, "Y-yes."

A cool hand touched his brow. It was soft and tender. Blinking again, he attempted to focus on the woman who was speaking to him. Little by little her face became clear. It was a young and beautiful face. She was smiling at him. The face of a goddess, he thought. It was framed in lovely swirls of hair the color of spun gold.

Her eyes were sky-blue, with long natural lashes, and her smile deepened the dimples in her cheeks.

"Well, Captain," she said, tilting her head, "I'm glad to see you are still with us. For a while there, I thought you were going to sleep through the duration of the war. Dr. Pierce will be glad to know you've regained consciousness. Your men will be happy to learn of it too."

"My men...Oh, my men!"

In a flash, it came back. McGraw was carrying Bobby Brinson toward the thick brush with guns roaring all around and bullets buzzing through the smoke-filled air like angry bees. Suddenly he was down and Hap Hazzard was lifting Brinson off him. Jim Henry Hankins was kneeling beside him, then...then came the whirling blackness.

The lady in white was saying something about his thirst and placing a tin cup to his lips. He drank lustily until she withdrew the cup, saying he must not drink too much at a time.

Swallowing what water was in his mouth, he asked, "Where am I, ma'am?"

"You're in a Confederate hospital in Birmingham."

"Birmingham? How'd I—? Oh, yes. In a wagon."

"You remember that?"

"Only a few seconds of it. I was out again pretty fast."

"They had you heavily drugged. That's why you've been so long in coming around. They gave you laudanum for your pain while transporting you here."

"How long have I been here?"

"Four days. Of course, you had surgery as soon as you arrived, but Dr. Pierce didn't have to administer much laudanum for that—you were so far under, anyway."

Ryan recalled, then, that he had been hit in the upper left side of the chest. Suddenly he realized his left arm was in a sling. Looking down at it, he asked, "How bad is it?"

"You took a bullet near enough your shoulder that it dislocated it, and high enough that it chipped your collarbone. The bullet almost went all the way through. It was so close under the skin on your back that Dr. Pierce cut through and took it out on that side."

"Will I—will I be able to use my arm and shoulder again? I mean just like before?"

"Dr. Pierce will talk to you about it," she said quietly. "Now, you need to stop talking and rest. You've been through a lot."

"But what about my men? Do you know how many were killed? What about Bobby Brinson? Where's Judd Rawlings? Is he okay? And what about—"

"Captain," the woman said, placing a finger to his lips, "I said you need to stop talking and rest."

"But—"

"I can tell you this much, then you're going to settle down. We have five Sharpshooters here in the hospital other than yourself, and they're all doing fine. I understand Private Bobby Brinson is not actually one of your men, but he is coming along real good, too. The bullet that passed through his thigh just barely chipped bone. He'll be fine. I can't tell you exactly how the battle ended, but I think our Rebels put the Yankees on the run. At least that's the way I got it from listening to your lieutenant friend tell it to Dr. Pierce."

"So Judd's okay? He didn't get hit in the battle?"

"If he did, he's hiding it quite well," she chuckled. "He's been to see you several times a day, along with about a million other of your roughnecks. A person would think you're their father or something."

"Well, in a sense I am, ma'am. I have to watch over them like a father." He paused, then asked, "You haven't heard Judd say how many of our men were killed?"

"No. I hope there were none. Do you think some might have been killed?"

"It's possible. I saw two of them fall. There was so much smoke in that ravine, I couldn't tell who they were or how bad they were hit."

"Maybe those two are among the five we have here in the hospital."

"I hope so," breathed McGraw. Brow furrowing, he said, "You haven't told me your name, ma'am."

Her dimples deepened as she gave him an appreciative smile. "Dixie is my name, Captain. Dixie Quade."

"Dixie, eh?" he grinned. "There's some south in the way you talk. Where are you from?"

Picking up the tin cup and moving it toward his mouth, Dixie said, "That's all the talk for now, Captain McGraw. Drink this."

The cup was about a quarter full. McGraw finished it and smacked his lips. "Thank you, Miss—or is it Mrs.Quade?" As he spoke, his eyes trailed down to her left hand. There was no wedding band.

"It's Miss Quade, for your information. Now, Captain, you are going to rest. I'll see that some food is brought to you shortly."

Setting the cup on the small table beside the bed, she lifted his head gently, fluffed up the pillow, and said, "Close your eyes, now. Dr. Pierce will be in to see you after 'while. I'll let him know you're back with us."

As Dixie headed for the door, McGraw said, "I want to see my men. Where are they?"

"They're close by," she called back over her shoulder. "You'll see them in due time. No more talk." With that, she closed the door behind her.

Ryan McGraw closed his eyes, wondering about his men...then about the beautiful nurse. He visualized her fascinating features, her smile, her dimples, and dwelt on the soft sound of her voice.

Soon he was dozing.

A half hour later, Dr. Jeremiah Pierce entered the sunlit room, expressed his joy that the patient had come around, then described in detail the wound and the surgery he had done. He encouraged McGraw by saying he would get the full use of his arm and shoulder back again, but might be bothered somewhat by pain from time to time. It would not hinder his work as leader of the Sharpshooters.

Relieved, the captain asked when he could see his men. Pierce told him three of them were waiting near the front entrance of the hospital, and that Private Brinson, who was four doors down the hall, was wanting to see him. The doctor added, however, that Bobby would have to wait till tomorrow, and that the three men outside would be allowed five minutes once the dressing had been changed on the wound and McGraw had eaten.

The captain was happy to see nurse Quade enter the room. She was there to help Pierce change the dressing. When that was done, the doctor told his patient that he was healing as expected.

Twenty minutes after Pierce and the nurse had left, a chubby woman with her hair done in a scarf came in, carrying a tray of hot food. She placed it on the small table beside the bed and promptly left. McGraw looked at it from where he lay flat on his back, and wondered how he was going to manage getting to it. Even if he could work his way into a sitting position on the bed, it was going to be difficult to reach it and get the food to his mouth with one hand. All he could do was try.

It took him two or three minutes to get in a sitting position, and when he did, the room was spinning around him. At that moment, the door came open and the Miss Quade hurried toward him, saying, "Captain, you shouldn't be doing that by yourself."

Grinning sheepishly, he said, "Sorry, ma'am, but the little gal left the food and disappeared. I figured it was up to me to—"

"Pauline was supposed to let me know when she was ready to bring your meal to you. I'm sorry."

She helped brace him up in the bed, then stood beside him and fed him. When he had all he could handle, she helped him lie down, picked up the tray and said, "Do you feel like seeing your three friends, now? If not, I'll—"

"Yes!" he said quickly. "I want to see them."

"You do remember that Dr. Pierce said it could only be for five minutes?"

"Yes, ma'am."

"I will warn your visitors of that, too," she said, heading toward the door. Opening it, she paused, looked at him, and commanded, "I want you to take a nap as soon as they are gone."

Ryan grinned. "Yes, ma'am."

"You have a beautiful smile, Captain. One would never think you could show such warmth to hear your men talk about how tough you are."

The captain's grin broadened. "That's because they only see my tough side, ma'am. Don't dare show them that I have a warm side. I save that strictly for pretty nurses."

Dixie's features tinted, and without another word, she was gone.

Moments later, Lieutenant Rawlings and Sergeants Hazzard and Cloud filed into the room. They greeted their leader, elated to know he would be all right. To his pleasure, McGraw learned that none of the Sharpshooters were killed in the fight, and that the five who were wounded were out of danger. Three of them were wounded seriously, and would be mustered out of the army for medical reasons.

Rawlings told him how a division of Sixth Alabama came to their rescue only moments after he and Brinson were carried into the brush by Hap and Jim Henry Hankins. The Yankees were put into immediate retreat. Several had been killed and many wounded.

McGraw asked where the Sharpshooters were camped. Rawlings informed him they were bivouacked on the south side of town, then gave him the news that General Maury had ordered them to move south to Union Grove. Federal forces were collecting there, and a battle was brewing. They were to pull out in the morning. The trio was to greet McGraw for all of the men, and wish him a speedy recovery. They wanted him back at the helm. In the meantime, Rawlings would be in charge.

The door came open and Dixie entered. Her mouth was turned down in mock anger as she looked at Judd Rawlings and said, "Lieutenant, you promised me."

Rawlings wiped a hand across his mouth, grinned, and said, "Has it been five minutes already nurse?"

Dixie placed her hands on slender hips and said flatly, "It has been thirteen minutes, Lieutenant."

"Well, time sure gets by, doesn't it?" exclaimed Rawlings, acting surprised.

Hap Hazzard gave her a wide smile and said, "Really, ma'am, if you knew just how tough Cap'n McGraw is, you wouldn't worry about a matter of a few minutes. Why, he—"

"Out!" she spat, pointing at the door. Her eyes showed that she was having fun at their expense.

"Yes, ma'am!" gulped Noah Cloud, feigning fear. "We wouldn't want to rile you. No siree! C'mon, guys. Let's vacate this place before the cute little lady decides to throw us out!"

Dixie folded her arms and fixed them with widened eyes. All three quickly shook hands with McGraw and hurried toward the door, saying they would see him soon.

Moving slowly toward the bed and smiling, Dixie said, "Some bunch, Captain. Are they like this all the time?"

"No," replied McGraw. "They're dead serious when they're fighting Yankees."

CHAPTER FIVE

★

Early morning sunlight was seeping through the window in Captain Ryan McGraw's room when he awakened at the sound of busy feet and a rustling skirt. Opening his eyes, he saw nurse Dixie Quade laying out soap, washcloth, and towel on a chair next to the bed.

McGraw was captivated by her beauty as she smiled and said, "Good morning, Captain. The night nurse told me you slept well. I'm glad."

"Me, too," he grinned. "What's going on?"

"I'm getting things ready for your bath. You'll eat breakfast first, then we'll get you washed up all nice and clean."

"My bath?"

"Mm-hmm."

"In a tub?"

"No, not yet. Just a good washing with soap, hot water, and a cloth."

"It's...ah...it's going to be sort of difficult for me to handle with one arm in a sling, but I'll do my best."

"Oh, you won't have to do it yourself. I'll take care of it."

The captain's face crimsoned. "Y-you *what?*"

There was devilment in Dixie's eyes as she said smiling, "I told you...I'll take care of it."

"Now, wait a minute. You...you're not going to give me a bath!"

Hands on hips, Dixie said, "Oh now, really, Captain. Certainly you're not *that* shy!"

Clearing his throat and looking obviously uncomfortable, Ryan replied, "No female has bathed me since my mother did when I was a baby, ma'am—and that's the way it's going to stay."

"Oh, really," snickered Dixie, about to burst into laughter. "Who do you think bathed you yesterday, and the day before, and the day before that?"

Ryan's red face suddenly drained to white. "You didn't!"

Turning toward the door and smiling to herself, she said, "Pauline will bring your breakfast in a few moments. I'll be back to feed you, then we'll take care of that bath."

Pauline came with the tray of food, laid it on the small table, and was gone in a flash. Seconds later, Dixie returned to feed him. McGraw's dread of his bath caused him to chew his food very slowly, attempting to put off the inevitable as long as possible.

When he was finished eating, Dixie picked up the tray and said, "One of the orderlies will bring in a pail of hot water in a few minutes, Captain. I'll be back shortly."

"Yes, ma'am," he said weakly.

The orderly arrived within three minutes and set the pail on the table. He was a beefy, middle-aged man with bald head, ample belly, and hulking shoulders. Smiling, he asked, "Feeling better, Captain?"

"Yes. Somewhat."

"I'm Harold Schamberg. I've been giving you your bath every day since you've been here. Glad to see you awake."

Ryan felt a sudden mixture of emotions. He was relieved to know it was Schamberg who had bathed him, but at the same time he was ashamed of himself for letting Dixie make him a victim of her sly intimidation. Laughing within, he thought, *That little scamp! She had me scared spitless, and she knew it!*

Schamberg had been gone about half an hour when Dr. Pierce came in to check on his patient. He was pleased that McGraw was looking better, commented about it, and left. Shortly afterward, the door came open and Bobby Brinson appeared in a wheelchair, being pushed by a pale, skinny orderly who looked like he ought to be a patient himself. The orderly said he would come for Bobby in twenty minutes.

The two soldiers shook hands warmly as Bobby leaned forward in his wheelchair, then young Brinson said, "Captain, I want to thank you for what you did the other day. You saved my life twice...both times at the risk of your own. Words fail me, sir, but I want you to know I appreciate it."

"All in the line of duty, Bobby," Ryan grinned.

"Not so, sir. What you did was above and beyond your duty. Please accept my apology for the way I conducted myself. There's no excuse for a soldier to let the death of his close friend push him over the edge like I did."

"Don't be too hard on yourself. You're only human. I've seen men much older than you and a lot more experienced in combat go off their keel when somebody close to them was killed." He paused, then asked, "You going to request dismissal from the army?"

Bobby shook his head. "No, sir. That experience has made a man of me, Captain. I want to fight again when this leg heals up. The doctor says I'll be able to."

"Great! I'm proud of you. You'll do all right from here on out. I'm sure of it. I assume you've linked back up with your unit."

"Yes, sir. There are some other men here in the hospital from the

Fourth Alabama. Colonel Stedham—that's my commander—was here yesterday. He had already learned about the way I acted at Guntersville Lake."

"What was his attitude?"

"Same as yours, sir. He didn't scorn me at all. Said I'd be a better soldier because of it."

"Good. Doc say how long you'd be in here?"

"Couple weeks. Then I have to go easy for about another six weeks. After that, I can get back into action."

There was a brief moment of silence, then young Brinson said cautiously, "Ah...Captain McGraw, sir?"

"Yes?"

"Did you really mean what you said—that you think I'll do all right as a soldier from here on out?"

"You bet. Why?"

"Well, sir...I...ah...I would like to join your Sharpshooter unit. That is, if you'll have me."

"How good are you with guns? Rifles *and* pistols? The way this war is, I don't have time to teach men how to shoot. General Maury only sends me men who are already crack shots. They also have to convince him they're Sharpshooter material. Most of the time, he'll take the word of their commanding officer for that."

"Well, sir, I've been handling rifles—or muskets—since I was ten, and revolvers since I was fourteen. The officers in Fourth Alabama call me 'dead-eye.' I don't say this to boast, but I'm known throughout my division as being a crack shot. Even Colonel Stedham is aware of it. He'll tell you that I'm speaking the truth. I can have him come in and talk to you. And I'll give you a demonstration just as soon as—"

"Hey, hey!" cut in McGraw, raising his free hand, palm forward. "I have no reason to doubt your ability with guns. It'd be rather foolish for you to sit there and tell me all this, then be found out a liar on the shooting range. Right?"

"Yes, sir." Light danced in his eyes as he asked, "You'll let me become a B Company Sharpshooter, then?"

McGraw grinned. "I'd be proud to have you in my outfit, Bobby. Of course, the transfer will have to be approved by General Maury. He'll do that only if Colonel Stedham—"

"The colonel already said he'd recommend it, sir. Depending on if you say you want me, that is."

"You'll have to go through some pretty tough training. You ready for that?"

"Yes, sir!" responded young Brinson, eyes shining. "It'll be an honor to serve with you!"

"Then consider it done," said McGraw. "We just lost three men to irreparable wounds, so we'll need new blood. I'll have General Maury leave a spot open for you. As soon as the doctor clears you for duty, we'll sign you up in B Company Sharpshooters."

"Thank you, sir."

Bobby was telling the captain about his parents and his childhood when the skinny orderly came back to return him to his room. McGraw asked Bobby to come back and see him soon. Agreeing to do so, Bobby gave the captain a parting smile as he was wheeled through the door.

Ryan lay quietly, letting his mind drift to his lovely nurse. He had never met anyone quite like her. She was not only beautiful on the outside, but she was equally beautiful on the inside. Her sense of humor was fabulous. He recalled the devilment in her eyes when she was "setting him up" for his bath. Dixie's inward beauty also consisted of tender compassion, which he could read in her expressions. And there was a wholesomeness about her—sweet, pure, fresh wholesomeness.

The captain was dozing when a gentle hand on his arm coincided with a familiar voice saying, "Captain McGraw, time for your medicine."

Looking up at her, McGraw blinked and put a mocking stern look on his face. "Oh, it's *you*," he said gruffly. "The nurse who likes to frighten poor, wounded soldiers to death."

Dixie was holding a cup of water mixed with powders. She giggled so hard, some of the water spilled over its rim.

McGraw's stern mask melted into a warm smile as he said, "I'll find a way to get even with you, Miss Quade!"

Giggling again, Dixie said, "Better not try it, Captain. That will only cause me to reciprocate...and I don't get even. I get *ahead*."

"I'm scared."

"You *were*," she laughed. "Did you have a nice bath?"

"Lovely."

"Wonderful," she said, placing the cup to his lips. "Drink it all down like a good little boy."

Ryan looked at the cup, gave her a scowl, and obeyed. When the cup was empty, she stood over him, looking down silently. There was an ineffable something in her sky-blue eyes. Something he could not name. Was it a special admiration for him, or was he just wishing it so?

To break the silence, Ryan asked, "Miss Dixie, I've been wondering about you."

She arched her eyebrows. "What about me?"

"Well...why you're not married."

"Oh?"

"I don't mean to be nosy, but most twenty-one-year-old ladies are married."

"Twenty-one? You flatter me. I'm twenty-four."

"Really? A *young* twenty-four."

"Thank you."

"That even enhances my curiosity. How can a young woman as lovely as you not have been snatched up by some knight in shining armor?"

"Quite simple," she replied. "I've had my share of would-be suitors, but when they learn the truth about me, they run away as fast as they can go."

"And what is that?"

"I turn into a frog at midnight."

McGraw laughed and laid a hand on his wounded chest. "Oh, don't make me laugh like that. It hurts."

"It's no laughing matter," Dixie said, pushing her lips into a pout. "How would *you* like to turn into a frog every night?"

Adjusting his arm in the sling, the captain said, "Okay. Now, seriously. There's a reason why you've gone this long without some knight in shining armor getting you to the altar to make you his blushing bride."

"You're right, Captain. And that reason is...I've yet to meet my knight in shining armor. So far, every man I've met and spent some time with has a chink in his armor."

"Oh. Looking for the perfect man, eh?"

"No, just the *right* man. Maybe I've been too busy to find him."

"What do you mean?"

"When I went to nurses' school, I was too occupied to get involved with a man. And since the war started, my duties here at the hospital have put me in the same position. I have some male friends, but no serious relationship.

Dixie studied him for a moment, then asked, "How about you, Captain? I happened to see your papers in the office the other day when they were out of the file. You're not married. Now, how is it that a handsome twenty-five-year-old man like you is not married?"

"Now, who's flattering whom? I'm twenty-eight."

"Really? A *young* twenty-eight."

"Thank you."

"To quote a famous Confederate captain, that even enhances my curiosity. How can a man as handsome and dashing as you not have been snatched up by some beautiful young maiden?"

Ryan's mouth pulled tight and his features paled. "Well, it...it's like this, Miss Dixie," he replied grimly. "I was married once, but my wife left me for another man."

"Oh, I'm so sorry," she said, putting her hand to her mouth. "Please forgive me."

"It's all right. I'm the one who started this question-and-answer session."

"But, I—"

Ryan reached out and took hold of the hand that held the empty cup. "It's all right, Miss Dixie. I'm completely over her now. It's been five years since she left me."

"Do you...have any children?"

"No. Thank the Lord. Children are the ones who suffer the most when a home is broken up." Sighing, he said, "I had suspected that she was seeing someone else, but there was nothing concrete. Just little things that happened now and then. We were living in Hattiesburg at the time. That's where I was born and raised. By the way, you never told me where you're from."

"Right here in Alabama. Tuscaloosa."

"So you really are a southern belle."

"That's what they say."

"Well, anyhow, back to my ex-wife—one day I came home from work and found a note staring me in the face. It said that she had left me for a better man. They would already be out of Hattiesburg by the time I came home. I never did learn who she ran off with. Several months later I received divorce papers, along with a brief note that she was marrying the man. I haven't seen her nor heard from her since. The letter came from Fort Payne, Alabama. She might've married a soldier. I don't know. And to tell you the truth, I don't care."

Dixie spoke quietly. "It's good that you can feel that way, Captain. Saves a lot of pain. But I'm sure it hurt plenty deep at first."

"Yes. I loved that woman a whole lot. But that love is dead."

Dixie was silent for a few seconds, then she asked, "Do you think you'll ever fall in love again?"

Ryan looked up at Dixie, meeting her gaze. He wanted to say, "Dixie, I think I'm falling in love with *you*," but after a brief moment he replied, "I sure hope so. Man needs a woman to love."

That ineffable something Ryan had seen in Dixie's eyes a few minutes earlier was there again...or was he imagining it? Was she having feelings toward him like he was having toward her? Was Dixie wanting to express them like he was wishing he could?

"It's only natural," she commented softly, then took a deep breath and said, "I'd better be going, Captain. The rest of my patients will think I've forgotten them."

When she reached the door, Ryan called after her, "Miss Dixie..."

"Yes?"

"Thanks for the medicine."

Her dimples were drawing him like a magnet as she smiled and said, "You're welcome, O mighty leader of Sharpshooters."

Dixie Quade was the bright spot in Ryan McGraw's life for the next couple of weeks. When he was able to leave the bed and sit in a wheelchair, she took him for rides up and down the halls, which gave him opportunity to meet other wounded Rebel soldiers.

Word came of his Sharpshooters from time to time. They were in battles and skirmishes in many parts of Alabama and eastern Mississippi under the capable leadership of Lieutenant Rawlings.

Private Bobby Brinson was sent home as scheduled to recuperate from his leg wounds, and would become part of B Company First Alabama Sharpshooters when army doctors pronounced him ready.

At the end of his second week in the hospital, McGraw was on his feet and getting his strength back. Once he was able to move around on his own, he saw little of the lovely nurse, who was busy with newly wounded men.

On New Year's Day, 1863, when McGraw had been at the hospital for just over four weeks, he was visited by Major General Dabney Maury. The general was glad to see him doing so well, and was pleased to hear that he was due to be released from the hospital on January 4. Maury said Lieutenant Rawlings was doing a fine job leading the Sharpshooters, but he was eager to see McGraw back with his men.

On the morning of January 4, Captain McGraw was in a fresh new uniform, getting ready to leave. He would meet his unit at Montgomery, where they were taking a much-needed rest. An army wagon was waiting at the front door of the hospital to take him to the depot where he would board a train for Montgomery.

The captain's mind was on Dixie Quade as he picked up his hat and crossed the room where he had spent so many hours talking to her. He was just reaching for the doorknob when it turned and the door swung open. It was Dr. Jeremiah Pierce, followed by the lovely nurse.

The doctor smiled and extended his hand, saying, "Well, Captain, I guess this is good-bye."

Meeting his grip, McGraw returned the smile and said, "Yes, sir. I appreciate what you've done for me. You did a good job patching me up."

"Just see to it I don't have to do it again."

McGraw chuckled. "I'll do my best, sir."

When the doctor had gone, Dixie moved into the room, closing the door behind her. She stepped close and Ryan saw that same look come into her eyes as they misted up. Did she really care that he was leaving?

Towering over her, he nervously turned his hat in his hands as he said, "Well, Miss Dixie, it's time for me to move on."

Blinking to cover the thickening moisture in her eyes, she spoke softly, "We'll miss you around here, Captain."

Ryan was wishing Dixie had said *she* would miss him. Her eyes seemed to be saying it, but she hadn't voiced it. He must not allow his imagination to give him a false impression. Yes, there were tears visible, but maybe she was this way with all the soldiers she had nursed back to health.

Trying to smile, he replied, "I'll miss all of you, too. You're a great bunch of people."

"I...I'm glad I got to know you."

From somewhere deep inside Captain McGraw there arose a strong compulsion to take her in his arms and kiss her. But he refrained, struggling against his desire. Inwardly he scolded himself for even thinking of kissing her. She had been kind to him, but he had no reason to believe he stood on special ground with her.

"Same here," he nodded, forcing a smile. He was still twirling his hat in a circle by the brim.

Dixie laid a hand on his arm and said, "Take care of yourself, won't you?"

It was like an electric current was running through him from where her hand rested on his arm. "Sure."

"Maybe...maybe someday we will meet again."

"I'd like that." Angling himself to step around her and head for the door, Ryan said, "Good-bye, Miss Dixie."

She let him move past her, then asked, "Could I walk you to your wagon?"

"I'd be honored."

Together, Dixie Quade and Captain Ryan McGraw strolled down the hall to the front of the building. The sun was shining, but the January air was cool. Ryan stopped at the door, looked through the glass at the army wagon that waited for him, and said, "You'd best not go out there without a wrap, Miss Dixie. I'll just say good-bye again right here."

A touch of sadness showed in Dixie's eyes. "Good-bye, Captain," she said, almost choking on the words.

Ryan donned his campaign hat and opened the door. He was about to pass through it when he heard her say, "Captain..."

"Yes?"

Without a word, Dixie moved close, raised up on her tiptoes, and planted a soft, tender kiss on his left cheek.

Captain McGraw was at a loss for words. Touching his hat brim, he walked to the wagon and climbed in next to the private who held the reins. As the wagon pulled away, he looked back to see Dixie waving at him through the window. He waved back, and as soon as the wagon had carried him out of sight, he touched the spot she had kissed with his fingertips.

The memory of that magnificent moment brought Captain McGraw back to the present. He was flat on his back aboard the Mobile-bound military train...and found his fingertips touching that sacred spot on his left cheek.

He breathed Dixie's name and wondered if she was still taking care of Rebel soldiers at the Birmingham hospital. It had been a year and a half since he'd last seen her. Not a day passed without her beautiful face crowding into his mind. Dixie Quade deserved love and happiness. Maybe by now that right knight in shining armor had come into her life. Maybe she had fallen in love with one of her patients and married him.

McGraw's attention was drawn to the train itself as it began to slow. He sat up and looked out the window. Darkness still prevailed. Certainly they weren't nearing Mobile yet. At the same instant, the front door of the coach burst open, and fireman Andreasen came in out of breath, saying, "Captain, we've got trouble!"

Lieutenant Rawlings stirred and sat up, blinking his eyes as McGraw rose to his feet and said, "What's the matter?"

"I think the Yankees have set a trap for us!"

"What do you mean?"

"There's a fire on the track about a mile ahead. Charlie told me to come and get you."

McGraw turned to his lieutenant and said, "Get the men awake and ready for action, then come to the engine."

"You bet," said Rawlings, following the captain and the fireman through the door.

Men were stirring and the two sergeants were on their feet as McGraw dashed through the cars with Andreasen on his heels. When they asked what was happening, McGraw said, "Do what Lieutenant Rawlings tells you!"

Plunging into the cab of the big engine, the captain found Charlie leaning out the window with his hand on the throttle. Swinging out from the rear of the cab and looking ahead, McGraw saw the flames on the track, brilliant against the surrounding darkness. Clouds had covered the moon, shutting off most of its light.

"It's Yankees, all right," McGraw said to the engineer. "They've got an ambush set up, sure as anything."

The fire on the tracks was now about half a mile away, and Coggins had the train barely moving. "What shall we do, Captain?" he asked.

"I don't know much about trains, Charlie. Can you ram that pile of burning wood without derailing us?"

"Maybe. The cow-catcher on this engine is set quite low. It'd be better that I hit it a little more than half of full speed. Any faster, and it could jumble the timbers and throw some of them underneath us."

Lieutenant Rawlings drew up to McGraw's side and asked, "So what's the story?"

"Yankees have set up an ambush."

Swinging out to see for himself, the lieutenant breathed, "Sure enough. What's your plan?"

"Charlie's gonna ram the barrier at better than half of full speed. Tell the men to get set. There'll be bullets flying out of the darkness from both sides of the train any minute. They need to stay as low as possible and fire back through the windows. All they can do is shoot at the flashes from the enemy guns. If we should derail, and they've got a large number of men out there, this could be a bad one. If we make it through the barrier, we'll be long gone before they can do too much damage to us."

"Let's hope it's the latter," clipped Rawlings and turned to leave.

"Lieutenant..." called McGraw.

Pausing, Rawlings looked back at him.

"Better put some men in the third car. If we get derailed, we for sure have to defend our ammunition and supplies."

"Yes, sir," nodded Rawlings, and was quickly on the catwalk of the coal car.

Turning back to the engineer, McGraw said, "Give the men a few seconds to get ready, Charlie, then shoot the steam to it."

Coggins nodded his agreement, then said to his fireman, "Lou, throw some more coal in the firebox."

While Andreasen was doing so, Coggins said, "Captain, how do you suppose them dirty Yankees found out this train was coming through to Mobile?"

"Hard to say, what with that bridge on fire earlier, and now this. When we found the bridge burning, I figured it was probably just a random piece of Yankee destruction. But what we're facing here is purposeful ambush. Maybe we'll never know how they found out we were coming. War always leaves a lot of questions unanswered."

Just as Andreasen was closing the big iron door of the firebox,

Sergeant Hazzard came around the side of the coal car and said, "Cap'n, we're about ready. Lieutenant Rawlings wanted me to tell you that he's distributed the men evenly in the three cars, and that he's commanding the third car."

"Thanks," said McGraw. Then to Coggins, "Okay, Charlie, let's go." Turning back to Hazzard, he said, "Hang tight back there, Hap. This could get rough."

"I'm thinkin' maybe I should send a couple men up here with you, sir."

"I don't think that'll be necessary. However, how about sending me a repeater rifle and some ammunition?"

"Will do," said Hazzard, and hopped onto the catwalk.

The train was picking up speed as McGraw said to the fireman, "Lou, I want you to climb in the coal car and keep your head down."

"I'd rather get my hands on a gun and help fight, sir," countered Andreasen.

"I appreciate that, but you're a civilian, and you're my responsibility. You'll be safest in the coal car. I'd put Charlie in there with you if I thought I could handle this thing when it hits that barrier."

"Do what the man tells you, Lou," cut in Coggins. "He's only tryin' to save your hide."

"I know," said the fireman. "I appreciate that, but I just want to do my part."

"Do your part by relieving my mind about you," came McGraw's firm words.

Saying no more, Andreasen climbed into the coal car and sat on the bottom in the black dust, behind the huge pile of coal.

Leaning out the window behind Coggins, McGraw looked at the blazing blockade on the tracks and asked, "How fast will we be going when we hit it?"

"About thirty-five miles an hour."

"Guess that'd be a little too fast for Yankees to run alongside and try to get on board."

"Yep."

"Of course if they've got horses, they could ride up and try to get on."

"Yep."

"Captain McGraw," came a voice from behind him.

Turning around, McGraw found himself looking at Corporal Bobby Brinson. Extending a Henry repeater and a small canvas sack loaded with cartridges, he said, "Sergeant Hazzard said I should bring these to you."

"Thanks, Corporal."

His features solemn, Brinson said, "Sir, I would like to respectfully request that I be allowed to stay here with you. It's not good that you should be here in the cab without some protection."

"I'll be fine. You get back to your post."

"Yes, sir."

When the corporal was gone, McGraw thought again of the day he had saved Bobby's life...and of the time in the Birmingham hospital when the bright-eyed youth had asked to become a part of the Sharpshooters. He had proven over and over again that his bloody experience at Guntersville Lake had been the making of him. Bobby had proven himself courageous and capable of operating under fire on many occasions since becoming a McGraw Sharpshooter.

The train was drawing close to the burning barrier on the track. Charlie Coggins spoke over his shoulder while keeping his eye on it and said, "Better brace yourself, Captain. Hard to tell just how big that pile of wood might be. May give us a good jolt when we hit it."

McGraw laid the sack of cartridges on the floor of the cab, levered a cartridge into the chamber of the Henry, and went to the other window, holding the rifle in one hand and bracing himself with the other.

Suddenly there was gunfire on both sides of the cab, and bullets were ricocheting angrily off the hard metal of the cab. In the vague surroundings along the track, McGraw could see horsemen charging toward the train firing repeater rifles. He turned to tell Coggins to duck down, only to see him draped out the other window. Dashing to him, McGraw pulled him inside the cab and laid him on the floor. One of the first bullets in the volley that had come out of the night had struck him in the right temple. Charlie was dead.

McGraw caught sight of a rider drawing up beside the cab, raising his rifle. Reacting quickly, the captain fired. The Union cavalryman stiffened and peeled from the saddle as the slug tore into his chest .

McGraw hopped to Charlie's window, laid his hand on the throttle, and looked ahead on the track. The blazing pile of timber was no more than fifty yards away. The sounds of rapid gunfire behind him were forgotten for the moment as he braced himself for the impact.

CHAPTER SIX

The locomotive slammed into the burning timbers with a thundering roar, scattering fiery missiles in three directions. Sheets of flame fanned into the night air, along with a massive shower of bright-red sparks, some flying thirty feet above the ground.

The impact slowed the train slightly, jarring everyone on it, but it began to pick up momentum seconds later. Ryan McGraw breathed a prayer of thanks that the stack of burning wood had not been too large. The Yankees had apparently hoped to delude the engineer into thinking it would be too dangerous to attempt plowing through it. A train was a wicked thing to be aboard when it went off the tracks.

McGraw looked back where the blazing timbers were scattered, and saw the Yankees on horseback making a wide circle around the flaming debris, intending to catch up to the train. Already the Rebels in the three coaches were firing at them.

Just as McGraw squared himself with the cab, he saw more riders coming at a gallop from both sides of the track up ahead. The wide swath of the engine's single headlight showed them clearly. He hated to do it, but he called over his shoulder to the fireman, asking him to leave the coal car and come to the cab.

When Lou Andreasen reached the cab and saw the engineer lying on the steel floor, he gasped, "Charlie!"

"He's dead, Lou," McGraw said sadly. "Nothing we can do for him now. Do you know how to run this thing?"

"Yes," nodded Andreasen, unable to tear his gaze from his dead friend.

"Okay. Take over. I've got to put my gun to use. Keep down as low as you can, but watch for any more obstacles on the tracks."

With the fireman at the controls, Captain McGraw leaned out the opposite window and shouldered his rifle. Two riders were drawing near from up ahead. The one in the lead lifted his carbine and fired at McGraw. The captain pulled his head inside just in the nick of time. The bullet struck the coal car and careened off with a shrill whine. At the same time, McGraw returned to his spot and fired, hitting the rider square in the chest. The sudden lurch of the man's body threw his animal off stride, causing it to stumble. When it went down, the horse behind it was unable to avoid it. Man and beast did a somersault, slamming the ground savagely.

At the same instant, Andreasen shouted, "Captain! Behind you!"

McGraw whirled about to see a man in blue coming up the steel steps at the cab's rear on the right side. His horse was just veering away. The muscular Yankee was gripping a revolver and bringing it to bear. McGraw had levered a fresh cartridge into the chamber of his Henry, but there was no time to bring it around. He leaped aside a split second before the gun discharged and the slug buzzed past him through the glassless window.

Before the Yankee could cock the revolver for a second shot, McGraw kicked it out of his hand. It went flying into the night. The Yankee was no novice at fighting. He leaped for McGraw, gripped the Henry with both hands and attempted to wrench it from its owner. The two enemies struggled for supremacy, each knowing that if he didn't kill his man, he would be the one to die.

The first volley of unexpected shots had dropped three Sharpshooters—two in the first coach and one in the second. One of the two in Sergeant Hazzard's coach was dead with a slug in his head. The other lay wounded with a bullet in his shoulder. The man in Sergeant Cloud's coach was still alive, with a mangled, bleeding ear. A Yankee bullet had taken part of it off.

The rear door of the third coach had no window, which allowed a couple of Union cavalrymen to ride up at the rear and leap aboard without being seen. Each wore two revolvers on his hips. One was a corporal, the other a sergeant. The sergeant tested the door and found it locked. "Okay," he said, "we've got about thirty seconds before the engine hits the fire. The door is plenty thin. We empty our guns through the door, then put our backs to the rear of the car and brace for the impact. The barrier won't stop the train, but it'll slow it down. That's when we jump."

"Gotcha," nodded the corporal.

"Okay," said the sergeant, pulling both guns, "on the count of three!"

Inside the third coach, Lieutenant Rawlings had his men hunkering on the floor at the windows, between the seats, firing at the riders. Rawlings was at one of the rear windows, using a repeater. He had just shot one of the Yankees from his horse when he noticed the wave of riders veering away from the train. A glance to the other side showed him the same thing. The horsemen were easy to see now, because of the huge blaze on the tracks.

Rawlings knew the engine must be about to slam into the burning barrier. Lifting his voice above the din, he shouted, "Brace yourselves, men! We're about to hit that pile of timber!"

Even as the last words were coming from Rawlings' lips, a barrage of shots came plowing through the rear door, scattering splinters everywhere. The lieutenant saw one of his men near the front of the coach take a slug that came through the door. Rawlings flattened himself on the floor and began firing through the door as fast as he could work the lever on the Henry. While he was peppering the door, suddenly the coach seemed to skid on the tracks, throwing every man forward.

Sheets of flame, sprays of sparks, and flying pieces of blazing timber could be seen through the windows. Every man in the coaches knew the train had survived the impact against the barrier and had come through without being derailed. Already it was picking up momentum.

In coach number three, Lieutenant Rawlings scrambled to his feet, drew his revolver, and eased up to the bullet-riddled door. He slid the bolt and jerked it open. By the dim light of the lantern behind him, he saw two Union soldiers lying dead on the small platform. Rawlings was about to throw the bodies off the train when more riders came thundering in, guns cracking. He leaped back inside, slid the bolt to lock what was left of the door, returned to his window, and picked up the Henry.

Inside the second coach, the Sharpshooters were readjusting their positions after being thrown forward when the train hit the flaming barrier. Sergeant Cloud looked around and asked, "Everybody all right?" There was a chorus of yeses.

Corporal Jim Henry Hankins was at a window reloading his repeater rifle and saw the dark forms of Union horses and riders drawing close to the train once more. "Sergeant!" he called out. "Here they come again!"

"Over here, too, Sergeant!" shouted Luther Mangus on the opposite side.

"Let 'em have it, boys!" bellowed Cloud, gripping his rifle and diving for the window he had occupied before the train hit the barrier. Rifles began to bark and bullets slammed into the coach. The rocking and swaying of the train made it difficult to hit the riders, especially in the dark, but from time to time the vague form of a Yankee could be seen falling from his saddle.

Private Brad Thacker squatted down to reload his rifle when he saw the rear door of the coach come open. At first he thought it was one of the Sharpshooters from the third coach, but when he caught sight of a gun muzzle being thrust through the opening and a blue uniform behind it, he realized that one of the Yankees had boarded the train from the back of his horse.

Thacker's heart froze. His rifle was out of service. The door was ten feet from where he was positioned between two seats. Reacting by instinct, he threw his weapon at the protruding gun barrel and shouted, "Back door!"

The Yankee's gun discharged, but its slug went wild because Thacker's rifle slammed against it. It took a couple of seconds for the other Sharpshooters in the car to respond. Several guns roared, sending hot lead through the opening and into the door.

When the firing stopped, Sergeant Cloud dashed to the door, but the Yankee was not in sight. He picked Thacker's rifle up, handed it to him, and said, "That was fast thinking, pal."

"Thank you, sir," grinned Thacker.

"Don't call me 'sir', boy. I'm not an officer."

"Yes, sir. I...I mean, yes, Sergeant."

Suddenly there were heavy thumping sounds directly above them. Cloud knew where the Yankee had gone. Raising his rifle, he shot through the ceiling of the coach. Working the lever rapidly, he fired several more times. A "whump" sounded overhead, then a corpse tumbled onto the small platform where the rear door stood open.

"Got him!" shouted Cloud, moving onto the platform. Using his foot, he shoved the dead Yankee off the train.

A new wave of riders was coming in, guns blazing. Two slugs chewed wood near Cloud's head. Dashing inside, he slammed the door and slid the bolt. The Sharpshooters quickly resumed their positions at the windows.

Brad Thacker, who had been with McGraw's Sharpshooters since October of 1862, returned to his window and bent low to finish loading his rifle. The sound of booming guns was deafening. Bullets were striking the coach from both sides. Suddenly a slug ripped through the wall of the coach and hit Thacker in the right side. He groaned and doubled over on the floor.

In the first coach, Sergeant Hazzard and his men were blasting away at the shadowed horsemen who came and went in waves. Several riders had come up close, fired point blank into the coach, then swept away quickly. Two of the Yankees had left their horses and grabbed onto the platform just behind the coal car. They found the door locked. One turned to the other and said, "Let's get 'em from the side!"

The platform was built so a person hanging onto its railing could swing out and look into the windows. The closest window on either side was a mere two feet from the vehicle's front end.

With revolvers in hand, the Yankees each took a side and swung out far enough to hang onto the rail with one hand and stick his gun through the window with the other.

Sergeant Hazzard happened to be at the first window on the right side. The Yankee on the left side was in position first and fired. The Sharpshooter at that window took the slug through the head and keeled over.

While the same Yankee was drawing a bead on the next Rebel inside the coach, the one on the other side stuck his hand through Hazzard's window. The Sergeant had just witnessed the shooting of his man across the aisle and was bringing up his gun to fire at the enemy who had shot him when some sixth sense caused him to turn toward his own window. The muzzle of the Union revolver was just coming inside.

Hazzard dropped his weapon, seized the revolver, and swung it upward. It fired and the bullet went through the ceiling. Hazzard's powerful hands twisted the gun from the man's fingers, and he put a steely grip on his wrist.

Across the aisle, the other Yankee fired again, hitting another Sharpshooter in the back. A split second later, Corporal Brinson's rifle fired through the window of the coach and tore into the Yankee's forehead. He dropped instantly from sight.

While the other Sharpshooters were firing at the riders, an angry Hap Hazzard had pulled the Union soldier halfway through the window. Gripping the man's arm, Hazzard stood up and brought it down violently against his up thrust knee. Bone snapped loudly. The Yankee released a blood-curdling wail, and Hap let him fall to the ground.

In the engine, Lou Andreasen stood at the controls and watched the death-struggle between Captain McGraw and the enemy soldier. Andreasen wanted to jump in and help subdue the big man, but to do so would leave the engine unattended. Such a move could result in a disaster to the entire train.

While guns popped beyond the coal car, McGraw and his enemy grappled for control of the Henry on the steel floor of the engine. They moved in jerky circles, stumbling repeatedly over the lifeless body of Charlie Coggins.

The Yankee was heavier than McGraw, and was trying to use his weight to proper advantage. He found, however, that the smaller man was a mountain of strength. Only by his bulk had the Yankee been able to stay in the fight. McGraw's shoulder wound was giving him pain, but he ignored it. He must overcome the big man and kill him.

At one point, the Yankee was able to swing McGraw around, putting his back toward the coal car. He was trying to shove McGraw backward so that he would fall off the engine and be ground to death beneath the wheels. He would gladly let go of the rifle to let it and the Rebel captain fall to the tracks.

McGraw knew what the man had in mind. When he felt himself being forced toward the edge of the cab, he stiffened and dug his heels into the engine's floor. They were again meeting strength for strength. When the Yankee saw that he could not break McGraw's stance, he suddenly jerked backward to throw him off balance. It didn't work. The seasoned Sharpshooter planted himself quickly, and drove the bigger man against the firebox, pinning him there. Their hands quivered as they gripped the Henry between them.

The husky man did all he could to force McGraw backward, but found himself without leverage because he was flattened against the firebox. The struggle continued while the engine picked up speed. Within thirty seconds, the Yankee was well aware of the rising heat on his back side. Sweating, he growled and grunted, trying to push away, but the smaller man seemed to be made of raw steel.

When the Yankee's blue pants began to smoke, he let out a howl. McGraw took advantage of his pain to wrest the rifle from his hands, let it fall, and surprise him by chopping him savagely on the throat and the left side of the neck with the edge of his hand, a move he had learned from the Japanese gardener of his childhood.

The Yankee gagged from the throat chop and went numb on the left side of his body. Momentarily defenseless, he felt himself hurled across the steel floor of the cab. A wild scream came from his lips as he sailed over the edge, bounced off the coupling between the engine and the coal car, then went under the merciless wheels.

The moon had reappeared and was spraying the land with silver light. Sucking hard for breath, McGraw looked back along the train and saw that the Union cavalrymen had given up the chase. The train was now traveling at nearly fifty miles per hour.

Picking up his rifle, the captain found Andreasen smiling at him. "That was some kind of fighting, sir."

"Not the kind I'd want to do every day," gasped McGraw rubbing his aching shoulder. "Keep this choo-choo steaming toward Mobile, Lou. I'm going back to check on my men."

When Captain McGraw had been in all three coaches and totaled up the damage, he found that three of his men were dead and four wounded. Four lives had actually been lost with the death of engineer Charlie Coggins.

At 5:20 A.M., the train pulled into Mobile's depot. McGraw had been told by General Maury that a unit of men would be there from Fort Morgan to meet them and transport them south to the fort.

The unit of twenty men had camped nearby and were on hand when the train pulled in. Their leader was Lieutenant Wesley Hall, who was pleased to meet the famous Captain Ryan McGraw, but saddened to learn of the ambush and its drastic results. The bodies of the dead Sharpshooters would receive proper burial at Fort Morgan's cemetery.

When Andreasen advised McGraw that Charlie Coggins had no surviving family, Hall said he could be buried with the soldiers. The bodies were placed in an army wagon. Another wagon would take the wounded men to Mobile's hospital, where Rebel soldiers wounded in other battles were recuperating. The army had hired a steam-engined barge to transport the wagons carrying Sharpshooters, weapons, ammunition, and supplies the twenty-eight miles south on Mobile Bay to Fort Morgan.

When Captain McGraw told Hall that he was going to deliver his wounded men to the hospital, the lieutenant said, "Oh, that won't be necessary, sir. I'll send one of my sergeants with them."

"I appreciate your willingness to offer the sergeant's services, Lieutenant, but this outfit operates a little different than the rest of our Confederate army units. These men look to me as a father. Now, would a father just send his boys over to that hospital, or would he *take* them there?"

Hall cleared his throat. "He would take them there, of course, sir. I understand."

"I appreciate that."

Hall forced a smile. "It's all right, then, for the rest of your men to go on down to the fort?"

"Yes. My lieutenant, Judd Rawlings, here, will remain with me."

"Very well, sir," nodded Hall. "The same wagon that takes you and your men to the hospital will be here to carry you down to the dock at whatever time you choose. The army has a couple of ferry boats that move us up and down the bay whenever needed. I'll make sure one is waiting for you. I'll explain all of this to General Page and tell him you'll be along as soon as possible."

"Thank you," said McGraw.

"Yes, sir. We're mighty glad to have you and your men at Fort Morgan with us, sir."

"We're honored to be a part of the team," nodded the captain.

McGraw stood before his men and explained the situation. Others wanted to stay with the wounded, but the captain told them it was best if they went on to the fort. He assured them he would see to it that the wounded men received the very best of care, and that he would not leave them until he was completely satisfied.

Captain McGraw delivered Corporal Dean Bradbury, Corporal Vince Udall, Private Clint Spain, and Private Brad Thacker into the hands of the hospital's chief surgeon, Dr. Glen Lyles, who examined them immediately upon arrival.

Udall had been shot in the back and the bullet had lodged in his lung. He was prepared for surgery immediately, since he was in the most danger. Bradbury had a bullet in his shoulder and would be operated on by a second surgeon within a few minutes. Private Thacker had been creased in the side by a Yankee bullet that had passed on through. Another doctor would clean the wound and patch him up. Private Spain had a tattered ear, which was bandaged upon his arrival at the hospital. The doctor who worked on Thacker would do what he could for Spain once he had stitched up Thacker.

McGraw and Rawlings stayed until all four had been attended to and the doctors had reported their condition. Udall would be the longest of the four to recover, but Dr. Lyles pronounced him out of danger after doing the surgery.

After talking to Lyles in his office for several minutes, the two Sharpshooter officers thanked him for the good care he was providing their wounded men and made ready to leave. The doctor walked them to the office door and stepped into the hall. He chatted with them about the festering situation at the mouth of Mobile Bay, then returned to his office.

Corporal Udall was in a private room with a special nurse to look after him. McGraw and Rawlings went to the room to see how he was doing. The nurse would not let them in, but said she would tell Udall they were inquiring about him. McGraw asked her to convey the message that he would be back in a day or so to see him. She assured him she would pass it on, and closed the door.

Bradbury, Spain, and Thacker had been placed in a four-bed room together, along with another wounded soldier who had lost his left arm in a battle on the Alabama-Mississippi border a week previously. He was Sergeant Marvin Staples of the Ninth Alabama Cavalry.

Upon entering the room, McGraw and Rawlings found Bradbury and Thacker asleep, still feeling the effects of the laudanum. Spain was awake and glad to see them. He was also glad to hear that Udall was going to be okay.

Spain introduced the captain and the lieutenant to Sergeant Staples. The sergeant had heard of McGraw. He shook hands with both officers, saying that he was glad the Sharpshooters were going to be at Fort Morgan when the Union navy decided to make a move on Mobile Bay. McGraw and Rawlings felt sorry for the man, who had only a bandage on his shoulder where his left arm had been, but they did not show it. No wounded soldier wanted to be pitied.

Telling Spain he would be back as soon as he could and to pass the message on to the "sleeping beauties," McGraw headed for the door with Rawlings on his heels. Pausing before moving into the hallway, he said, "Clint, I don't want you chasing any pretty nurses around this place. Understand?"

Grinning, Private Spain cupped a hand to his bandaged ear and said, "Eh? I'm deaf, Captain. Cain't hear a word you're sayin'!"

McGraw laughed, waved him off, and moved into the hall.

As the two Sharpshooters moved along the hall, they were noticed by a nurse working on a patient in one of the rooms. Near the front door of the building, they ran onto Dr. Lyles, who was in conversation with the surgeon who had operated on Dean Bradbury. McGraw and Rawlings spoke briefly to them, then passed through the door and climbed into the army wagon that waited for them.

Dr. Lyles turned to walk back to his office. He was almost there when he looked up to see one of the nurses trotting toward him. He saw that she was excited and said, "You look like one of your patients just had a miraculous healing, Dixie."

"It's almost as good as that, Doctor," she said breathlessly, brushing a lock of honey-blond hair from her forehead. "I just saw you talking to Captain Ryan McGraw!"

CHAPTER SEVEN

✦

D r. Glenn Lyles noted the dancing beads of light in Dixie Quade's eyes, and said, "You know Captain McGraw, I assume."

"Yes sir," Dixie replied, realizing how excited she had sounded. Clearing her throat, she covered her elation a bit and said, "The captain was a patient of mine at the Birmingham hospital about a year and a half ago."

"Got pretty well acquainted with him, eh?"

"Well, he was under my care for several weeks. We did get to know each other. Why is he here?"

"He and his famous Sharpshooters have been assigned to Fort Morgan because of the Union naval buildup off the Gulf coast. While coming down here from Montgomery on a special train, they were ambushed by Union cavalry. Three of his men were killed, and four were wounded. He and his lieutenant brought the wounded ones in for treatment. Couple of them had to have surgery."

"I recognized Lieutenant Rawlings, too," smiled Dixie. "Are the wounded Sharpshooters all in the same room?"

"Three of them are. Room twenty-seven. The other one is in worse shape. He's in room fourteen."

"I see. Thank you, Doctor. Well...I have to get back to work."

Dixie's heart fluttered as she made her way along the hall and entered a room to change the dressing of an elderly woman who had been burned severely with boiling water. The patient was under heavy sedative and was barely aware that the nurse was working on her. With no one to interrupt her thoughts, Dixie let her mind run to the handsome Rebel captain. She recalled the day he was brought into the Birmingham hospital. She had watched over him like a mother hen for four days after his surgery while he lay under the influence of laudanum, wondering what color his eyes might be.

While dabbing the elderly woman's burns with ointment, Dixie smiled to herself, remembering the morning Ryan awakened and opened his eyes. When she saw they were a magnificent pale blue, she told herself they fit perfectly with his sandy hair and mustache.

Dixie had also wondered for four days what his voice might be like. She was sure it would be strong, deep, and masculine...his entire makeup was so manly. And sure enough. When he spoke, he sounded exactly as she had imagined.

Was that when she fell in love with him? She thought so. If not, it came the next morning when she made him think she was going to give him a bath. *He was so darling,* she thought. *His face turned such a deep shade of red. Then when I made him think it had been me who had bathed him every day since he had been in the hospital, he went white as a sheet!*

One thing Dixie knew for sure—she had fallen head-over-heels in love with Captain Ryan McGraw almost from the first moment she met him. She thought of how it had bothered her when he began to get better and they had less time together. During their all-too-infrequent visits, they had experienced some precious moments together. At least they had been precious to Dixie.

While wrapping new dressing on the elderly woman's burns, Dixie recalled many of the moments she had enjoyed with Ryan until the very day they had to say good-bye. She remembered how she had looked for some sign in his eyes...anything that would tell her they had become more than just nurse and patient. For a moment there seemed to be an indication that he wanted to take her into his arms, but it quickly faded.

Feeling a sharp disappointment, she could only lay a hand on his arm and tell him to take care of himself, then remark that maybe someday they would meet again. He was kind enough to say he would like that, but gave her no hope that it would come to pass.

Dixie discarded the old dressing and put things away in the small cabinet. Making sure her patient was comfortable, she left the room and hurried down the hall to the nurses' "powder" room. Finding it unoccupied, she let herself recall that last moment, when at the hospital door she had kissed Ryan's cheek to show her affection for him, then waved good-bye through the window as he rode away.

Tears filled Dixie's eyes as she remembered how she wept that night in her bed—and many nights thereafter—missing the handsome captain who had unknowingly stolen her heart and realizing that she might never see him again.

Using a hanky to dry her tears, Dixie thought, *But here he is...assigned to Fort Morgan, less than thirty miles from me, and no doubt intending to return to the hospital to see his men!*

Pulling herself together, she returned to duty. Ryan was on her mind constantly for the rest of her shift. When her day was over in late afternoon, there was one more thing she had to do. Maybe some of the wounded Sharpshooters had been with the outfit when Ryan was in the Birmingham hospital. If this was so, she wanted to know it. Maybe she could learn a vital thing or two.

Dixie made her way to room twenty-seven and opened the door. The first face she saw belonged to the man with one arm. She had tended to Sergeant Staples the first couple of days he was at the hospital. When her gaze met his, she said, "Hello, Sergeant. How are you doing?"

"Fine, ma'am," grinned Staples.

"Good. I've been working the other end of the hospital and haven't had time to stop and see you."

Before Dixie could scan the faces of the three Sharpshooters, one of them exclaimed, "Well, I declare! Miss Dixie, is that you?"

The owner of the voice had a familiar face, and by the fact that he recognized her, she knew he had to have been among the Sharpshooters a year and a half previously. Moving up to his bed, she smiled and said, "I know your face, soldier, but the name escapes me."

"I'm Corporal Brad Thacker. Well...I was *Private* Brad Thacker when you knew me."

"Congratulations on your promotion."

"Thank you, ma'am." Turning to his comrades, who lay looking on, Thacker said, "Fellas, I'd like you to meet the most beautiful and charming nurse in the business. Miss Dixie, this is Corporal Dean Bradbury next to me, and that guy over there is Private Clint Spain."

"Pleasure to meet you, ma'am," said Bradbury and Spain.

"The pleasure is mine," smiled Dixie. "You'll have to excuse the corporal's accolades about me. As I recall, he thinks any young lady in starched white dress and nurse's cap is beautiful and charming."

"Aw, Miss Dixie," Thacker retorted mildly, "that just ain't so."

"Dr. Lyles told me about the ambush you Sharpshooters had on your way down here," said Dixie. "Looks like you tough guys will survive, though."

"Sure we will," said Thacker. "We've got another Sharpshooter here, too. He got shot up a little worse than us, so they've got him in a private room."

"So Dr. Lyles told me. Is he anyone I know?"

"No, ma'am. He's like these two guys here. He came along after our esteemed leader had been in the hospital." Eyes widening, he said, "Did you see the captain when he was here earlier?"

"Well, yes and no. I saw him from a distance—he and Lieutenant Rawlings—but I didn't get to talk to him. I asked Dr. Lyles what Captain McGraw was doing here, and he told me about the ambush and you men being brought in."

"Well, he'll be back in a day or so, ma'am," said Thacker. "He'll sure be glad to see you, that's for sure."

Dixie's heart thudded against her rib cage. Hoping to hear Brad Thacker say that the captain had mentioned her often over the past year and a half, she queried, "Oh? Why do you say that?"

"Because when Captain McGraw was in the hospital there in Birmingham, he mentioned lots of times that your smile and cheerful ways were hastening his recovery."

A feeling of disappointment washed over Dixie like cold water. "Oh. I see. Well, I'm glad to know that." She paused, then asked, "Does his shoulder wound bother him any more?"

"Sometimes. I've seen him rubbing it quite often. S'pose maybe it'll always give him pain now and then."

"It could." There was another question she had to ask. Mustering up the courage, she braced herself and asked, "Brad, has the captain...has he...well, has he gotten married since I saw him last?"

Grinning, young Thacker replied, "No, ma'am. He ain't even got a girlfriend. I guess the war's been keepin' him too busy."

Dixie masked her relief and said, "That's probably it. He'll no doubt find a woman and get married once this horrible war is over."

"I hope so, ma'am. The captain seems like sort of a lonely man sometimes. What...ah...what brought you down here? Run out of sick people in Birmingham?"

"Not quite," she giggled. "It's the Union naval buildup on the Gulf. As you know, General Lee is working hard making preparations for Mobile's defense. You Sharpshooters are part of those preparations. The general is confident the Federal forces are planning an all-out effort to destroy Fort Morgan and Fort Gaines and to capture Mobile. With the potential warfare pending here, experienced medical help will be needed. Like myself, many nurses are being brought in from Confederate hospitals all over the South to beef up the staff in this one."

"I bet they're not all as pretty as you, Miss Dixie," Private Spain said. "I wish they'd let you take care of me. I'd get well faster."

"Aren't you sweet?" she said, blushing.

"Not sweet, ma'am. Just honest."

Brad said, "You still are Miss Dixie, aren't you, ma'am? I don't see a wedding band on your finger."

"Yes," she sighed. "It's still Miss Dixie."

Thacker grinned broadly. "Good. Tell you what. Maybe when I get out of here, you and I could take a Sunday walk together, or somethin' like that. Maybe have dinner some night, too."

"That's a nice thought, Brad," she said warmly, heading for the door. "But once you knew the truth about me, you'd run away like a scared rabbit."

"The truth about you?"

"Mm-hmm," she hummed, pausing with one foot in the hallway. "I turn into a frog at midnight."

Thacker snickered.

Spain grinned and said, "I'll bet you're the prettiest little girl frog a feller ever saw, though."

Dixie laughed, said, "See you *fellers* later," and vanished.

The afternoon sun shone down on the rippling waters at the entrance of Mobile Bay as Captain McGraw and Lieutenant Rawlings stood on the deck of the small ferry and watched Fort Morgan come into view. With the chug of the steam engine in their ears, they surveyed the two-thousand-yard-wide mouth of the bay, letting their eyes sweep southward. Visible on the gleaming horizon of the Gulf of Mexico was the Union fleet, waiting for more vessels to join them before they launched the attack.

"Like a bunch of blood-hungry vultures," Rawlings said bitterly.

"Yeah," nodded McGraw.

The ferry was moving southward about a mile off the eastern shore of the bay, and began to angle to the left toward the tip of

Mobile Point, where Fort Morgan's lighthouse lifted its towering head against the azure sky. Letting his gaze rove westward to Dauphin Island where Fort Gaines lay in the heat of the sun, McGraw ran the two-thousand-yard expanse to massive Fort Morgan on the east. "Morgan's a lot bigger than Gaines," he commented.

"I'd say so!" Rawlings reacted with enthusiasm. "I never realized Morgan was so large."

"General Maury said Morgan's got some plenty big guns, too."

"They'll need 'em," responded Rawlings, lifting his hat and running splayed fingers through his dark-brown hair.

Fort Morgan was an old brickwork fortress built in the shape of a pentagon. Its formidable walls were topped with six feet of sod, which added to their strength. Grass even grew from the sod. Notched in the thick, five-angled parapets were rectangular slots where the muzzles of the big cannons loomed, waiting for Union targets.

With the warm sea breeze caressing his face, McGraw pointed toward Dauphin Island and said, "According to Maury, General Page's men have driven wooden pilings beneath the surface from just off shore to some spot out in there. Any ship trying to come through that area will find its hull being ripped up."

"Good thinking," remarked the lieutenant.

"I told you about the torpedoes. They'll protect the rest of the entrance."

"S'pose he's already got them in there?"

"Don't know, but if not, I'm sure they will be soon."

The ferry, which also bore the army wagon and driver, was gliding up to the dock. The pilot told McGraw and Rawlings to brace themselves. Seconds later, the ferry bumped the dock, and a soldier on the dock caught the rope tossed toward him by the pilot.

As the officers stepped onto the dock, the soldier saluted and said, "Captain McGraw, General Page is waiting for you. I'll take you to his office."

McGraw and Rawlings followed the soldier up the sandy slope, past the lighthouse, and through the heavy gates. Inside the walls, the open area was pentagonal shaped. The commandant's office, the dining hall, and the barracks were located on the eastern side of the impressive structure. Their guide led them to the open door of the commandant's office, halted at the threshold, and knocked on the wooden frame.

A voice inside said, "Yes?"

"I have Captain McGraw and Lieutenant Rawlings here, sir."

"Well, show them in, Williams!" blared the gusty voice.

McGraw and Rawlings entered the relatively cool office to find Brigadier General Richard L. Page on his feet, coming around his worn and faded desk.

Page was a stout man in his sixties with a thick head of silver hair and a handlebar mustache. He stood five feet nine inches tall, but his breadth and booming voice made up for whatever he lacked in height. After introductions and handshakes had been taken care of, Page said, "Gentlemen, I guess I don't need to tell you how glad I am that you and your Sharpshooters are with us. I've got a hundred and twenty good men here, but an additional ninety-four sure looks good. Your presence here has raised the morale of my men."

"So my men told you about the ambush and our casualties, I see," said McGraw.

"Yes. I'm sorry about that. Too bad the engineer was killed, too. How's the fireman going to get home?"

"Don't know for sure, General. He's staying at a Mobile hotel right now. Said he'd get himself back to Montgomery one way or another. Can't take the train back with the bridge out, that's for sure."

Stepping outside with the two officers following, Page gestured toward the barracks and said, "I've given you and your men separate quarters, Captain. At the end of the barracks. I thought it would make it more convenient for you to command your men."

"Thank you, sir," smiled McGraw. "It will."

Page called to a corporal passing by and asked him to find the fort's other officers and send them to his office. Taking McGraw and Rawlings back inside, the general sat them down and eased into the chair behind his desk. He was commenting on all the good reports he had heard about the fighting prowess of the B Company Sharpshooters when three men drew up to the open door.

"Come in, gentlemen!" boomed Page, rising to his feet.

McGraw and Rawlings also stood, and were introduced to Colonel DeWitt Munford, who was second-in-command at the fort, and Lieutenants Wilson March and Frank Cooley.

As the group sat down, General Page eased back in his chair, which groaned from his weight, and said, "We also have a captain attached to the fort. His name is...ah...Lex Coffield."

McGraw and Rawlings both detected a distaste for Coffield in the way the name came off Page's tongue, but neither commented.

Proceeding, Page said, "Captain Coffield is on assignment right now upriver...Tuscaloosa. He'll be back in a few days."

The mention of Tuscaloosa brought Dixie Quade to Ryan McGraw's mind. He felt a sharp pang in his heart at the thought of her. He hoped she was well and happy.

General Page discussed the chain-of-command arrangements with the officers, as stipulated in written orders by General Lee. The Sharpshooters were to remain under the jurisdiction of Captain McGraw and to be commanded only by him. The Sharpshooters were a separate fighting unit and would act as such. Page explained to his officers that this was the reason he had given McGraw and his men a separate section of barracks. Page ran his gaze over the faces of the men and said, "Naturally, because of my rank and position, B Company will follow my orders, but only as I give them through Captain McGraw." Pausing briefly, he asked, "Any questions?"

When there were none, the beefy general looked at McGraw and said, "Now...something that I find it necessary to do."

"Yes, sir?" said McGraw.

"I must warn you and Lieutenant Rawlings about Captain Coffield. The captain is very short-tempered and all business. He's not always easy to get along with. Has a lot of pride. He's a West Point graduate, a distinction none of the rest of us in this room can boast about. He's got a sharp mind...very intelligent. I just wanted to raise a red flag about his temper. If he'd learn to control that thing, he'd be a general."

"I see," nodded McGraw.

"So, what I'm asking, Captain, is that you and Lieutenant Rawlings work at trying to get along with Coffield, and please stress the same to your men."

"Will do, sir," said McGraw.

After breakfast the next morning, a group of men were standing around in the open area inside Fort Morgan, waiting for assembly time. General Page had put out word that he wanted to meet with all the men, including McGraw's Sharpshooters, shortly after breakfast. At the moment, Page was outside the walls in the lighthouse, having taken Captain McGraw with him. With the coming of dawn, the watchmen in the lighthouse had reported seeing new ships in the Union fleet on the horizon. Page wanted to take a look for himself.

A few Sharpshooters were talking with Fort Morgan men, getting acquainted. When Noah Cloud introduced himself to a couple of men, one of them smiled and said, "You say your name's Cloud...C-L-O-U-D? Like them white cottony things in the sky?"

"That's it," grinned big Noah.

Hap Hazzard chuckled, "Only with him, it's not always white. Most of the time, it's like *storm* clouds—you know, dark and ugly."

Noah gave Hazzard a sharp look. "Says you, carrot-head!"

"Yeah, says me!" snapped Hazzard. Looking around at the men in the group, he said, "You fellas all know the Bible story about the big flood. Must've been some kind of dark ugly storm clouds when all that rain was falling, wouldn't you say?"

A few of the men nodded their agreement, not knowing whether to smile or not.

"Well, let me ask you fellas," continued the redhead, "what was the gentleman's name who led his family and all those animals on that big boat?"

"Noah," came a quick reply from the group.

Hazzard reared back and gave a big belly laugh. "See? What'd I tell you? Ol' Noah Cloud here may have hair the color of straw, but like those clouds in the day of his namesake, he's dark on the inside and ugly on the outside!"

"Oh, yeah?" roared Cloud, swinging a haymaker and connecting solidly on Hazzard's ruddy jaw.

Hap's feet left the ground and he landed on his back. Mumbling words that no one could understand, he got up shaking his head, and growled, "You're gonna be sorry for that!"

While the Fort Morgan men looked on askance, the Sharpshooters in the group showed no surprise or excitement.

Taking a boxer's stance, big Noah rasped, "And just how are you gonna make me sorry, carrot-head?"

Spitting into his palms, Hazzard doubled up his fists and hissed, "I'm gonna mash your face into a bloody pulp and make you better lookin'!"

"Bah!" bawled Cloud. "Do it, *then* talk about it, big mouth!"

At the same instant, Lieutenant Wilson March appeared and said, "Hold it, you two! The general doesn't allow fighting amongst the troops!"

"I respectfully submit that we're McGraw's men, sir," said Cloud. "We *gotta* fight. Especially now, because that mutton-brained big mouth has asked for a good lickin'."

"General's coming, Lieutenant!" came a voice from the fringe of the group.

March swung his gaze to the front gate. Page and McGraw were moving through the wide opening with the blue waters of the Gulf of Mexico behind them.

Keeping his voice low, Lieutenant March said to the would-be combatants, "That will be enough. You two break it off right now."

Cloud dropped his hands to his side and said to the big redhead, "We'll finish this later, pal."

"We sure will," Hazzard said through his teeth.

Brigadier General Page assembled the troops and informed them that three new warships had just joined Admiral Farragut's fleet, making a total seventeen. He voiced his opinion that the Yankees would not attack until they had strengthened the fleet a good deal more...especially with ships equipped with greater firepower than those he had just viewed through a telescope. Farragut was no fool. He knew his fleet would have to bowl its way into Mobile Bay under the heavy guns of Fort Morgan, as well as those lighter ones at Fort Gaines. He would not make a move until he felt he had the firepower to make a successful attack.

Assuring the men that the attack was probably at least two or three weeks away, the general said, "Men, I want to explain the function of the Sharpshooters as I have laid it out for Captain McGraw. It is three-fold. First, they are to plant explosive mines known as 'torpedoes' in the bay. We don't have them on hand as yet, but I planned this so as to coordinate the arrival of B Company with that of the torpedoes. From what I know about Captain McGraw's men, I feel such a task will be to their liking."

"We can handle it, General!" called out one of the Sharpshooters.

Page smiled at him, then continued. "The torpedoes will be planted under the direction of Captain Coffield, who is in Tuscaloosa where the explosive devices are being assembled. Coffield will soon be returning. He is bringing a healthy supply of the torpedoes down the river in small boats."

Adjusting the gray campaign hat on his silver head, the bulky general proceeded. "Second, when the Union fleet moves in, the

Sharpshooters will position themselves on the east side of the bay so as to snipe at sailors on the decks of the Federal boats. You are all aware that we have driven huge pilings into the bottom of the bay from Dauphin Island to a point just two hundred yards from where we stand. We'd have done it all the way across, but the water's just too deep at that point. We can't do it. The torpedoes will have to take care of the two-hundred-yard channel.

"Admiral Farragut no doubt is aware of the depth of the bay's mouth, so he's probably figured out that we're using pilings. If he hasn't, he'll know it when he sees some of his ships hung up on the pilings while they're taking in water. Our Fort Morgan men will be firing their big cannons at the Union fleet as it approaches the channel. Even if we're highly accurate, the blue-bellies are going to get some ships into the bay. You Sharpshooters will be there to open fire and take out their deck crews."

One of the Fort Morgan sergeants lifted his hand for recognition.

"What is it, Sergeant Clary?" asked Page.

"Sir, I don't mean any offense at all, but are these B Company Sharpshooters really that good? I mean, if very many ships get past our big guns, some of them will get into the bay, then turn rudder and head toward the other shore to get out of rifle range. Granted they'll be slow-moving, but can these men be accurate, shooting three, four, five hundred yards?"

"Let me assure you that they are the best riflemen in the world, Sergeant," said the general. "They'll do their job. However, let me explain that those waters will also be infested with torpedoes. If they do as you say, they won't get very far before they find themselves in a fourth of July celebration. Those devices will be going off all over the place."

Rubbing the back of his thick neck, Page said, "Let me say to all of you Fort Morgan men—according to General Lee, no army on the face of this earth has an outfit as tough and capable as these McGraw men."

There was an outbreak of cheers from the men of B Company. A man didn't have to be too observant to see that this was a close-knit, hard-fighting bunch. Fort Morgan's troops were impressed.

"Furthermore," continued Page, "let me inform you what else General Lee has reported about these men. He says that not only are they the very best with rifles and pistols, but they are equally skillful at fighting with knives and bare hands. I would advise all of you not to rile them."

Laughter swept through the crowd.

Smiling broadly, the general said, "Now, I want to get back to the three-fold function of the Sharpshooters. General Lee believes the Yankees will also come along the narrow strip of beach to the east that leads to the mainland and hit us from behind. I've asked him to give us more men, but the way the war is going, he is not promising to do it. Our Confederate troops are in short supply on so many fronts. So— function number three—I have asked Captain McGraw to give me a couple dozen men to help guard the rear of the fort. We've got plenty of cannon power, but it sure won't hurt to have some dead-eye rifle-men on the parapets putting bullets into blue uniforms."

A Fort Morgan private lifted his cap over his head, waved it, and shouted, "Three cheers for the Sharpshooters!" Waving their gray hats and caps, the entire force of Fort Morgan's troops joined in a rousing cheer.

CHAPTER EIGHT

★

Morale was running high at Fort Morgan as General Page dismissed the men. Captain McGraw reminded his Sharpshooters to clean their guns, then turned to General Page and said, "Sir, I've noticed that there are some riding horses in the corral behind the fort, as well as those that pull the wagons. Would you mind if I borrowed a horse and saddle?"

"Of course not. You need to go somewhere?"

"Yes, sir. I need to go to Mobile. I realize you've made the ferries available, but I could ride up the shore on horseback a lot faster. I'd like to check on my wounded men at the hospital, and I also need to send a wire to General Maury."

"Of course. Certainly Maury needs to know about the ambush."

"Yes, sir. General Lee wants my unit to always be brought back to a hundred men plus myself when we have losses. General Maury has to know about my losses so he can send replacements."

"Take the bay gelding with the white stockings. Good horse. You'll find McClellan saddles in the feed shed."

"Thank you, sir. I'll be back as soon as I can. I've already made it clear to my men that anything you need done, they are to do it."

"Fine. See you when you return."

McGraw found his lieutenant at the barracks, making ready to clean his revolver and rifle. Most of the men had gone out into the open area to do their gun cleaning.

Rawlings was sitting on his cot, removing cartridges from his revolver when he looked up to see McGraw standing over him. "I'll clean yours, too, Captain, if you want me to," he offered.

"That's okay," smiled McGraw. "I'll do it myself when I get back from Mobile. I'm going to ride one of the horses up the shore and see the men at the hospital. Have to wire General Maury, too. Let him know about the ambush and that he needs to send us some replacements."

"Tell you what," said Rawlings, punching the cartridges back into the cylinder. "I'll just borrow one of the other horses and ride up there with you. I'm sure the general wouldn't mind."

"No need. I think I can find the way by myself."

"I don't doubt that," said the lieutenant, shoving the loaded revolver into its holster as he stood up. "I just think it's best that you not go alone."

"You think I need a nursemaid, is that it?" McGraw chuckled.

"Call it what you want, but I'm going with you."

McGraw shrugged his wide shoulders. "Okay, nursemaid. Let's ask the general for another horse."

When McGraw and Rawlings stepped out into the sunshine, they spotted General Page standing at his office door, talking to one of his colonels. The colonel turned and walked away just as McGraw and Rawlings were drawing up. The captain explained that they would need another horse. Page smiled and said, "Take your pick, Rawlings. The red roan's a good one. You gentlemen have a nice ride and I'll see you—"

The general's words were cut off by a bellowing voice across the sunbaked yard. They turned to see Hap Hazzard and Noah Cloud mixing it up in a furious fight. Page's men were forming a circle around them.

"Looks like a couple of your boys are in some kind of dispute," said Page. "Better stop it."

"It's best that I don't, sir," replied McGraw. "You have to know Hazzard and Cloud to understand, but they're the two toughest men I have. They're fighters by nature. If they don't have Yankees to fight just about every day, they'll fight each other. That ambush didn't last long enough. Just as well let them get it out of their system."

The general rubbed a hand over his mouth and said, "Well, I've got a hard and fast rule about my men fighting each other, but since you're our guests so to speak, I'll leave your men strictly to you on this." Grinning, he added, "I like a good fight, myself. Since you're going to let them go at it, I just as well watch."

McGraw and Rawlings exchanged glances and smiled. Knowing none of the Hazzard-Cloud bouts lasted very long, they walked with the general to where the fight was in progress and joined the Fort Morgan men as they looked on. The Sharpshooters had seen more than their share of Hap and Noah battering each other. They were paying no attention to the fight. The Fort Morgan men were divided as to whom they wanted to see win the contest. Half were shouting encouragement to Hazzard, and half were doing the same for Cloud.

The two combatants were locked in a hand-to-hand struggle, rolling in the dirt. When they slammed into the legs of the excited spectators, Cloud came up on top. Gritting his teeth, he popped Hazzard square on the jaw. Hap took the punch as if it were nothing and arched his back, bucking Noah off him.

Cloud rose to his feet, balled his fists, and breathing heavily, said, "C'mon, big mouth! Get up!"

Hazzard came off the ground as if catapulted and drove his head into Cloud's belly, knocking the wind from him as they both hit dirt and rolled about, stirring up dust. They came up on their knees and Hap quickly threw an arm around Noah's neck, grabbed his wrist with the other hand, and compressed it with every ounce of his strength.

Noah's face turned beet-red. It was a hot day, and both men were sweating profusely. Noah rammed an elbow into his opponent's ribs. Hazzard grunted, but kept his hold on Noah's neck. Noah dug his elbow into the ribs again, harder this time. It hurt enough to cause Hazzard to ease up slightly on his hold. Cloud twisted within Hazzard's grasp, putting his back to him, reached behind him, took hold of Hazzard's head, and flipped him over his back.

Hazzard was on his feet quickly and went after Noah. He missed with a roundhouse right, and caught a hard fist on the chin. They stood there toe-to-toe, trading blows. Finally, Cloud took a step back and said, "I've hit you with everything I've got, you big ugly ape! Why don't you go down?"

"Me?" gasped Hazzard. "It oughtta be *you* goin' down!"

"Hah!" roared Cloud, moving in and punching him on the jaw again. "You're the ugliest, not the toughest!"

Hazzard staggered slightly, then lunged in and returned the blow. "Oh, yeah?" he boomed, knowing he was going to be hit again, and not even attempting to dodge it.

The men of Fort Morgan were dumbfounded. They had never seen the like. It was as if Hazzard and Cloud enjoyed being punched.

"Use some of that Oriental stuff on him, Hap!" shouted one of the soldiers.

Hazzard gave him a dirty look and said, "I don't want to maim the man, I just want to make him prettier!"

The crowd laughed, and the combatants began laughing. Hazzard and Cloud each put an arm around the other and stood there, heads thrown back, roaring with laughter.

General Page turned to McGraw and asked, "Does it always end this way?"

"Always. Those two are the best of friends. They just have to let off steam once in a while. If they can't let off steam on the enemy, they work each other over. What you just saw will last a day or two, then it'll happen again."

Page chuckled, shaking his head. "Those two are crazy."

"I've told them the same thing, sir, and they always have the same answer. Watch." Speaking to Hazzard and Cloud, who still stood there with an arm hooked over the other man's neck, McGraw said, "Hap! Noah! You two are crazy!"

"We know, Cap'n," laughed Hazzard, "that's what keeps us from goin' insane."

There was a big round of laughter, then the soldiers went about their business. McGraw and Rawlings saddled the bay and the roan and headed for Mobile.

Receptionist-secretary Rebecca Worley was working on a stack of papers at her desk, enjoying the slight breeze coming through the open window. The early afternoon sun had just gone behind a bank of clouds, easing the summer heat a little.

Rebecca allowed herself a moment to watch the dozen or so recuperating Confederate soldiers as they sat in the shade a few yards away. She wondered how many more Southern men would be brought in to Mobile's hospital before the horrible war came to an end. She had seen several hundred come and go...some to the local cemetery. Many had returned home missing arms and legs. Others had left blind or maimed. Still others had walked past her desk and out the door to return to combat.

Rebecca's heart was heavy as she beheld one young soldier with bandages over his eyes, walking across the hospital grounds, being led by a nurse. Suddenly her attention was drawn to a young mother plunging through the door, carrying a small boy in her arms. There was a bloody makeshift bandage on the child's right arm and a look of apprehension on the mother's pale features.

Rebecca stood up and stepped around the desk to meet the woman. As she drew up, Rebecca said, "Looks bad, ma'am. Is the cut deep?"

"Yes," she gasped. "Can a doctor see him right away?"

"Of course. Follow me."

The bleeding boy immediately had the attention of nurses in the examining room, and a doctor was summoned. While the worried mother stood close, the nurses removed the bandage and examined the four-inch gash on the child's upper arm.

The boy's eyes showed fear, and in an attempt to calm him, one of the nurses said, "Don't you worry, little fellow, the doctor will be here shortly and get you all fixed up. What's your name?"

"Tommy," came the reply, riding a whimper.

"How did you get this cut, Tommy?"

"Fell out of a tree and hit the picket fence."

"He sure did," spoke up another nurse. "I can see some tiny splinters in the cut."

"Oh, I thought I'd gotten them all out," the mother said shakily.

"It's all right, ma'am," said the nurse. "Dr. Bentley will do a thorough job on it." She looked toward Rebecca, who stood near the door. "Rebecca, I'm sure you need to get some information from this lady. Why don't you take her to your desk?"

"Right," nodded Rebecca. "Please come with me, ma'am. Tommy is in good hands."

Brow furrowed, the mother moved close to the table and said, "Tommy, you'll have to be Mommy's big brave boy now. Okay?"

Lips pulled tight, the boy nodded.

"I'll be just down the hall, honey. When the doctor gets you all fixed up, these nice nurses will let me know, and I'll take you home."

A bit frightened but wanting to show his mother that he was made of brave material, Tommy nodded, but showed no inclination to cry.

As they walked together down the hall, Rebecca said, "That's a fine boy you have there, ma'am."

"Thank you."

Rebecca, who was rather plain and had mouse-brown hair, looked on the attractive woman with envy as she gestured for her to sit down on a chair in front of the desk. She wore a pale yellow dress that held her tightly at waist and breast, and her glossy black hair dropped in a long fall behind her stately head. Her eyes were like ebony bits of marble, giving a hint that they could spark with anger or mesmerize a man with innate power. Her features were clear and exquisitely formed.

Taking a printed form from a drawer, Rebecca picked up a pencil and said, "Okay, I need to get some information from you."

The woman told Rebecca her name was Victoria Manning Coffield, that Tommy was her son, and that she was the wife of Captain Lex Coffield of Fort Morgan. The Coffields had a house in Mobile so the captain could be close to his family.

While telling the receptionist that Tommy was five years old and giving his birth date, Victoria glanced anxiously toward the closed door down the hall where her son was being treated.

Rebecca noted it and said, "Mrs. Coffield, I understand that you are concerned about Tommy, but really you needn't worry. He'll be fine. Dr. George Bentley is one of the very best."

Victoria smiled and replied, "I'm sure of that, Miss—" her eyes dropped to the small name plate on the desk—"Miss Worley. It's just that I've been upset about some other things lately, and...well, this sort of came at the wrong time. I'm afraid I'm not handling it very well."

"I'm sorry, ma'am. I hate to bother you with all of these questions, but it's routine, you know."

"I understand."

At that instant, Victoria's attention was drawn to the front door of the hospital as two Confederate officers entered, looking sharp in their gray uniforms. Her mouth fell open when the officers removed their campaign hats, and she recognized the tall, handsome man with the sand-colored hair.

Rising to her feet as the captain and the lieutenant drew near, Victoria Coffield felt her heart thundering in her breast. It took the captain only an instant to find her familiar face. Shock registered in his eyes. He stopped quickly, his face slightly losing color.

Ryan McGraw had not seen his ex-wife for over six years. She was twenty-one when she walked out of his life, and had matured a great deal. She was still beautiful, and her maturity somehow made her beauty more clearly defined.

Victoria's hands shook as she said with dry mouth, "H-hello, Ryan."

The captain felt a tremor run through his body. He struggled to control his emotions. He thought he had his ex-wife out of his system, but even though she had torn his heart out six years ago, he found something deep within him responding to her presence. Forcing a calm into his voice, he said, "Hello, Tori. You're...you're looking well."

"You...you, too," she responded, looking him up and down. "You really do a lot for that uniform. And...you're a captain, I see."

"Army's desperate," he said shyly, looking uncomfortable.

Judd Rawlings, who knew the story on Victoria, took a step closer, and said, "Captain, if you need a little time to talk, I'll go on and visit the men."

Pulling his gaze from his ex-wife, Ryan set it on Judd and replied, "Sure. Do that. I'll be along shortly."

As Judd walked away, Victoria cast another anxious glance toward the door down the hall.

Rebecca realized an awkward situation had befallen the distraught mother. Rising to her feet, she said, "Mrs. Coffield, if you and the captain need to talk privately, there's a waiting room two doors down the hall to your left. It is unoccupied at the moment. We can finish up with these details on Tommy when you're through."

The name "Coffield" rang a hard bell in Ryan's mind. Was Victoria married to this Captain Lex Coffield who was in Tuscaloosa gathering torpedoes?

Setting expressive black eyes on her ex-husband, Victoria asked, "Would you like to talk for a few minutes, Ryan?"

"I guess maybe we should."

"If there is any word from the doctor before you're through, I'll let you know, ma'am," spoke up Rebecca.

Victoria thanked her and walked slowly down the hall with Ryan. When they entered the room, Ryan closed the door and pointed to a couch, telling her to sit down. As she dropped onto the couch, he took a straight-backed wooden chair and sat down facing her.

"Tommy..." said Ryan. "Is that your son?"

"Yes," nodded Victoria, clasping her shaky hands. "He...he fell out of a tree and cut his arm. I've told him a thousand times to stay out of that tree, but you know how boys are."

"Yes. I used to be one. Trees just seem to beckon to a boy. Not much he can do if he's all boy but give in."

"I suppose," she said, relieved that he was not unleashing a tirade of scorn upon her. "Tommy's that, all right."

"I heard the receptionist call you Mrs. Coffield. Your husband happen to be Captain Lex Coffield?"

"Yes," she replied, looking surprised. "You know him?"

"No. My men and I just arrived at Fort Morgan yesterday, and General Page told us about him. I understand he's up in Tuscaloosa right now, collecting torpedoes for the upcoming naval battle in the bay."

"Yes. I...figured you'd be in the army, with the war and all, but I never dreamed you'd be a captain. Lex is a graduate of West Point, and that's as high as he has gone. You've done all right for yourself."

Ryan shrugged his wide shoulders. "Like I said, the army's desperate."

"You lead a unit of men?"

"B Company. First Alabama Sharpshooters. You heard of us?"

"No," she replied, wringing her hands. "I don't pay much attention to the war. Are you at Fort Morgan because of Admiral Farragut's gathering fleet? I know about him because Lex talks a lot about him being out there in the gulf."

"Yes. We're here to bolster the defenses. Some of my men got shot up in a Yankee ambush while we were traveling to Mobile from Montgomery. We left them here at the hospital yesterday. My lieutenant and I decided to ride up and check on them."

"I see," Victoria said, brushing at a lock of hair that had fallen on her forehead.

There was a heavy, blank silence. Victoria could hardly breathe.

Ryan's memory was torturing him. He was picturing the raven-haired beauty in her exquisite white wedding dress and remembering how utterly happy he had been the day she became his bride.

Feeling the pressure to break the silence, Victoria said, "Ryan, I know I was wrong to just leave a note when I ran off with Lex. At least I should have told you face-to-face that I was leaving you. It's just that...well, I did it in that sudden manner, feeling it was best to make it quick and clean."

Fixing her with ice in his pale blue eyes, Ryan said acidly, "Leaving the note wasn't where you were wrong, Tori. It was leaving *me*. You stood at the altar the day of our wedding and vowed before God and man that you would keep yourself only unto me as long as we both lived. You broke your vows."

Victoria avoided his gaze.

"So you married him at Fort Payne, eh?" pressed Ryan. "That's where the divorce papers came from."

"Yes," she replied, staring at the floor. "That's where he was stationed when we happened to meet in Hattiesburg. Do you want to know how we met?"

"No. I don't care."

A pained look pinched her face. Still avoiding his gaze, she said, "The reason we're here is because when the war broke out, Lex declared his loyalty to the South. He was immediately assigned to Fort Morgan. We've maintained a home here in Mobile so Tommy and I could be close by."

"I guess that's as it should be."

Raising her eyes to meet his, Victoria said, "This will sound inane, Ryan, but I'm going to say it anyway. It's good to see you...and I'm glad to know you're at the fort. It will be nice having you so close."

Ryan wanted to hate her, but he couldn't. Memories of their sweet times together were racing through his mind. Part of him felt the desire to lash out at her for daring to say it would be nice to have him so close, but another part wanted to show her kindness. He was reading something in her eyes...something that told him she was under a heavy strain.

"Tori, are you happy?"

Tears surfaced and her anguish etched itself on her face. Her lower lip quivered as she replied, "Not that you should even care, but I am very *un*happy. Lex is not at all what I thought he was."

Leaving the couch, Victoria fell to her knees at her ex-husband's feet. Tears were now spilling down her cheeks as she laid a hand on his forearm and said with breaking voice, "Oh, Ryan, the last several months I have thought of you constantly. I have relived so many wonderful memories. I...I made such an awful mistake! You're right. The worst thing I did was break my vows. I deserve anything bad that happens to me. You have a right to hate me."

Breaking into sobs, Victoria pulled a hanky from the sleeve of her dress and dabbed at her eyes. Struggling to gain control of herself, she looked up at Ryan from her kneeling position and said, "Oh, darling, you don't hate me, do you?"

Victoria's use of the word darling tore at Ryan McGraw's heart. He was wishing their paths had not crossed in the hospital. Barely moving his lips, he said, "No, Tori, I don't hate you."

Swallowing hard, she closed her eyes and willed herself calm. Speaking with a level voice, she said, "Ryan...?"

"Yes?"

Victoria was looking into his eyes searchingly. "Have you remarried?"

"No," he replied flatly, rising to his feet and towering over her. "I'm not married, but you are. I had best be going."

Jumping up, she clutched both his arms. "Ryan, I need your help!"

"You've gotten along without my help for six years, Tori."

"Please!" she begged. "Living with Lex is unbearable! He's a hot-tempered brute! He mistreats Tommy. He's mean and selfish. He wants everything his own way."

Ryan looked at her blandly. "That was your problem, too, Tori. At least it was the last year we were married. You changed from what you were when I married you. Suddenly everything had to go your way, or you threw tantrums and pouted like a spoiled brat. Remember?"

Victoria did not reply. She just stood there gripping his arms and looking at him through a wall of tears.

"I suppose that's why you left me for this Lex Coffield," continued Ryan. "You thought he would give you your way all the time. I can see why you're miserable. Two selfish, self-centered people in a marriage can put a strain on things. There's nothing I can do to help, Tori. You made your bed, now you'll have to lie in it."

Shaking her head and struggling to keep from losing control of herself, the troubled brunette sniffed and said, "I deserve anything you say to me, darling, but you can't just walk away and leave me. I need your help!"

"You're asking the impossible, Tori. I can't butt into your marriage."

Abruptly, Victoria wrapped her arms around him, laid her head against his muscular chest, and said with trembling voice, "It will help me immensely if we can just see each other now and then."

Ryan was about to say that they could *not* see each other when there was a knock at the door. Pulling away from his ex-wife, he went to the door and opened it.

Rebecca Worley said, "Excuse me, Captain. Dr. Bentley is about finished with Tommy. He wants to speak with Mrs. Coffield."

Dabbing at her eyes with the wet hanky, Victoria moved up beside Ryan and said, "Thank you, Miss Worley. Tell the doctor I'll be right there."

Rebecca nodded and walked away.

Turning to Ryan, Victoria said, "I want you to meet Tommy."

"Maybe some time later, Tori. Right now, I need to look in on my wounded men."

Laying a hand on his arm, she gave him a certain tender look that had been something special to Ryan when they first fell in love. "Do you still feel something for me?"

"Tori, I must get to my men," said Ryan, and moved into the corridor. "I hope your son is all right."

With that, he walked away from her and did not look back. As he moved briskly down the hall, he was troubled by his encounter with the woman he had once loved with all his heart. When he neared room twenty-seven, he slowed his pace and drew a deep breath. Pausing a moment in front of the closed door, he composed himself, then pushed it open and entered the room.

Lieutenant Rawlings was sitting on a straight-backed wooden chair in the middle of the room so he could talk to all four men at once. When the captain entered, he stood up.

Grinning at him, McGraw said, "Sit down, Lieutenant. I'm not a general yet."

Rawlings grinned back and said, "I wasn't standing up for *you*, Captain, but for the lady behind you."

McGraw turned around to see a pretty redheaded nurse on his heels, carrying a tray with four spoons and a large bottle containing dark liquid. She smiled and said, "So you're the famous Captain Ryan McGraw."

"I don't know about the famous part, ma'am, but I do answer to that name."

"I'm Betty Wells," she said, setting the tray on a small table next to Brad Thacker's bed.

McGraw was carrying his hat. He quickly placed it on his head, then removed it, bowed, and said, "I am so glad to meet you, Miss Wells. It is *Miss* Wells, isn't it?"

"It better be, Cap'n," spoke up Clint Spain, who was propped up in his bed. "If she's got a husband, your lieutenant here is in deep trouble."

"Oh?" said McGraw, arching his eyebrows and setting his gaze on Rawlings.

"Aw, Captain, I haven't done anything but talk to her."

"And drool over her," interjected Dean Bradbury, who was also sitting up in his bed.

Rawlings' face tinted.

"He also chased her down the hall, Captain," put in Brad Thacker, who lay in his bed on his good side.

"I didn't do any such thing!" blustered Rawlings. "All I did was follow her down the hall so's I could get some water for Sergeant Staples."

Betty stuck out her lower lip, looked at Rawlings, and said, "Is that all you were following me for? Phooey. I thought you *were* chasing me, Lieutenant!"

There was a round of laughter in the room, then Betty said to McGraw, "Your boys told me a lot about you, Captain, but they neglected to tell me that you were so young."

"What do you mean?" asked the captain.

"Well, they said you were sort of like a father to them. I pictured this tottering, silver-haired old man."

"It was Lieutenant Rawlings who gave her the old man idea, Captain," said Spain. "He really worked on it. Of course, we know why. He wants her all to himself."

McGraw laughed. "Guess you're not the only one I should have cautioned about chasing the pretty nurses, Clint. Sounds like I should also have given the word to my gruesome lieutenant!"

Again there was laughter, then Betty said, "I'll let you gentlemen visit without interruption in a moment, but first I must give my patients their regular medicine."

"Oh, no!" gasped Sergeant Staples. "Not that awful stuff again!"

"Yes. This awful stuff again."

"We haven't had any of it, ma'am," spoke up Dean Bradbury. "What is it?"

"Exactly what I said—it's your *regular* medicine. It'll keep you that way. Good old syrup of pepsin," chuckled Betty, picking up the bottle and one of the spoons. "Who wants to be first?"

An argument ensued as to who should take the black liquid first. Taking control of the situation, the pretty nurse started with Staples and moved methodically from bed to bed. When it was done, she picked up the tray and said, "All right, gentlemen, I'll be out of your way now."

"You're not in the way," said Rawlings. "You can stay longer if you want."

"Sorry, but I'm leaving early today, and it's time for me to go. One of the other nurses will see to these fine gentlemen when they have any needs."

Rawlings walked her to the door and said, "Would it...ah...be possible, Miss Betty, for a gruesome fellow like me to take you to dinner some time?"

"Maybe. Next time you're here at the hospital, look me up and we'll talk about it."

"You really mean it?" asked Rawlings, his heart aflutter.

"Try me," said Betty, and moved away quickly.

When Rawlings turned back into the room, McGraw asked, "Have you looked in on Vince Udall yet?"

"Yes, sir. He's not too alert, but he knew who I was. The nurse that's staying with him said he's doing all right. She let me say a few words to him, then chased me out."

"I'm glad to know he's doing well. I'll look in on him myself in a little while."

The captain talked to each of his wounded men, showing sincere interest in their condition. He was standing next to Brad Thacker's bed with his back toward the open door when Thacker looked past him and saw someone in a starched white dress standing in the corridor.

Looking up at McGraw, Thacker said, "Captain, you'll never guess who's here at the hospital."

"What do you mean?"

"I mean, there's somebody here that you really like."

Brow furrowed, McGraw asked, "You mean as a patient? Some soldier friend of mine who's been wounded?"

"No, it's not a soldier, sir. It's a nurse."

"A nurse?"

"One that took real good care of you at the hospital in Birmingham."

The other men followed her movements as Dixie Quade stepped up behind McGraw and said, "The captain probably doesn't even remember me, Private Thacker."

Ryan McGraw knew the voice instantly. He whirled around and looked into Dixie's sparkling eyes above a warm smile that emphasized her dimples. The shock of seeing her momentarily blocked his throat. By this time his emotions were totally in a whirl.

Ryan had just seen his ex-wife, and suddenly here was the young woman he had carried in his thoughts and dreams for over a year. He had given up ever seeing Dixie again.

Unaware of Ryan's emotional strain, Dixie was expecting more of a reception than a stunned look. Her smile slackened as she said, "Captain, aren't you glad to see me?"

"Yes, of course!" he exclaimed, taking both of her hands in his. "I am *very* glad to see you, Miss Dixie. It's just that...that...well, you've taken me totally by surprise! I never...I never...well, I never—"

"Expected to see me here?" she finished for him.

"Yes! This is such a pleasant surprise, it's just left me speechless."

"Your men tell me you still have some pain in your shoulder now and then," said Dixie, allowing the captain to regain his composure.

"Uh...right," he nodded. "Sometimes. What—how—why are you here?"

"To beef up the medical staff for the battle in Mobile Bay. I was certainly amazed to learn that you and your Sharpshooters had been assigned to Fort Morgan. Maybe we will have a chance to spend a few moments together and talk over old times."

"That would be great," he said, releasing her hands. "I'll be back in a few days to check on my men again. Is this your normal shift?"

"It switches around every week, but if you're back by Saturday, I'll be on duty at this time."

"Then I'll make it a point to be back by Saturday," he grinned.

"See you then," she chirped, and left the room.

As the captain turned back to his men, Judd Rawlings gave him a wolfish grin and said, "You tried to get the little nurse out of your system, didn't you, O dauntless leader? But your ol' pal, here, can tell. There's still some Dixie in your blood, isn't there?"

CHAPTER NINE

On June 20, 1864, thirteen hundred Union soldiers of the Sixth Illinois Cavalry First Battalion were bivouacked in a dense Mississippi forest some sixty miles northwest of Mobile, Alabama. They had been there for three days, camped on the Black River, waiting for Major General Edward R.S. Canby to arrive.

The forty-eight-year-old Canby was commander of the Union Military Division of West Mississippi, and was to arrive on that day from his main camp in western Mississippi near Natchez.

It was midmorning, and the birds were singing in the trees overhead while most of the Union soldiers were washing their clothes in the sun-dappled river. In charge of First Battalion was Colonel Perry Stone, who sat in his tent with his five officers, smoking a pipe and discussing their most recent battle. Amid the officers was Captain Leonard Whittier, a fierce and rugged fighter on the battlefield.

The conversation was interrupted when one of the sentries looked through the opening where the flap was laid back and said, "Colonel Stone, General Canby is here."

Stone rose from his chair, thanked the sentry, and while the officers stood, said, "Gentlemen, let's go give a warm welcome to our commander."

The Union officers filed out of the tent into the warm sunshine. A light breeze was coming from the north, softly washing through the treetops.

On his long-legged chestnut gelding, General Canby threaded through the thick trees, followed by some forty-five riders in blue uniforms. Once Canby and his escort had dismounted, the men of First Battalion welcomed them, offering hot coffee from a series of steaming pots at the cook site near the river's edge.

After chatting for a few moments about how things were looking in west Mississippi, General Canby said to Stone, "Colonel, as my messenger told you, I have a plan concerning Fort Morgan. It will involve Captain Len Whittier. I need to get down to business on it so I can head north of here on some other matters."

"Certainly, sir," nodded Stone. Turning about, he let his eyes roam amid the deep surrounding shadows until he spotted Whittier in conversation with two of the men who had ridden in with the general. They each held a steaming tin cup of coffee.

"Captain Whittier!" the colonel called out.

"Yes, sir?"

"General Canby wants to meet with the two of us at once."

Whittier excused himself and hurried to where the general and the colonel waited.

"We can talk in my tent, sir," said Stone as Whittier drew up.

"You have a table in there?"

"Yes, sir. There are two, in fact—a small one with my lantern on it, and a larger one I use for my meals."

Canby turned to a young corporal who stood a few feet behind him and said, "Corporal Burris, I need that map in my left saddlebag."

Burris hurried toward the general's horse while Stone and Whittier walked him to the tent.

As they entered the tent and sat down at the table, Canby said, "I've worked out a plan concerning Fort Morgan, and it's been approved by General Grant and Admiral Farragut. As you know, Farragut is gathering his fleet off the Gulf coast at Mobile Bay. I don't have to tell you that it is absolutely necessary that we take Mobile and plug up the bay."

"Yes, sir," chorused Stone and Whittier.

Corporal Burris arrived with the map, placed it in the general's hands, and moved just outside the tent to be at Canby's beck and call. While the general spread the map out on the tabletop, he said, "Captain Whittier, I picked you specifically for this mission because I believe you are the best man for the job."

"Thank you, sir."

"Of course, Colonel Stone has to be in on this because he is your commanding officer, and the men who go with you are under his command."

Whittier nodded.

"Before we look at the map," said Canby, "let me explain what I have in mind. You gentlemen know that when Admiral Farragut leads his fleet into Mobile Bay, his greatest obstacle will be Fort Morgan. According to our latest intelligence report, they've got some plenty big guns in that place."

"What about Fort Gaines, sir?" queried Whittier.

"It won't be much of a problem. Farragut says he can level it in short order. He figures General Page will drive pilings into the mouth of the bay near Dauphin Island to force his ships to draw nearer to Morgan. So it's Morgan we're concerned about."

Colonel Stone eyed his pipe on the small table, which had gone dead. "General," he said, "do you mind if I smoke my pipe?"

Canby, who was a no-nonsense type, eyed him levelly and clipped, "Yes, I do mind. Can't stand the smell of tobacco in any form. You ought to give that stuff up, Colonel. Bad for your health."

"Yes, sir," nodded Stone, smiling weakly.

Whittier knew the rebuke had cut. He avoided looking at Stone.

"The latest intelligence report also informs us that Page has about a hundred and ten, maybe a hundred and twenty men in the fort," continued Canby. "So here's my plan. Captain Whittier, I want you to take a hundred and seventy men and capture Fort Morgan."

Without blinking, Whittier replied, "You want this done when, sir?"

"As soon as possible." Looking at Stone, he said, "Give him the best men you have, Colonel. This won't be an easy task. What you'll have to do, Captain, is build some rafts and transport them in wagons by land as far as the little town of Chickasaw. You know where that is?"

"I think it's due east of here on the Mobile River, sir."

"Correct," said Canby, running his finger across the map. "Right here."

Leaning close to get a good look, Whittier nodded. "So we float down the river on the rafts all the way to the bay, then paddle the rafts down the bay to Fort Morgan. Right?"

"Yes. You'll have to travel at night with the wagons and hide yourselves as much as possible during the day. You and your men will be on foot. I figure three wagons ought to be able to carry the rafts you'll need. Stash the wagons when you reach the river. You'll have to do all your floating at night, too. If the Confederates find out you're headed for the fort, you're in trouble."

"Yes, sir."

"You'll make your attack at night, also. I'd like to have a larger unit make the assault, but it's going to be hard enough to keep a hundred and seventy from being spotted. At least with that many, you'll reasonably outnumber the force at Morgan. You've got to go in there and take it, Captain. With Fort Morgan in our hands, Admiral Farragut will be able to move into the bay and on to Mobile with ease. President Lincoln and General Grant have both emphasized how important it is that we plug up the bay and capture the city. If we're successful, it could mean the beginning of the end for the South. They won't be able to fight us if we cut off their final means of supply. With General Sherman's march on Atlanta coming in a few weeks, this war could be over before autumn."

"You say, General," spoke up Stone, "that Farragut will be able to move into the bay with ease if we occupy Fort Morgan. But what about the Confederate fleet?"

"They don't have much. I'm sure they'll bring what they can down the Mobile River against us, but I don't think it'll amount to much. I did hear that Admiral Buchanan is trying to get some kind of ironclad ram put together, but that will take time. I hope we'll have the fort, the bay, and the city in our hands before he gets it done."

Captain Whittier was studying the map. Pointing to Mobile Bay, he said, "I figure we'll have to paddle down the bay just off the east shore. It's close to thirty miles according to the legend, here. It'll probably take all of one night and part of another. We'll have to go ashore at dawn after the first night and stay in hiding till dark. We should arrive at the fort in the middle of the next night."

"That's the way I had it figured," nodded Canby. "The element of surprise will give you a sharp edge. I want that fort under your control by sunup. You are to fire three cannons at fifteen-second intervals. That will tell our navy out on the gulf that Morgan is in Union hands. Farragut will move in immediately and bombard Fort Gaines."

"Is Farragut ready for such an assault?" asked Colonel Stone. "I thought he was still building up his fleet."

"He is, just in case this little project should somehow be foiled. But he won't need more and bigger ships if Fort Morgan is vanquished. This is why Captain Whittier and his men must not fail. Admiral Farragut can have Mobile Bay locked up for our side in a hurry."

Whittier was scrutinizing the map again. Without looking up, he said, "General, I estimate that it will take us about five days to get down there, take the fort, and have things ready for the fleet to move in. That is, if we don't run into trouble on the way."

Canby nodded. "Okay. Set your sights to have the fort in hand by no later than the twenty-ninth. Colonel Stone will send his best men with you. If you do run into trouble, you should be able to squelch it in a hurry. I want this job done by sunup on the twenty-ninth."

"We'll do it, sir," Whittier said with a note of confidence.

"That's the kind of attitude I like," smiled Canby. "One other thing."

"Yes, sir?"

"Since you're going to enter the fort at night, it would be a good idea to have all of your men wear white arm bands. That way you won't be shooting each other in the battle."

"I've heard of that tactic being used before, sir. Thanks for reminding me."

Canby rose to his feet and said, "You can keep the map. It'll be of use to you."

"Yes, sir, it will."

When the general had ridden away with his escort, Colonel Stone and Captain Whittier sat down with a list of the men in First Battalion and began picking out names.

During the ride back to Fort Morgan on June 28, Lieutenant Judd Rawlings could tell his friend was deeply disturbed. They had ridden at a steady trot for some fifteen miles without a word between them when they reached a stand of heavy trees and were forced to weave their mounts among them at a walk.

With only the muffled sound of hooves on soft earth in their ears, Rawlings said, "Ryan?"

McGraw turned his head and set troubled eyes on him. "Yes?"

"Want to talk about it?"

"About what?"

"Come on, friend. I hit the nail on the head when I said there's still some Dixie in your blood, didn't I?"

A half-grin curved McGraw's mouth. "You think so, eh?"

"I don't *think* it, I *know* it. The only way it could've been plainer is if you'd blurted out that you were in love with her right there in front of everybody."

"You think you know everything, don't you?"

"Oh, I guess there are a few things I don't know, but there's not much about you I don't know. We've been friends long enough that we read each other like a book, and that's the honest truth. Now, c'mon. Spill it. You'll feel better. You're in love with her, aren't you? Been carrying that torch all this time."

McGraw was quiet for a long moment. Then he said, "She deserves better than me, Judd. That's why I didn't pursue anything with her when we were at Birmingham. I already messed up one marriage. She doesn't need a man like me. She deserves the best."

"Aw, quit kicking yourself. You didn't mess up your marriage. Victoria did that." Rawlings paused, pulled at his handlebar mustache, then said, "Did Victoria do or say something that got to you? Must've been difficult for you, seeing her after all these years."

"Wasn't the easiest thing I ever did," admitted McGraw.

"I hope you told her off good. She deserves it."

"What would that accomplish? It's all over and done with."

Shaking his head, Rawlings said, "Good ol' Ryan McGraw. Tough as rawhide on the outside...soft as a feather pillow on the inside. She needs to be told off but good."

"I was firm with her about breaking her marriage vows, Judd, but there's no sense in trying to hurt her. Besides, she had her son in there getting a bad cut stitched up. She was under stress already."

"Her son, eh? You find out who she married?"

"Yeah. And when I tell you who her husband is, it'll knock you right out of the saddle."

Looking down at his saddle, Rawlings said, "This is a McClellan, so it doesn't have a saddlehorn. Nothing to get a grip on."

"Tori is Mrs. Lex Coffield."

Judd's jaw slacked. "Coffield! Mr. Popularity? I hope she likes him better than I think they like him at the fort."

Ryan thought of Victoria's miserable plight, but decided to keep it to himself. "I hope so, too. Be pretty miserable for her if she didn't."

"This'll put some strain between you and the illustrious captain, won't it?" remarked Rawlings.

"Not unless he chooses to make it that way. What's done is done. Let dead dogs lie. That's my philosophy."

"Well, I sure hope the dead dog stays dead. A resurrected dog might be plenty mean."

At midnight, Captain McGraw lay on his cot wide awake. He and his lieutenant had been given a private room adjacent to the long room where the Sharpshooters were sleeping. A closed door separated the two rooms, but the captain could hear a discordant chorus of snores through the door. More prominent was the reedy, nasal sound coming from his friend in the cot beside him.

McGraw's emotions were strung tight as a fiddle string. He thought of Dixie Quade and the joy he felt at seeing her. She certainly showed that she was glad to find him there. She seemed even more beautiful than ever...if that was possible. *What a sweet, unselfish, lovely flower of femininity,* he thought. *Any man would be plenty fortunate to have her as his wife.*

Wife! The word snapped his thoughts to Victoria. *What kind of fateful hand had brought her back into his life? Why did her husband have to be stationed at Fort Morgan?*

Ryan McGraw had been so certain that everything he ever felt for Victoria had long since died. But now—having seen her—he was not so sure. Even though she had become so greedy and self-centered that last year of their marriage, he still had loved her. After what she had done, Ryan felt he should despise her. But that emotion was not there. He only had that strange, unnamed *something* stirring within him for having been in her presence.

It was a warm night, and the room's two windows were open. The soft sound of the gulf's waves washing up on the beach met his ears as his thoughts drifted back to the first time he laid eyes on beautiful Victoria Manning. He was twenty. She was eighteen. Both of them were attending a community ball in Hattiesburg, Mississippi. Their dance partners were friends. The two friends decided to dance a number together, which left Ryan and Victoria on the sidelines. Ryan asked her if she wanted to dance, and she coyly accepted. They whirled across the floor to Johann Strauss's *Donaulieder* waltz.

While the music played, Ryan and Victoria became fascinated with each other, and they planned a time to meet again. Within a short time, they had fallen in love. Soon an engagement was announced, and they were married a few months later, in September of 1856. At their wedding reception, they danced again to what had become "their special number," the *Donaulieder*.

The first year was a happy one. Then Victoria began to change. Ryan's father, Thomas McGraw, was a wealthy land developer in the Laurel-Hattiesburg area, and had taught his son the business. Ryan had established his own just before he and Victoria were married. The area was growing, and the young firm was getting a good start by the time Ryan and Victoria celebrated their first anniversary. The business took a great deal of Ryan's time, but the future looked promising. Ryan was beginning to make a decent living, but little by little, he found he was unable to satisfy all of Victoria's wants. She was developing rapacious tastes and began to demand things he could not afford. She also insisted that he devote more time to her than his young thriving business could allow.

In an attempt to give his demanding wife more of his time, Ryan took in a partner. This satisfied Victoria for a while, but soon she became more demanding. She wanted a larger, more expensive house, better furniture, and more costly clothing. In a serious discussion with her, he made it clear that she was asking for too much. Victoria must learn to live within the limits of his income.

Almost immediately, Victoria began to grow cold toward Ryan. As time passed, he suspected she was seeing another man, but since he could come up with no proof, he never accused her. Then one day in June of 1858, he came home and found the note. Victoria had run off to some unknown place with an unnamed man.

Sweat beaded Ryan McGraw's brow as he lay in the dark, remembering what Victoria had done to him. He rose from the cot and dressed while Judd Rawlings snored. He would get some cool night air in his lungs.

There was a pale, hazy moon as he stepped out into the yard. Four sentries walked the walls, silhouetted against the sky. Moving across the yard with the sound of the surf in his ears, McGraw reached the gate, where a sentry stepped out of the shadows and said in a half-whisper, "Good evening, Captain. Going for a walk at this hour?"

"Yes. Can't sleep. Thought a little fresh sea air might help."

"All right, sir," said the sentry, opening the gate. "I'll be watching for you to return."

"Thank you. Probably be a half-hour or so."

McGraw's boots crunched on the sand as he walked toward the beach at the southern tip of Mobile Point. Fort Morgan's lighthouse loomed over him, standing some fifty feet in height. The glass-enclosed turret at its top was dark. General Page knew that with the Union fleet off shore, a beacon would only be a tempting target for Admiral Farragut.

The captain was bareheaded, and the sea breeze toyed with his sandy locks as he shoved his hands in his pockets and walked a circle around the towering stone structure. Breathing deep, he let the salty air fill his lungs. While circling the lighthouse, McGraw glanced south-ward where he could make out the shapes of Union ships on the watery horizon. He wondered when Admiral Farragut would make his daring move into the mouth of the bay. Would the Confederate forces be able to stop him?

Soon the captain was moving along the shore, heading north. With the soft surf washing close to his feet and the dull moonlight dancing on the surface of the dark water, he tried to sort out his feelings. Was that the old tingle he had felt today when he looked into Tori's eyes?

McGraw argued with himself. Of course it was not the old tingle! Whatever was once between himself and Victoria was over and done with. And even if it was the old tingle, she was married to this Captain Lex Coffield. Unhappily married to him for sure, but still married to him. And now she had that little boy, too. He had no desire to meet the child. Why should he care about some little boy who—"

Suddenly Captain McGraw stopped in his tracks. Movement in the distance upshore had seized his attention. He dashed to a large rock and hunkered down, peering over its top. A mile or so northward, several dark objects were floating toward him, barely off shore. Squinting to bring them into focus in the soft moonlight, he realized they were rafts, carrying men in dark uniforms. *Yankees!*

Quickly, McGraw darted into the shadows of the heavy brush near the shore. His heart pounded. The Yankees were coming under cover of darkness to swarm Fort Morgan and take it! Peering toward the rafts again, he tried to count them, but they were too closely knit and too far away for him to be sure. He estimated that there were about fourteen of them. How many men would each raft carry? That, too, was impossible to figure. The only thing he could do was run into the fort, alert the men, and get them ready to fight.

Leaving the shadows and praying the Yankees would not see him, McGraw made a mad dash for the gate. As he drew near, the sentries on the wall were watching him. Holding his voice low, but making himself heard, he said, "Yankees coming on rafts! Get everybody up!"

Within five minutes, the ninety-four Sharpshooters and Fort Morgan's one-hundred-twenty-man force were dressed and ready for action. General Page stood with McGraw and Lieutenant Rawlings near the gate as the men crowded close, weapons ready. McGraw had strapped on his knife and revolver and was working the lever of his Henry repeater as Page said, "We may just have the edge here, Captain."

"What do you mean, sir?"

"I doubt Federal intelligence could have reported yet that you and your Sharpshooters are here in the fort. Whatever force is on those rafts probably is numbered according to how many men are usually here in the fort. If that is correct, they are in for a surprise. We'll give them another little surprise, too. While you were going after your weapons, Captain, I ordered two of my cannon crews to get ready. Colonel Munford is up there on the wall with them. Lieutenants March and Cooley will lead our men behind you and the Sharpshooters. Just before you rush out to meet them, those two cannons will each fire a shot directly into the rafts. That ought to shake them up and give you a chance to start mowing them down before they can return fire."

"Good!" exclaimed McGraw. Then turning to his battle-hungry bunch, he said, "Okay, men! We'll lead off, and General Page's troops will follow. We'll wait in the shadows of the walls until Colonel Munford fires two cannon shots. The instant those cannons roar, we give off a Rebel yell and attack. Let's go!"

CHAPTER TEN

✦

Clustered tightly on the dark waters of Mobile Bay, the fifteen Union rafts glided steadily southward, hugging the shoreline. On the lead raft, Captain Leonard Whittier adjusted his white arm band and spoke in a low voice to Lieutenant Chet Noltey, "I'm glad General Canby thought of using these. It's going to keep us from shooting our own men."

"I'm for that," nodded Noltey. "In an operation like this, we're going to have casualties. We for sure don't need to cause any to ourselves."

Whittier ran his gaze over the obscure faces of his one hundred seventy men, then squared himself with the raft and looked on the walls of Fort Morgan in the distance. In the hazy light of the moon, he noted the towering lighthouse looming against the night sky. Moonlight glinted vaguely from the glass panes atop the tall stone structure.

The sound of numerous paddles slapping water filled Whittier's ears as he studied the pentagonal-shaped Confederate bulwark, now no more than a half-mile away. He could make out the Confederate flag waving lazily in the sea breeze above the fort's southernmost corner.

The captain's blood was racing as he anticipated the honor it would bring him to be the man who led the capture of Fort Morgan, which would result in the downfall of the last Rebel seaport. What Whittier accomplished tonight would ring the death knell for the Confederacy. With Fort Morgan under his command, Admiral Farragut could level Fort Gaines and steam up the bay toward Mobile. Ground forces would be alerted and move in from the north. Soon the city would be in Federal hands. When the last avenue of supply was cut off, the Confederacy would be forced to surrender.

Whittier smiled to himself as he envisioned the coming day of glory when at the war's end he would stand at attention before President Abraham Lincoln and General Ulysses S. Grant. Thousands of admirers would look on as Captain Leonard Whittier received a presidential commendation for capturing Fort Morgan, and they would applaud when he was given a promotion to major.

Turning to Noltey, Whittier said, "Lieutenant, pass the word along that we'll haul up and go ashore about two hundred yards from the fort. According to the map, the shoreline curves inward about fifty or sixty feet at that point, and there's plenty of brush. We should be able to get ashore without being spotted. We'll move into the brush and go the rest of the way on foot."

Noltey quickly turned and gave the message to the soldiers at the rear of the raft, telling them to pass it to the other rafts, which followed closely three and four abreast.

Corporal J. B. Burris, who sat directly behind Whittier, patted his Henry repeater rifle and said, "I can't wait to get me some more Rebels. So far in this war, I've killed exactly forty-seven of 'em. I'm goin' for at least three tonight."

"Hog!" chuckled Private Bill Temple, who sat next to him. "There's only a hundred and twenty or so. If you kill three, that'll mean some of our bunch won't get to kill any."

"So what? If the rest of you guys don't want me killing that many, then get to 'em before I do!"

"That's enough talk," said Whittier over his shoulder. "Get ready. We're going ashore in about thirty seconds."

A half-minute later, the captain gave signal for the rafts to haul up on the beach. His raft was first to touch ground. Just as he jumped ashore, a huge cannon roared from the wall of Fort Morgan. The ball plowed into one of the rear rafts and exploded, throwing bodies in every direction. Whittier was about to bark a command for his men to head for the brush further up the beach when a second cannon boomed. Another raft was blown to bits, with bodies scattered into the water and onto dry ground.

"Captain!" shouted Lieutenant Noltey. "How'd they spot us?"

"I don't know!"

Just as the captain shouted for his men to follow him into the brush, a blood-curdling Rebel yell came from outside the walls of the fort, and what seemed to be a huge swarm of enemy soldiers came from somewhere in the deep shadows.

As Rebel rifles barked, their muzzles blossoming orange in the gloom, Whittier raised his rifle and fired, then ran toward the brush for cover. Lieutenant Noltey was beside him, with Corporal Burris on their heels. Just behind them was Private Temple.

Temple heard a bullet whiz past his head at the same instant Burris took a slug in the chest and went down. Guns were booming all around as Temple knelt beside the fallen corporal. Burris's face was buried in the sand. When Temple took hold of his shirt and turned him over, it was evident that he was dead. "No more Rebels for you, J. B." he breathed. "I'll get your three and a couple for myself!"

As the Sharpshooters led the way around the fort's wall and pierced the night air with their Rebel yell, Captain McGraw raised his rifle and fired first. Instantly, the men-in-gray who followed opened fire, and men in dark uniforms with white bands on their arms were falling like flies.

With less than fifty yards between them, Rebels and Yankees fought it out in the pale moonlight. Rifle fire was a thundering roll, punctuated with loud commands, cheers, yells, and the cry of wounded and dying men.

Soon repeater rifles and revolvers were empty. With no time to reload, the battle became a hand-to-hand conflict. The Yankees found to their amazement that they were outnumbered, and when they clashed with the Sharpshooters, they were outclassed in fighting prowess. Knives flashed in the moonlight, and the smell of blood permeated the air.

Lieutenant Rawlings stayed close to his captain, using his knife, feet, and fists to stun, wound, and slay the enemy. At one point, Rawlings had used an Oriental-style kick to crack the jaw of a Yankee and drop him hard, when he saw another dash up behind McGraw, ready to drive a knife in his back. The captain was busy, battling two men.

Rawlings yelled and pounced on the Yankee. When their bodies collided, they rolled down the sandy beach to the water's edge. The Yankee swore at Rawlings and tried to stab him, but he was too slow. Rawlings drove his own knife into the man's heart full-haft, killing him instantly. Yanking the knife out, the lieutenant charged back up the slope to help McGraw. It didn't surprise him to find that the captain had already killed one of his assailants and was just finishing off the other one.

The Yankee whose jaw Rawlings had cracked was sitting up, groaning, and loading his rifle. When he saw the Rebel lieutenant coming, he tried to close the chamber, but Rawlings was on him with his knife. The Yankee lay dead as McGraw drew up and said breathlessly, "Thanks, pal. That blue-belly you took out a minute ago would've had me for sure."

"Don't mention it. You've saved my hide plenty of times."

Suddenly they saw a couple of Fort Morgan men in trouble, and dashed to their aid.

At the water's edge, Sergeants Noah Cloud and Hap Hazzard were fighting side by side. The Yankee soldiers were no match for them. Five Yankees were already dead on the shore. Four more had lunged in to put down the two husky Rebels. Hazzard sidestepped a hissing knife blade, kicked his assailant in the groin, and met the second man with a hard left, driving his knife into the Yankee's side as he staggered from the punch.

The two men-in-blue who were after Noah Cloud were swinging their deadly knife blades in wide arcs, but found the big man to be surprisingly agile. Noah dodged them three times, then drove a swift kick into the chest of one, putting him down with the wind knocked out of him.

The second Yankee lunged at Noah with his knife. Noah adeptly evaded the hungry blade, then slashed him across the back with his knife as the man attempted to regain his balance. He yelped with pain and pivoted, just as Noah rammed his knife into his chest, burying it deep. He was dead before he hit the sand.

Noah was about to jerk the knife out when he saw the first Yankee coming at him, his knife poised for the kill. The big Rebel leaped aside, jumped the Yankee, and put a lock on his head with powerful hands. One sharp twist, and the Yankee was dead of a broken neck.

As the battle raged, Captain Whittier faced the grim fact that he and his men would all die unless they surrendered. He was on his knees near a thick bush with a cut on his upper left arm when he whipped the white cloth loose and began waving it wildly over his head, shouting for his men to stop fighting and surrender. Three more Yankees were dead before they all heard and complied.

The Yankees, many of them battered and bloody, threw their hands over their heads in surrender. Whittier looked around at the great number of his men who lay dead on the beach and whose bodies bobbed in the water near the shore. His heart sank. They had failed to accomplish their mission. His visions of glory were gone. They were now prisoners of the hated Rebels.

Still holding his bloody knife in a death-grip, the Sharpshooter leader approached Whittier and said, "I am Captain Ryan McGraw. In the name of the Confederacy, I am taking you and your surviving men as prisoners of war. You will be treated as such."

Whittier was holding his slashed arm. Tiny trickles of blood were running between his fingers. His jaw slacked as he said wide-eyed, "You are McGraw as in McGraw's Sharpshooters?"

"The same."

"But...but we had no idea you and your men were in the fort. We thought—"

"You thought that you'd outnumber General Page's men?"

"Yes. As a matter of fact, we did."

"Good military strategy, but your source of information must be a little slow. Too bad for you. What's your name, Captain?"

"Leonard Whittier. First Battalion, Sixth Illinois Cavalry."

Running his gaze over the Rebel soldiers who now surrounded the Yankees, McGraw said, "All right, men, let's escort Captain Whittier and the rest of our prisoners into the fort."

"What about my wounded men?" asked Whittier.

"Have some of your soldiers carry them," replied McGraw. Then to Lieutenants March and Cooley he said, "Will you two see that our wounded men are brought in?"

"Yes, sir."

"Have some of the men count our dead and identify them, too, will you? General Page will want a report as soon as possible."

Five miles due south of Fort Morgan, in the moon-glazed waters of the Gulf of Mexico, the Union fleet huddled in silence. Aboard the flagship USS *Hartford*, Fleet-Captain Percival Drayton entered the admiral's quarters carrying a lantern. The ring of light showed him Admiral David G. Farragut asleep in his bed. He was snoring, and the yellow glare reflected off his balding head.

Gripping Farragut's shoulder, Drayton said, "Admiral,

sir...Admiral..."

The sixty-three-year-old navy veteran snorted, rolled his head, and opened his eyes. Blinking against the bright lantern, he focused on Drayton's face and asked, "Did we get the signal?"

"No, sir, but I thought I should awaken you anyhow. I think something must have gone wrong at the fort."

Farragut threw back the light covering and sat up. "What do you mean?"

"Well, sir, at exactly 2:40, there were two cannon shots. They were about fifteen seconds apart, but since there were only two, I knew they couldn't be the prearranged signal. Not only that, but there has been a battle going on ever since those two cannons were fired. Up until a minute ago, so many rifles were firing, it sounded like a Chinese new year's celebration. You know, firecrackers going off all over."

Farragut glanced at the bell-shaped clock on his dresser, and saw that it was ten minutes after three. Lifting his trim six-foot frame off the bed, he crossed the room in his long-johns and began dressing. Without looking at his fleet-captain, the admiral said, "Go keep an eye toward the fort, Drayton. I'll be there in a moment."

The sea was calm and the night breeze light when the admiral joined Drayton and two other officers on deck. All three were looking toward shore through telescopes. No sounds could be heard coming from the fort. Farragut noted that officers aboard the ships that flanked the *Hartford* were doing the same thing. One of them called across the fifty-foot space between the ships and said, "What do you make of it, Admiral?"

"Only one thing *to* make of it," replied Farragut. "Those rafts weren't carrying cannons. Drayton said there were two cannons fired before the gun battle began. Captain Whittier and his men were obviously discovered before they were able to pull their surprise attack on the fort. Since no signal shots have been fired since the gun battle stopped, I must assume that Whittier and his men are now dead or prisoners of General Page. Looks like we have no choice now but to steam into Mobile Bay and take what Page throws at us."

Drayton lowered his telescope and asked, "How soon will we launch the attack, sir?"

"I'm not sure. I want more ships than we have at the moment. When we go in there, I want to be dead sure we can overcome all obstacles and converge in full strength on Mobile. We *must* take Mobile if we're going to win this war."

At Fort Morgan, General Page ordered lanterns lit and crowded the beaten Yankees together in the open yard. There were only twenty-nine survivors. Of that number, seven were wounded, five of them seriously.

Three of General Page's men were dead, and eight were wounded seriously, including three of McGraw's men. Others among the Rebel soldiers had minor cuts and bruises. The wounded men on both sides were carried into the fort's small infirmary. Rebel soldiers did what they could to stop the bleeding of wounds, and used what medical supplies were available to make the battered men as comfortable as possible.

As General Page looked the wounded men over, he concluded that most of them could not stand a boat trip to Mobile. He quickly dispatched two soldiers to ride to Mobile and bring medical help.

When the riders had gone, Page took Colonel Munford, Captain McGraw, and Lieutenants Rawlings, March, and Cooley into his office. As they took seats, the general eased into the chair behind his desk and said, "Gentlemen, I'm proud of you and the men in this fort. My heart aches for the brave men who died in battle tonight, and for those who were wounded, but the enemy was defeated. Fort Morgan is still in our hands."

"Wish I could see Ulysses S. Grant's face when he receives word of it," Munford chuckled.

"I'd give a month's pay to see that myself," grinned Cooley.

Lieutenant March asked Page, "General, what are we going to do with the prisoners? We don't have room for them here."

"How about the jail in Mobile?" spoke up Cooley. "It could probably hold them."

Shaking his head, Page said, "No. We can't ask the law in Mobile to be responsible for that many men. They'll have to be taken to the nearest prison camp, which as you know is at Jackson, Alabama, sixty miles north of here."

"It'll have to be in wagons, sir," spoke up Colonel Munford. "What about their wounded men?"

"Once our medical people have patched them up and done what they can for them, the wounded Yankees will have to make the trip. If they're in real bad shape, they'll have to be taken to the Mobile hospital as soon as possible. But the rest of them will be placed in wagons and taken to Jackson, along with their comrades."

While Page and Munford were discussing what to do with the wounded Yankees, Captain McGraw thought of his three wounded men, hoping they would be all right. Suddenly it came to him that he had forgotten to wire General Maury at Montgomery and ask for replacements. He had been so emotionally shaken after seeing Victoria and Dixie, it had completely slipped his mind. He would need to ride to Mobile at sunup and get it done. However, instead of asking Maury for seven new men, he would now need ten.

McGraw waited for a break in the conversation, then he said, "General, with my ranks being cut down some more, I'll need to ride into Mobile come daylight and wire General Maury for additional replacements."

"Fine," nodded Page. "We want your unit to be up to full measure. If you and your men hadn't been here tonight, this fort would be in enemy hands."

"That's right," said Munford. "We're mighty glad you're here, Captain."

McGraw thanked them, then asked, "How soon will you be

sending the Yankees to Jackson, sir?"

General Page rubbed his chin. "Well, as soon as I know how many of their wounded—if any—can't possibly make the trip. We've got to get all of them out of here. I have enough on my mind with Farragut out there on the Gulf gathering gunboats. Since this little Yankee venture failed, he'll no doubt choose to steam his way in here in spite of our big guns."

"You think he'll come right away, sir?" asked Lieutenant March.

"Hard to tell," Page replied, pulling at an ear.

"You going to call off the dance, General?" The question came from Colonel Munford, whose wife was living in Mobile.

"Nope. I don't think ol' 'fair-guts' will come that soon."

"What dance is this?" Ryan asked.

"Guess I forgot to mention it since you and your men arrived, Captain," said Page. "I felt like our men needed a little boost in morale, so about ten days ago, I made arrangements for Mobile's small orchestra to come out here tomorrow night and play for us. Many young ladies of the town are planning to come. Your men will have to share dance partners with my men, but I think everybody will get a dance or two during the evening."

"General," spoke up Lieutenant Cooley, "how many of our men will you be sending to take the prisoners to Jackson? We don't dare cut ourselves too low here."

"I hate to cut any at all, but it has to be done. They could run into Yankee patrols, so I'll have to send at least a dozen. I wish Captain Coffield was here. I'd send him to lead the wagons."

"He's due back in another four or five days, sir," said Cooley. "Can't it wait that long?"

"No. Those Yankees have to be out of here before that."

"If you would like, General," put in McGraw, "I will be glad to take a dozen of my Sharpshooters and deliver the prisoners to Jackson."

General Page smiled. "I appreciate that, Captain, and I will take you up on it. I mean no disrespect to my own men, but a dozen of your Sharpshooters will be more likely to handle trouble than a dozen of any other Confederate soldiers. We'll know when to plan for the trip once the doctor from town has seen their wounded men."

The general stood up and said, "Well, gentlemen, I'll dismiss you so you can go get a little rest before sunup."

McGraw waited until the other men were gone, then said, "General, I need to talk to you for a moment."

"Certainly," nodded Page, easing back into his chair.

"What can you tell me about Captain Lex Coffield, sir?"

Page's face froze. "Why do you ask?"

"It's important that I know, sir."

"You'll be working with him, placing the mines in the bay. His personal traits won't matter that much. I've already warned you and your men that he's a bit hard to get along with."

"That's not what I mean, sir. What do you know about him as a family man?"

The general's brow furrowed. "Why are you interested in that?"

"Because his wife, Victoria, used to be *my* wife, sir. I have never laid eyes on the man, but six years ago he took Victoria from me and they ran off together. She sent me my divorce papers and a brief note saying she was marrying someone else. I never knew who he was until I ran into her at the hospital in Mobile yesterday. We talked for a few minutes and she told me the man is unbearable to live with. She even said he mistreats their son."

General Page scrubbed a palm over his face and sighed. "Sit down a minute, Captain. Since Victoria has told you this much, I'll fill you in a little."

As McGraw settled his muscular frame on a chair, Page said, "It is common knowledge both in Mobile and here at the fort that Captain Coffield is rough on Victoria and Tommy. It is a concern to me, and to the men of this fort, but there's nothing we can do about it."

"Does he beat on them?"

"I know he causes a lot of mental anguish. And I assume he abuses them physically, but I don't know it for a fact. There have been bruises on both of them, but Victoria always gives some explanation for them...an explanation that absolves Coffield from guilt."

"What would you do if you had proof that such a man under your command was beating on his wife and son?"

"I haven't given it much thought. But with proof, I'd probably have him court-martialed and thrown out of the army."

"That wouldn't keep him from beating his wife and son. Wouldn't it be better to keep him in the army so he's under government authority, and lock him up?"

Nodding, Page said, "Well, yes. It would. I guess that's what I'll do if I ever get proof. Lex Coffield is an enigma, Captain. He is courageous and tough in battle. He's got a sharp mind and is a good soldier. But he's got a couple of quirks that play against him. With his West Point training and military experience, he should be a colonel by now. But his dogged stubbornness to do things his own way and his short-fused temper have kept him from being promoted."

"Did you know he was like this before he was assigned to your command?"

"Only just before. The army sent him to me to get him out of the way at Fort Payne. A letter of warning preceded him by twenty-four hours. They said that in spite of his bad traits, he was good with explosive devices. I'll give him this much—the man does know his stuff about torpedoes."

"Too bad he doesn't know his stuff about wives and children. Even though Victoria hurt me when she ran away with him, I don't like to see her miserable, nor do I like to hear of that little boy being mistreated. I can't stick my nose into their business, but if he ever abuses either one of them in my presence, I'm not too sure I'll be able to just stand by and watch."

"Well, I hope that won't ever happen. By the way, yours truly is escorting Victoria to the dance tomorrow night. Captain Coffield is ordinarily quite jealous over any man who even goes near Victoria, but since I'm a widower and old enough to be her father, he asked if I would take her to the ball."

"I see," nodded McGraw, recalling the night he met the beautiful brunette at a ball. Crowding the memory from his mind, he stood up and said, "Thank you for filling me in on Coffield, sir. I'll go check on my wounded men now."

The Alabama sun was detaching itself from the earth's eastern edge when Dr. Ralph Bender, one of Mobile's prominent physicians, and nurse Betty Wells arrived with the two soldiers who had gone after help.

The wounded men—Rebels and Yankees—had spent the night on cots in the fort's crowded infirmary. As Dr. Bender and nurse Wells were led through the gate, there were whistles and catcalls. Lieutenant Rawlings happened to be in the infirmary talking to the three wounded Sharpshooters when the sounds met his ears. He knew immediately that medical help had arrived, and that at least one nurse had come.

Stepping to the door, Rawlings felt his heart leap when he saw Betty Wells heading toward the infirmary with General Page and a tall man carrying a black bag. Rawlings stepped out to greet her and saw a broad smile capture her face.

As they drew up, Rawlings touched his hat and said, "Good morning, Miss Betty."

"Good morning to *you*," she replied. Betty had already inquired of the two messengers concerning Lieutenant Rawlings and was secretly thankful he had not been one of the casualties.

Betty introduced Dr. Bender to Rawlings, then said, "We might need some help while working on the wounded men, Lieutenant. Would you be available?"

Rawlings had planned to ride into Mobile with Ryan McGraw,

but the prospect of being close to Betty for a few hours was too inviting to pass up. "Why, of course," he replied warmly. "I need to talk to Captain McGraw for a moment. He's about to ride into town. I'll be right back."

Rawlings hurried across the open area to the room he and McGraw occupied. The captain was strapping on his holster and knife sheath. Grinning at his best friend, he said, "I know. You want me to find somebody else to ride to town with me."

A puzzled look came over Judd's lean face. "How did you know?"

"Simple. When I heard all the whistling out there, I took a look. The instant I saw that cute little redhead, I knew you'd want to stay here."

The lieutenant's features crimsoned. "Aw now, Ryan, it isn't like that at all."

"No?"

"Of course not. I was still planning to ride with you until Betty up and asked me if I could help her and the doctor with the wounded men. They need me pretty bad. I mean...how can a true son of the South refuse to help patch up his wounded comrades?"

"Why, he can't," grinned McGraw. "That'd be dishonorable." Clapping on his hat, he said, "It's all right, pal. I understand. I'll be in town for a while. Got to send the wire to General Maury, then spend some time with our boys at the hospital. If I'm not back by the time Betty and the doctor are ready to go, why don't you ride to town with them? That way, you can escort me back to the fort from town, or wherever we happen to meet on the trail."

"How about you taking Hap or Noah along?" insisted Rawlings.

McGraw shook his head. "I'll be fine. Those two need a rest after the way they fought last night. Tell Betty 'hello' for me."

Rawlings made his way to the door and watched McGraw cross the open area, taking long, swift strides. When Ryan had passed through the gate, the lieutenant hurried toward the infirmary, his heart drumming his ribs.

CHAPTER ELEVEN

✦

It was nearly nine o'clock when Captain Ryan McGraw left the telegraph office, mounted his horse, and rode across Mobile toward the hospital. As he observed children playing in their yards and people moving about the streets he felt heavy in his heart. If somehow the Union fleet out there on the gulf was able to steam past Forts Morgan and Gaines—and if Union land forces were able to converge with them—this happy town would be plunged into the depths of despair. There would be no joy in Mobile if it fell into enemy hands.

Dismounting in front of the hospital, the captain observed several soldiers sitting in wheelchairs with nurses nearby. None of them were his men.

Just as he reached the door, he met a wheelchair bearing a soldier with bandages over both eyes. He held the door open and smiled at the nurse who was pushing the chair. She smiled in return and thanked him. As the chair moved past him, McGraw said, "Good morning, soldier. Captain Ryan McGraw. How's it going?"

The bandaged face lifted upward and the wheelchair stopped. "Captain Ryan McGraw? Of the B Company First Alabama Sharpshooters?"

"That's right."

Reaching up a pale hand, the soldier said, "Am I glad to meet you, sir! I'm Private Ollie Mears, D Company, Third Alabama Infantry."

McGraw took the hand gently, squeezed a little, and said, "The pleasure's mine, Private Mears."

"Thank you, sir, but it's really mine. I've admired you from afar for a long time. I was planning on getting some experience under my belt, then asking to join your Sharpshooters."

"Well, maybe you still can, Ollie," said McGraw, looking at the nurse. She slowly shook her head.

Mears smiled. "Yeah, maybe I can," he said with a lilt in his voice. "Dr. Lyles is good. He's gonna make it so I can see again."

The nurse was still shaking her head, her eyes misting.

"Well, you just keep believing that, Ollie," said the captain. "And when you're seeing good once more, look me up and we'll pull a few strings. Okay?"

"Okay—thanks!"

The nurse rolled the chair away, moving around the corner of the building. McGraw kept his eyes on them until they vanished from sight, then stepped inside. Just as he was passing the receptionist's desk, Rebecca Worley called out, "Captain McGraw!"

Halting, he said, "Yes? Good morning, Miss Worley."

Rising, Rebecca smiled, "Good morning," and extended an envelope toward him, saying, "Mrs. Coffield was in earlier. She left this for you. She said you'd be back to look in on your men sometime soon, and when you did, I was to give it to you."

Accepting the sealed envelope, Ryan thanked her, then proceeded down the hall. When he saw there was no one in the waiting room where he had talked with Victoria the day before, he stepped in and opened the envelope. He removed the folded note and read it silently.

Ryan Darling,

I live at 124 E. Evans Avenue. Please come to the house while you are in town. I have something very important to tell you.

All my love,

Tori

Ryan McGraw was once again troubled as he continued down the hall. His old flame for Victoria was struggling to rekindle itself. He placed the note back in the envelope and stuffed it in his shirt pocket just before turning into room twenty-seven. When he shoved the door open, the disturbance he was feeling over Victoria subsided at the sight of Dixie Quade, who was standing at Private Clint Spain's bed, facing the door.

The beautiful blonde's face lit up when she saw Ryan. She was changing the bandage on Spain's head. Smiling, she said, "Good morning, Captain."

"And a good morning to you," McGraw smiled in return. "Are my boys being good?"

Dixie pursed her lips, looked at the ceiling, and said, "Wel-l-l-l…"

"I don't like the sound of this, boys," the captain said, running his gaze from face to face.

Each of the three was grinning.

Settling his gaze on Dixie, McGraw asked, "Okay, nurse Quade, what have they been doing?"

"They've been giving the other nurses and myself a hard time about taking their syrup of pepsin. I think a lecture from their commanding officer would be appropriate."

Sergeant Marvin Staples spoke up. "Now, Miss Dixie, you shouldn't tattle on these boys."

Dixie gave him a mock glare. "It's for their own good, Sergeant. If they don't take it, they're in for real trouble."

McGraw gave each man a stern look. "You Sharpshooters had

better take your medicine and not give the nurses a hard time about it, or you'll answer to me. Understand?"

"Yes, sir."

"All right," said the captain. "Now, on a more serious note, I need to tell you about a sneak attack the Yankees tried to pull on Fort Morgan last night."

The Sharpshooters, Sergeant Staples, and Dixie listened intently as McGraw told them of the battle and its results.

Private Brad Thacker asked, "Do you think the Yankee navy will still try to get into Mobile Bay, sir?"

"General Page seems certain they will. It's just a matter of time. Probably a few weeks yet. Farragut's still building up his fleet."

Dixie completed Spain's fresh bandage and said, "Well, gentlemen, I have some other patients to tend to. I'll see you later."

As she rounded the bed and moved toward McGraw, he said, "I'll be here a while, ma'am. I've got to look in on Corporal Udall, also. I'd like to talk to you for a few minutes before I ride back to the fort."

"Of course," she nodded, showing her twin dimples in a warm smile. "I'll be here till four o'clock. Look me up, and I'll take a few minutes off."

"Will do," grinned McGraw, feeling a warm sensation wash through him. Forgotten for the moment was the old flame toward Victoria that had been struggling for life within him. Dixie's sky-blue eyes had him enthralled. He watched her till she passed from view, then turned back to his men.

After spending an hour with Bradbury, Spain, and Thacker, the captain went to Vince Udall's room and spent an hour with him. He was glad to see Udall feeling better and in good spirits. After giving him the story of the foiled Yankee attack, McGraw headed down the hall, glancing about for any sign of Dixie. He was almost to the front door when she came out of a room carrying a medicine tray.

"Hello, again," he said, feeling the ecstasy of her presence.

Dixie's heart was beating hard. "Hello, yourself," she smiled. "Are you leaving?"

"Not until I have a few minutes with you."

"Okay. Let me take this tray to the supply room. I'll be back momentarily."

Dixie was back in three minutes. Drawing up to Ryan, she said, "I can take a few minutes now. Would you like to take a walk outside?"

"Sure," he nodded. "I'd like that."

Ryan and Dixie strolled slowly over the hospital grounds keeping to the shade of the giant oak trees as much as possible. The summer sun was bearing down, and the shade felt good. As they walked together, Dixie asked, "Was there something special you wanted to talk to me about, Captain?"

"Yes, ma'am. I assume you're aware of the dance at the fort tomorrow night."

"Yes. Quite a few of the single nurses who are on days this week are planning to go. I'm one of them."

"Oh, good! General Page hadn't thought to tell me or my men about it until early this morning. As soon as I knew about it, I thought of you."

"Oh?"

"I...ah...didn't know if you'd be going or not, but I was going to...well, I'd like to be your escort when you arrive at the fort. Would you honor me?"

Inwardly, Dixie was all aflutter. Outwardly, she showed calm and replied with a warm smile, "I would be delighted to have you as my escort, Captain."

"Wonderful! I'll be the envy of every man in the fort!"

"I doubt that," she giggled, "but as long as you think so, that pleases me."

Ryan walked Dixie back to the hospital door, thanked her for giving him the time, and told her he would see her at the ball.

Dixie watched him walk to his horse, mount up, and trot away. Just before passing from her sight, he turned and waved. She waved back, sighed, and went inside, trying to calm her heart.

Captain McGraw road away from the hospital thrilled that Dixie so readily accepted his request. He turned around in the saddle, expecting to glance at the spot where he had last seen her, and was surprised to find her still standing there watching him. He raised his hand and waved. Just before the horse carried him beyond her line of sight, Dixie waved back.

Ryan memorized the sight of her standing there in her white nurse's dress with the white jumper apron. Beneath her small cap, the sun shone on her golden hair. There was a feminine grace about Dixie that he found hard to describe. She had a delicate elegance and charm flowing out of her that influenced everything and everyone she touched.

As McGraw rode southward through Mobile, he thought of the note in his pocket. Though the image of sweet Dixie was still fresh in his mind, there was something deep inside him, urging him to stop and ask someone how to find 124 East Evans Avenue. What important thing could Tori want to tell him?

Ryan shrugged it off. He must not let himself get involved with his ex-wife. Tori was married to another man. What could be important between them now?

At dusk on July 1, 1864, final preparations for the dance were being made in the dining hall at Fort Morgan. The men had come up with a few decorations to brighten the place, and even a clean galvanized bucket to serve as a punchbowl. The crude tables had been moved out into the open area to allow space for couples to dance.

At the same time, General Page and Captain McGraw were in Page's office finalizing plans for the journey to Jackson. McGraw had chosen a dozen of his Sharpshooters to take with him. There would be six privates, plus Lieutenant Rawlings, Sergeants Hazzard and Cloud, and Corporals Alex Zale, Chad Ewing, and Bobby Brinson.

Rising to his feet, McGraw said, "I guess that about does it, sir. Three wagons will be plenty. I figure the wounded men can make do in one wagon, and the rest of them can cram into the other two."

"I'm glad we're getting rid of all of them," said Page, standing up. "My conscience won't bother me since Dr. Bender said he'd patched up the wounded ones so they could travel, too."

"We'll pull out at dawn in the morning, then."

"Fine. McGraw, I want to thank you for volunteering yourself and your men to do this."

"Glad to do it, sir. We'll make the trip as fast as we can, just in case ol' 'fair-guts' decides to come in sooner than we're thinking."

"I appreciate that."

"However, let me say this sir...if the Yankees come steaming in here before we get back, the men I have left you are all tough, resourceful, and capable."

"I don't doubt it for a minute. I'm hoping, though, that Captain Coffield will get back here with those torpedoes, and we can get them in place before 'fair-guts' comes barging in here."

"Yes, sir. Me, too," McGraw said, running his fingers through his mustache. Turning toward the door, he added, "I'll go advise Whittier of the plan so he and his men will know what's in the making."

McGraw strolled across the open area to the crowded barracks where the Yankee prisoners were being kept under guard. Entering the lantern-lit room, he found Whittier standing over his wounded men, talking to them. There was a bandage on his left arm. Lieutenant Chet Noltey stood beside him.

McGraw said, "Captain, I believe you are aware that Dr. Bender said your wounded men can travel."

Whittier's eyes narrowed into angry slits. "That's what I would expect from a Rebel doctor. What does *he* care if they die along the way?"

McGraw's cheeks reddened. "He used *Rebel* medicine and *Rebel* bandages to patch them up, didn't he? I didn't hear you complain about that. Maybe I should remind you, Captain, that you and your men are trespassers! You invaded *Southern* territory, paddled your way down here on *Southern* waters with the intent of taking over a *Southern* fort. Three of our men are dead, and eight of them are wounded because of your assault. You want a hug and a kiss for that?"

Whittier lanced McGraw with red-hot eyes, and sneered, "You'll never get us to Jackson, Rebel! The woods are infested with Union troops. When they see you hauling us in those wagons, they'll annihilate you!"

McGraw stepped close to Whittier and growled, "I assure you, we'll get you to Jackson. You'll rot in that *Southern* prison till this bloody war is over. You and your men will be fed breakfast at four-thirty in the morning, Captain. We're pulling out at dawn."

McGraw winked at two of the Rebel guards as he passed through the door.

It was almost eight o'clock when four ferries docked at Mobile Point, bearing several carriages. Forty-three young ladies alighted from the vehicles as they pulled up to the gate at Fort Morgan. Sentries looked on from the top of the walls, knowing that halfway through the evening, they would be replaced so they could attend the ball.

The eleven-piece orchestra had arrived an hour earlier by ferry and were set up in the dining hall. Their instruments were tuned, and they could be heard playing as the soldiers gathered at the gate to greet the women. Extra lanterns had been placed around the fort's open area to provide plenty of light.

General Page stood just inside the gate and welcomed the women as they filed into the fort, then turned and offered his arm to

Victoria Coffield, complimenting her on her hair and her dress. Victoria smiled, thanked him, then took his arm. As they moved toward the dining hall, her eyes roamed through the crowd for a glimpse of her ex-husband.

Ryan fleetingly saw Victoria take the general's arm as he elbowed his way through the crowd, for just behind her came Dixie Quade and Betty Wells, side by side. Judd Rawlings had informed his friend that Betty was to be his partner for the night. Ryan stood transfixed as he beheld Dixie while Judd and Betty joined hands and walked away.

This was the first time Ryan had seen Dixie in anything but her white nurse's dress. She was in a high-necked, cream-colored, full-skirted dress with ruffles on the sleeves. The high top was fringed with soft lace, and above it she wore a delicate cameo on a black ribbon that encircled her neck, emphasizing its slender gracefullness.

Dixie had done her long golden hair with tiny ringlets across her forehead and an upsweep that ended in long curls on the back of her head. When she saw Ryan, her eyes glowed and her lips parted in a warm smile.

Dixie's appearance took the captain's breath. As he moved toward her, she held out both hands. He took them in his own, bowed, clicked his heels, and lightly kissed them both. "Miss Dixie, there's no doubt about it. If they were electing a queen of the ball tonight, you would win hands down. You are absolutely the most beautiful sight I have ever beheld."

"Why, thank you, Captain. That is the nicest compliment I have ever had."

Victoria Coffield was standing at the door of the dining hall with General Page as he introduced her to every Sharpshooter who came near. She nodded idly at each man, but her attention was on Ryan McGraw and the honey-blonde he was greeting near the gate. She felt her blood heat up when Ryan bowed and kissed both of the woman's hands.

Victoria had dolled herself up exclusively for Ryan's sake. She fixed her hair his favorite way, and wore a pair of diamond earrings he had bought her for their first anniversary. Lex Coffield was not aware that she had kept them. Ryan had never liked her in a low-cut dress, so she had worn one with a high neck that was frilly and extremely feminine. Victoria told herself Ryan would get a gander at her pretty soon. When he did, that blonde hussy would look like a ragamuffin in comparison.

The music was light and cheerful coming through the door. When there was a break between Sharpshooters who were filing by, the general said, "Shall we go in now, Victoria?"

Ryan's ex-wife wanted him to see her as soon as possible. From the corner of her eye, she saw that he and the blonde were drawing near, moving arm-in-arm toward the dining hall's only door. Glancing quickly at Page, she said, "Let's wait just a few more minutes, General."

Page nodded, then noticed that Ryan and Dixie were almost to the door. A quick look at Victoria told him why she was reluctant to go inside. Though she was trying to conceal it, he could tell she was concentrating on the handsome couple.

As Ryan and Dixie drew up, Ryan felt his throat tighten. Victoria had inched away from Page and was practically blocking the door.

Flashing her ex-husband a toothy smile, Victoria breathed, "Hello, Ryan, darling. Did you get my note?"

Dixie blinked at the word darling.

"Yes. I was at the hospital today. Miss Worley gave it to me."

Victoria laid a frigid glare on Dixie, then looked back up at Ryan and said, "It *is* important, darling. Make it soon."

Visibly uncomfortable, Ryan said, "Victoria, this is Miss Dixie Quade. She is a nurse. She brought me back to health a year and a half ago at the Birmingham hospital when I was seriously wounded in battle. She's stationed now at the Mobile hospital because of the impending invasion of the Union navy. Miss Dixie, this is Victoria Coffield.

Her husband is Captain Lex Coffield. He's part of the fort personnel here, but is away on assignment."

Showing a dimpled smile, Dixie said, "I'm happy to meet you, Mrs. Coffield. I'm sorry your husband couldn't be here for the ball."

Ignoring her, the brunette looked up at McGraw and said, "Ryan, darling, don't call me Victoria. You have always called me Tori."

Miffed at his ex-wife for the way she was snubbing Dixie, Ryan chose to ignore *her*. Turning to Dixie, he said, "Miss Dixie, this is General Richard Page."

The general took Dixie's hand, clicked his heels, bowed, and touched it to his lips. "I am very happy to meet you, Miss Quade," he said in a dignified manner. "Welcome to Fort Morgan, and welcome to the ball."

"Thank you, General," she smiled. "I am very happy to be here."

"Well, Victoria," said the general, "let's go inside."

Victoria's gaze clung to Ryan's for a brief moment, then she gave Dixie a feline smile and walked into the dining hall on Page's arm.

When they were out of earshot, Dixie looked up at Ryan and said, "Captain, I assume Mrs. Coffield is someone you know quite well."

Ryan cleared his throat nervously. "Yes. Quite well." Taking a deep breath, he said, "Come on, Miss Dixie. There are some Sharpshooters in here that you'll remember...and some you need to meet."

Ryan escorted Dixie to the punch table first, where Corporal Bobby Brinson was filling a cup for one of the young women. Bobby greeted Dixie warmly, and found quickly that she and the young lady already knew each other. From there, Ryan moved around the room with Dixie on his arm, introducing her to Sharpshooters she had not met, and allowing her to renew her acquaintance with those she had not seen in a long time.

Soon the music stopped, and General Page stepped up beside the orchestra conductor. When he had welcomed everyone once more, he thanked the men in the orchestra for donating their time on behalf of the men of Fort Morgan, and said, "All right, ladies and gentlemen, let the dancing begin. Maestro! Music, please!"

As the evening progressed, Dixie was ecstatic about being whirled around the floor in the arms of Ryan McGraw. She noted, however, that though Mrs. Coffield was dancing with General Page and other men, she kept looking at Ryan.

After an hour of dancing, Ryan went to the punch table and poured two cups full. Carrying them to where Dixie was sitting, he handed her a cup and sat down beside her. Taking a sip of punch, he smiled and said solemnly, "Miss Dixie, I meant what I said."

"You've said many things tonight, Captain," she replied softly. "To what do you refer?"

"I refer to what I said when you first came into the fort tonight. You are absolutely the most beautiful sight I have ever beheld."

Dixie swung her eyes to Victoria, who was on the floor with General Page, and said, "Even more beautiful than your friend Mrs. Coffield? She *is* striking, Captain."

"Yes she is," he admitted, "but she can't hold a candle to you."

Dixie looked deep into his eyes, loving him, but unable to say it. "Thank you. To hear such words coming from you means more to me than I can begin to tell you."

Neither Dixie nor Ryan noticed that the song had come to an end, and that seconds before the next one started, Victoria spoke briefly to the conductor, who nodded in assent. This was the most intimate moment they had experienced together. Ryan's heart hammered in his chest as he touched her hand and said, "Miss Dixie, I—"

"Well!" Victoria's voice cut across Ryan's words as she suddenly appeared, standing over them. "I see you two are sitting this one out." Fixing Dixie with hard, penetrating eyes, she said, "Miss Quade, you won't mind if I borrow the captain for a dance, will you? I mean, since you are not using him for the moment."

"Tori," Ryan said in a strained voice, rising to his feet, "Miss Dixie is my partner for the evening. It isn't proper for me to leave her here alone and dance with you. I've noticed that you've had an abundance of partners. Surely if General Page is growing tired, you can find someone else." With that, he sat down.

Putting on a pout, Victoria took hold of his arm and whined, "But, darling, the orchestra is going to play something special when this number is over. I want to dance it with you for old times' sake. Ple-e-e-ease!"

Graciously, Dixie patted Ryan's hand and said, "It will be all right, Captain. I'll give you up to Mrs. Coffield for just one number."

"See?" said Victoria. "You have permission, now. Come on."

Ryan's brow furrowed as he gave Dixie an "I'll get this over with and be right back" look. Standing up, he said, "All right, Tori. Just one."

Victoria took the cup from his fingers and handed it to Dixie, saying, "You can hold this while I hold *him*, sweetie."

Dixie had the sudden urge to lash out, but suppressed the desire for Ryan's sake. She wondered what kind of hold this woman had on him. What did she mean, "for old times' sake"? Was she an old girl-friend?

Bobby Brinson and his partner drew up to Dixie as Victoria led Ryan away by the hand. They sat down and struck up a conversation about how good the orchestra was. Dixie entered the conversation, but kept one eye on the man she loved.

Victoria held Ryan's hand at the edge of the dance floor, waiting for the present number to finish. While she waited, she said, "Darling, you must come to the house tomorrow."

"I can't. I'm busy."

"Well, get unbusy," she insisted. "It is very important."

"Why can't you just tell me about it right now?"

"Huh-uh," she said, shaking her head. "I have to tell you at the house. You'll understand when it happens. Trust me. Just please come tomorrow."

"Tori, I—"

"Oh, Ryan, the song is ending," she blurted, dragging him onto the floor. "Come on. Let's get ready for the next one."

Victoria took hold of both his hands as the orchestra started to play the *Donaulieder*.

Ryan looked down at Victoria and said stiffly, "Tori, you shouldn't have asked them to play that."

Victoria laughed flirtatiously, reached up and stroked his cheek in a tender manner, and said, "Darling, there's nothing wrong in stirring up a few old memories." Taking her stance for a waltz, she laid her left hand on his shoulder, placed her right hand in his left, and said, "Come on."

Ryan and Victoria were unaware that many of Fort Morgan's soldiers were watching them. Dixie also watched as they whirled round and round the floor. Bobby Brinson and his partner were back amid the dancers.

Presently, General Page sat down beside Dixie, holding a cup of punch. He noted that Dixie was following every move Ryan and Victoria were making. Assuming that Dixie knew who Victoria was, he said, "I see she took him away from you. Victoria *is* a bit forward, isn't she?"

"To say the least."

"Does it...ah...bother you to see them together like that?"

"Not really," she replied, pulling her eyes from the whirling couple and placing them on Page. "It's only for one number. Guess I can give him up for a few minutes to an old flame. That's what she is, I assume—a girlfriend from his past?"

The general realized that Dixie had not been told of Victoria's previous relationship to Ryan. Rising quickly, he said, "Excuse me, dear. I see a man I need to talk to."

Dixie watched the general move away quickly and approach one of the fort's officers at the punch table. Her line of sight soon strayed back to the dance floor.

When the waltz was over, everyone on the floor applauded the orchestra, which then began to play a slow, moody song. Ryan turned to leave the floor, and Victoria grabbed his arm. With a strange look in her eyes, she half-whispered, "One more, darling. Please."

"Victoria," he said firmly, "Dixie granted us one number. Now, I must get back to her."

As Ryan spoke, he glanced toward Dixie, who politely looked away when their eyes met. At the same instant, Victoria pressed against him and said, "Hold me close, Ryan. Like you used to. Our old song touched your heart, even as it did mine. I know it."

"Victoria, I—"

"Don't call me that," she clipped. "My name is Tori to you. It always has been and it always will be. Hold me, darling. Hold me tight."

"Tori, don't," he said, taking a step back. "There's no sense in this."

Forcing herself close again, she stood on her tiptoes and whispered, "Be honest, darling. It's still there, isn't it? You still love me, don't you?"

Gripping her shoulders and pushing her back, he said, "This has to stop, Tori. We mustn't see each other any more. You have a husband and a son. There is nothing between us any more."

Taking hold of both his upper arms, Victoria's black eyes bored into him as she countered, "You *are* still in love with me. I can feel it. And you can see it in my eyes. I am still in love with you. I made a mistake, darling...an awful mistake. Leaving you was wrong...terribly wrong. Please help me. I want to be yours again."

"Tori, two wrongs never made a right. Think of your son. Think what a broken home would do to him."

Victoria dug her fingernails into his arm. Eyes flinting, she said, "I wrote that note to you because there is something very, very important you need to know. Whatever you have planned for tomorrow, shorten it, or cancel it, but come to my house!" With that, she broke away from him and threaded her way among the dancers to where General Page was in conversation with Colonel and Mrs. DeWitt Munford. Within seconds, she had Page on the dance floor.

Approaching Dixie and sitting down beside her, Ryan said, "I'm sorry, Miss Dixie. Mrs. Coffield is a troubled woman right now. Her husband has been away for some time. She's lonely."

True to her nature, Dixie smiled sweetly and remarked, "The way she clung to you, it's evident that she's *quite* troubled. Can something be done to help her?"

"I'm sure it can, but I'm not the one to do it."

Cautiously, Dixie asked, "Captain...how well do you know her?"

Ryan took a deep breath, looked squarely into Dixie's eyes, and said glumly, "Mrs. Coffield is my ex-wife."

Dixie was stunned. Since Ryan's ex-wife had disappeared so long ago from his life, she had not thought of that possibility. All she could do was release a weak, "Oh."

Rising, Ryan took her by the hand and said, "Come on. The music is going to waste."

On the dance floor, Dixie said, "Captain, I don't mean to pry, but I have to ask you something."

"It wouldn't be like you to pry unnecessarily, ma'am," he said, holding her gently. "Ask your question."

"Are you still in love with her?"

"No."

Relieved at Ryan's prompt reply, Dixie was able to enjoy the rest of the evening. When the last dance was over, the orchestra and the female guests began boarding the carriages outside the gate. The ferries waited at the dock below.

Ryan walked his partner to her carriage, and before helping her in, he took hold of her hand and said, "Thank you for letting me be your escort tonight."

"You're welcome," she smiled. "It's been my pleasure."

"Not half as much as it's been *my* pleasure," he said softly.

"When will I see you again?"

"It'll be a few days. A dozen of my Sharpshooters and I are taking our Yankee prisoners up north to the prison camp at Jackson. We're pulling out at dawn in the morning. We have to take them in wagons because the railroad tracks between Mobile and Jackson have been destroyed by the Yankees. We can't float them up the Mobile River without making ourselves perfect targets... so the safest way is to move through the thick forests all the way up there, where at least we will have some protection."

Dixie frowned. "But even that is going to be very dangerous. Couldn't the prisoners just stay here?"

"No. General Page wants them out of his hair when Farragut comes in here, guns blazing.

Dixie nodded. "I can understand that." Ryan was still holding her hand. She squeezed his fingers and said, "Please be careful. I don't want anything to happen to you."

The captain's pulse picked up pace. "I'm glad for that. I promise I'll do my best to take care of Mrs. McGraw's boy."

Dixie smiled at his homespun way of expressing himself. The carriage driver spoke up, announcing that all the ladies should get on board.

Ryan took both of Dixie's hands in his and said, "When I get back, I'll be in to see you. Could I...could I take you to dinner?"

"Of course," she said softly.

Pulling her hands close to his chest, he said, "If it's all right with you, I want to see a lot more of you in the days to come."

Now it was Dixie's pulse that was beating faster. "Yes, it's all right with me."

At that instant, Victoria brushed past them and said, "Tomorrow, Ryan. I'll be waiting for you." She moved on to another carriage, not giving Ryan time to tell her that he was leaving for Jackson at dawn.

Dixie boarded her carriage, told Ryan she had had a wonderful evening, and waved as the carriage pulled away. Captain McGraw stood watching the carriage carry Dixie down the gentle slope toward the dock, and wrestled with his emotions. He could almost swear he was falling in love with the beautiful blonde. He had even come to the point that he wanted to be in love with her and make her his wife.

Yet, he asked himself, *how could I be feeling true love for Dixie when I am so stirred by the presence of Tori?*

CHAPTER TWELVE

✦

Before dawn the next morning, several Rebel soldiers prepared the wagons while the Confederates and Yankees who were going to make the trip to Jackson were eating breakfast in the dining hall.

Captain Leonard Whittier ate quickly, then made his way to the table where Ryan McGraw was eating with Judd Rawlings and Bobby Brinson. Standing over the Confederate officer, Whittier said with grit in his voice, "You shouldn't be making my wounded men take this ride, McGraw."

"We've already been over that, Captain. They're going."

"I'm telling you again, Johnny Reb. You'll never get us to that prison camp. There are plenty of Union troops out there in those forests. They'll cut down every man in a gray uniform in short order."

"You'd better hope not," was McGraw's blunt reply.

"And why is that?"

"Because you and your men are going to be wearing gray."

Whittier's jaw slacked. "What're you talking about?"

"When you made your little threat yesterday about the woods being infested with Union troops, you said, 'When they see you hauling us in the wagons, they'll annihilate you.' Remember?"

"Yeah. So what?"

"You planted an idea in my head. I happened to know that there were several old and tattered Confederate uniforms in a store room here in the fort. General Page was glad to let me have enough to dress each of you blue-bellies in gray. All of you will be wearing Rebel uniforms on the way to Jackson. We'll put your wounded men in gray, also. They'll ride in a wagon together, and the rest of you will fill up the other two."

Whittier's eyes bulged. "You can't do this!"

"Oh, but I can. Your men will drive the wagons while my men and I ride horseback. Every one of your able-bodied men will have a rifle...but no ammunition, of course. With all twenty-nine of you in gray uniforms, we'll look like a detachment of thirty-five Confederate soldiers hauling seven of our wounded men somewhere. Since the Union scouting units are always made up of a dozen men or less, your blue-bellied comrades won't want to tackle a squad of thirty-five."

Whittier measured McGraw with a look of cold fury. "If our troops *do* attack, me and my men will be helpless! They'll cut us down—"

"This is war, Captain Whittier. You threatened me with Union troops coming after us in the woods, so I came up with a way to try to ward them off. If they open fire on you and your men, that's the way it is in war."

"If it happens, it'll make you a murderer."

"It won't be *me* pulling the triggers. You'd better pray your blue-bellied friends leave us alone. I might also add, Captain, that if any of your men try to escape, they will be shot. They're all listening over there right now. You better make sure they understand I mean what I say."

Just before dawn, Captain McGraw led the procession out of Fort Morgan, heading northward along the edge of Mobile Bay.

Captain Leonard Whittier rode on the seat of the wagon that bore his seven wounded men. It galled him to see his men humiliated by having to wear Confederate uniforms, and he especially hated the one on his own body. The Rebel who had worn it had been shot in the chest. The ragged bullet hole was still there. He gripped the empty Henry repeater he was forced to hold and cursed Captain McGraw under his breath.

McGraw's dozen Sharpshooters surrounded the three wagons on their horses. Each man wore a sidearm and knife, and carried a repeater rifle. Private Bus Williams was sent ahead to ride point. Lieutenant Rawlings rode beside the captain, with Sergeants Hazzard and Cloud directly behind them. Corporal Bobby Brinson rode directly behind wagon number three. The other privates and corporals chose their places on both sides of the procession.

As the sun began to rise in the sky, it gave promise of a hot, humid day. Soon the procession was deep in the woods, veering away from the bay. They had been traveling for some three hours when Noah Cloud adjusted himself in his McClellan saddle and griped, "I wish I had a good western-type saddle with a saddle horn. I hate this dumb thing some lame-brained Northerner invented."

"General George B. McClellan designed it," said Hap Hazzard. "That's why it's called a McClellan saddle."

Cloud looked at Hazzard askance and said, "You're plumb crazy. That numskull McClellan was the first guy to use it. He didn't design it. They call it McClellan because he endorsed it, and he's a hot-shot. That's all."

"Talk about bein' a numskull. Don't you ever read anything but nursery rhymes? I'm tellin' you...McClellan designed this here saddle back in 1858. In 1859 the United States War Department adopted it as the army's official saddle because it takes less leather than the western kind, so it's cheaper to make."

Noah spit in the well-shaded dirt and guffawed. "Hap Hazzard, do you think everything you read is true? When would McClellan have time to invent a saddle? You got it wrong. It's like I said—he only endorsed it."

The driver of the first wagon, who was directly behind the arguing sergeants, spoke up. "The big redhead is right. I've been in the U.S. Army for a long time, and I know General McClellan personally. He *did* design that saddle in 1858, just like he's telling you."

Noah jerked around in the saddle and spat, "Shut your mouth, Yankee! Nobody gets in on our arguments! Understand? If my friend here wants to believe everything he reads and be told what to think by someone else, let him! But you butt out! The war between me and him is a private one. Got it?"

"Okay," shrugged the Yankee, turning to look at his captain, who sat beside him.

Whittier's face was like solid granite as he glanced at the two Rebel sergeants and said, "Don't bother with them, Oates. Save your energy for more important things."

Victoria Manning Coffield busied herself about the house all morning long, keeping it straightened up in spite of the continual litter left about by her five-year-old son. From time to time, she found herself going to the front door or the parlor window and looking toward the street.

After a while, Tommy noticed her frequent glances outside and asked, "Is Lex coming home today, Mommy?"

Turning away from the front door, which stood open because of the heat, Victoria looked down at the sandy-haired boy, thinking how much he looked like his father, and replied, "No, honey. It'll be three or four more days before Lex comes home."

"Good. I wish he'd never come home."

Tommy had voiced Victoria's own feelings. She did not reprimand him.

"Why do you keep looking outside if Lex isn't coming home? Is someone else coming to see us?"

"Somebody very special, honey. Somebody I've wanted you to meet for a long, long time." She cast another glance out the door, then turned back and said, "Tell you what. I'm trying to keep the house neat for our guest. Why don't you go out and play in the back yard? Maybe Eric and Rollie are in their back yards and will play with you."

"Naw, they ain't. Both of 'em left a while ago with their dads."

Frowning at him, Victoria said, "Tommy, I told you not to use the word *ain't*. You say 'They *aren't*.'"

"Yes, ma'am," replied Tommy, ducking his chin. He paused a moment, then unwittingly ripped at his mother's heart by saying, "I wish I had a *real* dad, like Eric and Rollie. They're always asking me why Lex doesn't take me boating on the bay and other stuff like their dads do. I keep telling them it's because Lex ain't—aren't—*isn't* my dad. He doesn't want to do things with me 'cause I'm not his son."

Victoria bit her lower lip as she saw the hurt in Tommy's pale-blue eyes. There was a tiny tear in the corner of the left one.

Clearing her throat, she said, "Honey, go out back and ride your stick horse that Grandpa Wiley made you."

"Okay," the boy said. He started toward the rear of the house, then halted and looked back at his mother. "Mommy, Grandpa Wiley isn't really my grandpa, is he? And Grandma Wiley really isn't my grandma, is she?"

Clarence and Myrtle Wiley, the elderly couple who lived next door, had taken a special liking to Tommy, and had asked Victoria if they could "adopt" her son as a grandchild. Their own grandchildren lived in Tennessee and South Carolina. Victoria's parents had been dead for over ten years, and since Tommy would never meet his paternal grandparents, she granted their request. To their delight, Tommy was even allowed to call them "Grandma" and "Grandpa."

"No, honey," the young mother answered, fighting a lump in her throat, "they're not your real grandparents, but they love you as much as if they were. Go on, now. Play in the back yard. I'll call you when our special guest arrives."

Wheeling, the boy broke into a run. He was almost to the kitchen when Victoria called, "Tommy!"

Skidding to a halt, he looked back. "Yes, ma'am?"

"Don't get dirty. I want you presentable when he gets here. And be especially careful with your bandage. We have to go to the hospital later this afternoon and get it changed. I don't want Dr. Bentley to see a dirty bandage. Understand?"

Tommy said he understood and was quickly out the back door.

When Ryan had not shown up by noon, Victoria called Tommy in for lunch. To her dismay, he was covered with dust and the sweat on his face and neck had turned to mud. Amazingly enough, the bandage on his arm was relatively clean. She washed him up, changed his clothes, combed his hair, and fed him lunch. One of the neighbor boys had returned home, and Tommy was eager to rejoin him in play.

The hours dragged by. Twice Victoria heard the sound of hooves on the dirt street out front and ran to the door expecting to see her ex-husband. Disappointment gripped her when she saw it was not Ryan.

Four o'clock came. Frustrated and a bit angry, Victoria called her son in and washed him up again. Together, they walked the three blocks to Mobile's hospital. Approaching the receptionist's desk, Victoria said, "Miss Worley, I have Tommy here to see Dr. Bentley."

"All right, Mrs. Coffield," smiled Rebecca. "Just have a seat. The doctor is with a patient now, but will be able to see Tommy shortly."

"Thank you," nodded Victoria. Before turning toward the waiting area, she asked, "Has...ah...has Captain Ryan McGraw been in today?"

"Not that I know of, ma'am. I was away from my desk for about twenty-five minutes while I had lunch, but I didn't see the captain earlier or later, so I doubt that he's been in. He stays quite a while when he comes to see his men."

"Is nurse Quade in?"

"Yes. She's about to leave, but someone called for her to help with a patient down in room forty-one a couple of minutes ago. It's straight down the hall and to the left. She should be coming out momentarily."

"All right. I need to talk to her briefly. I'll take Tommy with me so you won't have to watch him. If Dr. Bentley is ready for him before we get back, come and let me know."

Rebecca nodded with a smile.

Leading her son by the hand, Victoria reached the hall and turned left. Just as they rounded the corner, Dixie was coming out of room forty-one, along with another nurse. When Dixie saw Victoria, she could tell by the look on her face she was wanting to speak to her. Dixie excused herself to the nurse, who proceeded on down the corridor, and waited as mother and son drew up.

Dixie's attention was drawn to the boy immediately. There was no doubt who his father was. She wondered why Ryan had never told her he had a son.

Dixie smiled at the boy, then looked up at his mother. Face stolid, Victoria asked sharply, "Miss Quade, are you expecting Captain McGraw to be here at the hospital today?"

"No, Mrs. Coffield. He left Fort Morgan at dawn this morning. He's taking some Yankee prisoners to the prison camp at Jackson. He'll be gone for a few days."

Anger flushed Victoria's face. "Why didn't Ryan tell *me* he was going to Jackson? I've been waiting for him to show up at my house all day!"

Dixie did not reply. She simply turned and started down the corridor in the opposite direction.

The move infuriated Victoria. "Wait a minute!"

Dixie kept on walking.

Tommy watched with wide-eyed concern as his mother ran ahead of the nurse and blocked her path. Dixie stopped abruptly, fixing the furious woman with an impassive look and struggling to keep her composure.

Fiery rage flashed in Victoria's black eyes as she blared, "Don't you walk away from me! I'm not through talking to you!"

Dr. Glenn Lyles emerged from a room a few feet down the corridor. His brow furrowed as he stepped close and asked, "Is there a problem, nurse Quade?"

"Nothing that I can't handle, Doctor," Dixie answered calmly.

"Is this lady upset about something that's happened here in the hospital?" pressed Lyles.

"No, sir. It's a personal matter."

Turning to Victoria, the doctor said, "Ma'am, if you have some personal dispute to settle with Miss Quade, it shouldn't be done here at the hospital while she is on duty."

Victoria had to bite her tongue to keep from snapping at the doctor. Suppressing her anger for the moment, she said, "I...I didn't come to the hospital for the purpose of having a confrontation with Miss Quade, Doctor." Gesturing toward Tommy, who stood where she had left him, she added, "I came to have Dr. Bentley examine my son's arm and change the dressing."

Lyles glanced at the boy, then said, "It might be best if you take your son to the waiting room until Dr. Bentley can see him."

"I will, Doctor, but it is very important that I talk to Miss Quade while I am here."

"Then do it privately and when Miss Quade has the time," said Lyles, and walked away.

When he was out of earshot, Victoria was about to speak to Dixie again when two nurses came out of a room a few doors down and headed their direction. When they had greeted Dixie and passed on by, Victoria put her face close to Dixie's and said, "You know who I am, don't you?"

Dixie knew what she meant, but said tartly, "You are Mrs. Coffield. Captain Lex Coffield's wife."

The cold insinuation was wasted on Victoria. Acidly she snapped, "Did Ryan tell you he was once married to me?"

"Yes, he did. You'd best remember that you're not married to him any more."

"You're in love with him," Victoria said levelly. "I saw it in your eyes when you were in his arms on the dance floor last night."

"That's really none of your business."

"Oh, really? I have a right to know what's going on in Ryan's life."

Temper flashed in Dixie's sky-blue eyes. "No you don't! You forfeited that right when you ran out on that wonderful man and divorced him. But since you brought it up, *Mrs. Coffield,* I will tell you straight. Yes, I am in love with Ryan, but why should you care? You've got a husband."

Ignoring Dixie's heated words, Victoria asked pointedly, "Do you think Ryan is in love with you?"

It's none of your business, Mrs. Coffield. None of this has any connection with you."

"Well, let me tell you, miss blond prissy, Ryan McGraw is still in love with me! And I'm serving notice right now...I am going to have him back!"

Dixie's temper grew hotter. It shook her throat as she spoke. "What is your husband going to say to that?"

Looking around to see if anyone was in earshot, and seeing no one, Victoria put her nose within inches of Dixie's and hissed, "I'll handle Lex in my own way and my own time! And if you tip anything to him, or try to stand between Ryan and me, *I'll kill you!*"

While her words hung threateningly in the air, Victoria spun around and stomped down the corridor. Grabbing Tommy by the hand, she led him into the waiting room, making sure the receptionist saw them. When they sat down, the boy said, "Is that nurse a bad lady, Mommy?"

Patting his head, Victoria replied, "Yes, honey. She is a *very* bad lady."

The day wore on as the three wagons and their mounted escort wended their way through the dense Alabama forests. The sun beat down mercilessly, and though they were in deep shade most of the time, every man's shirt was stained with sweat.

Private Williams was some fifty yards ahead, his eyes carefully searching the woods. McGraw and Rawlings were still riding side by side ahead of the lead wagon. Hazzard and Cloud had dropped back and were chatting with a couple of other Sharpshooters.

Raising his hat and mopping sweat with a bandanna, McGraw observed two squirrels chase each other around the base of a giant oak tree, then dart up its trunk and disappear into the thick foliage overhead. Giving his lieutenant a sidelong look, he said, "I happened to observe you and Betty off and on during the dance last night. Seems to me things are thickening up pretty fast between you two."

Judd grinned and said, "Does that statement require a comment, sir?"

"Well, I guess you wouldn't say a comment was *required*, but since I am your superior in rank, I do request a comment."

"Okay. I won't beat around the bush. I'm falling in love with her."

"Really? What about Betty? She showing signs of feeling the same about you?"

"Mm-hmm. *Good* signs."

"Yeah? And what are they?"

"Unless I get a direct command to answer, sir, you ain't gonna find out."

"Guess I'll leave it alone."

"Thank you," grinned Rawlings. He waited a few seconds, then said, "Captain, are you aware of the talk among the Fort Morgan men after the dance last night?"

"No. What kind of talk?"

"Well, some of them were discussing the way you and Victoria danced awfully close there at the last. They said that when Captain Coffield returns, he'll no doubt hear about it."

"Probably will," McGraw said dryly.

"They're saying you'll probably have a fight on your hands."

McGraw stuffed his bandanna back in his hip pocket, but said nothing.

Judd proceeded. "The men at the fort say Coffield has a wicked mean streak. They say he has a hot, hair-trigger temper, and that he's insanely jealous over Victoria. He has already maimed two civilian men in Mobile for being too friendly with her."

When the captain still did not reply, Rawlings said, "None of the men at the fort like Coffield, Captain, and to a man they said they won't tell him about the way—as they put it—you and Mrs. Coffield were cuddling. But they're sure he'll find out about it. Could be real trouble."

"I've faced real trouble before. The hot-headed captain can come after me if he wants to, but the cuddling was Victoria's doing, not mine."

"None of those fort men know she used to be your wife," said Rawlings. "The women who attended don't either."

"That really shouldn't enter into the picture, Lieutenant. Victoria's very unhappy in her marriage and is trying to win me back. I shouldn't even have danced with her. She was so insistent, and Dixie was nice enough to tell me to go ahead and give Victoria one dance. After that one dance was over, she threw herself at me. I should have shoved her away the instant she moved so close, but she'd have made a scene. I know her too well."

"So what are you going to do about her?"

Before Ryan could answer, Private Donnie Jim Michaels pulled up on his opposite side and said, "Captain, you told me to ride up and relieve Williams on point at three o'clock. It's time."

"Fine," nodded McGraw. "Go right ahead."

"I wanted to tell you something, first, sir."

"Yes?"

Leaning close and lowering his voice so Captain Whittier could not hear him, Michaels said, "There's a lot of whispering going on in the last wagon, sir. Corporal Brinson asked me to tell you he thinks those blue-bellies are going to make a run for it. We both think maybe you'd better tell them one more time we'll shoot them down if they try to escape."

"I told them once. They're not children. I'm not telling them again. I gave all of you men your instructions. One warning shot if they try to run. If they don't stop, you shoot to kill. Remember?"

"Yes, sir."

"Brinson and the others will remember, too. Go on up and relieve Williams."

Michaels said, "Yes, sir," and touched heels to his horse's flanks. The animal went into a trot.

As Michaels drew close to Williams near a creek up ahead, Rawlings said, "I think I'll drop back and join Brinson for a while...just in case those blue-bellies decide to make a run—"

The lieutenant's words were cut short as the report of a rifle split the hot afternoon air. McGraw and Rawlings turned to see the eleven Yankees in the last wagon peeling over the sides and running in two directions. Corporal Brinson's smoking Henry was cocked and ready to fire a second time as he shouted to the fleeing men, "Halt! Halt or you die!"

The warning shot had caused most of them to stop, but two of the Yankees were still running to the left, and one to the right. Brinson, Hazzard, and Cloud fired, dropping one, and at the same instant, six more rifles barked, cutting the other two down.

Captain Whittier was swearing at the Rebels and started to get out of his wagon. Jerking on the reins, McGraw wheeled his mount in a tight circle and shouted at Rawlings, "Make him stay in the wagon!"

As McGraw headed back along the line, Rawlings swung his rifle on Whittier, who was halfway to the ground and blared, "Back in the wagon, Captain, or you'll get what those three men of yours just got!"

Whittier froze, eyes blazing. As he moved back into the seat, he swore and bawled, "Murderers! They just murdered my men!"

The Rebel captain rode past the second wagon, telling his men to shoot the first Yankee who threw a leg over the side. When he reached the last wagon, four Sharpshooters were holding rifles on the would-be escapees who were fearfully climbing back into the wagon.

"Good work, all of you!" said McGraw, turning his horse so each of his men could hear him. "Corporal Zale, you and Private Stelling take six men from the second wagon and escort them as they pick up their dead comrades and carry them back here."

Suddenly Whittier stood up in his wagon and screamed at the top of his voice, "McGraw! The whole bunch of you are murderers! You'll pay for this! I guarantee it! You'll pay for this!"

"Shut up, Captain!" Rawlings shouted, urging his horse closer to the first wagon."

Corporal Zale and Private Stelling were collecting the six Yankees from the second wagon, and Corporals Brinson and Ewing were holding guns on those in the last wagon, along with Private Koop. Hazzard and Cloud positioned themselves so as to cover troublemakers in any of the wagons.

Captain McGraw trotted up to the first wagon, reined in, and said to Whittier, "Nobody murdered those men, Captain. I remind you that all of you were warned that if you tried to escape you would be shot. Corporal Brinson fired a warning shot, and even called out to them, but they still kept running. They were fools for trying to escape."

"My men are just scared, McGraw. They're spooked about being sitting ducks in these gray uniforms! They're also worried about being locked up in one of your filthy Confederate prison camps. Who can blame them for gambling an escape? Your men didn't have to be so eager to cut them down. They didn't have to kill them! They could've shot them in the legs."

"Sure," snorted McGraw. "Like you would have done to us if the tables were turned. They were duly and properly warned, and were given two chances to halt. They kept running. It was their own fault they got killed. I don't want to hear any threats from you."

"I don't care what you want to hear!" Whittier roared. "You'll never get us to Jackson. In spite of these stinking Confederate uniforms, we'll find a way to overcome you. And when you're *our* prisoners and I have the upper hand, I'm going to give you some of your own medicine. You're going to rue the day you were born!"

McGraw did not see Sergeant Hazzard dismount and head toward the lead wagon as he nudged his horse close to Whittier and said, "Do as Lieutenant Rawlings told you, Captain. Shut your mouth. Now, sit down and cool off."

Whittier's cheeks were red as brick dust in the dappled sunlight that filtered through the trees. There was insolent contempt in his voice as he snarled, "I'll sit down, shut up, and cool off when I'm good and ready, McGraw!"

Suddenly big Hap Hazzard yanked Whittier from the wagon seat and let him drop to the ground. Whittier's empty rifle clattered on the seat, then fell to the floor of the wagon. The Yankee captain gasped for breath and started to rise. Hap sank powerful fingers into his sweaty shirt, lifted him to eye level, and growled, "You can forget try-ing to make my captain rue the day he was born. By his own medicine, I assume you mean you would kill him. Let me tell you something, big-mouth! Captain Ryan McGraw don't kill easy! A lot of men have tried...and a lot of men have died. Are you listenin' to me?"

Whittier clamped his mouth shut, giving his countenance an insolent mien. Hap's face grew redder. He shook the man and said, "I asked you if you're listenin' to me!"

Whittier swallowed hard. "I'm listening," he choked.

"Okay, you listen good. Even if somehow you succeeded in killing my captain, you'd have *me* to face. You know what I'd do, big-mouth? Do you?"

Whittier's face was paling. He was helpless in the hands of the muscular sergeant and was embarrassed in front of his men. Licking his lips, he said, "No."

"I'd tear off both your arms and beat you over the head with 'em. Then I'd tear off both your legs and stuff 'em down your stinkin' Yankee throat. Then you know what I'd do, Whittier?"

"No," came the weak reply.

"Then I'd kill you!"

The Rebel soldiers burst into laughter. Captain Whittier eyed them with hatred as Hazzard dumped him back on the wagon seat in a heap.

CHAPTER THIRTEEN

★

The blazing sun made its arc across the sky and dropped toward the western horizon. The horses' ears were drooped from the heat, and the sweaty men rode in relative silence.

Captain Leonard Whittier sat glumly on the wagon seat. Confederates and Yankees alike let their eyes roam the woods around them, aware that Union soldiers could come at them any time. The thought of dying under the guns of their own army was almost more than the Yankee prisoners could bear.

At sundown, Captain McGraw and Lieutenant Rawlings saw Private Michaels trotting toward them from his point position. Reining in, Michaels said, "Captain, there's a bubbling spring just ahead, and it's at the edge of a small clearing. Be a good place to camp for the night."

"Sounds good. We'll do it."

As the wagons hauled up in the clearing and the Rebels dismounted, the able-bodied prisoners were allowed to stretch their legs and drink from the spring. Canteens were filled and the wounded men were given water. When they had taken their fill, they were helped out of the wagon and laid out on the ground.

One of the wounded Yankees looked up at McGraw, and said, "Captain, riding in that wagon is killing us. Every time it hits a hole or runs over a rock, it jars us and shoots pain through our wounds."

"Soldier, I'm sorry about your pain, but there's nothing I can do about it."

"You could just leave us here. Wouldn't be long till some of our troops would come along. They'd take care of us."

"You ought to know I can't do that, soldier. It's my duty to deliver you to the prison camp. I don't enjoy seeing anyone suffer...not even Yankees. You and your wounded pals just have to face it. War is made of pain and discomfort."

Together the enemies ate a cold meal. McGraw did not want to draw attention by building a fire. Lieutenant Rawlings took charge of assigning sentries for the night. Three men would be on duty at all times, and would work in shifts. The Yankees were huddled together in one spot and lay on the warm ground. McGraw and his men encircled them, and as darkness fell, everyone in the camp was asleep except the sentries.

Dawn came. Privates Southard, Barnes, and Koop awakened the other Sharpshooters, then began rousting out the Yankees. As a matter of caution, Koop began a head count of the prisoners. Coming up one man short, he counted again. When it was confirmed that one prisoner was missing, Koop dashed to McGraw, who was in conversation with Sergeant Hazzard and said, "Excuse me, Captain, but I've got some bad news."

"What bad news?"

"One of the Yankees is missing."

Frowning, McGraw asked, "Are you sure?"

"Yes, sir. I counted all of them. Dead ones, wounded ones, and the rest of them. We're one prisoner short. Somehow one of them slipped past the sentries during the night and got away."

McGraw turned toward Alex Zale and Doug Stelling, who stood near the spot where the horses had been picketed, and called, "Alex, are all the horses there?"

Zale turned, and began a quick count. After a few seconds, he called back, "Yes, sir. They're all here, including the wagon teams."

"Thanks," said McGraw, and wheeled, stomping toward Leonard Whittier with Hap Hazzard on his heels. Koop followed close. The rest of the Rebels caught on that something was up and began looking toward their leader.

Whittier was on his feet, checking the bandage on his arm as McGraw drew up and said, "One of your men is missing."

Whittier had heard McGraw asking his men about the horses, but had paid little attention. His head jerked up. "What?"

"I said one of your men is missing. I want to know who it is."

A wide grin split Whittier's face. "Really?"

"Really. Who is it?"

"Did he take a horse?"

"No. He's on foot."

Looking around with the grin still wide, the Yankee leader said loudly, "You hear that, guys? One of our men was smart enough to get away!" There was an instant cheer from the Yankees.

Fixing McGraw with hard eyes, Whittier smirked, "Well, Captain, it won't be long now. My man will bring Yankees swarming down on you like mad hornets! They'll know about us being in these gray uniforms, too."

"Who is it, Captain?" queried one of the wounded Yankees who lay on the ground.

Whittier ran his gaze over the faces of his men for a few seconds, then replied, "It's Bill Temple."

"He take a horse, sir?"

"No. He was probably afraid if he tried it, one of them would nicker and give him away. He's on foot."

"That'll be no problem, Captain," spoke up another wounded Yankee. "Bill's a fast runner. He'll bring help soon!" There was another cheer from the prisoners.

Bus Williams was standing near. "What shall we do, Captain?"

Before McGraw could reply, Hap Hazzard said, "I'll go after Temple on horseback. I know a little about trackin'. If I can run him down before he finds some of his blue-bellied buddies, this whole episode will be over before you can bat an eye."

"I'll go with you," nodded McGraw. "Lieutenant Rawlings, you're in charge. Don't let anybody move till Hap and I get back."

While a couple of the men were saddling McGraw's and Hazzard's horses, the captain followed Hap as he walked the perimeter of the camp, studying the ground. It took him only a minute to find footprints leading through the trees eastward. Kneeling down and examining the prints closely, he said, "By the way these blades of grass are pressed down, I'd say Temple hasn't been gone more than an hour, Cap'n. Probably made his move just before dawn."

"Let's go," breathed McGraw.

As the two Rebels rode out at a trot with Hazzard's keen eye tracking the escapee, the captain said, "Stands to reason that unless Temple knows of a Union camp somewhere around here, he'll find himself a horse to ride."

"I was thinkin' the same thing," replied Hazzard. "If he spots a farm, he'll beeline for it."

Moments later, they broke out of the woods into open country, and spied a farmhouse with barn and outbuildings about a mile away. "C'mon!" said McGraw, goading his mount.

Their horses' hooves threw up turf as McGraw and Hazzard put them into a full gallop. Just as they were thundering into the yard, they saw an elderly man bound out the front door of the weather-worn farmhouse. He stumbled and fell as he jumped off the porch, and at the same moment, a revolver boomed at the door. The bullet chewed dirt next to the old man's head. The gunman saw the two army officers closing in, and ducked back, slamming the door. In the second or two that it took for him to do it, McGraw and Hazzard recognized Bill Temple in the gray uniform.

Skidding their mounts to a stop, both men vaulted from their saddles, rifles in hand, and picked up the old man. Hurrying, they dragged him behind a huge oak tree close by and sat him down. Sensing danger at the house, the horses followed and stood by the tree.

As the elderly farmer looked into their faces, eyes wide, McGraw said, "Sir, I am Captain Ryan McGraw of B Company, First Alabama Battalion Sharpshooters. This is Sergeant Hap Hazzard. You probably know by now that the man inside your house is not a Confederate soldier."

"Yes," gasped the old man. "That devil Yankee fooled me at first. He knocked on my door and told me he had escaped from a Yankee camp where he was bein' held prisoner, and needed a horse. He couldn't find one in the corral or in the barn. He got angry when I told him I don't keep horses any more, that my son down the road does the farmin' for me with his horses. Then he points that rifle at me and enters my house. Once't he's inside, he grabs my revolver off'n its hook on the wall and points it at me. Come to find out, his rifle is empty. I figure he's a Yankee in disguise an' he admits it. 'Bout that time, he heard you men gallopin' in. I made a dash out the door and he took a shot at me."

"Is there anyone else in the house, sir?" asked McGraw.

The old man drew in a raspy breath, his eyes widening. "Yes, my wife! But she's bedridden. He...he wouldn't hurt a crippled old woman, would he?"

Before McGraw could comment, Temple's voice cut the air. "Captain! Can you hear me?"

McGraw removed his hat and peered cautiously around the tree. The Yankee stood in the doorway, holding the revolver to a small, elderly woman's head. He was supporting her entire weight with his free arm. A look of terror was on the woman's face.

"I can hear you," replied McGraw. "Put the woman down!"

"I will! All you have to do is throw out your guns. I want those horses. I'll ride one and take the other one with me so you can't follow. Do as I say, and nobody will get hurt."

"Can't let you do that, Temple. The lives of my men are at stake. You'd bring your blue-bellied friends down on us."

As he spoke, McGraw levered a cartridge into the rifle's chamber, edged the muzzle around the rough-barked trunk and lined it on what he could see of Temple's head behind the woman's.

Hazzard did the same thing on his side of the tree. "Cap'n," he said in a low tone. "I think you've got a better angle than I do."

"Mine's pretty good," said McGraw.

"Hey!" boomed Temple. "Are you listening to me out there? I said throw your guns out and nobody will get hurt!"

"What's he doin' to my wife?" asked the old man, his voice quavering.

"He's got your revolver to her head, sir," said McGraw, "but in the excitement, he's forgotten to cock the hammer. He's an infantryman and doesn't handle revolvers much."

"Oh, don't endanger her life, Captain, please! Don't try to shoot him if he's using her as a shield!"

"What's your name, sir?" Hap asked.

"Clive Holman. Wife's name is Elsie."

"Mr. Holman, the Yankee *is* using your wife as a shield, but he's exposing half of his head so he can see us with one eye. Captain McGraw is an expert marksman. When he thinks he's got a clear shot, he can take the man out. If we wait too long, that Yankee is going to realize the hammer isn't cocked. Once he cocks it, even if Captain McGraw drills him perfectly, his reflex could pull the trigger on that revolver."

Clive Holman started praying in a half-whisper.

"McGraw!" bellowed Temple. "My patience is running out!"

Elsie could be heard whimpering.

Voice low, McGraw said, "Hap, tell him one more time to put her down. I'm holding my breath to steady my aim."

The old man was weeping as he prayed.

Looking at the Yankee down the barrel of his Henry, Hazzard shouted, "Temple, give it up! Ease Mrs. Holman down carefully and drop the gun."

"You stupid Rebs are gonna get her killed!" shouted Temple. "Now, throw those guns out or—"

Ryan McGraw's rifle barked and the slug tore through Bill Temple's right eye. Elsie fell backward on top of the dead man.

"See to her, Hap," said McGraw, reaching down to help the old man to his feet.

"Is she all right?" choked Holman.

"Yes, sir. She's fine."

"Oh, thank you dear Jesus!" the old man sobbed as McGraw steadied him and helped him around the tree.

Hap was standing over Temple's body and cradling Elsie in his arms as the captain and the farmer drew up. Tears were dripping from her chin and staining her cotton nightgown. Reaching past the big sergeant's muscular arm, Clive Holman hugged his wife's neck as they wept together.

A cheer went up from the Rebels when they saw Captain McGraw and Sergeant Hazzard ride up with the dead Yankee's body draped over Hazzard's horse. The prisoners eyed each other with dismay and looked toward their captain, who walked up to the corpse as Hazzard and McGraw were dismounting and eyed the gaping scarlet hole in the back of Temple's head.

McGraw had moved up behind him. Before Whittier could vent his wrath, McGraw met him with a cold stare and said, "Don't say it, Captain. He forced his way into the home of an elderly farm couple, took their revolver, and shot at the old man when he ran from the house. We arrived just as the old man was coming out the door. Your big, brave soldier, here, dragged the farmer's crippled wife from her bed, put the gun to her head, and demanded we give him our horses. He was going to kill her if we refused."

"I don't believe it!"

"Well, that just cuts me deeply," retorted McGraw. Shoving his way past the Yankee leader, he called to the prisoners, "Okay, we're pulling out. Put your wounded men in their wagon and pile in your own. Let's go!"

The dead Yankees were carried in wagons one and two, with nothing to cover them. McGraw figured it was best that way. Maybe the sight of the corpses would be a constant reminder of what it cost to attempt escape from McGraw's Sharpshooters.

Travel was resumed. The wounded men complained of their discomfort, but to no avail. At noon, when they stopped beside a babbling brook to eat and fill the canteens, McGraw announced that they were halfway to Jackson. By sundown the next day, they would be at the prison camp. Soon they were on the move again. From time to time they caught a glimpse of the Mobile River glistening in the harsh sunlight a mile or so to the west.

Some fifteen miles southeast of Jackson, a squad of a dozen Union soldiers was camped in a wooded thicket as the sun was going down. They were clustered in a tight circle, sitting on the ground, as Sergeant Eli Garrett stood over them.

"So what do you think our assignment will be, Sergeant?" asked one of the soldiers.

"I could guess two or three things," replied Garrett, who chewed on a dead cigar. "But no sense in going through them. Just be a waste of breath. We'll know for certain when Lieutenant Blake gets back."

"I'd like to go over there to that stinking Confederate prison camp at Jackson and free our men in there," spoke up a corporal.

"Take more men than we have here to do that," said Garrett. "I understand it's a virtual fort."

The sound of a horse blowing met everybody's ears. Grabbing their guns, they leaped to their feet. They were traveling on foot and had no horses; the sound meant someone was coming. Seconds later, five riders in blue uniforms emerged from the dense woods and greeted them. Amongst them was Lieutenant Erven Blake, their leader.

After exchanging a few words with the four men who had escorted him from Major General Edward R.S. Canby's camp in Mississippi, Blake bid them good-bye. When they had ridden out of sight, Blake tied his horse to a bush and told the men to gather around.

When everyone was seated on the ground, Blake stood before them and said, "I know you're all eager to find out our assignment, so here's the story. Within the last day or two, a special unit made a night assault on Fort Morgan at the mouth of Mobile Bay. There is no word as yet as to the result of that mission. The unit was to capture the fort and hold it, which would eliminate most of the danger Admiral Farragut and his fleet would encounter upon entering the bay. I say *most* of the danger, because there's also Fort Gaines to reckon with, but it is held by only a few men and can be overcome by land *or* sea quite easily."

Blake lifted his campaign hat, mopped sweat from his brow with a dark-blue bandanna, and continued. "If General Canby learns that the Fort Morgan mission was successful and that the fort is now in the hands of Union forces, he will hasten to send a large number of troops toward the city of Mobile by land. This is where we come in. Our assignment is to move from here toward Mobile and rendezvous with a couple hundred of our troops bivouacked about ten miles north of Mobile."

"Sir," spoke up Sergeant Eli Garrett, "where will General Canby obtain enough troops to capture Mobile? It'll take a whole lot more than two hundred plus us."

"General Canby is working on that right now. From what he said, I think he's going to send Major General Gordon Granger and his Cumberland Fourth Corps. They've got over five thousand men. Right now, Granger's bunch are in a hot battle somewhere north of here, but it looks like that one will be won shortly."

Garrett spoke again. "Lieutenant, what's the time schedule, then? If Fort Morgan is now in our hands, how soon does General Canby plan to move on Mobile?"

"I'd say it'll be about two weeks."

"But what if that assault on Fort Morgan didn't come off as planned? Then what?"

"General Canby and I discussed that. He figures that without control of Fort Morgan, Admiral Farragut will want to beef up his fleet some more before steaming into Mobile Bay. If Fort Morgan is still in Confederate hands, we're probably looking at the first week of August for the big move. So that'd be about another four weeks." Blake paused to mop sweat again, then said, "If the mission was successful, then as I understand it, Admiral Farragut has already run his fleet into Mobile Bay and overpowered Fort Gaines, too. He'll wait until our land forces are ready to close in on Mobile from the north, then move on the city from the bay. This will give the Union a sure-fire victory, and Mobile will then be in our hands."

"So we won't know about all this until we get word from General Canby," said Garrett.

"Right," nodded Blake. "Once Canby hears from Farragut, he can plan accordingly. Our job is to be at the spot ten miles north of Mobile whenever word comes."

"So we move out at dawn. Right, sir?"

"Right. Now let me say something else. General Canby told me that the war is definitely turning in favor of the Union. We're winning more and more battles everywhere. President Lincoln and General Grant are in agreement that once we occupy Mobile and the bay, the end of the war can be hastened."

There was instant joy among the soldiers. They shook hands, patted each other on the back, and laughed heartily, saying they could soon go home.

Blake proceeded. "The reason it'll hasten the end of the war is because having the use of the Mobile seaport will enable the Union to bring in troops, weapons, ammunition, and supplies to the degree that we'll have what it takes to overpower the already weakening Confederate forces."

With spirits running high, Lieutenant Blake and his men ate their evening meal and talked of going home. Soon darkness surrounded them, and they bedded down for the night. At sunrise Blake mounted his horse and headed southwest with his men following on foot. Blake sent Corporal Benny Middleton to move out ahead and walk point. Middleton stayed in sight of the others about fifty to sixty yards ahead.

It was nearly midday when the sun-blistered Yankees saw Middleton waving at them from the top of a heavily wooded rise. He had seen something and wanted them to hurry. Lieutenant Blake trotted on ahead.

When the others arrived, they found Blake and Middleton looking at movement in a shallow valley about two thousand yards below. The lieutenant was leaning against a tree, using binoculars to study the faraway scene.

As the men gathered close, keeping well within the shadows, one of them squinted down into the valley and asked, "Is it Rebs, sir? Looks like gray uniforms, but with the heat haze, it's hard to tell."

Without taking the binoculars from his eyes, Blake replied so that all could hear, "It's Rebels, all right. There are three wagons loaded with them, and thirteen of them on horseback. Can't tell exactly how many are in the wagons, but I'd say at least twenty-five ...maybe thirty. They're all bearing what look to be repeater rifles."

Sergeant Garrett stood at Blake's shoulder and said, "They're headed due north across that open meadow, sir. They'll be in the woods ahead of them in a short while. Are we gonna go after them?"

"There's no way we can just rush them. Be foolish to try to swap lead with that many men. We need to hasten on ahead of them, lay wait for them in the forest, and take them by surprise. Without the element of surprise, we'd be committing suicide. We'll try to avoid a gun battle if possible, since we're so outnumbered. If we can get the drop on them, we can take them as prisoners. Looks like they just might be coming from Mobile. I'd sure like to squeeze some information out of them."

Corporal Ken Southard was riding point as the blazing sun neared its zenith. The wagons and mounted Rebels were some eighty yards behind him, moving steadily across an open meadow. Southard studied the dense woods ahead of him and wished for more open spaces. The forests were extremely dangerous because it offered the enemy a place to hide and spring an ambush.

In the procession, Captain McGraw rode alongside the lead wagon, listening to the Yankee leader complain while he gripped his empty rifle.

"You should've let us bury our dead, McGraw," griped Whittier. "It isn't good for my men to have to ride with those bodies. Pretty soon they'll start to stink."

"We're not taking time to bury them, Captain. That'll be taken care of as soon as we arrive at the prison camp. Besides, as I said earlier, having those corpses in the wagons will be a good reminder of why they died. Nobody is going to get away from us. My job is to deliver all of you to the prison camp. I'll do that whether it's dead or alive."

"I'm wondering if dead isn't best," mumbled Whittier.

"Certainly prison camp is better than death, isn't it?"

"Since it's a Confederate prison camp, that's debatable. I've heard some pretty bad things about your prison camps."

"Well, I've heard some bad things about yours, too."

Ignoring McGraw's comment, the Yankee captain said, "You know the South is licked, don't you? There's no way you can win this war."

"That's your opinion."

"It's more than an opinion. You Southerners are short on supply, and you know it. You can't make guns and ammunition out of cotton fields and peach orchards. The North has the advantage. We have factories. We can produce weapons and ammunition in a way the South cannot. Face it, McGraw, the Confederacy is doomed. It's only a matter of time."

Captain McGraw was nobody's fool. He knew what Whittier was saying about the factories was right. This was what made Mobile Bay and the city of Mobile so important. A few foreign countries were shipping in needed supplies via the Gulf of Mexico for the Confederacy's use in the Western Theatre. If the Union navy was allowed to capture the bay and the Union land forces found a way to capture Mobile, all necessary supplies would be cut off.

The Confederates had managed to last this long because of the foreign supplies and the fact that after so many battles in which the stubborn Rebels had been victorious, they were able to confiscate Union guns and ammunition. Confiscation by itself, however, would never keep them in the war. They had to have the supplies that came up the bay to Mobile.

The procession moved into the heavy timber, and the deep shade cast by the foliage overhead was a welcome relief from the heat of the sun.

Having true Southern doggedness in his makeup, McGraw would have the last word of the discussion. Leaning slightly from the saddle, he held Whittier with a penetrating stare and said, "Don't count your chickens before they're out of the eggs, Captain. We've still got Mobile Bay. Never underestimate the South's determination to wear you Yankees down till you turn tail and run back home. We've got grit you haven't even seen yet." With that, McGraw nudged his horse forward and rejoined Judd Rawlings at the front of the procession.

A half hour later, the wagons were rattling amid the thick trees when suddenly a dozen men-in-blue leaped out from the shadows, guns ready, surrounding the procession. Riders and drivers pulled rein.

A single Yankee up ahead jumped from behind a tree, threw his gun on Ken Southard, and commanded sternly, "Drop the rifle, Reb!"

Southard reprimanded himself for being taken by surprise, leaned over and carefully dropped his Henry repeater. When it hit the soft forest floor, the Yankee snapped, "Okay, out of the saddle!"

Southard looked around for more Yankee soldiers, but saw none. As he slowly dismounted, he wondered why the Yankee hadn't shot him out of the saddle. When he touched ground, the enemy soldier said crustily, "Okay, Reb. Turn around and head back where you came from."

What Southard saw in the thick woods some seventy yards behind him filled him with fear. The wagon procession was stopped and surrounded by blue-bellies, wielding repeater rifles.

"Let's go," said the Yankee, prodding him with the muzzle of his weapon.

Standing his ground, Southard said over his shoulder, "What about my horse?"

"Don't fret," replied the enemy soldier, prodding him again. "We'll be taking him for ourselves."

Lieutenant Blake planted himself in front of the two lead horses, holding his service revolver on McGraw and Rawlings, whom he recognized as officers. "You two dismount!" he directed sharply, waving his gun with authority.

McGraw hated that the Yankees had gained the advantage on them, but knew it was impossible to totally protect themselves when traveling in dense timber. He and his men had been in tight spots before. If a natural opportunity didn't quickly present itself for them to turn the tables, the Sharpshooters would create one. As McGraw and Rawlings were throwing their legs over their saddles, the natural opportunity came unexpectedly.

Eager to identify himself and his men as Union soldiers, Captain Whittier stood up in his wagon, holding the empty rifle, and said excitedly, "Lieutenant, these men in the wagons are Union army! I'm their Captain! My name is—"

The sudden move startled Lieutenant Blake. He raised his gun and eyed him skeptically, expecting a trick. "Sit down, soldier!" he snapped, "and drop that rifle! Union soldiers don't wear gray uniforms!"

Men on both sides tensed.

Frustrated that the Union officer did not believe him, Whittier looked down at the rifle he held and stammered, "It...it isn't loaded, Lieu-Lieutenant." In his frenzied eagerness to prove his point, he jerked the rifle up for Blake's inspection.

A tense Union soldier misunderstood the quick move, reacted by natural reflex and fired his rifle, hitting Whittier in the chest. There was instant bedlam.

Sharpshooters went into action. Guns roared. McGraw and Rawlings had their rifles in scabbards on their saddles. There was no time to grab them. Instead, they hit the ground and whipped their revolvers out of their holsters, firing at the first blue uniforms they saw. They both fired once, and two Union soldiers fell dead. McGraw caught a glimpse of Captain Whittier hanging over the edge of the lead wagon with his head down and a foot caught under the seat. There was a bullet hole directly over his heart. His eyes stared vacantly into space. The empty rifle lay on the ground beneath his head.

Rawlings saw a Yankee dive under the wagon for cover. He trained his revolver on the man's face with the hammer cocked. A split second before he dropped the hammer, he saw the knowledge of death in the surprised Yankee's eyes. The gun bucked against his palm and the Yankee died instantly with a slug in his forehead.

The woods clattered and echoed with the harsh gunfire. Bullets hissed and hummed deadly songs, hitting men and splintering the bark off trees. Horses were neighing and stomping their hooves as the battle progressed. Smoke filled the air, giving off its bitter odor.

Captain McGraw rose up on one knee, hunting for a target, when through the smoke he saw Noah Cloud and Hap Hazzard fighting side by side, using rifle butts to crush Yankee heads. Suddenly a Union corporal dashed through the smoke and vaulted into the saddle of McGraw's horse. McGraw swung his revolver on him just as he took hold of the reins, and fired. The Yankee jerked with the impact as the bullet plowed into his chest and fell to the ground like a rag doll.

The Yankee who walked behind Private Southard kept prodding him with the muzzle of his rifle as they moved toward the wagons. Captain McGraw had taught his men how to take the gun away from an assailant who had it pressed against your back. Southard waited to feel the hard metal against his backbone one more time. They were some thirty yards from the wagons when it came simultaneously with the shot that killed Captain Whittier. Southard moved with the quickness of a cat, taking the Yankee by surprise. When he jerked the rifle from the Yankee's hands, it discharged, sending the bullet into the trees.

Southard planted his feet and swung the rifle by the barrel, cracking the Yankee's head with the butt. The Yankee hit the ground, and Southard brought the rifle around in a second arc, connecting with his head in a savage blow. The man in blue fell flat with a cracked skull. For him the war was over forever.

Flipping the rifle in his hands, Southard worked the lever and ran toward the fight.

The battle was less than a minute old when the Sharpshooters began to take control. In another three minutes, it was over. When the smoke cleared, ten of the men in blue were dead, including Lieutenant Blake and Sergeant Garrett. The other three were seriously wounded. Two Sharpshooters had minor cuts and scratches.

Captain Whittier's body was placed in a wagon with his own dead men, and the procession moved out, carrying the dead blue-clad Yankees and the three wounded ones.

Late that afternoon, Captain McGraw and his men delivered the prisoners to the prison camp. The wounded ones received medical attention, and the dead ones were buried.

At dawn the next morning, the Sharpshooters headed back for Mobile, some on horseback, and some driving the wagons. The impending battle at Mobile Bay was on their minds.

CHAPTER FOURTEEN

R yan McGraw and his dozen Sharpshooters had been gone from Fort Morgan four days when Captain Lex Coffield returned at noon from Tuscaloosa. The torpedoes were being unloaded onto the dock by the boatmen, who would quickly begin their return trip.

Coffield walked briskly up the sandy slope and was greeted without enthusiasm by the guards at the gate. He cursed at them under his breath as he headed for General Page's office to report his return with the torpedoes. His attention was immediately drawn to the unfamiliar faces intermingled among the regular men of the fort.

A private named Hank Webb noticed Coffield's puzzled expression and said, "We got some help while you were gone, Captain."

"So I see," nodded Coffield. "Who are they?"

"B Company, First Alabama Battalion Sharpshooters."

"B Company?"

"Yes, sir!" exclaimed Webb, grinning from ear to ear. "We done got us the famous McGraw's Sharpshooters!"

Lex Coffield stiffened. His features went pale and stony as he breathed through tight lips, "Ryan McGraw? *He's* here?"

"Well, not at the moment, sir. Right now, Captain McGraw and a dozen of the Sharpshooters are on a mission to Jackson. We had some excitement here while you were gone. I'm sure General Page will tell you all about it."

Without a further word, Coffield stomped away, unaware that every eye was following him. When he disappeared into the general's office, the soldiers went back to what they were doing before Coffield made his entrance.

General Page looked up from his desk at the sound of rapid footsteps approaching the open door. Without waiting for permission, Captain Coffield entered and said stiffly, "General, why wasn't I informed about B Company Sharpshooters being sent here? Certainly you knew they were coming before I left for Tuscaloosa."

"I didn't think it was necessary to tell you."

Dark eyes flashing, Coffield snapped, "I'll bet the other three officers knew, didn't they?"

Page cleared his throat. "Yes. Yes, they did."

"What is it with you, General?" Coffield boomed. "Why am I the step-child in this place? Why do I have to learn what's going on around here from the lowly enlisted men?"

The general rose to his feet, his own features flushed. "When you start acting like you're a captain and like you're one of us in this place, Coffield, you'll be treated as such! Now, come off your high-horse and tell me how many torpedoes you brought with you."

Coffield pulled a bandanna from his hip pocket, took a deep breath while wiping sweat from his face, and said, "Almost two hundred. A hundred and ninety-one to be exact. They're being unloaded on the dock right now."

"Good," nodded Page, sitting down.

Coffield dropped onto a chair in front of the desk, clutching the bandanna.

The general asked pointedly, "Is your ire stirred because I didn't inform you that we were getting additional men...or because the additional men are led by Captain Ryan McGraw?"

The captain studied him for a moment, then said, "I take it you know about Victoria having been married to McGraw."

"Yes."

"She tell you?"

"No. He did."

"I see. So I'm even lower in your estimation than I was before."

Page did not comment. Easing back in his chair, he said, "I have informed Captain McGraw that his men will be helping you place the torpedoes in the bay."

"All right. We'll begin after lunch. Hank Webb said we had some excitement around here while I was gone, and that McGraw and a dozen Sharpshooters are in Jackson on a mission. I assume the excitement and the mission are related."

Page told Coffield of the Union attack on the fort and that McGraw had volunteered to take the prisoners to the prison camp. He added that they should be showing up soon.

The general impressed on Coffield that it was important to get all the torpedoes in the water as soon as possible, since he was expecting Farragut to come steaming in once he had built his fleet sufficiently. Coffield said he would work with the Sharpshooters all afternoon, then ride into Mobile in time to eat supper with Victoria.

Page noted that Tommy wasn't mentioned. He had assumed that the boy was Coffield's son until he learned that Victoria had been married to Ryan McGraw. It didn't take the general long to recognize that Tommy was the spit and image of McGraw. From that moment, he understood why the self-centered Coffield showed no love for the boy.

After lunch, Captain Coffield changed his clothes and led the Sharpshooters down to the dock. They worked until the sun was lowering in the sky, then Coffield dismissed them for the day, saying they would begin again in the morning. Planting sea mines was a slow and tedious task.

Coffield made his way to the stables and was saddling his horse when he overheard a group of the fort's regular men talking on the other side of the thin wooden wall. One of them said, "Did you see the look on his puss when he heard Hank say 'B Company, First Alabama Battalion Sharpshooters'?"

Laughter followed. Then another chuckled, "Yeah! And did you notice his eyes when he said, 'Ryan McGraw? *He's* here?' "

"One thing for sure, fellas," said another. "Coffield and McGraw know each other. And unless I'm mistaken, they ain't pals."

"Well, from what we saw at the dance the other night," put in a fourth voice, "Mrs. Coffield knows McGraw, too."

"I'd say real well," agreed one of them. "Maybe McGraw was her beau and Coffield came along and stole her away."

"I'll bet that's it!" the one who had spoken first said with elation. "The way the two of them were cuddlin' on the dance floor, it was like they'd done it before."

Another laughed and said, "Coffield would've swallowed his tongue if he'd walked in on that! With his temper, he would probably have shot both of them!"

"He might yet if he finds out about it," said another.

"Well, he ain't gonna find it out from *me!*" laughed another.

Victoria Coffield and her son were just finishing supper in the kitchen of their two-story house when they heard a horse blow in the back yard. They looked at each other, knowing what it meant, and Tommy said glumly, "It's Lex."

Victoria rose from the table and looked through the open back door. Coffield was leading the horse into the small corral beside the barn. Victoria had acted bravely in front of Dixie Quade when she snapped that she would handle Lex in her own way, but in truth she was terrified of him. He was big, strong, and could be dangerous when his temper was riled.

Tommy pushed away from the table and said half to himself, "I wish he'd never come home." As he spoke, he hurried toward the parlor, wanting to be absent when Coffield entered the kitchen.

Victoria stood at the door, dabbed at her hair, smoothed her dress, and forced a smile as the captain approached the porch. She waited till he passed through the door, then threw her arms around his neck, saying, "Hello, sweetheart. I missed you! I'm so glad you're home."

As she turned her lips toward his, Coffield exploded. Face beet-red, he sank powerful fingers into her hair, jerked her head back until he knew it was hurting her neck, and growled, "Don't *sweetheart* me, Victoria! Missed me, did you? Glad I'm home are you?"

"Please—you're hurting me!"

"Don't lie to me!" he hissed. "You didn't miss me...not with Ryan McGraw around!"

"Lex, it's not my fault he was assigned to the fort. You can't blame me—"

Shaking her head violently, he spat, "I can blame you for dancing with him the other night! And I can blame you for cuddling close when you did it!"

"Lex, I—"

"Don't deny it, woman! I overheard some of the men talking about it at the fort!"

"Please!" she begged. "You're hurting me!"

"You think I don't know that? I'm hurting you on purpose. You're *my* wife, Victoria! I gave you permission to go to the dance as partner of the fat old man. You knew I meant for you to stick with him only. So did you and your ex-husband step out into the moonlight? Did you kiss him? Huh? Did you?"

"No, we didn't go out into the moonlight, and no, I didn't kiss him," she said, her voice shaking.

Shaking her head by the hair, he asked, "Why'd you dance with him, Victoria?"

Wincing, she said, "I tried to avoid him, Lex, but he followed me around till he cornered me at the punch table. He wanted a dance 'just for old time's sake,' he said. Your fellow-soldiers were there. I would have had to be rude to refuse. None of them know he's my ex-husband. I didn't want the wife of Fort Morgan's captain to appear rude. So, to be polite in front of everyone, I told Ryan I would, but for only one number."

"Yeah? Then what about the cuddling? Why didn't you make him keep his distance?"

Victoria gasped, "I don't know what those men you overheard were talking about. There wasn't any cu—"

"Stop lying, Victoria!" he shouted, snapping her head back again. "I heard those soldiers say if I'd walked in on you two, I probably would have shot both of you. Now tell me the truth! You were snuggling him, weren't you?"

At that moment, Tommy appeared, weeping, and cried, "Let go of my mommy! You're hurting her!"

"Shut up, brat! Go back to wherever you were! Go on!"

Tommy's cheeks glistened with tears and his breathing was ragged as he backed slowly toward the door to the parlor.

Turning his attention back to his wife, Coffield railed, "You *were* snuggling him, weren't you? Tell me the truth!"

"No! I mean...it wasn't me who did it! Ryan surprised me by suddenly pulling me close. I tried to push him away, but he's stronger than I am. I—"

"Liar! Those soldiers I overheard said the way you and him were cuddling, it was like you'd done it before. That doesn't sound like you were fighting him off to me!"

Coffield let go of Victoria's hair and slapped her. She went down hard, screaming. Leaning over, he began slapping her repeatedly. When she raised her arms to protect herself, he batted them away and slapped her harder. She whined and wept, jerking with each blow.

Suddenly the maddened captain felt a sharp pain in his right thigh. Looking down, he saw Tommy gripping his leg and biting him through the pantleg. Swearing, Coffield struck the boy across the top of the head, breaking his hold and flattening him on the floor. The child sprang to his feet, showing hatred in his pale blue eyes and screeched, "Leave my mommy alone! Leave my mommy alone!"

When Lex turned and slapped Victoria again, Tommy lunged at him and sank his teeth in another spot on his thigh. Coffield swore again and struck him with his fist, knocking him loose. The boy struggled to his feet. Coffield placed his foot against Tommy's chest and gave a hard shove. The five-year-old sailed across the room, slammed the wall hard, and slumped to the floor.

Victoria dashed to Tommy and gathered him into her arms. Looking up at Coffield with her nose and mouth bleeding, she screamed, "You've killed him! You've killed him! You beast! You killed my son!"

There was a knock at the front door. Coffield pointed a stiff finger at Victoria and warned, "You stay here!"

While Coffield hurried toward the parlor, Victoria looked down at Tommy. He was limp in her arms. She opened her mouth to wail, but checked it when she saw his eyes roll under the lids. "Tommy!" she gasped, shaking him mildly. "Tommy! Speak to Mommy!"

The lids fluttered, then the eyes that were exactly the same color as Ryan McGraw's looked up at her. They were glassy, but he focused them on her as he spoke with slurred tongue, "Did...did he go away, Mommy? I want him...to go...away."

Victoria held him close and wept. Suddenly she noticed that the gash on his arm had been torn open. Blood was trickling down his arm in two thin streams.

Lex appeared, standing over them. "What's the matter with you?" he said harshly to Victoria. "The kid isn't dead."

Rising to her feet and sniffing at the blood oozing from her nose, she glared at him and said, "It's not your fault he isn't dead! He's got a big knot on his head, and his arm's bleeding again. We've got to take him to the hospital so they can stitch it up. Who was at the door?"

"Our big-nosed neighbor, old man Wiley. He heard you carrying on and decided to come see if there was anything wrong. I had to placate him a little, but he's satisfied everything's all right. We aren't taking the kid to the hospital. You can fix him up."

Victoria's concern for her son overshadowed her fear of Lex. "The wound is torn open, Lex. I can't stop the bleeding! He's got to have a doctor's attention—I'm taking him to the hospital!"

Moving to block her way, Coffield grunted, "I said *you* can fix him up. If the Wileys see you carrying the kid out of here bleeding, the old man will think I lied to him."

"Well, didn't you?" she rasped as she stepped around him, her jaw set in grim determination.

As the inflexible mother headed for the front door, Lex shouted, "Victoria! Come back here!"

She never broke stride. When she opened the door, he bellowed, "Victoria! I'm commanding you to come back here!"

Pausing halfway across the threshold, she turned her bleeding face toward him and said tightly, "I'm not one of your lowly privates, *Captain*. Don't command me!"

Victoria heard the angry man call her a vile name as she moved swiftly across the yard to the street.

A soldier on crutches with his right foot bandaged was coming out the hospital door as Victoria arrived, carrying Tommy. Quickly he hopped out of the way and held the door open, eyeing the blood and purple marks on her face and the blood on the child's arm. She thanked him and hurried to the reception desk. An older woman

Victoria had not seen before greeted her. When the receptionist saw the blood on both mother and son, she quickly ushered them down the corridor, saying that Dr. Glenn Lyles would see them right away.

Victoria thanked her and followed her into the examining room. Dr. Lyles was in conversation with Dixie Quade at a desk. Both looked up at the same time. When Victoria saw Dixie, she cursed under her breath.

"Dr. Lyles," said the matronly receptionist, "this lady and the little boy need your attention."

Lyles immediately recognized Victoria as the woman he had reprimanded for giving Dixie trouble in the hospital corridor. He scrutinized them quickly and gestured toward the examining table. "Put him right over here, ma'am," he said.

As Victoria laid Tommy on the table, Dixie headed for a cupboard to fetch the necessary materials. The anxious mother quickly explained to Lyles that Dr. George Bentley had stitched up a bad gash on her son's arm several days earlier, and that the boy had fallen and reopened it.

"Did *both* of you fall?" queried the doctor, focusing on Victoria's blood-caked nose and mouth.

Dixie was carrying a tray toward the table. The eyes of the women met fleetingly. "Uh...no," Victoria replied.

The doctor looked down at his small patient and touched the bloody bandage. As he examined it closely, he said without looking up, "Miss Quade, see if you can help Mrs.——" He looked around and said, "I don't know your name, ma'am."

"Victoria Coffield. Captain Lex Coffield of Fort Morgan is my husband."

Lyles nodded. Then to Dixie he said, "I'll need that dried blood cleaned off Mrs. Coffield's face. Looks like her lip may need a stitch or two."

"I don't think so, Doctor," said Victoria. "It's cut on the inside, but it doesn't seem too bad."

"We'll know when your face has been washed," said Lyles, then he turned back to the boy, who was studying him with wide eyes, and asked, "What's your name, son?"

"Tommy," the boy said softly.

"Tommy Coffield, eh?"

"No, sir. Tommy *McGraw*."

Lyles shot a glance at Victoria, who had turned to look at Tommy. When her eyes swerved to the doctor's, she said calmly, "Captain Coffield is my second husband."

Lyles nodded, then said to the boy, "Did Dr. Bentley hurt you when he sewed up your arm before, Tommy?"

"A little bit."

"Well, I might have to hurt you a little bit too, but you're a big boy, aren't you?"

"Yes."

"Good. Nurse Quade and I will have you fixed up here in no time."

Tommy's mouth pulled down. He glared at Dixie and said, "I don't want her to help you. She's a bad lady."

"Why would you say that, Tommy? Did nurse Quade help Dr. Bentley when you were stitched up before?"

"No, she talked real bad to Mommy once here at the hospital. She's a bad lady. A *very* bad lady."

Dr. Lyles said he believed Miss Quade was a very *nice* lady, and that if Tommy knew her better, he would think she was nice too. He then noted the knot on the boy's head and asked, "How did you fall, Tommy?"

"I didn't."

"I thought your mommy said you fell?"

"Lex kicked me and I hit the wall."

Lyles set quizzical eyes on Victoria.

Her face pinched. She looked at Dixie, then at the doctor. "My...my husband...he...he has a bad temper. He—"

"Lex is a mean man!" Tommy cut across his mother's words. "He hurt my mommy!"

Dr. Lyles asked, "Why did your daddy kick you against the wall, Tommy?"

"He's not my daddy! I hate him! He hit me on the head, then kicked me against the wall because I bit his leg. He was hitting Mommy. I bit him to make him stop hitting her."

There was a moment of silence. Then Dixie broke it by saying, "Dr. Lyles, Mrs. Coffield won't need any stitches. The cut is on the inside of her mouth as she said. It has stopped bleeding, and so has her nose. I'll put some salve on these bruises, and she'll be all right."

Lyles was pressing firmly on the boy's reopened gash to stay the bleeding while cleaning around it. "Good," he said. "As soon as you finish, we'll take care of Tommy." Then he spoke to Victoria. "Mrs. Coffield, we've found that it's best to work on children without their parents present. You can go down to the waiting room. Once I've closed the wound, nurse Quade can complete the work on Tommy. I'll come to the waiting room. I'd like to talk to you for a few minutes."

"All right, Doctor."

Dixie was finished within a few minutes. Victoria did not thank her for the treatment. She stepped to the table and said, "Tommy, you be a brave boy, won't you?"

"Yes, Mommy," he replied shakily.

"That's my big boy," she said, patting his shoulder. Leaning over, she kissed him on the forehead, then headed toward the door. Opening it, she looked back, waved to Tommy, and stepped into the corridor.

She was halfway to the waiting room when she saw a rather homely young nurse coming toward her. As they drew close to each other, the nurse noticed Victoria's battered face. Stopping, she said, "Hello. Aren't you Captain Lex Coffield's wife?"

Victoria halted and nodded. "Yes. Do I know you?"

"Not really," smiled the nurse. "My name is Florence Dillon. I was one of the girls who went to the fort for the dance the other night. You probably didn't notice me."

The inelegant face was suddenly a bit familiar to Victoria, so she said, "Come to think of it, I do remember you."

Studying Victoria's bruises, Florence asked, "What happened, ma'am?"

Victoria knew it was none of the nurse's business what had happened, but since she just might talk to Dixie or the doctor, she decided to tell her the truth. "My...my husband has a bad temper, Miss Dillon. He got angry over something and batted me around a little."

"Oh, I'm sorry," said Florence. Then in a catty voice, she asked, "Was it because of the way you and that handsome Captain McGraw were holding each other at the dance? I'll bet someone tattled to your husband, didn't they?"

Victoria realized too late that Nurse Dillon was nothing but a busybody. "It really doesn't concern you!" she snipped, and walked away. When she reached the door of the waiting room, she looked back and saw Florence Dillon enter the examining room where Dr. Lyles and Dixie Quade were working on Tommy. *Oh wonderful,* she thought. *Now the busybody will find out that Lex beat on Tommy, too.*

Florence Dillon stepped into the examining room, unaware that the doctor had a patient, and said, "Oh, excuse me, Dr. Lyles. I didn't realize you were busy. I'll come back later."

"Fine," Lyles told her without looking up. He knew Florence's grating voice quite well.

Dixie was intent on what she was doing and did not bother to look up, either.

Florence glided up close and eyed Tommy. "Who's this cute little guy?"

When neither doctor nor nurse answered, the boy said, "My name's Tommy."

"What happened to you, Tommy?"

Dr. Lyles knew Florence could be an irritating snoop, and was about to tell her to go find something to do, but Tommy let it out before he could speak.

"Lex kicked me against the wall."

Dixie and the doctor exchanged glances.

"Oh," said Florence, realizing who the boy belonged to. "I just saw your mother in the hall. She told me about your daddy beating up on her, but she didn't say anything about him beating on you, too."

Tommy was about to say that Lex was not his daddy when he felt a sharp pain and winced.

"You're doing fine, Tommy," the doctor said calmly. "Sorry this has to hurt, but we're almost done."

Unable to subdue her curiosity, Florence said, "Tommy, your daddy was angry about the way your mommy was acting with a man at the dance, wasn't he?"

Tommy's attention was on his arm. "Yes," he said, hoping the nosy nurse would quit asking him questions.

Dixie flashed a hot glare at Florence.

Dr. Lyles was disgusted with the way Florence was pumping Tommy. Pausing in his work, he set hard eyes on her and said in a stern voice, "Nurse Dillon, you must have work to tend to elsewhere."

Florence stiffened and said, "Well I guess I could find something to do."

"Then do it."

Florence walked to the door and disappeared into the hallway.

During the repair work on Tommy's arm, Dixie smiled at the boy frequently and made sure he knew she was doing everything she could to ease his pain. She even held his hand while the doctor was finishing up, which was the most painful part.

Telling Dixie to bandage his arm while he talked to Mrs. Coffield, Lyles left the room.

Dixie stood over Tommy and took his hand again. "You're a brave young man, Tommy," she smiled. "You were real good for Dr. Lyles."

Tommy did not reply. He was confused. The bad lady didn't seem bad at all. She had talked sternly to his mother that day in the hospital hallway, but she didn't do that today. Maybe she had changed. He liked the way she looked at him and the way she held his hand.

In the waiting room, Dr. Lyles sat down facing Victoria Coffield and said, "Ma'am, I have to tell you that I'm quite concerned with this situation."

Victoria had developed a severe headache. Pressing the fingertips of both hands to her temples, she asked, "Will Tommy be all right, doctor?"

"The gash stitched up fine. You'll just have to make sure it doesn't get opened again."

"I'm thinking more of that big bump on his head. I don't know whether it came from when my husband struck him on the head or when he hit the wall. It really frightened me. I thought he was dead. He was unconscious for probably a minute, and he didn't breathe, either. Could there be any serious damage?"

Lyles rubbed his chin thoughtfully. "I doubt it. His eyes are quite clear, now. If he should show any signs of abnormality, bring him in immediately, but I think he'll be all right. What I'm concerned about is his being subject to this kind of treatment...and yourself, too, for that matter. Has this happened before?"

Victoria set her gaze on the floor. Rubbing her temples again, she nodded without looking up and replied shakily, "Yes. Not to this degree with Tommy, but Lex has manhandled me many times and slapped the boy around. He...like I said, he has a bad temper."

"Well, he's going to have to get control of it, Mrs. Coffield, or something serious is going to happen. I'd like for him to come in and let me talk to him."

"He'd never submit to it, doctor. Lex is a proud and stubborn man."

"Are you aware that if the army learns that he is beating you and your son, they will take action?"

"No."

"Well, it's so. The captain could find himself in the brig for quite a long spell if they learn about it. Such conduct is looked at as very unbecoming for any soldier, but much more for an officer. If this kind of thing happens again—even if you don't care about yourself—for Tommy's sake, you'd best report it to General Page."

Victoria nodded, thinking that her best solution was to let Ryan know he has a son and alert him to the kind of treatment Lex Coffield was giving him. She thanked the doctor for his help and advice, and took Tommy home.

CHAPTER FIFTEEN

★

C aptain Ryan McGraw and his twelve men arrived at Fort Morgan at one-thirty in the afternoon on July 5. General Richard Page welcomed them back. He congratulated them when he learned of the attack and how they had handled it.

Page explained to McGraw and the others that the rest of the Sharpshooters were out in the bay planting torpedoes with Captain Coffield, who had returned from Tuscaloosa the previous day. He told them that the Union navy had added more ships to their fleet on the Gulf. A naval invasion was imminent, and he felt certain that a ground attack would come, if not simultaneously, shortly after the ships began their assault. Every man in the fort must stay alert.

General Page advised the weary Sharpshooters to rest for the remainder of the day and plan to join the others in the bay the next morning. Captain McGraw said he wanted to ride to Mobile and check on his men in the hospital.

Arriving at the hospital shortly after four o'clock, the captain was happy to see that his men were doing well. Private Brad Thacker and Corporal Dean Bradbury would be released to go home for further recuperation within a week or so.

When McGraw looked around for Dixie Quade, he was told it was her day off. Leaving the hospital, he went to the apartment building a half-block away where the nurses lived. By asking a couple of nurses he met in front of the building, he learned Dixie's apartment number. Hurrying to the door of the apartment, he removed his hat and knocked lightly.

There were soft footsteps inside, then the latch rattled and the door swung open. The lovely young woman with the golden hair showed him a warm smile and said, "Well, hello, Captain! I'm glad you're back safely."

"Thank you," he grinned, feeling a fiery sensation wash over him at the sight of her. His arms ached to embrace her and his lips longed to kiss her, but he made no move to do so.

"Would you like to come in and sit down?" she asked.

"I'll be glad to come in, Miss Dixie," he said, drinking in her beauty, "but if it's all the same to you, I won't sit down. I've been sitting in that saddle for so long, I just need to stand for a while."

"I can understand that," she said, stepping aside so he could enter. When he passed her, she closed the door and asked, "Can I get you something?"

"No," he said raising a palm. "I'm fine. Please. Don't stand just because I am. Go ahead and sit down."

"Actually I was standing when you knocked. I was putting new paper on the shelves of my cupboard above the counter. Mind if I finish while we talk?"

"Of course not."

Ryan followed Dixie into the kitchen of the small apartment and watched as she resumed her work. "Can I help?" he asked.

"No, that's not necessary." She used a pair of scissors to cut the paper to size. "When did you get back?"

"We arrived at the fort about one-thirty."

"Run into any trouble?"

"Yes."

Turning to look at him, she asked, "What happened?"

"Small unit of Yankees caught us flatfooted on the way to the prison camp. We were in thick timber, which is always risky. Thing that saved us was that I had put all the prisoners in gray uniforms and made them carry empty rifles. Gave the illusion that there were about thirty-five Rebels in the bunch."

"Smart idea."

"It worked, anyway. The Yankees figured since we outnumbered them, they wouldn't start shooting, but rather, would jump us with their guns ready. That way, they'd disarm us and we'd be their prisoners. But the Yankee captain we had captured was so eager to let his fellow blue-bellies know he was one of them that he made a sudden move to show them his rifle was empty. The Yankees were jittery, and one of them shot him. It was instant gun battle...and the Sharpshooters, as you know, are good at what they do. Anyway, we delivered the prisoners—some dead and some alive—and came back to the fort."

Cutting paper again, Dixie asked, "Did you see Captain Coffield at the fort?"

"No. He and the rest of my men are planting sea mines in the bay. Explosive devices we call torpedoes."

"I've heard of them. So you've yet to lay eyes on Coffield."

"That's right. And to be honest, I wish I never had to."

Dixie had thought a lot about the situation that had developed between Ryan and his ex-wife. There was no question in Dixie's mind that Victoria had been pregnant with Tommy when she ran off with Lex Coffield, but did not know it. When the baby was born, Ryan was never notified. This was why he had never told Dixie he had a son. He was not aware of it...and still did not know. Dixie felt he had a right to know, but it was not for her to tell him. She would leave that to

Victoria. One thing for sure, she thought, if Ryan gets one look at Tommy, he'll know he has a son.

"I sure can't blame you for that," she said. "Lex Coffield has to be just about the lowest—"

Dixie's words were interrupted by a knock at the door. Laying the paper and scissors down, she said, "Excuse me, Captain. I'll be right back."

Ryan gave her a warm smile as she left the kitchen.

Dixie opened the door to see Florence Dillon standing there, holding an empty sugar bowl. "Hello," she grinned. "I'm out of sugar. Could you spare some?"

Dixie was not happy to see the nosy nurse, especially with Ryan in her apartment. Florence was also a long-tongued gossip. She would make something juicy out of it if she knew he was there.

Taking the bowl from Florence's hand, Dixie said, "My kitchen's a mess. You wait here and I'll fill the bowl for you."

Florence nodded and leaned against the door jamb, folding her arms.

Ryan had heard every word, though he could not see the apartment door from where he stood. When Dixie came in, she gave him a "you don't want to meet this woman" expression. He smiled at her, nodding that he understood.

While Dixie was filling the bowl from a cloth sugar sack, Florence's loud, grating voice came from the front door, "What did you think about that poor little Coffield boy, Dixie? Sad, huh? How could a father be so mean to his son? I mean, maybe Mrs. Coffield deserved the beating he gave her, but that little boy...I'll never understand it."

Dixie's nerves tightened. A glance at the captain told her he was taking it all in. She knew if she didn't answer immediately, Florence would come traipsing into the kitchen to repeat what she had just said.

Over her shoulder, she called back, "Terrible thing, Florence. Such a sweet little guy. A brave one, too. He took a lot of pain last night. He'll be okay, though."

"I hope so. Somebody oughtta take that Captain Coffield out behind the barn and give him a good threshing."

Hurriedly placing the lid on the sugar bowl, Dixie headed back to the unwanted guest, saying, "I agree, Florence. Somebody ought to give him some of his own medicine."

Florence thanked Dixie for the sugar and was gone. Dixie closed the door and returned to the kitchen. "Whew!" she sighed. "That mouthy woman makes me nervous."

"A fellow-nurse, I assume?"

"To my sorrow, and the sorrow of the rest of the hospital staff."

"Mind telling me what happened?"

Returning to the cupboard, Dixie picked up the scissors. "Of course not. You'd no doubt learn about it from Victoria one of these days, anyway. I...didn't think it was my place to tell you. That's why I didn't say anything about it."

"Certainly. But since your loudmouth friend told it to everyone in the building, I'd like to know the details."

Dixie finished cutting a length of paper and placed it on a shelf, adjusting it to fit. "It was about seven...maybe seven-fifteen last evening when Victoria carried Tommy into the hospital. She had some pretty bad bruises on her face and was bleeding from the nose and mouth. She admitted to Dr. Lyles and me that Lex had lost his temper and beat her. Tommy had a large knot on his head and a cut on his arm from a few days ago that had been reopened. Dr. Lyles had to stitch it again. Nosy Florence was on duty last night, and apparently had a talk with Victoria in the corridor."

"So this is how she knew about it."

"Plus she came into the examining room and began pumping the boy while Dr. Lyles and I were working on him. Tommy told her—and us—that Lex had kicked him against a wall. Tommy had told us earlier that Lex had also hit him in the head."

"Dirty bully."

"To put it mildly. From what Tommy told us before Florence showed up, he had bitten Lex's leg to stop him from hitting his mother. This was no doubt when he got clobbered on the head and kicked against the wall."

"Did you learn why Lex was beating Victoria?"

"Not until Florence questioned Tommy. You see, Florence was at the dance the other night. I never did see her on the floor, so she had plenty of time to gawk around from the sidelines. Before Dr. Lyles finally ordered her from the room last night, she asked the boy if his daddy was angry at his mommy because of the way she had been acting with a man at the dance. Tommy said yes."

"Me, right?"

"She didn't snuggle close to anyone else."

"And somebody told Coffield about it when he returned to the fort yesterday."

"Must have."

Ryan rubbed the back of his neck. "Victoria shouldn't have pressed me into dancing with her, but no harm was done. Certainly it didn't call for a beating from her husband." Sighing, he added, "In a way, I'm responsible. I did dance with her."

"But the snuggling wasn't your doing."

"I know, but I let her get me in a position so it could happen. Some of the blame is mine. I'm going to their home and see about Victoria and the boy....and express my regret that I've been a source of trouble."

Dixie moved close to him, laid a hand on his arm, and said, "Captain Ryan McGraw, you are a good man."

"You could get an argument on that from some people."

"I mean it. If that no-good Lex Coffield hadn't stolen your wife in the first place, none of this would be happening. And still you're going to go over there and take your share of the blame for this."

Ryan shrugged his wide shoulders. "Just something I have to do."

"God bless you."

"He did, Miss Dixie. He brought you into my life."

While she blushed, Ryan asked, "Could I take you to dinner tonight?"

Dixie's pulse quickened. "Well, yes...of course."

"Know any good restaurants?"

"The Mobile Arms Hotel has an excellent one."

"Okay. The Mobile Arms it is. Seven o'clock all right?"

"Sure."

"Pick you up at seven."

"I'll be ready," she replied sweetly, and thought to herself, *with bells on!*

Mixed emotions stirred within Dixie as she watched the captain swing aboard his horse and ride away. She was thrilled that he wanted to take her to dinner, but felt the strain of knowing that Victoria had set her sights on ridding herself of Coffield and getting Ryan back. She also felt a twinge in her heart. Ryan McGraw was about to find out he was a father.

The sun was setting behind a bank of long-fingered clouds in a fiery blaze of color as Ryan dismounted in front of the two-story house at 124 East Evans Avenue. His nerves tightened as he stepped onto the porch and knocked on the door. Only seconds passed before the door came open, and in the orange light of sunset, Victoria appeared, smiling, and said, "Ryan! I'm so glad you've come!"

Ryan cringed at the sight of her bruises. Then she was embracing him before he knew it. She held him tight for a few seconds, pulled back, took his hand, and said, "Come in."

Ryan was only a couple of steps inside the house when he stopped and said, "Tori, I can only stay a minute. I...I found out about you and the boy being at the hospital for treatment last night, and that your husband had laid into you for the way we were acting at the dance. I just wanted to come by and tell you that I'm sorry to be the source of a squabble between you and Lex. It was you who pulled close to me that night, but it's as much my fault for letting you. I'm truly sorry."

Victoria frowned. "How did you find all this out? Couldn't have been from that...that blonde prissy or the doctor. I didn't tell them why Lex had beaten me."

"Dixie is not a prissy, Victoria," he said firmly. "She is a wonderful, unselfish, sweet young lady."

Victoria did not comment.

"There's an obnoxious nurse at the hospital who had also been at the dance. She saw you and me when we were close. She was on duty last night. Florence is her name."

"Yes," nodded Victoria. "I met her in the corridor. Florence Dillon. Has a big nose, if you know what I mean."

"Exactly."

"I talked to her there in the corridor for a few minutes while Dr. Lyles was stitching Tommy's arm. But I didn't tell her why Lex had beaten me."

"No, but Tommy did. She got it out of him that Lex was angry over the way you acted toward some man at the dance. Florence knew that man was me. I just want to say that I'm sorry my weak moment on the dance floor got you and your son a beating." Starting to turn toward the door, he said, "I have to go, now."

Taking his hand again, Victoria said, "Before you go, I want you to meet Tommy. He's upstairs in his room." Moving to the bottom of the staircase and pulling Ryan with her, she called loudly, "Tommy! Tommy!"

A small voice responded, "Yes, Mommy?"

"Come here, honey! There's someone I want you to meet."

There was the sound of running feet, then a diminutive form appeared at the landing above. The brilliant sunset flowing through a window near the bottom of the stairs cast a shadow above. The boy could not be seen clearly.

When Tommy remained in the shadows, Victoria said, "Come down, honey."

There was a pause. Tommy asked, "Is this the person who was supposed to come that other day, but didn't?"

"Yes. It's that very special someone I told you about. He couldn't come then because he was away on a trip. I didn't know it."

Slowly, Tommy moved to the head of the stairs and began to descend. Before he was halfway down, the glow of the sunset illuminated his face and hair.

Ryan McGraw's jaw slackened. A chill rippled through him. His mouth went dry. Seeing the express image of himself in Tommy stunned him.

While Ryan was attempting to find his voice, Victoria waited for the boy to reach the bottom step, then took his hand with her free one and said, "Ryan, I would like you to meet Thomas Manning McGraw. I gave him his first name after your father."

To the boy, she said, "Tommy, when you got old enough to understand, I told you Lex is not your father. I explained that you had a real father somewhere, but that you would never be able to see him or know him. Remember?"

"Yes."

"Well, honey, that has changed. This man is your real father."

Tommy's face lit up and a wide smile captured his mouth. "This is my dad?"

"Yes," nodded Victoria, tears welling up in her eyes. "I think it would be proper for you to give your dad a hug."

Ryan choked out hoarsely, "Tommy, until this moment, I didn't even know I had a son," and bent down with open arms.

Father and son stayed together in a long embrace. When Ryan released him, Tommy looked up and asked, "How could you have me and not know it?"

"When you get older, I'll explain it to you, honey," interjected Victoria. "But I want you to know that it isn't your dad's fault that he didn't know about you. It's mine."

Tommy smiled at the tall man who towered over him.

While Ryan thumbed away tears from his cheeks, Victoria said, "When I ran off—when I went away with Lex, I was carrying Tommy, but didn't know it. When Lex found it out, he was terribly angry. At first he was going to send me back to you. Then he had second thoughts and decided he loved me enough to marry me in spite of the baby."

"That was big of him," mused Ryan bitterly.

"When Tommy was born, Lex didn't want anybody to think the baby was his. He insisted he have his real father's name. I gave him my maiden name for his middle name. So he's Thomas Manning McGraw. Ever since I explained that Lex is not his father, Tommy has called him Lex."

"Dad," said the child, looking up with bright eyes, "are you gonna move in and live with us? Then the other kids who live around here will know that I have a real dad, just like them!"

Ryan felt a pang of sadness run through him as he knelt down, looked his new-found son in the eye, and said, "Your mommy and I used to be married, Tommy, but we aren't any more. She's married to Lex, now. That means I can't live here."

"Then mommy can send Lex away and be married to you again," said the innocent child. "I don't like Lex. He's mean to

Mommy and he's mean to me. *You* wouldn't be mean to us, would you, Dad?"

Ryan laid a tender hand on Tommy's head. The lump was still quite large under the boy's thick hair. Indignation toward Coffield welled up within him. He had to swallow hard to get the words to come out. "No. I wouldn't be mean to either of you, Son, but I just can't live with you."

Tommy's eyes glistened with tears. "Won't you ever come and see us?"

Ryan folded him into his arms, saying, "Sure I will, Tommy. I'll come see you often."

"Yes, he will, honey," said Victoria. "Now, I want you to go back upstairs to your room and play. I need to talk to Dad by myself."

"Yes, ma'am," replied the boy. He hugged Ryan's neck hard, then charged up the stairs.

When Victoria heard Tommy's door slam, she moved close to Ryan and said in a soft tone, "With Tommy looking so much like you, it has been a little bit like having you near, darling."

Still stunned from learning that he had a five-year-old son, Ryan's guard was down. Before he realized it, Victoria had her arms around his neck, and her warm breath was on his lips. In spite of the black and purple marks on her face, she was still beautiful.

Memories flooded Ryan's mind. He thought of the myriad times he had held her next to him...the times he had looked into those deep, meaningful eyes and kissed those lips. Suddenly they were locked in a fervid kiss. Victoria clung tight, digging her fingers into the thick hair on the back of his head. Though she felt pain from the cut inside her mouth, she held her lips to his with hungering force.

When they parted, Victoria laid her head on his chest with her arms around his slender waist and breathed, "Oh, Ryan you *are* still in love with me, aren't you? Say it, darling. It was in your kiss. I know it. Tell me you still love me."

Ryan loosed himself from her, his mind whirling. "Tori, I...I'm sorry. That shouldn't have happened. I've got to go."

Moving close again and looking deep into his eyes, Victoria said, "It can be us again, my love. Like old times. We have a child, you and I. Tommy is both of us. He needs you. Lex is mean to him—he resents him because he's *your* son. He puts marks on his head and face often."

Ryan let his gaze stray up to the spot at the top of the stairs where he last saw his son. Already his heart was full of love for the boy. Confused and upset, he shook his head and said, "I really must be going."

Realizing she could detain him no longer, Victoria said, "You told Tommy you'd come see us often. How soon will you be back?"

"I can't say right now, Tori. This is Lex's home. I'll have a talk with him. We'll work out some kind of agreement so I can visit Tommy on some kind of regular basis." Pausing, he said, "But it's not *us* I'll be visiting. It's *Tommy*."

Victoria's face paled. "But what about me?"

"I remind you that you are Lex's wife, not mine. I have no right to be seeing you."

Victoria broke into tears, gripping both his arms. "Please, Ryan!" she begged. "You've got to help me. I want to divorce Lex, but I'm afraid of him! With his violent temper, he could kill me! He might kill Tommy, too!"

Attributing such extreme fears to her emotional state, Ryan said, "You ran off with him and married him, Tori. You'll have to make the best of a bad situation. However, I will talk to Lex about his treatment of Tommy."

"But you don't understand!" she sobbed. "I want to be your wife again!"

"Tori," he said, heading for the door, "the water's already run under the bridge on that count. Tell Tommy I'll be back once I've worked it out with Lex."

Victoria stood at the door, her breath coming in tiny jerks as she watched through a wall of tears while Ryan McGraw rode away.

Less than a half-hour after Ryan was gone, Captain Coffield came home, tired and irritable. Victoria was cooking supper. He entered the kitchen, pecked her purpled cheek, and grunted, "What's for supper?"

Victoria was quiet and moody. "Grits and gravy," she replied without looking at him.

"Well, I hope there's plenty," he said crisply. "Being in and out of that water all day, planting those torpedoes, is hard work. I'm hungry."

"There'll be enough," she said coldly.

Coffield eyed her with disdain and went to the wash basin.

During supper, there was thick silence. After a few minutes of it, Lex set penetrating eyes on his wife and growled, "What's the matter with you?"

Putting a pained look in her eyes, Victoria met his gaze and replied, "You ought to know the answer to that. You beat me up last night, remember?"

"That was last night. This is tonight. Don't pout for the rest of your life over it."

Tommy looked up at the captain and said, "You're mean. You treat Mommy mean, and me too. My dad don't treat us mean."

Victoria's heart leaped to her throat. She had not thought to warn Tommy not to say anything about Ryan being there. She wanted Ryan to be the first to break it to him.

Coffield's heavy dark eyebrows arched. "Your dad?"

"Yes—he said he'd never treat us mean."

Fire leaped into Coffield's eyes as he looked at Victoria. "Ryan McGraw was *here*? At *my* house?"

Victoria's voice trembled as she said, "He learned from a nurse at the hospital that Tommy and I were there last night. He simply came by to see if we were all right. All he needed was one look at Tommy to know whose son he is."

One look at Lex's face and Victoria knew a storm was coming. Her heart sank into abysmal depths.

While the rage within him festered, Lex spat, "You didn't have to let him in the house!" Eyes bulging, he spewed out a string of profanity and demanded, "Why did you let him in my house, woman?"

Struggling to maintain her composure, Victoria answered, "Tommy has a right to know his father."

"It hasn't bothered you for over five years that he didn't know his father! So what's so important about it now?"

"Ryan wasn't near him then. He is now."

Victoria was seated directly opposite Coffield. Leaning halfway across the table and breathing raggedly with fury, he hissed, "I want to know if he touched you while he was in *my* house!"

Victoria's mind was racing. Ryan McGraw was twice the man Lex Coffield was. If she made Lex angry enough to go after her ex-husband, Ryan would handle him and would see what she was dealing with. Ryan would help her get rid of Lex.

Meeting Lex's glare, she said coolly, "I couldn't fight him off. He took me in his arms and kissed me with such passion, I was helpless."

Coffield swore vociferously and overturned the table, shoving it against a wall. Food, dishes, and silverware bounded, splattered, and rattled on the floor. Tommy was screaming in terror, and Victoria was trying to get to him when Lex stomped out of the house, slamming the front door.

Swearing to himself, the furious captain walked down the street at a fast pace. He walked for a half hour until his wrath had cooled, then headed back to the house. He had been gone a full hour when he entered the house and found Victoria on her knees in the kitchen, doing the finishing touches on cleaning up the mess. Tommy was up in his room.

Victoria rose from the kitchen floor with a rag and pail of water, glanced at him, and went to the cupboard, turning her back to him.

Holding his voice calm, Lex said, "Ryan McGraw is never to set foot in this house again."

Turning around, Victoria eyed him levelly. "You'll have to tell Ryan that yourself."

Jaw jutted and teeth clenched, he said, "I will!"

CHAPTER SIXTEEN

✦

As Dixie Quade and Ryan McGraw dined together at the Mobile Arms Hotel restaurant, Ryan did his best to show his interest in Dixie's childhood, her parents and family, and her years in nursing.

Dixie did not doubt his interest in her, but she could read through the facade. After they had finished the meal and she had answered for the third time why she had gone into nursing, she gave him a warm, dimpled smile and said, "Captain, your mind is somewhere else tonight. You're such a kind and good man. You're trying to make me feel important, and I appreciate it, but something's bothering you. All you told me when you came to pick me up was that you had learned that Tommy was your son. Did something else happen?"

Ryan took a deep breath, let it out slowly through his nose, and ran his fingers through his hair. "Miss Dixie," he said, thinking how beautiful she looked by candlelight, "you are important. I very much value the times we've had together...especially this one. The more I see of you, the more important you become in my life."

"Thank you," she said softly. "That means more to me than I can tell you. But I think I know you well enough to sense that there's something under the surface that's eating at you."

Ryan sighed again, looking at the candlelight that danced in her eyes. His heart was warmed by the tender, beautiful young woman. She was everything he wanted. He wished he could take her into his arms and tell her he was in love with her, and if she'd have him, he wanted to marry her. But he couldn't bring himself to do it.

Then Dixie, seeing the affliction in his eyes, leaned across the table and took hold of his hand. Setting her compassionate gaze on him, she said, "Captain, are you still in love with Victoria?"

He was shocked that Dixie could read him so well. He was fighting the inward battle over the way Victoria still rang a bell down deep within him. Until he could settle the dispute within himself, he couldn't pursue what he wanted with Dixie. She deserved better than that.

Placing his other hand on top of hers, he said, "This has been an emotional day for me, Miss Dixie. The way I'm churning inside, I don't even know what day of the week it is. I guess I'm still so stunned at learning about Tommy that I can't answer any question intelligently."

"I understand," she replied tenderly. "We'd better go. You've got a long ride back to the fort."

Dixie's heart was heavy as Ryan walked her home along a dimly lit Mobile street. She was in love with the man as much as any woman could be. She wanted him with everything that was in her, but she was afraid Ryan might still be in love with his ex-wife. Maybe he always would be.

At Dixie's door they talked briefly about the buildup of the Union fleet in the Gulf and the possibility of General Canby launching a land attack on Fort Morgan and the city of Mobile. Before leaving, Ryan said, "Miss Dixie, we don't know when the Yankees are going to come at us, but if they hold off a little longer...could we have another evening together soon?"

A cold hand seemed to squeeze her heart as she asked, "Do you really want it, Captain?"

Ryan felt his pulse quicken as he looked into her tender eyes by the light of a lantern that burned on the apartment porch. He wanted desperately to take her in his arms and kiss her, but refrained. He must not let himself go that far until the struggle over his feelings toward Tori was ended. If it would ever end.

"Yes, I really want another evening together," he assured her.

"Then I'll be at your beck and call," she smiled. She started to turn toward the door, then came back around and said, "Captain?"

"Yes, Miss Dixie?"

"Would you do me a favor? Would you drop the Miss and just call me Dixie?"

"If you'll drop the Captain and just call me Ryan."

Extending her hand, she said, "Let's shake on it."

Ryan took her hand, squeezed it for a moment, and said, "It's a deal, Dixie."

"Yes it is, Ryan," she breathed, then stood on her tiptoes and surprised him by touching his face with her fingertips and planting a kiss on his cheek.

As the sun was lifting itself from the earth's eastern edge the next morning, General Page had nearly all the men of Fort Morgan gathered in the open area for a briefing. The only men missing were two privates who watched the Union fleet out on the Gulf from the top of the lighthouse, and Captain Lex Coffield, who had not yet arrived from Mobile. He was often a few minutes shy of reporting in on time. Page explained that reports had come to him from Richmond that the war was not looking good for the South. The Union had blockaded vital seaports along the Atlantic coast and the Gulf coast. By fighting back at Savannah, Georgia, the Confederates had been able to reopen their seaport and had received arms shipments from England. The government of Great Britain had taken the Confederate side in the war and was sending arms and supplies as fast as possible.

Confederate intelligence reported that plans were being made in Washington, D.C., to send General William T. Sherman and a massive land force to capture Atlanta, then move on to Savannah and capture it. The only other seaport not already in Union hands was Mobile. President Lincoln had ordered that Mobile be taken, if at all possible, even before Sherman began his march against Atlanta and Savannah.

Page told his men that three small gunboats were now on their way down the Alabama River from Selma: the *Gaines*, the *Selma* and the *Morgan*. At Selma's shipyards, the Confederates were working around the clock to build a huge, well-armed ironclad ram. It would be called the *Tennessee*. If Farragut held off another three weeks, the *Tennessee* would be ready for battle, and could mean the difference between victory and defeat. The *Tennessee* was being built under the supervision of Admiral Franklin Buchanan, Commander of the Confederate Navy.

The general explained that the torpedoes were all in place in the bay, but that the Yankees would be coming with many boats. The torpedoes would stop a few, but once they had exploded and done their damage to the first boats entering the bay, those behind them would have smooth sailing. The few men at Fort Gaines would unleash what fire power they had, but it was going to be up to the men at Fort Morgan to carry the load. They must be ready to fight a full-scale battle.

While Page was talking, Lex Coffield appeared and stood at the rear of the group. Noah Cloud was standing next to Ryan McGraw and saw Coffield come in. Elbowing McGraw, he whispered, "The almighty Captain Coffield just showed up."

Ryan turned his head slowly and found the dark-haired man who wore the captain's bars. He pictured Coffield abusing Tommy and felt a tinge of anger.

General Page was reminding the men that the danger of land attack was also imminent. This was one reason the Sharpshooters were there. Page would lean heavily on them when it came.

When the briefing was over, McGraw waved a hand and said, "General, I have an announcement."

"Yes, Captain McGraw?"

From his place at the rear of the group, Coffield swung his hard gaze on McGraw.

Lifting his voice, McGraw said, "All Sharpshooters meet me over there by the north wall in five minutes! It's calisthenics time!"

Noah Cloud drifted toward the designated spot with McGraw as the men of B Company began to slowly gather. Cloud looked across the open area to catch another glimpse of Coffield, and said, "Cap'n, Coffield's coming this way." Ryan saw the man weaving his way through the milling soldiers.

From the side of his mouth, Noah said, "Workin' with that man is a real bucketload of agony, Cap'n. He thinks he's Robert E. Lee."

"He does, huh?"

"Yeah. He was bossing all us Sharpshooters around like he owns the world. Me and Hap got into one of our fights, and he threatened to put us under arrest if we didn't quit. That's rough on me and Hap. You understand, Cap'n. We just gotta blow off steam once in a while."

"Sure," nodded McGraw. "And Coffield hasn't the authority to arrest you, anyway."

"No?"

"No. This is a special setup here. The Sharpshooters are under General Page in the sense that he's commander of the fort, but even he can give you orders only through me. You boys are directly responsible to me and me alone. Remember our very first briefing? The general explained it so the men in the fort would know the situation."

"Oh, yeah," nodded Cloud, rubbing his chin. "Coffield wasn't here. Well, great! I'll tell Hap. Next time the almighty Captain Coffield tries to stop us, we'll just keep on fightin'."

Coffield drew up to McGraw with fire in his eyes. With a rasp in his voice, he said, "McGraw, I'm Captain—"

"I know who you are," cut in McGraw. "Noah pointed you out to me. What do you want?"

Nostrils flared, Coffield replied stiffly, "I want a private conversation with you."

"I want to talk to you, too," came the quick response, "but it'll have to be after calisthenics. I always work out with my men."

Coffield knew by the look in McGraw's eyes it would be useless to argue. "All right," he said. "How long will that be?"

"Exactly two hours."

"Meet you out at the lighthouse in two hours and three minutes."

"It's a date," McGraw said evenly.

For the next two hours, Captain McGraw led his men in a strenuous workout, including hand-to-hand combat practice. He wanted them to be in top physical condition and to keep their fighting skills sharp.

When it was over, McGraw made his way out the gate and found Coffield standing in the shadow of the weatherworn lighthouse. Knowing the structure was tall enough that the men in the glass compartment above could not hear them, Coffield spoke first. "I know about you and Victoria cuddling at the dance, McGraw, and I don't like it!"

"You probably got an enlarged version of it," countered McGraw. "It wasn't that much."

"Well, did I get an enlarged version of you going to my house and kissing her?"

"I don't know, but maybe I should remind you of what *you* did in Hattiesburg when Tori was *my* wife. Don't tell me you never so much as held her hand until the divorce was final and you two were married."

Coffield's face blanched and tiny sweat beads moistened his forehead. His tongue seemed to freeze to the roof of his mouth.

While Coffield was mulling that one over, Ryan said, "Now that I know Tommy is my son, I'm going to say something, and I'm only going to say it once. *Don't you ever touch that boy again.* You've put your last bruise on him, mister. Victoria is your wife, and I can't interfere there, but if I ever learn that you beat on that boy again, I'll pound you to a bloody pulp."

Coffield's tongue came loose. Bristling, he snapped, "I don't like threats, McGraw!"

"And I don't like men who beat on women and children! Only a low-bellied, cowardly snake would manhandle a woman or a child."

Coffield's natural impulse was to send a fist to the man's mouth, but Ryan's size and his reputation as the tough-as-rawhide leader of the Sharpshooters caused him to check it.

McGraw was ready if Coffield threw a punch. When it did not come, and neither did a retort, he said, "Now, I want to discuss Tommy with you, Captain."

"What about him?"

"He lives in your home, and I respect the sanctity of it. I would like your permission to see my son on a regular basis."

"Not in a million years."

"If you had respected the sanctity of *my* home, I wouldn't be asking your permission to see my own son in your home."

For the first time since stealing Victoria, Lex Coffield felt a pang of guilt. He took a step back, removed his hat, and sleeved away the sweat. While the sea breeze toyed with his dark locks, he pondered McGraw's request.

Seven or eight seagulls flew in from off the Gulf, swooped low over the heads of the two Confederate officers, then continued on to the top of the lighthouse. Coffield watched them in their flight, then looked at the rugged leader of B Company and said, "You're sure it isn't Victoria you want to see on a regular basis?"

"I'm sure."

"What about this kissing that went on in my house...and the romance on the dance floor at the fort?"

"Victoria was lonesome for you. We hadn't seen each other in a long time...and she reached for me in your place. I had a couple of weak moments. It won't happen again. Especially if you quit beating on her and show her some love and tenderness."

"You're sure you don't want her back?"

"I've had some old feelings surface. I can't really describe them. But I don't want her back. She's your wife now. I'll leave it at that."

"If I give you permission to see Tommy, will you let him meet you at the door? I don't want you inside alone with Victoria again. By alone, I mean without me there."

"I'll stay outside if that's your wish."

"That's my wish. You can take Tommy wherever you want to. Just don't go in the house with Victoria."

"All right."

"Then you have my permission. I'll talk it over with Victoria and we'll work out some kind of visitation plan."

"Fine," said McGraw, relieved that he would be able to see his son without resistance from Victoria's husband. "Just let me know."

Coffield nodded, placed his hat back on his head, and walked toward the gate of the fort. McGraw turned and set his gaze on the sunlit waters of the Gulf of Mexico. His heart throbbed with love for Thomas Manning McGraw...the son of his own image. He hoped the day would come when his parents could meet their fine little grandson. It would mean the world to his father that the boy was named after him.

Moving down the sandy slope to the water's edge, Ryan stood there gazing at the foaming shoreline for a long moment, then lifted his eyes heavenward and said, "Lord, I don't always understand Your ways...but in spite of all this confusion going on inside me, I want to thank You for letting me learn about Tommy. Already I love him as much as a father can love his son."

Ryan soon found himself focusing on the fleet of Union ships that seemed to hover like vultures on the horizon. How soon would they come, bringing death and destruction with them?

Just after breakfast on Saturday morning, July 9, General Page met in his office with Colonel DeWitt Munford, Captain Ryan McGraw, and Lieutenants Wilson March, Frank Cooley, and Judd Rawlings. Captain Lex Coffield had been informed of the meeting, but had not shown up.

Page stood over his desk where he had laid out a large map of Mobile Bay, and the officers gathered close. Using his index finger as a pointer, he showed them just how the torpedoes had been moored in the mouth of the bay by Captain Coffield and the Sharpshooters. Stretching from the pilings that covered the westward portion of the mouth at Fort Gaines all the way to a red buoy that bobbed in the water within a few feet of the shore under the ramparts of Fort Morgan was a triple line of the deadly torpedoes...a hundred and ninety-one in all.

"Looks like Captain Coffield did a good job," mused Munford.

"Yes," said Page. "Coffield does know his stuff about explosives. The way he has them situated, they'll take their toll on quite a few Union vessels." The general ran his finger to a spot up shore on the east side. "The *Selma*, the *Gaines*, and the *Morgan* are anchored right there, just beyond sight of the fort. They'll be ready to open fire on the ships that make it past the torpedoes."

McGraw ran a finger over his mustache, shook his head, and said, "That doesn't give us much fire power, does it, sir?"

"Not when you take a look at the number of ships and boats Farragut's got out there. Last count was twenty. We're going to have to rely a whole lot on those big guns out there on our walls."

"Even then, sir," spoke up Lieutenant Rawlings, "we're looking at a task that's next to impossible. Our B Company can snipe from the shore and kill a lot of men aboard those Union vessels, but we can't sink them. We need more sea power. Even if the *Tennessee* gets here in time, we're still horrendously outnumbered in the water. How about those rams I've seen docked at Mobile? Can't they be used?"

"No. Not a one of them is seaworthy. Their engines are shot. It would take more time, engine parts, and men than the Confederate navy has to put them into service. The *Tennessee* will do us more good than all of them put together. She's ironclad and well armed."

"I understand she looks a lot like the old *Merrimac*, sir," said Lieutenant Cooley.

Nodding, Page pulled a drawer open and produced a sketch of the *Tennessee*, which also listed the ship's specifications. Laying it on the desk in full view, he said, "You'll see she resembles the *Merrimac* in configuration. See? The sloping sides of her barn-like superstructure are very much like the *Merrimac*. However, the *Tennessee* is the most powerful casemated ironclad ram ever built by the Confederate navy."

"She looks like a floating fortress, all right," said Rawlings.

"See what it says here," commented Page. "The superstructure is plated with three courses of two-inch wrought iron armor, giving her a six-inch composite shield capable of resisting the heaviest fire that could be brought to bear against her. And look at this. Her battery consists of six heavy guns...four six-inch Brooke rifles in broadside—two on each side—and two seven-inch Brooke rifles on pivot mounts, one at each end of the casemate."

"That's some kind of gun vessel," said McGraw. "I just hope they get it down here before ol' ' fairguts' comes steaming in."

"Me, too," agreed Page. "The *Tennessee* is calculated to reduce any Union ships to charred flotsam in a head-to-head battle." The general paused as he placed the drawing back in the drawer, then sighed, "However, she does have one big problem. There wasn't time to build new engines for her, so I understand they cannibalized engines from a Yazoo River steamboat that are quite underpowered for her weight. She'll be slow in maneuverability."

"I guess that's where our other three boats will have to shine, sir," put in Colonel Munford. "At least they're quick and maneuverable."

The general nodded. "They'll have to shine *real good.* And so will the guns of Fort Morgan."

While the discussion continued in General Page's office, Captain Coffield arrived at Mobile Point, took his horse to the stables, and approached the gate. He could hear excited voices as the sentry swung the gate open. Moving inside, he saw a cluster of the fort's men looking on as Sergeants Hap Hazzard and Noah Cloud were whaling away at each other in a bloody-nose fight.

Coffield knew he was late for the meeting in the general's office, but decided he would just have to be a little more tardy. He had forbidden Hazzard and Cloud to ever fight again as long as they were at Fort Morgan, and was irritated to see them defying his orders. Coffield rushed to the battle zone, elbowed his way through the clot of spectators, and shouted, "Hey, you two! Stop this instant!"

Hazzard had just taken a blow to the mouth and countered with a roundhouse punch. Cloud's feet left the ground, and he landed on his back. Neither paid any attention to Coffield's command.

Hazzard stood waiting for Cloud to get up, breathing hard and wiping blood from his lips. As Cloud was scrambling to his feet, the angry captain moved between them, and waved his arms, shouting, "I said stop this fighting!"

One of the excited spectators said, "Aw, let 'em finish it, Captain!"

When Coffield turned to see who had just spoken, Hazzard stepped around him to meet Cloud, who was charging in. The two combatants came together, swinging wildly.

Unable to tell who had spoken, Coffield turned back again, only to find that the two big men were stumbling his way. Suddenly Hap Hazzard's meaty right fist caught him flush on the jaw. The captain went down like a decayed tree in a high wind and lay still. He was out cold. The spectators looked on open-mouthed and wide-eyed, wondering what would happen now.

Big Hap ran thick fingers through his mop of red hair, eyed the unconscious officer, then looked at his friend, and said, "Maybe I oughtta go make a quick report to Cap'n McGraw and the general."

Cloud sleeved moisture from his face and replied, "Yeah, I guess that'd be the thing to do."

"You guys are gonna be in trouble for sure," interjected one of the soldiers. "Coffield will have your hides for this."

The sergeants exchanged glances. Lying flat on his back, Coffield began to stir, rolling his head and moaning.

Hap looked toward the general's office, then back at Coffield. To the men around him, he said, "Maybe I better try to soothe the captain before I report to Cap'n McGraw and General Page. Somebody get a cup of water."

While one of the men ran to a water pail nearby, Hazzard knelt down, using his bulky body to shade Coffield's face, and asked, "Captain, are you all right?"

Coffield batted his eyelids, rolled his head some more, then focused on Hazzard's face as the sergeant was wiping blood from his own mouth. Eyes a bit glazed, Coffield put a hand to his jaw and grunted, "You're under arrest, Sergeant! You struck an officer of the Confederate army!"

As Coffield raised up to a sitting position, the soldier arrived with a cup of water and handed it to Hazzard. Hap took it, extended it to Coffield, and said, "Here's some water, sir."

Coffield swore and batted the cup from Hazzard's hand. Eyes blazing, he snapped, "Don't try to appease me! You're under arrest and so's your friend. Since Fort Morgan doesn't have a guardhouse, you're going to rot in the jail at Mobile!"

Suddenly two shadows were cast over Coffield as General Page and Captain McGraw drew up. The other officers had arrived on the scene also.

"What happened here?" demanded Page.

Struggling to his feet as he spoke, Coffield said, "Hazzard and Cloud were fighting, sir." He swayed unsteadily and jerked his arm from Hazzard's hand as he tried to help him. After burning Hap with hot eyes, he looked at Page. "I've warned these two before about their ridiculous fighting, General. I commanded them never to do it again as long as they're in this fort. When I arrived a few minutes ago, here they were fighting again. I commanded them to stop, but they ignored me." Gesturing toward the gray-clad spectators, he added, "These men can testify to that."

No one affirmed that they would.

Rubbing his jaw, Coffield went on. "Since they disobeyed my order to stop fighting, I stepped in to stop it myself. Next thing I know, I was lying on the ground. Hazzard knocked me unconscious, General. I have put both of them under arrest. I'm sure you will back me in that, sir."

General Page could not show it, but he was extremely glad the captain had been punched out. Though he wanted to grin, he kept a sober look and said levelly, "No, I won't, Captain."

Coffield shifted his stance to better steady himself and looked as if he had been slapped in the face. "Wha—"

"You have no jurisdiction over any of the Sharpshooters, Captain. B Company is strictly under Captain McGraw's command. Even I can command them only through Captain McGraw."

Coffield gasped, "But I—"

"These fine men are here on special assignment by General Robert E. Lee, and the stipulations are as I just told you. You have no authority to place Sergeants Hazzard and Cloud under arrest."

Coffield's features darkened. "But Hazzard struck me, General! You know what the book says about an enlisted man who strikes an officer!"

"You're thinking of the book you studied at West Point," Page countered quietly. "You ought to know there hasn't been time since the war began for a book to be written for our army. Besides...I'm sure it was an accident. You said that you stepped in to stop the fight. Apparently fists were flying. Sergeant Hazzard wouldn't strike you deliberately. Now, let's drop it right here."

Captain Coffield looked as though he had just swallowed a mouthful of dill pickle juice. "Yes, sir," he managed to say.

"Now, let's get back to our meeting, gentlemen," Page said to the officers. "Captain Coffield, I remind you that you are tardy."

Coffield did not reply. As he walked beside McGraw toward the general's office, he said in a low tone, "Victoria and I have worked out a visitation plan. You can see Tommy anytime and take him anywhere you want as long as Victoria says so...and with the stipulation that you never enter the house."

"Agreed," said McGraw.

When the officers were gone, Hap and Noah went to the water pail and washed their faces. The men gathered close. One of them said, "Hap, we're all curious."

"About what?" Hap said, wiping water from his face.

"Was it really an accident?"

The big redhead gave them a furtive smile and walked away. The men looked at Cloud, who shrugged his thick shoulders, grinned from ear to ear, and followed his friend.

CHAPTER SEVENTEEN

★

While the Union ships sat quietly on the watery horizon day after day—observed closely from the lighthouse at Mobile Point—Ryan McGraw made frequent trips into town to divide time between his son and Dixie Quade. He took Tommy for walks and ate meals with Dixie.

Each time Ryan went to the house for Tommy and Lex was absent, Victoria tried to lure him inside. Remaining true to his word, he reminded her that he and Lex had an agreement. He would not violate it.

On Sunday, July 17, the devoted father picked his son up after Tommy had eaten lunch. As they stepped off the porch with Victoria and Lex looking on from the door, Tommy said, "Dad, how about instead of us walkin', we take a ride on your horse? I've never been on a horse before."

Pausing, Ryan turned toward the boy's mother and asked, "Is it all right if he rides the horse with me?"

"Certainly," she smiled, "but don't take him too far."

"We'll just ride over to the hospital. I need to see my men who are still there. All but two have gone home. I'd like for them to meet Tommy."

Victoria wondered if Dixie was on duty. She didn't want Tommy being around her, but if she protested in front of Lex, he would question why. She dare not ripple the waters until she had Ryan ready to take her back and help her get rid of Lex. With Ryan on her side, she would not be afraid of Lex.

"Have a nice time," Victoria said, forcing a cheerful note into her voice.

Tommy giggled and squealed when his father hoisted him into the saddle, then swung up behind him. As they rode away at a trot, the boy laughed and said, "This is fun!"

Arriving at the hospital, Ryan led Tommy down the corridor and introduced him to Private Brad Thacker and Corporal Vince Udall, who were now in the same room. After chatting with them for a few minutes, he left and led the boy toward the nurse's station. He knew Dixie was on duty and would get off at five o'clock. They were to have dinner together that evening after attending a church service. Every church in Mobile was holding special services, invoking God's mercy in light of the impending invasion by the Union army and navy.

Dixie was just leaving the nurse's station as father and son drew up. She warmed Ryan with a dimpled smile, then kept it on for the boy, as she looked down at him and said, "Hello, Tommy. I see you're not wearing a bandage on your arm anymore. When did the doctor take it off?"

Tommy looked up at his father and beckoned with his finger for Ryan to bend down. Dixie looked on as Ryan put his ear next to the boy's mouth. Tommy's whisper was louder than he realized as he said, "I'm not supposed to talk to her. Mommy said she's a bad lady."

Ryan looked up, realizing Dixie had heard every word. "Why is she a bad lady, Son?"

"'Cause she talked mean to Mommy one day. Mommy says she's bad, and I shouldn't ever talk to her."

"Let's take a little walk," Dixie said, casting a glance at two nurses who were bent over a desk in the station.

As they moved down the corridor, Dixie said, "Victoria and I had a heated discussion here at the hospital the day after the dance. She... she doesn't like the fact that you and I see each other. It got a little hot. So I guess I'm a bad lady." Dixie would not tell Ryan of Victoria's death threat.

"I see." Kneeling down and looking his son in the eye, Ryan said, "Tommy, wasn't it this lady who helped Dr. Lyles fix up your arm the night Mommy brought you in here after Lex kicked you into the wall?"

The child's memory took him back to that night and he recalled how kind she was to him. He remembered thinking that she sure seemed nice. He also remembered how he liked the way she looked at him and the way she held his hand. "Yes," he nodded.

"Wasn't she nice to you?"

"Yes."

"Do you think she's bad?"

The boy raised his pale blues and set them on Dixie. There was a brief moment of thought, then he answered, "No. I think she is nice."

It was Dixie's turn to kneel down. Looking tenderly at the child, she said, "Tommy, I don't want to make you disobey your mother, so you don't have to talk to me. But I want you to know that I wasn't trying to be mean to your mother. We were both angry, so we didn't talk very nice to each other. I also want you to know that I think you are a very brave little boy...and I like you a lot."

Tommy smiled. "I like you a lot, too."

Standing up, Dixie asked, "How old are you, Tommy?"

He held up five fingers and said, "This many."

"Five?"

"Yes, ma'am."

"Well, it just so happens that we had some nice people come here to the hospital and leave us some candy to give to boys and girls who visit us. Do you like horehound candy?"

"Yes, ma'am!"

"Well, the pieces are small, so we give children one for each year they are old. So I'll get you five!"

As Dixie was turning away, Tommy said quickly, "I'm almost six!"

"Oh, is that so?" she laughed. "When is your birthday?"

Tommy looked at the floor. "Um...August...August..."

"August first," Ryan finished for him.

"I guess that's close enough to deserve six," Dixie said, laughing again and heading for the nurse's station.

With one piece of horehound in his mouth and five in his pocket, Thomas Manning McGraw left the hospital with his father...but not before volunteering a kiss for the nice lady. As Ryan watched the two together, he wished they could be a family. Dixie would make a wonderful wife and mother.

Admiral David Glasgow Farragut stood on the bow of the flagship USS *Hartford* at sunrise on Friday, July 29, 1864. With telescope in hand, he peered toward Mobile Bay and watched the CSS *Tennessee* steam down the bay and drop anchor just off the beach at Fort Morgan.

The long weeks had passed slowly for Farragut while he waited for the Union ships that would make up his attack fleet to arrive one by one. He now had twenty-one ships, but as he studied the ironclad *Tennessee* through the telescope, he knew he dare not engage the seemingly unconquerable vessel in shoal water without ironclads of his own.

The admiral had learned about the *Tennessee* being built at Selma just before the land attack on Fort Morgan a month previously by Captain Leonard Whittier and his unit. When Farragut received word that the assault had been a failure, he knew he must add more ships before attacking. Now with the new threat of the *Tennessee*, he would have to bring in at least four ironclads (also known as monitors) to feel secure about steaming into the bay.

The admiral had sent word to Washington, asking for the monitors to be sent as soon as possible. When ship number twenty-one, the USS *Lackawanna* had arrived in mid-July, it bore a message that three monitors would be sent within a few days. They were the single-turret *Manhattan* from the Atlantic and two twin-turret river monitors, the *Chickasaw* and the *Winnebago* from the Mississippi. They were due to converge on Farragut's fleet around the end of July. The same message also informed Farragut that the fourth monitor, USS *Tecumseh* was docked at Pensacola for repairs and would arrive no later than August 3.

When Farragut lowered the telescope, he found Fleet-Captain Percival Drayton standing next to him. "How's it look, sir?" queried Drayton.

"Like a formidable bulwark of iron and big guns," sighed the admiral. "It'll take a lot of firepower to overcome the *Tennessee*. It's everything we were told it was, and more."

"We can still capture the bay once our monitors join us, sir," Drayton said with confidence.

"We can and we *will*," remarked Farragut, raising the telescope to study the *Tennessee* some more.

Farragut had all the sagacity of an old sea-dog. At sixty-three, he had been a sailor for fifty-four years. When just nine years old, he became a midshipman in the United States Navy, and during the War of 1812—at the age of eleven—he was prizemaster of the USS *Alexander Barclay*. Thereafter, until the outbreak of the Civil War in April 1861, he held ship commands on various stations, fought in the Mexican-American War, and was the instigator for establishing the Mare Island Navy Yard in San Francisco Bay.

In December 1861, with fifty-one years of service under his belt, Farragut was appointed admiral of the newly formed Federal Western Gulf Blockading Squadron. During the next two-and-a-half years, his fleet developed into a primary strike force in the Gulf of Mexico and Mississippi Delta, carrying the war to the Confederates and capturing New Orleans, Galveston, Corpus Christi, Sabine Pass, and Port Hudson.

His next and primary goal was Mobile Bay.

At nine-thirty that same morning, monitors *Chickasaw* and *Winnebago* were seen on the western horizon of the Gulf, and within an hour had been welcomed as part of the fleet. Later that afternoon, the *Manhattan* steamed in from the east, and except for the promised *Tecumseh*, Admiral Farragut's floating strike force was complete. Once the *Tecumseh* joined the fleet, the Union commander would not hesitate to enter the bay and fight it out.

The *Manhattan's* captain delivered a message from Washington that Major General Canby was experiencing a heavy drain on his manpower, a result of having to send troops to the Virginia theatre. Canby could not yet release Major General Gordon Granger and his five thousand troops for the assault on Mobile. When Farragut's twenty-fifth ship—the *Tecumseh*—arrived, he was to proceed into Mobile Bay at once. His task was to bombard Forts Gaines and Morgan until they were defenseless, then pull out of the bay, leaving enough men and ships to occupy the forts and guard the bay. Land forces would move on the city of Mobile as soon as Canby could spare them.

Farragut's original plan called for a simultaneous attack on the forts by both land and naval forces. With this message from the Navy Department in Washington in hand, he sat down at a table in his quarters and worked out a new plan. When he had it complete, he called for the captains of all the ships gathered around him to come to the *Hartford* for a meeting.

With twenty-three captains and his Fleet Captain Percival Drayton assembled, Farragut used little wooden blocks to represent the Union ships and laid out his plan of attack. He carefully prescribed the position of each vessel in the task force and explained various tactical arrangements he wished to be observed.

The fleet was to form in two columns, the wooden ships in couples running side by side and the monitors in single file. Fourteen wooden ships were assigned to the main column, the number being equally divided between heavy battleships and lesser vessels. Each battleship was paired with a gunboat. Farragut had observed the

Confederates installing torpedoes. He knew some of his vessels would sustain severe damage, but this did not deter him. They must go ahead in spite of the deadly explosive devices.

Once a number of his ships had moved past the pilings and those vessels slowed or stalled by the torpedoes, the gunboats were to separate from the battleships to do their own damage to the forts. Some of the fleet would remain outside the mouth of the bay and bombard the forts from the south.

Originally, the admiral intended to lead the fleet into the bay in the *Hartford*, but when he saw the Rebels placing the torpedoes from the red buoy by the shore all the way to the pilings, he changed his mind. The battleship *Brooklyn* was equipped with four "bow-chasers"—cannons on special swivels that allowed them to blow up torpedoes before the ship struck them. The *Hartford* would run in behind the *Brooklyn*.

When the admiral was satisfied that his captains all understood the plan of attack, he said, "Gentlemen, once we have the forts in our hands, Mobile Bay is ours. General William Tecumseh Sherman will take Savannah, and we'll have the Confederacy totally blockaded. Without supplies from England and the other countries that've helped them, they can't last very long. We know they've got a lot of supplies stockpiled in Mobile, but once General Granger and his troops move in and take the city, those supplies will be out of reach. Within a few more months this war will be history."

"I'll vote for that," spoke up one of the captains.

"Me, too," said another. "I haven't seen my wife for nearly a year."

"It's been almost that long for me, too," put in another. "And I've got two grandchildren I've never seen."

Farragut smiled, then said, "Gentlemen, I have set the time of attack for one week from today...Friday, August 5th. We'll go in at dawn to take advantage of the early morning high tide."

The admiral, who was fond of red wine, had his cabin attendant break out tin cups and personally filled them from his well-stocked wine cabinet. While each man held his cup, Drayton poured for the admiral. Farragut then lifted the cup, swinging it in a half-circle toward his fleet leaders and said, "A toast, gentlemen. To the end of the war...and, of course, a Union victory!"

On the first day of August, Captain McGraw appeared on the porch of the Coffield house at dusk bearing birthday presents for his son. Victoria met him at the door, smiled, and said, "Mercy me! You're going to spoil that boy!"

"That's the idea," grinned Ryan. "He's the only son I have."

Tommy's father noted that Victoria was dressed up and had her jet-black hair styled in his favorite way. "You can come in," she said cheerfully. "Lex isn't here. He won't be home for a couple of hours."

The grin faded from Ryan's lips as he replied, "No, Tori. Lex and I have an agreement. I won't break it."

Tilting her head back and lowering her eyelids, she said, "Well, that's too bad. You won't be able to see your son on his birthday."

"Why not? He can come out on the porch."

"No, he can't. Tommy's got a fever and I've got him lying down."

"A fever? What's the matter with him?"

"Nothing serious. This happens to him once in a while. It's that way with some children. He'll outgrow it, I'm sure." Extending her hands, she said, "I'll take the presents and give them to him."

Frustration showed on Ryan's face. "Tori, I—"

"Yes?"

"Will you make sure Tommy understands that I didn't come in and see him because of the agreement I made with Lex?"

"I'll try, but he's only six years old. What does he know about a gentleman's agreement? He'll probably think you don't love him any-more."

"Aw, now, Tori, I can't have that. Can't you just bring him to the door long enough for me to explain the situation and assure him that I do love him?"

"No. When he stirs around, it makes his fever rise."

Ryan's love for his son outweighed even his sense of honor. "All right," he sighed. "I'll come in...but only for a couple minutes."

Carrying the packages, he followed Victoria into a small room at the rear of the house where Tommy was sitting up on a couch. His pale blue eyes widened and danced with glee when he saw his father and the armload of packages. Bounding from the couch, he laughed and said, "Hi, Dad! Mommy told me to stay back here and I'd have a big surprise. Oh, boy! Are those presents for me?"

"They sure are!" said Ryan, kneeling down and laying them on the floor. "Happy birthday! How about a big hug?"

When Tommy wrapped his arms around Ryan's neck, the concerned father placed an open palm against his brow. Letting go of Tommy and rising to his feet, he said, "Go to it, son. Open your presents."

While the excited child was tearing paper, Ryan looked at his ex-wife. "Tori, you lied to me. He doesn't have a fever."

Tears filmed her eyes as she lunged at Ryan, flung her arms around his neck, and planted a kiss solidly on his lips. Tommy looked up, then returned to his presents.

Breaking Victoria's hold, Ryan took a step back. The beautiful woman once again struck a nameless chord somewhere deep within him. "Tori, why? You tricked me."

Blinking to start the tears flowing down her cheeks, Victoria grasped both his hands and said, "I can't stand this marriage of mine any longer, darling! You've got to help me break free from Lex!"

"Oh, boy! A drum!" Tommy shouted.

Both parents looked down to see the child, eyes dancing, holding the toy drum. He beat on it for a few seconds, then laid it aside and reached up to hug his father. Tommy thanked him over and over as he squeezed hard on Ryan's neck.

When the excited boy returned to the other packages, Victoria took Ryan's hands again and pled, "Please, darling...you must help me!"

"Tori, I didn't help you marry Lex. I can't help you unmarry him."

"Oh, but you *can!*" she cried. "You can and you will because you're still in love with me. I know you are, Ryan! Why won't you admit it?"

Again, she lunged for him, attempting to wrap her arms around his neck. Ryan adeptly stepped back and seized her wrists. "No, Tori!" he said sharply. "We mustn't be in each others arms. You are Lex's wife...not mine."

"But I want to be your wife again."

"It's no good. I've got to go." Turning to Tommy, he said, "Son, I have to leave now. You have a good time with those presents, okay?"

"I will, Dad. Thank you!"

"You're welcome. Could I have another hug before I go?"

"Sure!"

Holding the boy, Ryan said, "Tell you what. If the Yankees don't attack the fort tomorrow, I'll come by and take you for another horse-back ride. Would you like that?"

"Yes, sir! I really like riding with you, Dad."

Tommy went back to his packages, and Victoria stood at the door and wept as she watched Ryan ride away.

Later that evening, Lex Coffield entered the house and found Tommy playing with his new toys in the middle of the parlor floor. Standing over him, Lex asked, "Where'd you get all this stuff?"

"From my dad for my birthday!" Tommy answered, reaching for his drum. "See my neat drum?"

"Where's your mother?"

"Upstairs."

Checking the staircase to make sure Victoria wasn't on it, Lex leaned close to the boy and asked, "Did your father come inside the house to give you your presents?"

"Yes," Tommy said without looking up.

Coffield's temper flared. "You're sure? You're sure he didn't just give them to you on the porch?"

"Hmp-mm. He brought them back into the sitting room. Mommy told me to wait there 'cause I was gonna get a surprise."

Lex heard Victoria coming down the stairs. Turning toward her, his anger showed. Victoria felt a fear pang as she reached the bottom of the stairs and moved toward her husband. "What's wrong?" she asked.

Lex's breath was hot. "I understand from your son that his father came inside the house to give him his presents."

Tommy stopped his playing, sensing Lex's anger. He looked on as the man moved close to his mother and said, "Well?"

Victoria's hands trembled as she said, "Ryan didn't think you'd care since it was Tommy's birthday. I told him Tommy could open the presents on the porch, but he thought it would be better if he was in the parlor."

Lex's dark eyes were suddenly savage. Victoria felt their striking power as he rasped, "Somebody's lying here! Is it you or the kid? He told me you had him waiting back there in the sitting room, promising him a surprise...and that his father brought the presents back there."

Victoria's lower lip quivered as she stammered, "It...it was m-me who invited Ryan in, Lex. I...I told him Tommy had a fever, and...and if he wanted to see him, he'd have to come in. I'm...I'm sorry. I just wanted Tommy to have a few special moments with his father on his birthday."

Looking down at the boy, Lex asked, "Tommy, when your father was in the house, did he and your mother hug and kiss?"

Tommy's fearful gaze shot to his mother. When he observed the terror in her eyes, he swallowed hard, looked up at Lex, and managed a weak, "No."

Jerking his head around to his wife, the furious husband blared, "The brat's lying! I can see it in his eyes! You and your lover boy were carrying on, weren't you?"

Before Victoria could make a reply, Lex hit her with his fist, knocking her across the room. She bounced off the railing at the staircase and tumbled to the floor. The maddened Coffield moved in and kicked her in the stomach. Swearing, he drew back his foot to kick her again when Tommy grabbed his right hand and sank his teeth into it. Coffield cursed him, jerked his hand free, and slapped him hard. Tommy fell to the floor, dazed, his mouth bleeding.

The anger-crazed captain kicked Victoria again, then wheeled and began stomping on Tommy's toys, cursing the name of Ryan McGraw. When he had destroyed the toys, he threw them out in the front yard. The last to go was the little toy drum. It was battered and broken.

On the way to Dixie's apartment, Captain McGraw rode slowly, wrestling with his emotions. He was having stronger feelings toward Dixie all the time, but there was still that strange, unexplainable stirring within him when he was with Tori.

How can I be in love with two women at the same time? he asked himself.

Ryan knew that even if Lex Coffield was out of the way and the road to Tori was clear, he could never take her back again. But as long as those powerful feelings toward his ex-wife were still alive, he would never be free to marry Dixie. It would be unfair to her.

But the way he felt toward Dixie, he couldn't just break it off with her. He was sure that if he never laid eyes on Tori again, the strange feelings would go away, and he could tell Dixie he loved her and ask her to marry him. But there was no way to avoid seeing Tori when he went to visit Tommy. *That* he could never give up. He had a sudden dreadful thought that once the Mobile Bay battle was over, he would be sent elsewhere to fight. When would he ever see Dixie or his son again? And what was Captain Ryan McGraw, who made fast and firm decisions in the heat of battle, going to do about his divided heart?

An emotional maelstrom was churning inside him when he arrived at Dixie's apartment. She had prepared a delicious dinner, which they sat down to eat by candlelight. While they ate and discussed the coming Union assault, Ryan found himself enchanted by Dixie's beauty of character and form. They were finishing up on apple pie when Dixie asked, "Did you visit Tommy today?"

"Mm-hmm. It's his birthday." He saw no reason to tell her about the way Tori tricked him into entering the house.

"Oh, this *is* the first! Bless his little heart. This had to have been his best birthday ever...having his daddy to celebrate it with him."

"I hope so," smiled Ryan. "I bought him some toys, including a drum."

"A drum?" she giggled. "I'll bet his mother appreciated that!"

"She didn't say," Ryan shrugged.

"You'll probably hear about it later."

"Probably."

Shoving her empty plate aside, Dixie set her soft gaze on the man she loved and said, "Ryan, there are a couple of things I want to do this evening while you're here."

He hurriedly chewed his last bite of pie and said, "Yes, ma'am."

"First, I have a present I want to give you, then I want to have a serious little talk."

"Okay," he said, blinking.

Leaving the table, Dixie went to a small table nearby and picked up a white envelope eight by ten inches in size. It had a slim pink ribbon tied around it, topped off with a fancy pink bow. She handed it to him, then returned to her chair on the opposite side of the table.

Giving her a suspicious look, Ryan opened the envelope and pulled out a daguerreotype of herself in the very dress she was then wearing.

Dixie could tell by the look on his face that Ryan was pleased, and as his eyes dropped to the handwriting in the lower right-hand corner, she said, "I had it done especially for you."

Ryan's heart was in his throat as he read the words, *I will always love you. Dixie.*

He was overwhelmed with the moment. "Dixie," he breathed. "It's...it's beautiful. I'll treasure it always. I—"

Dixie reached across the table and took hold of his hand. Suddenly they were on their feet, drawn together by a force so strong they had neither the will nor the way to resist. There was pure ecstasy in the room as their lips came together in a lingering kiss. When their lips parted, Ryan looked down into her expressive eyes, but could find no words. Dixie laid her head against his chest and embraced him for a long moment, then looked up and half-whispered, "Now for our serious little talk."

She led him by the hand into the apartment's small parlor where two lanterns burned low and sat him down on an overstuffed sofa. She eased down beside him, folding one leg under her so as to face him, and said, "Ryan, I meant what I wrote on that picture." Her eyes misted. She looked toward the ceiling and placed a hand over her quivering lips.

Reaching toward her, he said, "Dixie, I—"

Shaking her head, she threw up a palm. He waited.

After a moment, Dixie cleared the lump from her throat and began again. "I really meant what I wrote on the picture." She drew a deep breath, then said, "I must bare my heart to you."

Ryan opened his mouth to speak, but she cut him off by saying, "Please. Let me tell you what's on my heart, or I'll never get it out."

Ryan's love for her was expanding by leaps and bounds. "All right," he nodded.

Dixie thumbed away tears from both cheeks and said, "Ryan, I've been in love with you since the first time I saw you at the Birmingham hospital. I knew it almost instantly, and I've never doubted it since. Even when we didn't see each other for so long and I didn't know if we ever would cross paths again, I knew you were the only man I would ever love. No one but the Lord in heaven will ever know how happy I was the day you showed up here. I thought maybe somehow we'd get to see each other, and maybe...just maybe...you would fall in love with me."

As she spoke, Dixie could read in his eyes the desire he felt toward her. It warmed her heart.

He started to speak again. "Please," she said, motioning him silent. "I must get it all out before you say anything."

"I'm sorry. Go ahead."

"Ryan...I...know you are fighting an inward battle. I can see it in your eyes, and I felt it in your kiss that you have strong feelings for me. You've shown it in other ways. I...I want you to know that I understand what's going on inside you."

"You do?"

"Yes. You're not sure of yourself with Victoria. There is something down deep that won't let you quite let go of her, now that you've seen her again after all these years. Tell me I'm wrong."

Ryan said nothing for a brief moment, then nodded. "You're right."

"Thank you for giving me a straight answer. Now, the picture I gave you a little while ago is...is something to remind you of me. I'm leaving Mobile, Ryan," she said quietly. "I've asked for a transfer and it has been granted. I've been assigned to the hospital in Chattanooga. As you know, there is heavy fighting in that area. They are in dire need of more nurses."

"But...with the battle that's coming here—"

"I know. But I must leave, Ryan. I want to give you a chance to sort things out in your own heart. I love you with everything that's in me, but I have to know it's the same with you. If, when you get it sorted out, it's me that you want, you can contact me at the hospital in Chattanooga."

After a pause, Ryan asked, "May I speak, now?"

"Yes. I'm through."

Looking her square in the eye, he said, "Dixie, you don't know it, but I fell in love with you at the Birmingham hospital, also. I wanted so much to reveal it to you, but of course I didn't know how you felt about me. I told myself you probably showed the same warmth and kindness toward all the soldiers you attended. I thought of you constantly during that long period we were apart, and considered looking you up just to tell you that I loved you. But...but I couldn't bring myself to do it because...well, because I felt that since I had been married before and had somehow messed it up, I wasn't good enough for you. I felt you deserved better than me. And I still do."

"Oh, Ryan," Dixie whispered. More tears were surfacing. "There *is* no better than you."

Ryan leaned forward, looked at the floor, and rubbed the back of his neck. "You are the kindest person I know," he managed at last. Lifting his head, he set loving eyes on her. "Dixie, in the past few weeks I've started many times to tell you that I'm in love with you, and that if you'd have me, I want you for my wife. But I just couldn't bring myself to do it. This thing with Tori, I—"

"If Lex was out of the way, Ryan, would you take Tori back?"

"No. My problem isn't that I want her back. My problem is that there's a haunting *something* that I feel when I'm with her. I can't describe it, and I can't put a name on it. I guess...I guess it's the embers of a love that once was a blazing fire. But until it's gone, I can't come out and say, 'Dixie, I love you. I'll never think of Tori again, and I'll never feel a tingle for anyone but you...ever.' Do you understand?"

Laying a hand on his, the tearful Dixie said, "Yes, I understand. You have an honest streak in you a mile wide. I love you, Ryan McGraw. I always will. I would love to be your wife...but not with the ghost of an old love between us."

Ryan nodded silently, then asked, "When are you leaving?"

"Early in the morning. There's a medical team taking a boat up to Selma. I'm going with them. From Selma I can take a train to Chattanooga."

Squeezing her hand, Ryan said, "You're the most wonderful person God ever made. I mean that."

"Thank you." Dixie smiled, blushing.

Rising to his feet, Ryan said, "I'm sure you've got packing to do. I'd better get out of here and let you get to it."

They held hands while she walked him to the door. With his free hand, Ryan turned the knob and swung it open.

"Remember," she said, fighting tears, "I'll be at the hospital in Chattanooga."

"Don't worry, I'll remember," he assured her. There were a few seconds of silence, then he looked down at her and asked, "May I kiss you good-bye?"

"I wish you would."

The kiss was long and tender.

Dixie stood in the doorway, shedding silent tears as she watched the man she loved ride into the night.

CHAPTER EIGHTEEN

✦

L ate in the afternoon on August 2, Ryan McGraw rode into
Mobile, feeling an empty spot in his heart.
Dixie Quade was gone.

Ryan had hardly slept the night before. He had tossed and
turned, wrestling with his dilemma. For the time being, Dixie had
solved her portion of it for him. Her absence would allow him time to
give plenty of thought to the strange battle over his feelings for Tori.
Somehow he would solve the mystery and free himself so he could
hurry off to Chattanooga at the first opportunity and tell Dixie that
the ghost of his first love was gone. He would marry the beautiful
woman with the golden hair.

The Coffield house was third from the corner. When McGraw
turned his horse onto Evans Avenue, his attention was drawn to the
front yard. Tommy's toys were scattered about, battered and broken.

Dismounting, Ryan noted the little toy drum, lying off by itself.
Only one person in the Coffield household would have destroyed
Tommy's birthday presents and thrown them in the yard. Heading
toward the porch, McGraw hoped Lex was home.

McGraw was mounting the steps when the door came open and

Lex Coffield appeared. Moving halfway out the door, he rasped, "Get out of here, McGraw! I don't want you on this property ever again!"

"I promised Tommy I'd come by today and take him for a ride on my horse. I'm here to fulfill my promise."

Coffield cursed, backed up, and started to close the door.

Before the door could close, McGraw had his boot against the jamb, blocking it. Coffield swore again and threw his weight against the door, attempting to hurt McGraw's foot. Ryan lunged hard, hitting the door with his shoulder. The blow threw Coffield off balance, and McGraw was inside the house looking for Victoria and Tommy.

"Where are they?" demanded McGraw.

"Get out of my house!" bellowed Coffield. When he spoke, he inadvertently glanced toward the stairs.

Ryan saw it and bolted for the staircase with Coffield on his heels. McGraw took the stairs three at a time. Coffield followed, shouting for him to stop.

McGraw checked two rooms and found them empty. He threw open a third door and found himself in Tommy's bedroom. Victoria was sitting on the small bed holding Tommy in her arms. McGraw's first glance told him the story. Victoria's face had fresh bruises, and the scarlet color of iodine was on Tommy's swollen lower lip, covering a cut. There was also a black-and-blue mark on his cheek. Fear was evident on their faces.

Before mother or son could utter a word, Coffield barged in, blaring at the top of his voice, "Get outta my house, McGraw! I'll have you arrested!"

Wheeling, Ryan shouted, "You'll have *me* arrested? Do you know what the army does to officers who manhandle women and children? They lock them up and throw away the key!"

"You'll never make that happen," Coffield hissed.

"Don't bet on it. But for right now, I think I'll just keep the promise I made you. I told you if you ever laid a hand on my son again, I'd beat you to a bloody pulp. I'm going to give you some of your own medicine."

Even as he spoke, McGraw seized Coffield by the front of his shirt and yanked him through the door. Off balance, Coffield swore and tried to break free. It was useless. McGraw's grip was like spring steel.

"C'mon!" growled McGraw, dragging him toward the stairs. Stumbling helplessly, Coffield unleashed a string of profanity, calling the angry leader of B Company every vile name he could think of, and demanding that McGraw let go of him. Victoria and Tommy moved into the hall and watched the scene.

When they reached the top of the stairs, McGraw halted, still gripping the shirt, and breathed hotly, "Now, *Captain*, you can go down the stairs quietly, like a gentleman, or you can go down the hard way. Choice is yours."

"I'm not going down those stairs at all! Let go of me!"

McGraw swung him around so his back was to the stairs and the first step at his heels. "Oh, but you *are*," McGraw said. "You want me to let go of you? All right." With that, McGraw released his hold on the shirt and gave the man a hard shove.

Coffield sailed halfway down, struck stairs, rolled head-over-heels, banged his head on the banister, and fell in a heap at the bottom. Moaning and swearing, he was trying to gather himself when McGraw grabbed him by the shirt again and began dragging him toward the door. Seconds later, the two men were in the yard, amid the broken toys. Coffield had lost his footing while being pulled down the porch steps, and was on all fours.

McGraw stood over him and said, "Get up."

Coffield's head was throbbing and his whole body hurt from tumbling down the stairs. His face was heavy with hate as he looked up at McGraw. There was no question that McGraw was planning to give him a bloody threshing. Lex decided he might as well fight back.

Coffield swung a foot as hard as he could at McGraw's ankles. It happened so quickly, Ryan couldn't avoid the kick and it knocked his feet out from under him. When he hit the ground, Coffield was on top of him like a panther. He grabbed McGraw's throat with both hands and tried to crush his Adam's apple with his thumbs. McGraw brought his knees up violently under Coffield's rump and sent him sailing head-over-heels.

Coffield landed hard and rolled over, shaking his head. By the time he could get to his knees, McGraw was standing over him again, saying, "C'mon, big tough woman and child beater. Get up!"

The urge to destroy Ryan McGraw was a living thing in Lex Coffield. He leaped to his feet, ejected a wild animal-like roar, and charged him. The adept Sharpshooter dodged him. Coffield skidded to a halt, swore angrily, and spun around. The lust for battle flushed his dark features. He held up his fists and charged again.

McGraw drove the point of his elbow into Coffield's throat, setting him back, gagging and choking. He followed up with a lashing right to the jaw. Coffield was down again.

Shaking his head to clear the cobwebs, he cursed McGraw and got to his feet. Ryan glanced up as Tommy and Victoria came out onto the porch. The half-second his eyes were off Coffield was enough to allow Lex to barrel in and chop him high on the cheekbone. The blow was hard enough to throw Ryan off balance. He stumbled backward, and Coffield was after him like a wild beast.

Ryan brought his elbows up, blocking the barrage of blows. A quick punch through the barrage caught Coffield flush on the nose and staggered him. Water filled his eyes as he fought to stay on his feet.

McGraw eyed Coffield's lower lip at the exact spot where Tommy's was split. The child-beater would now get some of his own medicine. Coffield saw the fist coming and tried to avoid it, but the swiftness of the blow caught him on the targeted place. Skin split and blood spurted. The impact snapped Coffield's head to the side and a crimson spray also came from his nose. He went down once more.

This time, Ryan grabbed his shirt and lifted him to his feet.

"Let's find out how you look with black and blue marks on *your* face, Captain!" he rumbled, and cracked him on the cheekbone. Coffield's knees buckled, but Ryan held him by the shirt and hit him three times more before letting go.

Captain Lex Coffield was down again. His face was red from the smarting blows and crimsoned with blood from his nose and lip. Rolling to his knees, he glanced at Victoria and Tommy on the porch. Tommy was standing beside his mother, clinging to her skirt. Lex tried to summon something from deep within him. He had to get up and give McGraw more of a fight. He must show Victoria that he had the courage to battle back. Spitting blood, he grunted and rose to his feet, raising his fists.

McGraw came after him, dodged Lex's haymaker, and popped him solidly on the jaw, purposely pulling the punch enough to avoid knocking him out. He meant to give Coffield the bloody pulp beating he had promised, but wanted him conscious when it was over.

Lex swung again, but missed. Another McGraw fist snapped his head back, opening a cut above his left eyebrow. His bloody mouth sagged open and he stood there groggily swinging his fists. Ryan stepped in and slapped him hard over and over, rocking his head back and forth with each smarting impact. When he saw Coffield's eyes glaze up, he stopped. Lex Coffield's face was a bloody pulp, and Thomas Manning McGraw's father was satisfied. He stepped back and lowered his fists.

Coffield sank to his knees.

Neighbors were looking on, as they had been for some time. Ryan walked to the battered toy drum, picked it up and went back to Lex. Towering over him, he shook the drum in his face, and growled, "You're going to buy my son a new drum exactly like this one, Captain, and you're going to replace all the other toys you smashed. If you don't, you'll think what you and I just did was play a game of patty-cake compared to what'll happen next."

McGraw went to the porch and held out his arms to his son. Tommy reached for him, and Ryan hugged him. While he held the boy in his arms, he asked, "Do you feel like taking that horseback ride?"

"Sure do!"

Looking at Victoria, Ryan said, "Okay?"

"Of course, as long as you're back by dark."

"We'll be back in half an hour."

Victoria watched as father and son rode away, then turned and went into the house. The neighbors went back to whatever they had been doing before the fight began.

Captain Coffield struggled to his feet, wiped blood from his mouth, and began gingerly to pick up the broken toys.

On Wednesday morning, August 3, Ryan McGraw was sitting on his bunk after a strenuous workout with his men. Judd Rawlings was outside in a discussion on battle tactics with Colonel DeWitt Munford and several of the Fort Morgan men. Having a few moments of privacy, McGraw held Dixie's daguerreotype, looking at it dreamily, and missing her.

A dark form appeared at the door, silhouetted against the stark sunlight. "Captain McGraw, your new men have arrived."

Turning toward the voice, McGraw recognized one of the sentries. He thanked the man, then rose from the bunk and placed Dixie's picture under his pillow.

Emerging into the brilliance of the Alabama sun, McGraw followed the sentry toward the gate. Already, Sharpshooters and Fort Morgan men were welcoming the new recruits. As McGraw drew up to where the new arrivals were clustered, a rugged-looking sergeant smiled and moved forward, extending his hand. McGraw recognized him. They had fought together in a battle McGraw could not name at the moment. Returning the smile, he said, "Hello, Sergeant! I remember fighting side-by-side with you, but you'll have to jog my memory."

"John Grove's my handle, Captain," said the sergeant as their hands clasped. "Those cold three days in December of '61 up at Muscle Shoals near Wilson Lake."

"Oh, sure! Now, I remember. You got separated from your unit during the battle and fought with us."

"Right! You probably don't recall, but I told you then that if I ever got a chance, I'd do my best to get assigned to B Company. Well, here I am!" Handing McGraw a brown envelope, he said, "Here's the official papers from General Maury. He sent a dozen of us to give a little overlap. Said General Lee gave him permission."

"Fine," grinned McGraw, opening the envelope. "With the battle that's coming here, we can use every one of you." Pulling out the papers, he silently read the letter signed by Major General Dabny H. Maury. As the letter stated, on a separate sheet in the envelope were the names and ranks of the new men. Eleven were listed, then at the bottom of the sheet, this note: "One man in the dozen I'm sending you has no combat experience. I realize this is unusual. I have always given you men who have proven themselves in battle. He's also eighteen, younger than any Sharpshooter has ever been. I'm including him in the dozen for two reasons. First, he is the best marksmen I have ever seen. He'll do well as a Sharpshooter once you toughen him up. Second, he showed more enthusiasm for fighting under your command than any potential Sharpshooter has ever shown. I think you know him. His name is Johnny Ray Griffin."

The name brought McGraw's head up with a snap. Quickly he scanned the faces of the new group. At the rear of the knot of men was the boyish face of Johnny Ray. He was looking straight at McGraw, grinning from ear to ear. The grin faded when McGraw did not grin in return.

The Sharpshooter captain welcomed the new men, introduced Lieutenant Judd Rawlings, and informed them that Rawlings would see that they were bunked properly. There would be calisthenics and hand-to-hand combat instruction at three that afternoon. Just before dismissing them to follow Rawlings, he said, "Private Griffin, I want to talk to you immediately."

Griffin remained, looking sheepish as McGraw approached him. A slight smile curved McGraw's mouth as he said, "Johnny Ray, General Maury's note here says you're eighteen. Now, if memory serves me, you were fifteen when I met you. Correct?"

Johnny Ray's face tinted. He lowered his chin. "Yes, sir." Then raising it, he said, "I turned sixteen since then, Captain. And...you gotta admit, I'm tall for my age. I *look* eighteen. The sergeant at the induction center in Montgomery didn't question my age."

"What about your mother? I know she didn't give you permission to lie about your age and join up."

"Well...she got married a couple weeks ago. I...I don't like my stepfather. He sent Ben Rice away, and me and him don't get along. So I decided to run off and join up. When I showed them how good I could shoot and told them I wanted to fight in your company, they talked it over with General Maury. As you can see, he gave me permission to become a McGraw Sharpshooter."

McGraw sighed. "Johnny, General Maury gave his permission because he thinks you're eighteen. You know he wouldn't have if he knew your true age. Right?"

The boy bit his lower lip. "Yes, sir."

Laying a hand on Johnny's bony shoulder, McGraw said, "Johnny, I appreciate your willingness to fight for the Confederacy, and I double appreciate the fact that you want to fight under my command. But Confederate law says you have to be eighteen. Since I know the truth about your age, if I say nothing and let you stay in uniform, I'm breaking the law. Do you want me to break the law?"

"No, sir. I didn't think of it that way. I figured if I told you about my awful stepfather, you'd let me be a Sharpshooter anyway."

"I can't do it, son. You're too young to be out there in combat."

"I captured them Union soldiers. You know about that."

"Yes, and I commend you for it. But that has no bearing on this situation. You are under age, and I've got to send you home."

Johnny Ray looked like he was going to cry.

"There are some civilian clothes in our store room," McGraw continued. "I'll get you into them and take you to Mobile with me next time I go. Probably be tomorrow. I'll find a way to send you home from there."

"But I want to fight the Yankees, Captain McGraw. At least let me go back to Montgomery and get signed up in a unit where nobody knows me."

"Can't do it. I'll have to see that you travel with a military unit of some kind so I know they'll take you home."

Stubbornness showed on the youth's face, but he knew there was no hope of changing Ryan McGraw's mind. "Yes, sir," he replied dejectedly.

"For today, kid," said McGraw, patting his shoulder, "you can watch the Sharpshooters work out. You can bunk with Lieutenant Rawlings and me tonight. Now, let's get you out of that uniform."

Five minutes later, McGraw and the youth emerged from the store room with Johnny Ray carrying shirt and pants. They headed for the captain's quarters, and when they entered, they found Lieutenant Rawlings at his bunk, cleaning his revolver. "Hello, Johnny Ray," smiled Rawlings.

"Hello, sir," Johnny Ray responded glumly.

"Get your clothes changed," McGraw said. Then to Rawlings, "You get everybody situated?"

"Yes, sir." Judd set his curious gaze on the civilian clothing in the youth's hands and said, "I take it you're being sent home."

"Yes, sir."

"Can't let him stay," Ryan said. "He had a birthday since we saw him, but he's still only sixteen."

"Your ma didn't give you permission to do this, did she?" asked Judd.

"No, she didn't," Ryan answered for him.

"Bet she's plenty worried about you."

"No, she's not," replied Johnny Ray. "I don't matter to her any-more. She got married and she's got my dumb ol' stepfather."

Rawlings and McGraw exchanged glances.

"Just because she got married again doesn't mean your mother doesn't love you or care about you, kid," put in McGraw. "She's probably beside herself with worry right this minute."

Shrugging his narrow shoulders, the slender youth said, "Maybe."

There was a rap on the frame of the open door. It was a sentry from the gate. "Captain, General Page sent me to get you. He's in the lighthouse. Wants you immediately."

Captain McGraw hastened up the spiral stairs in the lighthouse to find General Page standing between two soldiers, looking south on the Gulf of Mexico through a telescope. Page lowered the telescope, turned to McGraw, and said, "Take a look at this, Captain."

Placing the telescope to his right eye, McGraw focused on the Union fleet. He saw that instead of bobbing on the water in loose fashion as they had been for weeks, they were lining up in formation. "Oh-oh," he said, still looking. "I think they're getting ready to come in."

"That's the way I see it," responded Page. "Looks like *we'd* better get ready."

"I would say so, sir," said McGraw, lowering the telescope.

"My men, here, spotted a new ship arriving out there about an hour ago," said the general. "It's a monitor. This gives Farragut a total of twenty-five vessels. Four are monitors. He must figure he's got enough, now."

"I agree, sir. You think they'll hit us right away?"

"I'd say they'll wait till tide and come in at dawn."

"Makes sense."

"You're not going to have but one session with your new men if I'm right about the attack coming at dawn.".

"We'll have to make do with that, then, sir. All but one of the new men have combat experience. That one is a sixteen-year-old I know personally who got past the induction center in Montgomery, lying about his age. I've already got him in civilian clothes. I was going to take him to Mobile with me tomorrow, but that's out. He'll just have to stay in my quarters during the battle."

Page nodded. "He's one of many hundred sons of the South who've lied their way into a uniform. That's all you can do with him, now." As he started toward the spiral stairs, Page said to the two men on duty in the lighthouse, "Let me know immediately if they should happen to start this direction."

"Yes, sir."

As general and captain walked together toward the fort gate, Page asked, "Have you seen Captain Coffield?"

"You mean, has he come in today?"

"Yes."

"Not that I know of, sir. But I...ah...I probably should tell you that he might not show up."

"Oh? And why's that?"

"I told you that I learned about Tommy being my son."

"Yes."

"Well, sir, I learned that Captain Coffield is known to manhandle Tommy and leave him black and blue at times. He does the same thing to Victoria."

"I'm aware of how he treats her, but I didn't know about him beating on the boy."

"Have you talked to him about beating on Victoria, sir?"

"No, because whenever I've seen the marks on her face, she won't admit he did it. If I ever get proof, I'll lock him up till the war's over, no matter how long it goes on. As you know, the Confederate army frowns hard on such a thing, especially when the guilty party is an officer. So what happened that Coffield might not be in today?"

"I saw marks that he put on Tommy, sir. I had warned him never to touch my son again. I lost my temper and worked him over pretty good. He's no doubt got a mighty sore carcass about now."

They were nearing the gate. General Page hauled up so they were still out of earshot from the sentries. Smiling, he said, "May I say something in response to what you just told me—just between us?"

"Of course."

"You have my utmost praise and admiration!"

"Thank you, sir," grinned McGraw.

Page cleared his throat and headed for the gate, saying, "Well, Captain, we've got to get ready to take on the Yankees, Coffield or no Coffield."

The Union monitor *Tecumseh* was sighted on the east horizon just before eight o'clock on the morning of August 3. An hour later it steamed in to the cheers of men on the decks of the other ships and drew up beside the *Hartford.* The *Tecumseh's* captain, Tunis A.M. Craven, was an old and close friend of Admiral Farragut. The balding fleet commander stood on the deck of the *Hartford* and invited Craven aboard.

When Farragut had filled his friend in on the attack plan over a glass of red wine, Craven returned to his ship. The *Hartford's* flag man then signaled for the entire flotilla to move into their assigned positions.

Standing next to Farragut on the deck as they watched the massive strike force line up, Fleet-Captain Percival Drayton said, "I like your idea, Admiral. We know they're watching us take formation. And I think you're right—since we're forming up now, General Page will figure us to come riding in on high tide at daybreak in the morning.

When we don't come, it'll sure enough give them something to think about. Time they've sweated it out till dark tomorrow night, we'll really have them wondering. They'll be a little shaken when we do come in on high tide the next morning."

"Maybe not much," grinned Farragut. "But even if it's a little, it'll help."

CHAPTER NINETEEN

Like many of the men in Fort Morgan, Captain Ryan McGraw found sleep hard to come by on the night of August 3. It was well after midnight when he rose from his cot, dressed while Johnny Ray Griffin and Judd Rawlings slept restlessly, and walked out into the cool night air. A strong wind was coming in off the Gulf, and it felt good.

Greeting the sentries at the gate, McGraw passed through and walked past the lighthouse to the beach. There was enough moon for him to be able to tell that the Union fleet had not come any closer. The enemy ships were lying in wait, dark and menacing shapes on the horizon. Standing just shy of the foamy line where the surf washed the sandy slope, McGraw let the wind ruffle his hair while he thought of Tommy, wishing the child had a better home life. Even greater than the fear he held for his son living with Lex Coffield was the fear that Union forces would move in and capture Mobile.

What would the Federals do to him? Tommy needed him, but duty would keep Captain McGraw at Fort Morgan until the battle in Mobile Bay was over. He could only pray that Tommy would not be harmed if Granger and his troops did take the city.

And then there was Dixie. He wondered if she had made it to Chattanooga safely and what kind of fighting was going on around that part of the South. His heart ached for her. "Someday, Dixie," he whispered. "Someday this horrible war will be over. Someday I'll get myself squared away and come for you with a marriage proposal on my lips."

Ryan lost all sense of time. He didn't know what time it was when he headed back for the gate, but a few men were stirring around the cannons at the parapets. When he moved inside the walls, he saw the vague forms of General Page and his three officers huddled together a few feet away. Page called to him.

Stepping to them, Ryan said, "Yes, sir?"

"You couldn't sleep, either, I see," said the general.

"No, sir. I've got Tommy on my mind, as well as what's about to happen here. I'm concerned about what could happen to him if Granger's troops move on Mobile."

"I understand," replied Page.

"Maybe if we whip the Yankees here in the bay, Lincoln will call off his dogs up north," put in Lieutenant Wilson March. "If we can sink enough of their ships to send what's left hightailing it out of here on the Gulf, Granger may not want to venture into Mobile. We could all rush up there and defend it."

"I'd like to believe that myself, Lieutenant," said Colonel DeWitt Munford, "but if Granger's got five thousand men like we've been hearing, our little handful here wouldn't scare him."

"All we can do is take what comes and make the best of it," said Lieutenant Frank Cooley. "Your wife's in Mobile, too, Colonel. I'm sure you're as uneasy as Captain McGraw is."

"Maybe more so," replied Munford. "The Yankees have been known to ravage our Southern women, but not harm the children."

"Well, there's one Yankee leader who doesn't mind harming children," said March, "and that's William Tecumseh Sherman. When he decided to take Pittsburg Landing over near Corinth, Mississippi back in March of '62, he blasted farm houses, knowing there were children as well as women inside. People in Atlanta are scared out of their wits with word that Sherman's going to march down there with blood in his eye this fall."

General Page realized the conversation was only serving to put a pall in the minds of McGraw and Munford, and that talking about the danger would not eliminate it. "It's almost dawn, men," he said. "I'm going to the lighthouse. Get the rest of the men up and in place. Farragut could be coming in here real soon."

When dawn broke, Captain McGraw and his Sharpshooters were out of the fort and positioned along the shore of the bay, beginning just below the lighthouse and strung along toward the north side of Mobile Point. They were spread out enough so they could begin sniping before the Union vessels had even broken the line between the two forts. While Fort Morgan's big guns fired over the Sharpshooters' heads, they would be blasting away with their rifles, shooting Union sailors off the decks. The Tennessee sat in the water some two hundred yards from the mouth of the bay, sided by the small gunboats, *Selma, Morgan,* and *Gaines.*

Inside the fort, General Page's men waited at the big guns to open fire on the Union fleet the instant they came within range. Nerves were stretched tight.

In Captain McGraw's quarters, Johnny Ray Griffin looked on the scene from a window. McGraw had ordered him to keep the door closed. In the youth's hands was a .44 caliber Henry nine-shot repeater rifle. On his waist was a sheath bearing a ten-inch knife. If the Yankees were able to get into the fort, Johnny Ray was ready to defend himself.

A heavy mist hovered over the Gulf. The men in the lighthouse strained their eyes to peer into the vaporous curtain, watching for any sign of movement.

The eastern sky came alive with a pink flush that soon turned orange, but no enemy ships could be seen steaming into the mouth of Mobile Bay. Soon the mists were gone, and in the lighthouse, General Page peered southward through a telescope to find that the Union fleet had not moved since lining up in formation the day before.

When Farragut's armada had not moved by nine o'clock, General Page called for his signalman on the wall to beckon the Sharpshooters back inside the fort.

Meeting with all the men at nine-thirty, except for those on the walls and in the lighthouse, Page stood before them with his officers and Captain McGraw beside him.

"I know you're all wondering why our enemy didn't ride the tide in with guns blazing," said the general. "You were ready to do battle, and no battle came. You're feeling rocks in the pit of your stomachs, and your nerves feel like they're going to snap. Well, gentlemen, this is what is known as psychological warfare. Ol' 'fairguts' is playing games with us. We mustn't let him rattle us. He may decide to come in here at midday without the benefit of high tide...or he may just wait and come at us at dawn tomorrow. Whenever he comes, we've got to be ready and be in control of ourselves. Now let's gird up our loins as the saying goes, and be ready to fight at any moment. What do you say?"

There was a rousing cheer, and a portion of the Fort Morgan men returned to their guns while the rest went to breakfast.

The day dragged on, with no movement out on the Gulf.

When night fell, the Rebel force talked of blasting the Yankees out of the Gulf at dawn. Certainly Farragut couldn't wait another day. Yankees didn't have steel for nerves, either.

At an hour before dawn on Friday, August 5, 1864, a heavy fog lay on Mobile Point and its surrounding waters. The Sharpshooters were back in place along the shore, the men of Fort Morgan were in their places, General Page was in the lighthouse, and Johnny Ray Griffin was in Captain McGraw's quarters.

At 5:45, a light breeze began to stir the fog, causing it to swirl about on the surface of the water in thin tendrils like filmy ghosts.

Once again, Rebel nerves were strung tight.

Suddenly, high in the glass compartment of the lighthouse, General Page peered through the thick mists and said to the two men on duty beside him, "They're coming! "

The dim outlines of the Union vessels were slowly emerging like phantoms in the fog. A lantern was lit and waved from the top of the lighthouse to signal the three gunboats and the CSS *Tennessee* to get ready. The long-dreaded battle was about to commence.

The Union fleet approached with the ships lined up two-by-two. As they drew nearer in the fog, the *Brooklyn* forged ahead of the *Hartford,* her bow-chasers fully manned.

Captain McGraw had placed Lieutenant Rawlings at the head of the line of Sharpshooters just below the lighthouse, and had placed himself in the middle of the long, curving line. He would fire the first shot, which would signal his men to unleash a barrage of rifle fire. From that point on, the Sharpshooters were to fire at will.

The fog began to lift at the same time the eastern horizon came alive with light. The Union fleet was closing in, with the *Brooklyn* in the lead. The Confederates naturally assumed the *Brooklyn* to be Farragut's flagship.

In the bay, just north of the minefields, the CSS *Tennessee* and her three gunboats were lining up, ready to begin firing once the Union ships breached the line between the forts.

General Page was now inside Fort Morgan to direct the firing of the big guns. His orders were that they would open fire when the first shot came from a Union ship or when the first enemy vessel struck a torpedo.

The tension grew stronger. Nerves were on edge. Every man knew this could be his day to die, but tried to shove that thought to the back of his mind while he waited...and waited.

Suddenly the Union monitor *Tecumseh,* commanded by Admiral

Farragut's old friend Tunis Craven, broke from the line and forged ahead at full speed. There was surprise on board the other Union vessels, including the flagship. At the same time, the *Tecumseh* opened fire with two of her fifteen-inch guns, aiming for the walls of Fort Morgan.

There was a strange feeling of relief among the Confederates the instant the first two shots were fired.

Along the shore, Captain McGraw drew a bead on one of the gunners in the bow of the *Brooklyn* and fired. The man stiffened, then fell to the deck in a heap. Instantly the Sharpshooters cut loose, aiming at other men aboard the *Brooklyn*, which they thought was the Union flagship. Bullets began dropping men all over the starboard side of the deck and were crashing through the glass windows of the captain's cabin.

At the same time, cannons from Fort Gaines and Fort Morgan were thundering and belching fire. The battle of Mobile Bay had begun.

The mouth of the bay was instantly bedlam. Guns roared, rifles barked, and men shouted at the thrill of battle. The bombardment blasted the walls of the Confederate forts and tore into the hulls of Union ships. The CSS *Tennessee* and her three gunboats stood ready to rake the advancing enemy vessels with cannonballs when they broke through the minefields.

The *Brooklyn* was suddenly stalled in the water only a few feet from the red buoy. Its captain and crew had been cut to pieces by McGraw's men. The *Tecumseh* sped past the *Brooklyn* and immediately hit a torpedo. The vessel shuddered with the explosion. At the same time, a barrage of cannon fire was unleashed on it from Morgan. As shot whistled through the monitor's hull and shells exploded around her, the *Tecumseh's* propeller churned the black water to white foam as it began to list to the starboard side. It was sinking fast. The torpedo had blown a gigantic hole in its bottom.

While the deafening thunder of the battle grew louder and the sky filled with black smoke, the crew of the *Tecumseh* was abandoning ship. Twenty-two of her men were dead. The others were leaping into the water and swimming frantically to avoid being sucked into the ship's whirlpool as it plunged beneath the surface. The last to leave her was Captain Craven.

The USS *Metacomet*, being the closest, steamed toward the *Tecumseh* crew, and under a deadly storm of shot and shell, began picking them up.

It was a critical moment for the Union navy.

The *Brooklyn* was lying across the narrow channel between the pilings to the west and the red buoy under the fiery guns of Fort Morgan. McGraw's Sharpshooters had reduced the *Brooklyn's* crew to a handful. There were bodies strewn all over the deck. Her engine had since died, and all her surviving crewmen could do was lie low on the port side and try to keep from being hit.

With the *Brooklyn* dead in the water, the whole Union fleet became a stationary target for the guns of forts Morgan and Gaines and the deadly rifles of the Sharpshooters.

Because of the *Hartford's* position, only her few bow guns could be used. A destructive rain of enemy fire was falling on her, and her men were being cut down by the guns of B Company. In the captain's cabin, Admiral Farragut was swearing at the situation, trying to get a clear look ahead amid the heavy smoke that clung to the water's surface like fog.

At the same time, the captains of Union ships *Monongahelah*, *Kennebec*, *Lackawanna*, and *Ossipee* were blasting away at Fort Gaines. The guns in the small fort were doing little damage to the Union fleet, but the four captains, through flag signals, agreed to knock it completely out of commission while they were waiting to move into the bay. It took only a matter of minutes to silence the guns of Fort Gaines.

Aboard the CSS *Tennessee*, Admiral Franklin Buchanan decided to get into the action while the Union vessels were stalled under the guns of General Page. Signaling for the three gunboats to follow, he steamed his huge ironclad forward. Soon all four vessels were firing into the bottled-up mass of ships whose masts were flying the Stars and Stripes of the United States.

At one forward gun on the *Hartford's* deck, a shell came crashing down and killed several men, blowing their bodies every direction. Some sailed over the edge and fell into the churning waters. Inside the *Hartford's* cabin, Admiral Farragut swore and said to Fleet-Captain Drayton, "We've got to move, but I can't see for the smoke! I've got to get out there and climb the rigging."

"But, sir, you'll be killed!"

"We'll *all* be killed unless we get moving," snapped Farragut, and charged out the door.

Drayton followed him, hunching low. The sixty-three-year-old admiral scurried up the rigging of the main mast hand-over-hand with the agility of a man in his twenties. He stopped at the futtock-shrouds, just under the towering top. Fearing for the admiral's life, Drayton stood below, observing him on the swaying mast. He was glad when he saw him coming back down.

When Farragut touched deck, he ran to the pilot at the wheel and shouted, "There's space enough for us to pass the *Brooklyn* on her port side. We'll take the lead. Hard a-starboard! Full speed ahead!"

"But, sir, with all that smoke, I can barely see the *Brooklyn.* I may ram her!"

"I said *hard* a-starboard!" snapped Farragut. "Do as I tell you, and you'll miss her. From what I saw up on the mast, once you're alongside the *Brooklyn*, you'll be able to see clearly."

"Yes, sir."

Drayton swallowed hard and faced Farragut. "Sir, I beg your pardon for speaking to you like this, but the smoke isn't the big problem. It's the torpedoes. You saw what happened to the *Tecumseh!*"

The admiral's deeply lined face turned to granite. With a steely look in his eyes, he bawled, "Damn the torpedoes! Full speed ahead!"*

Amid the fire, smoke, thunder of guns, and the sight of many of his men lying dead, General Page paced back and forth behind the guns of Fort Morgan, shouting encouragement. From time to time, the gunners answered back with a Rebel yell.

Down on the shore, the Sharpshooters lay flat and fired at the Union fleet as it moved forward into the bay behind the *Hartford*. Torpedoes were exploding and more Union vessels were being damaged and stalled, but many were steaming through. It was evident that their plan was to fire at Morgan from every possible angle.

Six Union ships remained outside the mouth of the bay to bombard the fort from the south side. The lighthouse was taking a beating. The glass was shattered in the compartment at the top, and two bodies hung on the edge. About halfway up, a large chunk had been blown out of the lighthouse's side.

Behind the *Hartford* came the *Octarora*, the *Metacomet*, the *Port Royal*, and the *Richmond*, with several small gunboats in their wake.

The tiny Confederate "fleet" of the *Tennessee*, the *Selma*, the *Gaines*, and the *Morgan* was firing at the approaching enemy vessels as rapidly as possible.

Sergeants Hap Hazzard, Noah Cloud, and John Grove found themselves shoulder-to-shoulder on the shore, alongside Captain McGraw and a half-dozen other Sharpshooters, including Bobby Brinson. The Union ships were moving in rapidly.

McGraw turned to Brinson and said, "Corporal, take four of these men and hurry farther north. Keep them sniping away at crewmen when they've passed us."

"Yes, sir," nodded Brinson. Quickly he chose his men and was gone.

Moments later, as McGraw was reloading his repeater, he heard a rifle firing rapidly from behind him and saw a Union sailor fall aboard the *Metacomet*—which was directly in front of him—for each shot that

*This famous quotation is included for historical accuracy

that was fired. Some Sharpshooter, McGraw told himself, was really finding his targets.

Looking around to see who the marksman was, McGraw was surprised to see young Johnny Ray Griffin. Griffin fired again, and another crewman of the Metacomet went down.

"Johnny Ray!" shouted McGraw. "I told you to stay in my quarters!"

Grinning, the boy levered another cartridge into the chamber of his Henry, took aim, and blew a Yankee sailor into the water.

"Johnny Ray!" McGraw shouted, punching the last fresh cartridge into the magazine of his own repeater. "I want you back in the fort! Now!"

"Please, Captain! I'm killing Yankees. Isn't that what *you're* doing?"

"Yes, but I'm a soldier. You're a civilian. Now do as I tell you. Get back inside the fort and stay in my quarters till this is over!"

The boy shouldered his rifle and took aim at a gunner aboard the next ship in line. The rifle bucked in his hands, and the gunner went down. "See, Captain!" argued Johnny Ray. "You need me!"

"I'm going to whip your britches, kid!" bellowed McGraw. "Now get out of here!"

Pouting, Johnny Ray got up and hurried away.

After firing at the Union crews for another fifteen or twenty minutes, McGraw found that he was taking the last cartridges out of his ammunition sack. Turning to John Grove, who was next to him, he said, "I've only got four bullets left. Can you give me some?"

"I'm almost out, Captain, but you can have what I've got."

"I don't want to take all of yours," said McGraw. Looking past Grove to the others nearby, he called, "Can you guys spare me some ammunition?"

To his dismay, he learned that every man near him was running low. Somebody would have to run back up to the fort and bring a fresh supply. Donnie Jim Michaels was on the far side of Noah Cloud.

Calling to him, McGraw told him to dash to the fort and bring more ammunition.

Donnie Jim hadn't been gone more than a couple of minutes when McGraw was out of bullets. He emptied his revolver at the passing ships, but with little effect. Soon the others were also out of ammunition.

Hazzard looked back through the clouds of smoke toward the fort and said, "Cap'n, I sure hope Donnie Jim hurries up. We're losin' time!"

McGraw noted a small gunboat with *Loyal* printed on the bow. "Tell you what," he said, removing his hat. "We could come by some fire power if we took over one of those gunboats."

"Novel idea!" exclaimed Hap.

Pulling off his boots, McGraw said, "Hap...Noah...come with me. Let's take the *Loyal*, right there." Leaving the others on the shore, the three men secured their knives in their sheaths and dived into the dark waters.

The *Tennessee* and her gunboats continued to fire at the enemy ships, and the fire was being returned. The guns of Fort Morgan continued to send screaming shells into the hulls and onto the decks of Admiral Farragut's fleet, though some of General Page's big guns had been put out of commission.

McGraw and his chosen partners swam under water until they reached the side of the slow-moving *Loyal*, then bobbed to the surface so close that the crew—who were firing at the *Selma*—could not see them. The deck was barely four feet above their heads.

McGraw blinked the water from his eyes and pulled his knife. Sticking the dull side of the blade between his teeth, he said, "Okay, boys, let's take us a Yankee boat!"

Suddenly a fourth head bobbed to the surface. It was Johnny Ray Griffin. He showed McGraw his long-bladed knife and grinned.

The noise of the battle was loud enough to cover his voice, as McGraw scowled and said, "Johnny Ray, I told you to go back to the fort!"

"I don't have to obey you, Captain. I'm a civilian, remember?"

"I'm telling you to get out of here! You're going to mess up this mission!"

"You have no authority over the bay, Captain," grinned Johnny Ray. "Anybody who wants to can swim in it. That's what I'm doing. Only I want to help you kill Yankees while I'm doing it."

There was no time for further argument. "Okay, kid," sighed McGraw. "You'll have to carry your own weight."

Johnny Ray flashed another grin and nodded. "Let's go."

The four Rebels—knives between their teeth—reached up, laid hold of the deck's edge near the stern, and pulled themselves aboard. The crew of five had their backs to them. The pilot was at the wheel and each of the others manned the four eight-inch iron rifles that were built on swivels and positioned at the bow. Two of the guns boomed seconds apart. The other two were ready to fire.

Cloud dashed across the deck, threw an arm around the pilot's neck from behind, and drove his knife into his heart. At the same time, Hazzard and Griffin went after the men who were just aiming their guns at the *Tennessee*. Being taken by surprise, they had no time to react. It took Johnny Ray two stabs to finish his man, but the Yankee was dead before he hit the deck.

At the same time, McGraw slammed one Yankee on the back of the head with an elbow hard enough to stun him, and as the other one wheeled around, he drove his knife into his heart. As he jerked the blade out, he shoved his victim overboard, then turned to find that Hap had already disposed of the dazed one. He was just heaving the lifeless form into the bay. When the entire crew was dead and overboard, Noah took the wheel and began turning the boat so they could fire at the Union ships.

While McGraw began reloading one of the guns, he shouted, "Hap, show the kid how to fire one of these things! Both of you be ready! We'll be squared around in a minute!"

"C'mere, kid," said Hazzard, planting himself behind one of the guns.

Johnny Ray obeyed quickly. The cannon was mounted on a small platform built on a swivel with thick round springs underneath to allow for recoil. There were small holes in the deck where a steel rod would drop in to steady the gun once it was aimed and ready to fire. Hap showed young Griffin how to aim it, drop the steel rod, and yank the strong, slender cord known as the lanyard to fire the gun.

As the *Loyal* was coming around to face the Union ships, Noah Cloud glanced at the Confederate vessels, hoping the *Loyal* was not in their gun sights. The gunboats were busy blasting away at ships nearer to them, and the *Tennessee* was firing at the *Hartford.*

McGraw had his iron rifle ready to fire just as the *Loyal* squared with the Union fleet. A gunboat called the *Oneida* was bearing down on them at a distance of about forty yards. McGraw's heart leaped when he saw her guns seemingly aimed right at them. When they did not fire, he knew the crew had not seen the takeover.

"Okay, fellas!" shouted the captain. "Aim right down those big hungry-looking barrels and let 'em have it!"

While Hazzard and Griffin prepared to follow the order, McGraw aimed his gun at the *Oneida's* bow, just above the water line. He could make out the faces of the gunners on the bow just before he yanked lanyard. They had picked up on the gray uniforms and, too late, realized they were now facing their own guns in enemy hands.

The *Loyal* shuddered as all three eight-inchers roared. McGraw's shell split the bow at the water line, but it wasn't needed. One of the other shots blew up the cannon and its men; the other one found the store of gunpowder. The *Oneida* became a huge ball of fire.

"Yahoo!" shouted Johnny Ray, shaking a fist over his head.

"Load up again!" shouted McGraw. Then to Cloud, "Noah, make a circle! We're too close to those other enemy ships coming in!"

The water in the bay was churning and the small gunboat bobbed as if it were in a storm at sea as Cloud gave it steam and began a wide circle. The three iron rifles were loaded before the circle was complete. McGraw, Hazzard, and Griffin each stood at his gun, ready to fire at the first enemy vessel that presented itself a likely target.

Suddenly from the west side of the bay, McGraw saw the battleship *Manhattan* coming at them. Her crew had spotted the Rebel uniforms on the *Loyal*'s deck and watched the destruction of the *Oneida*.

Johnny Ray was sighting in on another Union gunboat steaming their direction from the mouth of the bay. "Look, Hap!" he shouted. "Let's get that one!"

McGraw saw the *Manhattan*'s gunners swing two fifteen-inch Dahlgrens on the *Loyal*. Quickly he cried, "Jump, men! Jump!"

The other three looked and saw the Dahlgrens lining up on them. All three wheeled toward the edge of the deck. Ryan bounded for the water and dived in. While Hap and Noah dashed after him, Johnny Ray abruptly stopped and ran back to his gun. Maybe he could put a cannonball down the mouths of the *Manhattan* crew like he did the *Oneida*.

When McGraw, Hazzard, and Cloud surfaced and were swimming furiously toward shore, they looked back to see young Griffin still on the deck and aiming his gun at the *Manhattan*. Hazzard shouted something indistinguishable just as Johnny Ray yanked the lanyard. In the same split second, the big Dahlgrens boomed. The shells hit the *Loyal*'s deck and exploded, sending the guns into the bay and Johnny Ray Griffin into eternity.

McGraw and his two sergeants exchanged sorrowful glances and swam for shore. When they reached it, they looked back and saw the *Loyal* afire and sinking, but beyond it, the *Manhattan* was stalled in the water. Johnny Ray's shell had exploded directly between the Dahlgrens. They were off their bases, lying on their sides, and underneath a rising cloud of smoke, the gunners lay dead on the deck.

Hazzard stood dripping wet and said with choked voice, "For a civilian, the kid was quite a soldier."

McGraw swallowed the lump in his throat and said, "Yes, Hap. He was quite a soldier."

CHAPTER TWENTY

The sun rose into the sky as the battle continued on Mobile Bay, but it was obscured by a heavy pall of black smoke.

It had become apparent to the tiny Confederate fleet that the *Hartford* was Admiral Farragut's flagship. The *Tennessee* had unleashed a merciless barrage on the flagship, and was preparing to hit it some more when the monitors *Chickasaw* and *Winnebago* moved past Morgan's guns and made a beeline for her. Admiral Buchanan gave his pilot orders to wheel about and meet both ships head-on.

Seeing the *Tennessee's* sudden sharp turn toward the two monitors, the captain of the Confederate gunboat *Selma* swung directly in front of the Union flagship and raked her bow. At the same time, the other two Confederate gunboats were on the Hartford's starboard side, blasting away, but they received more damage than they were able to inflict.

The thick-ribbed *Tennessee* stood "toe-to-toe" with the *Chickasaw* and *Winnebago*, guns booming. Strange metallic sounds rang across the bay as cannonballs struck the heavy armor of the monitors. Some of the Union gunboats had spotted the Sharpshooters on the shore and began to train their cannons on them. When the guns belched fire, the men of B Company dived for cover and slowly made their way to the fort, where they found Captain McGraw carrying Lieutenant Rawlings up the sandy slope toward the gate. Rawlings had taken a chunk of shrapnel in his shoulder.

Inside the fort, the Sharpshooters gathered around their leader as he laid Rawlings on a cot and a couple of the fort's medics went to work. McGraw told his men they had done a magnificent job of sniping. Now that most of the Union fleet was inside the mouth of the bay, they would join the men of the fort at the cannons that were still operable and help keep them firing.

Several of the Sharpshooters were unaccounted for. A few were reported dead by their comrades, but there was still hope that the others would soon come into the fort. Captain McGraw prepared to go out and look for them.

The six Union ships outside the bay continued to bombard Fort Morgan as the day wore on. Captain McGraw moved along the shore, looking for his missing men, and the sea battle between the four ships of the Confederacy and the Union fleet remained hot. From the flagship, Admiral Farragut signaled for his destroyers to continue gunning the fort, while the gunboats and monitors stayed after the four Rebel ships.

Just before noon the Confederate gunboat *Gaines* took a series of shots from three Union ships and ran aground north of the fort, its hull filling with water. The crew jumped onto the shore and ran for the fort. They were barely out of danger when the small Rebel gunboat exploded. What was left of it lay on the shore burning.

The *Metacomet*, Farragut's fastest vessel, turned its attention on the *Selma*. A brief exchange took place, but the Union ship's guns were bigger and soon rendered the *Selma* unable to defend herself. She wheeled about and headed north up the bay. The *Metacomet* overtook her, firing relentlessly. When the *Selma's* captain was seriously wounded, a white flag was run up, and the crew surrendered. They were taken aboard the *Metacomet* as prisoners and the *Selma* was sunk.

Several Union ships converged upon the *Morgan*. The crew knew they had no chance. Running the boat to the shore under the booming guns of Fort Morgan, they hit the beach and dashed to the safety of the fort.

The *Tennessee* was now the target of all the Union monitors and gunboats still in action. Cannons thundered against her, but she fought on gallantly. Soon the bombardment against the invincible Confederate ironclad ram began to take its toll. While the battle raged, the *Tennessee's* flagstaff was shot away. Soon the smoke stack was riddled with holes, and finally disappeared.

Aboard the *Hartford*, Admiral Farragut commanded his pilot to pull back. The Union monitors and gunboats would soon have the *Tennessee* in hand. Standing on the deck of his battered flagship, the admiral watched the dramatic finish.

The monitor *Chickasaw* came up astern of Buchanan's ironclad and began pounding away with eleven-inch shells. At the same time, the fifteen-inch guns of the *Manhattan* pounded her port side, and the twelve-inch guns of the *Winnebago* blasted her starboard side. The *Tennessee* continued to fight back, blasting away at her attackers and maneuvering expertly in the water.

Suddenly the *Chickasaw's* shots cut the rudder chain of the Confederate ram, and the pilot no longer had control. The *Tennessee* began to spin in a tight circle. At the same time, the gunboats *Ossipee*, *Monongahela*, and *Lackawanna* joined the monitors, firing relentlessly at the *Tennessee*, bent on her complete destruction.

Inside the *Tennessee*, Admiral Buchanan was severely wounded when an iron splinter pierced his side. Immediately the ram's captain displayed a white flag, hoisted on an improvised staff through the grating over the deck. When Admiral Farragut saw the white flag, he commanded his signalman to flash a quick message of cease fire to all the ships.

Abruptly the thunderous cannonade began to diminish until even the guns concentrated on the fort went silent. The afternoon breeze carried the smoke away, and as the six ships outside the bay steamed around Mobile Point to join the fleet, cheer after cheer resounded from the decks of the Union vessels.

Inside the fort, the Rebels looked on dejectedly as the *Tennessee's* crew emerged into the sunlight. A wounded Admiral Buchanan surrendered his sword to the captain of the *Ossipee*, and was taken aboard as prisoner, along with his crew.

Captain McGraw stood with General Page and his two lieutenants and watched glumly as the *Tennessee* was towed across the bay to where the *Hartford* had dropped anchor.

"Looks like we're whipped, General," Frank Cooley said with a break in his voice.

Page stared at the Union fleet gathered in the bay. Though a few of their vessels lay on the bottom of the bay, and many of the others were severely damaged, he knew the fort was now under siege. Without commenting on Cooley's dismal remark, he said to McGraw, "Captain, I want you to take your men to Mobile under cover of darkness tonight. You can have the horses and wagons you need. We'll bury your six dead men for you. Since none of your four wounded men are in danger, take them with you. They'll get proper care at the Mobile hospital. I have six wounded men to send along with you."

"Sir, we can't go off and leave you and your men to face Farragut's guns. You need us."

"We'll be all right," Page replied, looking McGraw straight in the eye. "What I said was not a request. It is an order. We'll hold the fort as long as we can, but Mobile will be President Lincoln's next target. There'll no doubt be ground forces moving against it shortly. The people of Mobile need you and your Sharpshooters more than we do. Lieutenant Cooley is right. We're whipped, here. All we can do is grit our teeth and hold off the enemy as long as possible. The people of Mobile aren't whipped. Go do all you can to see that the Yankees don't take Mobile."

A solemn look etched itself on Ryan McGraw's face. "Yes, sir. We will."

Page scratched at an ear. "And when you see Captain Coffield..."

"Yes, sir?"

"Tell him to stay in Mobile and fight the enemy there. That's an order."

"I will convey the message, sir."

Travel in the darkness was slow. B Company and the fort's six wounded men arrived in Mobile at dawn. The wounded men were taken immediately to the hospital, where McGraw learned that General Maury had sent three hundred men of A Company, Third Alabama Infantry to defend the city. They were under the command of Captain Andrew Garrison and bivouacked just outside Mobile on the north side.

McGraw left the wounded men at the hospital and took the Sharpshooters to the army camp He was glad to know that Judd Rawlings was under the personal care of Betty Wells.

Captain Andrew Garrison listened intently as McGraw told him of the Confederate defeat at Mobile Point. He welcomed the Sharpshooters, saying he and his men would be honored to fight alongside them. Garrison explained that though General Maury was expecting the Federals to send a massive force against Mobile, he could send no more than the three hundred men of Third Alabama A Company to defend it.

McGraw asked if Garrison had any idea when General Gordon Granger and his troops would come. Garrison told him he did not. All they could do was send scouting patrols northward and hope that once it was learned that the Yankees were on their way, there would be time to evacuate the civilians from Mobile.

McGraw thought of Tommy and asked why they didn't evacuate the civilians now. Garrison explained that the waiting period could stretch into months. Being displaced for an extended time would work a hardship on the families, and if the bulk of Mobile's citizens were gone too long, it would destroy all the businesses.

McGraw then asked if Garrison had seen anything of Captain Lex Coffield. When Garrison replied that he had not, McGraw told him he would be back later. He must go and check on his son, who lived in Mobile.

Word was spreading fast over the city about Fort Morgan's defeat when Ryan McGraw knocked on the door at 124 East Evans Avenue. When the door came open, Victoria broke into tears and threw her arms around him, sobbing, "Oh, darling, I'm so glad you're all right! Our neighbor was here a few minutes ago to tell me that he heard about our defeat at Mobile Point. I was so afraid...so afraid you might have been killed!"

Ryan took hold of her shoulders and eased her back so he could look at her face. There were more bruises, and her left eye was puffy. Scowling, he said, "Another beating?"

Victoria's fingers went to the swollen eye. She nodded silently, tears spilling down her cheeks.

"Tommy?"

"He beat him again, too," she said weakly.

Ryan pushed past her and saw the boy standing in the middle of the parlor floor. The cut on his lower lip had been opened again and was covered with fresh iodine. The whole lip was swollen. There were also purple marks on both cheeks. Ryan dashed to Tommy, took him in his arms, and held him. While the boy sniffled, Ryan turned to Victoria and asked, "Where is he?"

"I don't know for sure. Probably at his favorite saloon, the Rusty Lantern. He got drunk Tuesday night after you brought Tommy home, and has stayed in a half-drunk condition ever since. When he didn't go to the fort on Wednesday, I asked him why. He swore at me and said he was hurting all over from the beating you gave him. He spent all day Thursday at the Rusty Lantern, came home in a stupor, and laid in bed till noon yesterday. When he did get up, he demanded breakfast. I had already fixed Tommy and me some soup for lunch, and I asked him in a nice way if he couldn't just eat some soup. He threw a tantrum and said if I didn't fix him pancakes and bacon, he would beat me up."

"So you refused his demand?"

"No. I fixed him pancakes and bacon. It was when I asked him if he shouldn't get back to the fort that he acted like a madman and started beating on me. Tommy...Tommy tried to stop him, and you see what he did to him. After he worked us over, he stormed out of here. Hasn't been back since."

Ryan put Tommy down, speaking soothing words to him.

Victoria asked, "Tommy, did you finish your breakfast?"

"No, ma'am. When I heard Daddy's voice, I wanted to come and see him."

Patting his head, she said, "Okay, you've seen him. Now go finish your breakfast."

As soon as Tommy was out of the parlor, Victoria pressed close to her ex-husband, clutched him by the arms, and said, "Ryan, I want to divorce Lex. You've got to help me. I'll need protection when I do it."

"Tori," he said, shaking his head, "there's nothing I can do. I'm going to be tied up who knows how long with this impending attack on the city. I—"

"What?"

"I just had a thought. As a Confederate officer, I can put Lex under arrest for beating you and Tommy again. I'll take him to the city jail and have him locked up till the war's over. General Page affirmed that it can be done. With Lex behind bars, you won't be in any danger."

"Wonderful!" Victoria exclaimed, throwing her arms around his neck.

"Tori," he said, reaching back and breaking her hold, "we mustn't be embracing. I'm not your husband anymore."

"But all that can be changed after I divorce Lex," she said, taking hold of his upper arms. "We can be married again."

"No, Tori," Ryan said, shaking his head. "It's no good."

Tightening her grip on him, she looked deep into his eyes and half-whispered, "Darling, it *is* good! It can be us again, just like it used to be. Don't you remember what we once had? Doesn't that mean anything to you?"

Certain words that had just come from Victoria's mouth echoed through Ryan's mind. *Just like it used to be...what we once had.*

That's it! he thought. *That's it!* The mystery of the strange stirring he had been feeling in Victoria's presence was solved! He *was* remembering what they had once had. His subconscious was latching onto what Tori *used to be* when he first met her and fell in love...before she became selfish and self-centered.

Ryan knew then that he had been in love with a *memory*. But that was past and gone forever. Relief washed over him. He was now free to unleash his love for Dixie...the love he had kept bottled up within him.

With this settled, Ryan McGraw's next move was to throw Lex Coffield in jail for the duration of the war. Breaking Victoria's hold on his arms, he said, "I've got to go find your husband."

"But Ryan, you didn't answer me. Doesn't what we had mean anything to you?"

"I have some good memories, yes, but you ran off, divorced me, and married another man, Tori. I can't just erase that out of my mind."

Tommy was chewing his food gingerly because of his split lip as Ryan entered the kitchen. Bending over, he kissed the boy's forehead and said, "I'll see you soon, Son. I love you."

"I love you, too," Tommy said around his food.

"Good-bye," Ryan said to Victoria and headed for the front door.

She followed him, saying, "You won't say you love me, Ryan McGraw, but I know you do. Why won't you say it?"

Ryan did not answer. His temper was white hot. Lex Coffield was going to pay for what he had done to Tommy.

That night, Captain McGraw was in his private tent just outside of Mobile, where the Sharpshooters were bivouacked with Captain Garrison and A Company. By lantern light, he sat down to write a letter to Dixie Quade. Ryan was feeling good. He had found Lex Coffield at the saloon and dragged him off to jail. Mobile's chief constable would keep Coffield confined until further notice.

Ryan was feeling even better about something else. Now he could tell Dixie he loved her with his whole heart. It was no longer divided.

In the letter, he told Dixie that he had sorted it all out, explaining that he had been in love with a memory. The link to the past was now broken. There was no ghost to come between them. He was head-over-heels in love with her, and was asking her here and now to marry him.

When he had finished the letter, Ryan wrote another one. It was addressed to Mrs. Mabel Griffin, General Delivery, Brewton, Alabama. He knew that even though she had remarried, everyone in Brewton knew her. She would get the letter. Wording it carefully, Ryan paid tribute to young Johnny Ray, telling her of the outstanding courage her son had displayed in the face of enemy fire. He had died a true soldier and a hero.

The next morning, Ryan posted the letters with a Confederate courier who was leaving immediately to carry messages for Captain Garrison.

The days passed slowly as the city of Mobile waited for word from army patrols of the enemy's approach. The patrol units were out one at a time, usually staying four or five days.

On August 24, Captain McGraw and his patrol unit of four Sharpshooters came riding in after a five-day tour to learn that General Page had finally surrendered Fort Morgan to the Federals the day before. The general and his remaining men were prisoners of war. Mobile Bay was now in the hands of the Union.

On September 12, word came from General Maury in Montgomery that Confederate intelligence had confirmed a report that General Gordon Granger's Fourth Corps had been whittled down by Rebel forces in battles a hundred miles north. Granger was now waiting for reinforcements before marching for Mobile. Maury cautioned Captains Garrison and McGraw to stay on the alert and keep the patrols out. There was no way to tell when Granger would get his replacements.

On Thursday, September 15, Captain McGraw was sitting in his tent, talking to Judd Rawlings, who had reported for active duty. His shoulder wound was sufficiently healed. Rawlings had also announced to his best friend that he had proposed to Betty Wells, and she had accepted. A wedding date had not been set. The circumstances of the war would affect that.

Ryan was congratulating Judd on the engagement when a shadow crossed the tent opening. Recognizing the regular courier, he stood up and said, "Hello, Wally. Got some mail for me?"

"One letter. It's from Chattanooga."

Ryan's heart pounded. "I'll take it!"

Returning to the bunk where he had been sitting beside his friend, he said, "I sent Dixie a letter better than a month ago, asking her to marry me. This will be my answer."

While Ryan tore the envelope open, Judd said, "As if there's any question that she'll say yes."

Ryan laughed, but his laughter faded as he pulled out the familiar envelope with his own handwriting, addressed to Dixie at the Chattanooga hospital. A small slip of paper was attached.

Seeing the look on Ryan's face, Judd said, "What's wrong?"

"The letter I just told you about..."

"Yeah?"

"It's been returned unopened. There's a note here from an official at the Chattanooga hospital."

Judd observed Ryan's countenance fall as he silently read the note. "Bad news?"

Ryan nodded, without lifting his eyes. When he finished, his face was ashen. "Dixie was serving in a tent hospital near Fort Oglethorpe, Georgia...just south of Chattanooga. On August 14, enemy artillery shelled the tent. Dixie's been wounded, but it's not known for sure what happened to her."

"Oh, no!" gasped Rawlings.

"Goes on to say that the Yankees took about fifty Confederate soldiers as prisoners, leaving our wounded behind. The wounded men said the gallant nurse continued to help them while she, herself, was bleeding. When the Yankees and their prisoners were gone, so was Dixie. They assume she was also taken prisoner."

Ryan lowered his head. Judd stood up, laid a hand on his friend's shoulder, and said, "It'll be okay. I can feel it in my bones. If Dixie was still helping wounded Rebels after she was wounded, it couldn't have been too bad. The Yankees have probably got her somewhere taking care of their wounded."

"Which means she's a prisoner."

"Yeah, but certainly they won't hurt her. They need her."

Ryan was silent for a long moment, then said, "Thanks for the encouragement."

"You're welcome."

The lieutenant stayed with his best friend for a good while, then excused himself, sensing that Ryan wanted to be alone.

Alone, Ryan McGraw battled with the helpless feeling that gripped him. There was no way to find out where Dixie was, or just how seriously she had been wounded. He was also grieved that she had not received his letter. If he never saw her again, she would never know the truth about his divided heart and that she had all of his love. Nor would she know he proposed marriage. Dropping to his knees beside the bunk, he wept and prayed.

The war raged on.

Months passed as scout patrols out of Mobile rode the hills and valleys, watching for Granger and his troops. The army and the citizens of Mobile prepared as best they could for the inevitable. The civilians prepared to evacuate on short notice and the soldiers prepared to fight.

News came to Mobile that the South was slowly but surely being beaten by the North.

In January, word came from Confederate intelligence that General Granger had been engaged in more battles without additional reinforcements. The cold weather had his army holed up some eighty miles northwest of Mobile, and they would not move on Mobile until Granger could muster more men.

During the agonizing wait, Ryan visited Tommy often, having to ward off advances from Victoria. He knew her temperament and dared not antagonize her. She might prevent him from seeing his son. So he avoided her advances, but in a way that made her assume he was preoccupied with the threat of attack on Mobile.

On January 31, word reached Mobile that Savannah had fallen into Federal hands under the leadership of the indomitable General Sherman. Things were looking bad for the Confederacy.

On March 28, Ryan went to the Coffield house to visit his son, and was told by Victoria that she had hired an attorney a few weeks earlier and had just learned that the divorce was granted. She would receive her official divorce papers within a week to ten days.

Victoria was hurt when Ryan did not show excitement about the divorce. She told herself that using Tommy as leverage at just the right time, and stirring Ryan's old longing for her, she would eventually be Mrs. Ryan McGraw once more.

As warm weather came, the people of Mobile waited apprehensively for General Granger and his beefed-up army. News continued to come that the South was losing ground fast. The Yankees were making greater inroads into Southern territory.

Victoria had known that Dixie Quade was gone almost from the time it happened, having learned it from hospital sources. Victoria thought Dixie's absence meant she had a clear shot at winning Ryan back. Although Ryan had not spoken of Dixie to Victoria, she had never left his thoughts. Many a time, in moments of privacy, he had held her picture and prayed for her safety. Someday the bloody war would end. When it did, he would find her.

On the morning of April 6, 1865, Captain McGraw rode out of the army camp with Sergeants Hap Hazzard, Noah Cloud, and John Grove for four days of scout duty. Three hours later, under a cloudy sky that threatened rain, Lieutenant Rawlings was patching a hole in the tent he shared with one of A Company's lieutenants when he looked up to see a familiar figure moving toward him. Dropping his needle and thread, he ran toward her saying, "Dixie! Dixie, how are you?"

She embraced him like she would her brother and said, "I'm fine, Judd."

"But...but we heard you had been wounded."

"I was, but I'm all right, now. Took some shrapnel in my left shoulder."

"I did the same thing in the Mobile Bay battle," he laughed.

Dixie's eyes were roving the area. "Does that make us twins?" she giggled.

"Not exactly. You're too good-looking to be my twin."

Still searching among the soldiers of the camp, Dixie asked, "Is Ryan here?"

"No. He left early this morning on scout patrol. Won't be back until the tenth. That is, unless he sees General Granger coming."

"They told me all about the evacuation plan over at the hospital," she said. "They also told me that Ryan had survived the bay battle and was stationed here."

"Guess you'll just have to wait a few days to see him. What brings you back here? And what happened to you? We heard you had been taken prisoner."

"Well, what brings me back here is that I've been assigned to the Mobile hospital again. I...ah...requested it. I didn't know if Ryan was alive, or even if he was whether he'd be here, but I figured this would be the place to come. I knew somebody here could tell me about him."

"So tell me what happened...I mean your being captured and all."

Dixie explained that she had been taken prisoner by the Yankees after the battle near Fort Oglethorpe and taken to a Federal camp near Dayton, Tennessee. There she was forced to care for wounded Yankees. On March 19, the camp was stormed and captured by Rebels. She returned to the hospital in Chattanooga, asked for the transfer back to Mobile, and it was granted. She had been traveling since then with some news people, who were coming to Mobile, planning to cover the coming attack.

The wind whipped up, and tiny raindrops began to fall. Bending her head against the wind, Dixie said, "Judd...has Ryan spoken of me any?"

Looking up at the falling rain, Judd said, "Step into my tent. Let's get out of this weather." Soldiers all over the camp were scattering for cover as Judd and Dixie moved beneath the canvas shelter.

"Now, to answer your question, young lady—Ryan talks about you constantly. The man is madly in love with you."

Dixie's heart leaped. Then she frowned and asked, "What about Victoria?"

"Oh, he still has to see her in order to see Tommy, but he's not interested in her, Dixie. That's as plain as a black wart on the face of an albino polar bear! It's you he loves. In fact—wait here a minute. I'll be right back."

"Where are you going?"

"To Ryan's tent. He has a private one since he's a hotshot captain. There's something I know he would want me to give to you."

Judd was gone but a moment, and returned with the unopened letter and the note from the hospital in Chattanooga. Pulling the envelope from under his shirt where he had placed it to keep it dry, he said, "Read the name and address on the envelope, then read the note. After you've read the note, open the letter Ryan wrote to you."

Dixie gave Judd a quizzical look, then examined the envelope. When she saw that it was addressed to her, she bit her lower lip and began reading the note from the hospital official. Glancing at Judd, she asked, "Do you know what's in the letter?"

"Sort of, but I never read it, of course. Go on. Read it."

Carefully, Dixie opened the envelope and took out the letter. Angling it toward the open flap to get better light, she read it slowly. By the time she was halfway through it, tears brimmed her eyes. She finished and tears flowed freely as she said with quivering lips, "Oh, Judd, he *does* love me! He *does!* And he wants me to marry him!"

"I know," Judd said with elation. "And I can't wait to see you two in each other's arms."

"I'll be living for that moment. Please...when he comes back, tell him I'll be at the hospital or at my apartment. It's number nineteen. I want to see him as soon as he comes in. Tell him, won't you?"

"Of course," grinned Judd.

Dixie looked outside at the falling rain and said, "I need to be going, Judd. Would you have something I could wrap this envelope in to keep it dry?"

"Sure, I've got a leather pouch over here I use in my saddlebags. You can take it."

Dixie took the pouch from his hand, thanked him, and placed the envelope inside.

As she did so, Judd said, "I've got some good news about Betty and me. We're engaged!"

"Wonderful! I'm so happy for both of you. You make a beautiful couple. Have you set a date?"

"No. The war and all, you know."

"I can't wait to see Betty and tell her how happy I am." Placing the leather pouch under her arm, Dixie said, "Well, I'll be going."

"Don't you want to wait till the rain eases up a bit?"

"No," she chirped happily. "I don't care how wet I get. I'll just sing in the rain all the way home! Good-bye."

"Bye," grinned Rawlings.

Dixie stepped out in he rain and started away, then stopped and turned back. "Judd!" she called, blinking against the rain.

"Yes?"

"I want Ryan to know how things are as soon as possible. Tell him my answer to the marriage proposal is *yes!* And tell him that I love him more than ever!" With that, she was gone.

CHAPTER TWENTY-ONE

O n Saturday, April 8, Lex Coffield was pacing the floor in his cell, cursing Ryan McGraw and cursing Victoria. Rage burned within him, firing the desire to kill them both. His mind was racing, trying to pick up some glimmer of an idea of how to escape and take care of both of them. *McGraw would die first.*

The sound of the cell block's door rattling halted Coffield in his tracks. Turning, he saw the door swing wide and the daytime jailer enter. The jailer, a short, fat man of fifty waddled up to the barred door with an envelope in his hand.

Coffield's dark eyes glanced at the revolver on his hip, then met his gaze and asked, "What's that?"

"Some gorgeous doll just came into the office and asked me to deliver it to you. Since I didn't nose into it, I don't know what it is."

Shoving the envelope through the bars, the fat man grinned and said, "You're in here for wife and child beating, Lex. That doll couldn't have been the wife you beat on, could it? Maybe this is a 'good-bye forever' letter."

Coffield scowled and took the letter. "Shut up!" he snapped. "It's none of your business." Without a word, the jailer grinned wolfishly and left the cell block.

Lex looked at the envelope. It was sealed, but nothing was written on it. Ripping it open, he found two folded sheets of paper. One was official-looking. Reading it first, he learned that Victoria had divorced him on the grounds of his mental and physical torture. His being in jail for that very thing had been enough for Victoria's attorney to convince the judge that a divorce was necessary.

The second sheet was a hastily scribbled note in Victoria's handwriting:

Lex—

The enclosed will document that you and I are no longer married. And I say good-bye and good riddance. I should never have left Ryan for you in the first place. That mistake has been rectified, now. We got married again yesterday.

V.

Coffield crumpled the paper and swore, his breath coming in short spurts. A cruel manifestation of diabolical hatred spread slowly over his face like some shadowy creature coming out of its lair. His pulse pounded in his temples as the thought froze in his mind, *No. Victoria dies first.*

Late afternoon the following day, Sergeant Hap Hazzard galloped into the Confederate camp just outside of Mobile and skidded to a halt in front of Captain Andrew Garrison's tent. Garrison stepped out immediately, and gray-clad men began to gather around.

Sliding from his saddle, Hap said breathlessly, "Captain, our scout patrol met up with a small Rebel unit about thirty miles north of here late this morning. They're on their way to some Confederate camp in southeast Mississippi. They told us they spotted General Granger and his troops about fifty miles due north of where we ran onto them. This was Friday morning, they said, and the Yankees are coming this way."

"They estimate how many?"

"Yes, sir. At least five thousand...maybe more. Most of them are on foot. They're bringing lots of wagons and cannons." There was a buzzing among the soldiers who were pressing close around Hazzard and Garrison.

The captain nodded solemnly and said, "That many men on foot, with the wagons and artillery you describe, can only move in that terrain at the rate of about fifteen miles a day. Since your friends spotted them on Friday morning, they'd be some forty-five miles closer by now. You say Captain McGraw's patrol is thirty miles from here?"

"They were when I left them, sir."

"Okay. That would mean Granger has to be about thirty-five miles from here right now. They'll be in here by sometime Wednesday. That means according to our evacuation plan, the hospital patients who are able to travel and the medical staff chosen to go along with them must pull out of here before sundown. We should have everybody gone by noon on Tuesday."

"Should be plenty of time," Hazzard said. "I assume you're still planning to send them all to Hattiesburg."

"That's right. Hattiesburg is the closest city with a good hospital, since New Orleans is in enemy hands. I hate to have to make those patients ride for ninety miles, but there's no choice. Since we're sending them there, I felt it's best to just send everybody to Hattiesburg."

"Captain McGraw said to tell you that they'd keep an eye on Granger from a distance today, and if there were any significant changes, he'd send another rider in to advise you. He and the patrol will be in here by dawn tomorrow morning."

"Good. We'll pretty well know about Granger's progress by then, and can plan accordingly."

At dawn the next morning, Captain McGraw and his two scouting companions rode into camp. McGraw went immediately to Captain Garrison's tent and made his report. Granger's army was two days away.

As McGraw left Garrison's tent for his own, Hap Hazzard rushed up and said, "Cap'n! Lieutenant Rawlings is in town saying good-bye to Betty. He told me if you rode in to tell you to come to him with all haste. He has something really important to tell you."

"He give you any idea what it's about?"

"Naw. He looks like the cat who swallowed a canary, but he wouldn't tell me nothin'."

McGraw would see what Judd had to tell him, then head for 124 East Evans Avenue. He was eager to see his son. Tommy was an early riser. He would be eating breakfast shortly after sunup.

Trotting his horse into Mobile, Ryan spotted the long line of wagons and soon caught sight of his best friend, standing beside a wagon talking to Betty. The occupants of the wagon were obviously hospital patients.

Judd saw Ryan coming and smiled broadly as he rode up and dismounted. The captain greeted Betty, then said to his friend, "Hap said you had something you were burning up to tell me."

"To say the least. I've got some terrific news. Would you like to sit down before I hit you with it?"

"I can take it standing. Hit me."

Ryan McGraw was stunned by the news that Dixie Quade had returned to Mobile. He was elated to learn that her wound was not serious and to hear the story of her escape from the Yankee prison camp.

Judd was saving the best till last, when Ryan said, "So long, Judd. I'm heading for the hospital. I've got to see Dixie right now!"

"She isn't there. She left last night for Hattiesburg with several patients, other nurses, and a couple of doctors. I assume you know about the order of evacuation."

"Yes. Captain Garrison told me. Tommy and Victoria don't leave until this afternoon." Frowning, Ryan said, "Oh, I wish I hadn't missed Dixie."

Betty spoke up. "I was supposed to stay here myself, Ryan, but the doctors decided these patients could make the trip to Hattiesburg after all. So I'm going along to care for them."

Judd was about to explode. "I have something else to tell you."

"Okay. Shoot."

"Dixie requested to be assigned back here because she wanted to find you."

"Really?"

"Mm-hmm. You...ah...you know that letter you sent to her that came back? I took the liberty of giving it to her. Hope you don't mind."

"You did? No—no I don't mind. How did she react when she read it?"

"Cried like a baby. She thought she'd be here when you returned, so she asked me to send you to her the minute you rode in. Said she wanted you to know her reaction right away. I was supposed to tell you, and I quote: *Tell him my answer to the marriage proposal is yes! And tell him that I love him more than ever!'* She repeated it last night just before she left, and told me to tell you she's sorry she couldn't be here when you got back. She tried to be one of the nurses who will be staying here, but the hospital officials insisted she go to Hattiesburg."

Ryan's heart was pounding his ribs. Suddenly it hit him. *Hattiesburg!* Dixie had been sent to his home town! The wagon train was about to pull out. Turning to Betty, he said, "You'll be seeing Dixie as soon as you get to Hattiesburg, right?"

"Yes."

"Tell her...tell her that I meant every word in that letter, and I'll do my best to come to Hattiesburg when this battle is over. Tell her to go to my parents' house and stay with them. Mr. and Mrs. Thomas McGraw. Everybody in town knows them. They can direct her to their house. It's just outside of town on the southwest side on top of a hill. It's white with two stories, and a huge porch that runs the length and breadth of the house. There are honeysuckle bushes all along the porch, and there are four big oak trees in the front yard. Got it?"

"Got it."

"Okay. Tell her to tell my parents our story and show them the letter...and that I asked that they take her in and let her live with them. She's also to let them know about Tommy. Since Victoria and Tommy will be going to Hattiesburg also, they'll get to meet him."

"Will do," smiled Betty.

Ryan thanked her, then said, "I know you two need to kiss good-bye or something, so I'll be on my way. Got to go see my boy."

The eastern sky was pink, but the sun had not yet put in an appearance when Victoria Coffield descended the stairs and headed for the kitchen. She would get breakfast going. Tommy was dressing himself in his room.

As she entered the kitchen, Victoria's heart lurched in her breast and a gasp escaped her mouth. Lex was sitting at the table with a revolver lying near his hand. His eyes glittered and she saw madness there. A venomous smile parted his lips as he said gratingly, "I had to strangle the jailer to come to you, Mrs. McGraw. But here I am."

Horror crawled up Victoria's spine and over her head, tingling her scalp. Thinking fast, she said shakily, "Ryan's upstairs, Lex. You'd better leave right now. If he finds you here, he'll tear you apart." Turning her head toward the kitchen door, she shouted, "Ryan! Lex is here! He escaped from jail and he's got a gun!"

"Won't work," Coffield said coolly. "I already looked in on you while you were asleep. He isn't here."

Eyes bulging, Victoria gusted, "I want you out of this house right now, Lex!"

"Well, you haven't always gotten everything you want, have you, dear?"

Victoria knew Lex Coffield could be a dangerous man, but she had never seen him like this. She knew he was there to kill her. He would kill Tommy, too. Her heart thundered, shaking her whole body. "Lex," she warned, mouth suddenly dry, "if you harm me, Ryan will kill you!"

The madman laughed. "This is your day to die, sweet Victoria. And after I've killed you, I'm gonna kill your new...or should I say your *old* husband."

Lex's hand was not touching the gun. In desperation, Victoria lunged for it with both hands. Her sudden move took Lex by surprise. She had a firm hold on it before he could stop her. He quickly closed his hands on her wrists and began twisting them to make her let go. His superior strength won out. Victoria yelped as the gun was jerked from her hands.

At the same instant, Lex was aware of sharp pain in his right thigh. Tommy, missing one shoe, was biting into flesh as hard as he could. Lex swore and swung the barrel of the revolver against the child's head. Steel met flesh and Tommy collapsed on the floor.

Victoria was on Lex like a mother cat, clawing and screaming at him. The angry man slammed her jaw with an elbow, then followed with a fist to her stomach. Victoria doubled over and fell to her knees. Lex eared back the hammer of the revolver, aimed at Victoria's head, and squeezed the trigger.

Trotting his horse, Ryan McGraw rounded the corner onto Evans Avenue, wondering where the shot had come from. It was a handgun and sounded as though it had to have come from inside a building.

Suddenly he saw an elderly man leave the house next door to Coffield's and dash toward the front porch. Digging heels into the horse's flanks, he sped into the yard just as Clarence Wiley pushed open the door. On his heels, Ryan bolted inside and caught up to the old man before he reached the kitchen. Charging past Wiley, he entered the room first.

Victoria's lifeless form caught Ryan's attention a split second before he saw Tommy lying a few feet away. Another quick glance at Victoria showed him the bullet hole an inch inside her hairline and the tiny trickle of blood that moistened her forehead. There was no question that Victoria was dead.

Clarence was saying something that was not registering in Ryan's ears as he moved to Tommy. When he found the boy breathing, he whispered a prayer of relief and examined the gash on his temple. It had only been a glancing blow and had not damaged his skull, but it was bleeding heavily. Tommy was beginning to stir.

"...her husband, Captain!" the old man's words finally penetrated.

"What did you say?"

"I said it was her husband! Lex! I heard the shot and came out of my house. I saw him charge out of the back of the house with a gun in his hand, and run down the alley!"

Ryan headed for the back door, saying, "See if you can stop the bleeding. I'm going after him. Which way did he go?"

"West."

Ryan dashed to the alley and looked westward just in time to see Lex Coffield cut into a back yard a block away, heading in the direction of Evans Avenue.

Wheeling, he ran to the front yard, leaped on his horse, and put it to an instant gallop. Up ahead, he saw Coffield plunge toward the street from between two houses, then skid to a halt and look at him. When Lex realized the galloping horseman was Ryan McGraw, he pivoted and disappeared quickly in the direction he had come from.

McGraw drove his horse between the houses and saw a man standing next to his back porch. Pulling rein, he asked, "You see a man go through here?"

"Yes. Is there trouble, Captain?"

"He just murdered a woman. Where'd he go?"

Pointing, he replied, "Across the alley. Into my neighbor's b—"

The hayloft door of the neighbor's barn came open and a shot was fired, barely missing McGraw, who dived from the saddle. The bullet chewed into the man's back porch. He yelped and flattened himself on the ground.

McGraw had his revolver out and was crouching low as Lex Coffield's face appeared at the loft door again behind a menacing weapon. A split second before the gun discharged, Ryan hit the ground, rolling. The slug hissed and struck earth where Ryan had just been.

From his prone position, the leader of the Sharpshooters took aim and waited for Coffield to show his face for another shot. His wait was brief. Victoria's killer had to see if he had hit McGraw. Using both hands to steady his gun, Ryan squeezed the trigger.

The slug plowed into Coffield's forehead. The revolver sailed earthward first, followed by Coffield's body.

At one o'clock that afternoon, Captain McGraw carried his son out of the Mobile hospital toward the line of wagons. The last of the civilians were about to depart for Hattiesburg. There was a bandage on Tommy's head.

Approaching the Clarence Wiley wagon, Ryan smiled at the elderly couple and said, "I sure appreciate this, folks."

"Glad to do it, Captain," smiled Clarence.

"We'll take good care of him," Myrtle Wiley said.

Looking into the boy's pale-blues, Ryan said, "Tommy, when Mr. and Mrs. Wiley take you to Grandma and Grandpa McGraw's house, you tell them I'll be along shortly, okay?"

Hugging his father's neck, the boy said, "I want you to come with me, now."

"I can't, Son. I've already explained it to you. I need you to be a big boy for me."

"I miss Mommy."

A lump rose in Ryan's throat. "I know," he said, squeezing Tommy hard. "You're so young to try to understand. Remember I told you a little while ago that when God lets someone be taken from us, He has a very good purpose, even though we don't always know what it is?"

"Yes."

"And remember...God loves little boys like you. He loves Tommy McGraw so much that He is going to give him someone else to love and take care of him. Right?"

"Yes."

"And who is that someone?"

"Miss Dixie."

"Right. You like her, don't you?"

"Yes. She's nice. And she likes me, too."

"That's right, Son. When you see her, be sure to tell her you like her, won't you?"

"Okay."

"Okay. Give Dad a big hug, now. It's time for you to go."

Ryan McGraw wiped tears as the line of wagons rolled out of Mobile. When the Wiley wagon passed from view, he took a deep breath and turned away, breathing a prayer of thanks that Dixie and Tommy would be waiting for him together in Hattiesburg. "Of course, Lord," he said audibly, "it's up to You whether I ever get to go to them or not."

CHAPTER TWENTY-TWO

The sun had been up about an hour on Wednesday, April 12, 1865, when the little band of less than four hundred Confederate soldiers and about a hundred and sixty townsmen looked northward over their crude handmade barricades and saw the Yankees appear in the distant grassy fields, moving like a swarm of ants.

Captain Ryan McGraw hunched behind an old wagon that had been flipped on its side. On his left was Lieutenant Judd Rawlings, and to his right were Sergeants Noah Cloud and Hap Hazzard. The rest of the Sharpshooters were scattered among A Company and the handful of civilians who had stayed for the fight.

Hazzard eyed the blue uniforms lining up two hundred yards in the distance and said, "Fellas, this is gonna be a tough one."

"Yeah," nodded Cloud, noting the cannons that were being set in place in the woods off to the east.

McGraw looked along the line of Rebels and focused on Captain Andrew Garrison. The captain raised a fist and shook it, indicating that he was ready to fight. McGraw gave him the same signal, then turned back to watch the enemy getting ready to attack.

Ryan thought of Tommy for a moment. He hoped the boy would not have to grow up and fight in a war.

As Ryan beheld the number of blue uniforms, he told himself it would take nothing short of a miracle to bring him through this battle. They were outnumbered more than ten to one...and they didn't have any artillery. His mind went to Dixie. It was the war that had brought them together...for a short time. Now it was the war that was going to tear them apart...forever.

Judd was having the same thoughts about Betty Wells.

Noah laughed hollowly, slapped his friend on the back, and said, "Sure wish we had time for one more good fistfight."

"Yeah, me too," chuckled Hap. "I've never told you this, ol' pal, but all these years I've just been playin' with you. If I'd wanted to, I could've whipped you till you could never fight again."

"Hah! It's the other way around, fella! I could've—"

"That's enough, men," cut in McGraw. "Here they come."

The Yankees were coming in a steady march, spread across the field in a phalanx, shoulder-to-shoulder. It appeared that the cannons were going to hold off firing until they were really needed. Their crews stood idly beside them and watched.

Captain Garrison stood behind the line and shouted, "When I give the signal, fire away, men!"

Every man in the line had his rifle ready. The enemy drew closer and closer. When they were within forty yards, Garrison cried, "Fire!"

The barrage unleashed by the Rebels took its toll. The front line of Yankees began to fall like flies. Abruptly, the swarm of soldiers fired back. Bullets hissed and whined, men shouted, and the battle was under way.

So gallantly fought the Rebels that the Yankees found it impossible to close in for hand-to-hand fighting. Though men behind the crude barricades were falling, they were taking a greater toll on the men in the field. After more than an hour of being held in check, General Gordon Granger gave the order for the cannons to open up.

McGraw had a bullet burn on his right cheek and a nick on his left shoulder. Rawlings was untouched. Hazzard was down with a bullet in his right leg, and Cloud had been creased in his left side, but was still firing.

When McGraw saw the cannon crews making ready to fire, he shouted along the line, "Cannons! Stay as low as you can!"

Captain Garrison looked around at the wounded and dead men and made a dash for McGraw. Hunkering next to him, he said above the din, "Captain, those cannons will finish us off. In my estimation, it's time to surrender. I hate to do it, but it's suicide for the rest of us if we don't."

Surrender went against McGraw's grain, but he nodded and said, "You're right, Captain. I hate the thought of a Yankee prison camp for the duration of the war, but the way it's been going the past few months, the end may not be too far off."

"I think you're right. We'll run up the white flag."

Garrison hoisted a large white cloth on the end of a long stick and waved it so General Granger could see it. "Stop firing, men!" Garrison shouted to the men on the line.

Almost simultaneously, Rebels and Yankees ceased firing.

General Granger rode in on horseback with six officers and dismounted. Under the watchful eyes of the Rebels along the line, Captains Garrison and McGraw stepped over the barricades and walked to meet him. When they both saluted, Granger saluted in return.

"Sir," said Garrison, "as the white flag indicates, we are surrendering."

A Confederate flag was flying on a mast at the end of the homemade barricade. Granger nodded, pointed to it, and said, "Please have your men haul down the flag."

The Rebels wiped tears and saluted as their flag was lowered by two of Garrison's men. Their hearts went cold as immediately a Union flag went up in its place.

A soft breeze blew across the fields and through the empty city of Mobile as General Granger said to the Confederate officers, "Gentlemen, you are now prisoners of war. In the name of the United States of America, I claim Mobile, Alabama, as Union territory. Before we take you and your men to our nearest prison camp, there is something I want to say."

Garrison and McGraw were standing at attention. "Yes, sir," they replied.

Granger lifted his hat from his head and said with emotion, "To you and your gallant men, I take off my hat. I have never seen soldiers or civilians anywhere who have fought with as much courage, valor, and determination as you have today. You are to be commended."

"General Granger," came the shout of one of the Union officers.

The general turned to see the officer pointing to a lone rider who was riding hard on a lathered horse across the field from the northeast. The rider was shouting and waving his hat. When he thundered to a halt, his blue uniform was flecked with foam.

Granger moved to him as he was dismounting and said, "What is it, Corporal?"

Breathing hard, the Yankee corporal said, "Sir, I've just come from our camp forty miles northeast of here. We got word this morning that General Robert E. Lee surrendered to General Grant at Appomattox Court House this past Sunday afternoon! The war has been over for three days!"

On April 18, 1865, the Mississippi sun was shining brightly in an azure sky as Captain Ryan McGraw and Lieutenant Judd Rawlings rode onto the hospital grounds in Hattiesburg. Betty Wells happened to be on the lawn in the shade of a large cypress tree, sitting on a bench. Next to her was an elderly person in a wheelchair.

When Betty saw the two riders approaching, she jumped to her feet and said something to the patient. She then moved into the sunlight and met the man she loved as he dismounted.

While Judd and Betty held each other, Ryan left his saddle and waited for them to finish their greeting. When they parted, Betty went to Ryan and gave him a fond embrace, saying she was glad both of them had lived through the awful battle. The news of the war's end had reached Hattiesburg on April 13.

Anticipation danced in McGraw's pale blue eyes as he asked, "Where can I find her, Betty?"

Smiling as she held Judd's hand, she said, "Dixie's on the night shift this week. Right now you'll find her at the big white house on the hill."

"Okay," he grinned. He paused a few seconds, then said, "I assume she and my parents have taken to each other all right."

"Oh, have they ever! They adore each other. Your mother can talk about nothing but the wedding, and your father keeps hugging Dixie and telling her how happy he is that she is going to be his daughter-in-law."

Betty anticipated Ryan's next question, and before he could ask it, she said, "And Tommy! Your parents say you and Dixie can't have him. Tommy has to stay and live with them!"

"Oh, no he doesn't!" Ryan laughed.

"I've been out to the house four times now, and it's so sweet to see Tommy and his grandfather together. Your dad thinks it's wonderful that Tommy was named after him. The two are inseparable."

Running her eyes between the two officers, Betty said, "How...how did it go in the battle with the Sharpshooters?"

Ryan replied sadly, "We lost some. A few were wounded and are in the Mobile hospital."

"How about...how about Hap and Noah?"

"They're among the wounded, but they'll be okay. In fact—" Ryan laughed—"they're in the same room, and when Judd and I left, they were arguing and building up to a fight."

"Well, at least if they hurt each other, they'll have medical help close by!"

The three friends laughed together, then Ryan excused himself, saying he needed to get going.

As he mounted up, Judd said, "Hey, how about a double wedding?"

Ryan smiled down at him. "If the girls like the idea, it's a deal!"

The happy couple waved as they watched Ryan ride away.

Birds were singing in the trees and squirrels were chattering as Captain Ryan McGraw emerged from the dense Mississippi forest, drew rein, and lifted his gaze up the long, green slope to the big white house on the hill. Standing a hundred and fifty yards away like a royal castle, it looked mighty good to the boy who had grown up there.

He nudged his horse forward at a slow walk. Within a couple of minutes, he could make out four people sitting in the yard in front of the long porch, enjoying the shade of the huge oak trees. Two of them had silver hair. There was a small boy sitting on the lap of his grandfather, and a beautiful young woman with hair like spun gold was laughing at something that had been said.

Ryan's heart drummed his ribs. He put the horse to a trot.

Seconds later, the elderly man pointed down the hill and stood up with the boy in his arms. The women rose to their feet, and the younger one started running down the hill amid the wild flowers that grew in the grass.

When Ryan was within fifty yards of Dixie, he slid from the saddle and ran toward her. Tears streamed down Dixie's face as she opened her arms. As the distance between them narrowed, the grass and flowers disappeared, the surrounding forest vanished, and they were floating in a remote and wonderful paradise on heavenly clouds. Far away and forgotten was the world of war and bloodshed and loneliness.

With outstretched arms, they reached for each other...and toward a future, bright with the promise of happiness, contentment, and unending love.

EPILOGUE

✦

The Battle of Mobile Bay was Admiral David G. Farragut's greatest victory, but it was bought at great cost. Union casualties were 319, including 145 men killed. The sinking of the *Tecumseh* and the destruction of several battleships and gunboats was the greatest single U.S. Navy disaster until World War II.

The fall of Fort Morgan had a crippling effect on the South. The Confederates were thrown back on their already overstrained and inadequate resources, and the resulting shortages weakened their strength of resistance. Coupled with other devastating losses all over Dixie, General Ulysses S. Grant's forces drummed the South's battered, hungry army into surrender.

As for the city of Mobile, her men fought gallantly alongside the courageous Confederate troops to the bitter end. The Yankee assault on Mobile cost the Union 1,417 casualties—dead and wounded combined—and caused General Grant to lament, "I had tried for more than two years to get an expedition sent against Mobile when its possession by us would have been of great advantage. We waited too long. It cost many lives to take it, but when its ultimate possession came three days after the war was over, it was of no importance."

A PROMISE UNBROKEN

✦

If you've enjoyed the love story of Ryan McGraw and Dixie Quade, you'll also want to read **A Promise Unbroken**, *the story of young lovers fighting jealousy and racial hatred in war-torn Virginia. The following excerpt from* **A Promise Unbroken** *begins as the valiant Web Steele attempts to diffuse a slave uprising on a neighboring plantation.*

Web Steeele whipped his head around as the flat report of the shot carried to him through the cool mid-October air. Jerking hard on the reins, he drew horse and buggy to a halt in the middle of the road. While the breeze carried the small dust cloud away, he peered past the imposing archway on his left that housed the gate to the Jason Hart plantation.

Another shot rang out, and Web felt a vast hollow in his stomach. Instinct told him that what he had been expecting to happen on both the Ruffin and Hart plantations was now in progress directly ahead of him. The gate beneath the archway was open. Snapping the reins, he sent the horse galloping under the archway, following the narrow, winding road.

The mansion was a quarter-mile from the road. As the buggy bounded into the spacious yard, another shot reverberated through the air, the sharp sound coming from the rear. Guiding the horse along the path to the backside of the house, Steele saw Jonas Hart and his two sons hunkered behind an overturned wagon, facing the tool and wood shed, which was close to the barn, about forty yards from the rear of the mansion. There were splintered places on the wagon where bullets had chewed wood.

Drawing the buggy to a sudden stop, Steele saw Mabel Hart, her oldest daughter, Mary Ann, and daughter-in-law, Chloe, collected on the back porch of the mansion with the butler and the maid. All were wide-eyed with fear.

As Web Steele jumped out of the buggy, he saw that Jonas was holding a revolver with one hand and a bleeding shoulder with the other. Sons David, twenty-two, and Daniel, twenty-one, were not armed. A group of slaves could be seen at the edge of a clearing some fifty yards further back, where their small cabins huddled in a circle. They too looked frightened.

Steele knew his instincts were correct. Hart had a slave revolt on his hands. Some of them were holed up in the tool and wood shed, and were armed. The absence of Hart's sixteen-year-old daughter and fourteen-year-old son might mean they were being held hostage.

Jonas Hart shouted, "Web, take cover! We've got real trouble here!"

Steele took one look at the open window next to the shed's only door and saw the barrel of a revolver glint in the sunlight. He dashed to where Jonas and his sons were clustered behind the overturned wagon. "Please tell me that Darrel and Melissa aren't in there!"

Jonas's voice was tight as he replied, "They're in the shed, all right, Web."

"How many slaves in there?" Web asked.

"Two."

"Do I know them?"

"Yeah. Dexter and Orman."

Eyeing the blood that was running between Jonas's fingers as he gripped his shoulder, Web said, "You'd better get to the house and let Mabel tend to that wound."

"Naw," growled the plantation owner, "it's only a scratch. It'll be all right. Main thing right now is to bring this situation to an end."

Looking back toward the shed, Steele said, "Dexter and Orman, eh? What do they want?"

Gritting his teeth in pain, Jonas replied, "To go free. They say if we'll let them go, they'll release the kids when they're a safe distance from here."

"What brought this on?"

"Nothing special, they just—"

"Tell him the truth, Pa," butted in David, who was slave overseer for his father. "I've been warning you this was going to happen."

"Shut up!" snapped Jonas. "If you'd be a little more stern with these lazy whelps, it wouldn't make me look so mean when I have to discipline them."

David Hart had been developing a distaste for slavery for the past two years. He and his father had had many heated discussions about it. Jonas accused him of becoming an "abolitionist Yankee" in his heart.

Before David could respond, a voice came from within the shed. "We's gettin' tired of waitin', Massa Jonas! We want those horses, and we want 'em right now!"

Web Steele recognized the voice of Dexter, whom he had known for several years. In a half-whisper, he said, "Jonas, Dexter knows me well. So does Orman. Do you think it would help if I talk to them?"

"Couldn't hurt, that's for sure," spoke up Daniel. "Both of them like you."

"What about it, Jonas?" pressed Steele.

"Go ahead. Talk to them. Like Dan said, it can't hurt for you to try."

"Massa Jonas!" bellowed Orman. "We saw Massa Web come in. Yo' can do yo' talkin' later. We want those horses, or we's gonna be forced to hurt dese chillin o' yo's!"

Jonas's anger broke. "You harm my kids and you'll wish you'd never been born, Orman!"

There was no response from the shed. Setting his gaze on Steele, Jonas said, "Well, do your talking."

"First I have to know what David meant when he told you to be truthful with me."

"Aw, I just found it necessary to give them both a good belt-whipping, that's all. They've been getting lazier by the day. David won't chastise them, so they just get continually worse."

"Pa, you expect too much of them," said David. "Their bodies get tired like ours do. If you'd only ease up on the load—"

Jonas swore, cutting off his elder son. "Young and strong as they are, they oughtta be able to do a whole lot more than they've been doing! There are other slaves on this place who put out more work."

"Yes, and there are other slaves who'll be doing this same thing shortly, too," responded David.

"Not if I make an example of these two," Jonas growled, sending a heated glance in the direction of the shed.

At that moment drumming hoof beats were heard in the direction of the road, and seconds later two riders came thundering around the corner of the mansion. The Hart men and Web Steele recognized Reed Exley, slave overseer of the neighboring John Ruffin plantation, and one of the Ruffin slaves, a handsome young man named Mandrake.

David Hart mumbled, "The last person we need here right now is Exley."

Web agreed. As with most people in the Richmond area, he harbored a deep dislike for Exley, who was married to wealthy John Ruffin's oldest daughter, Elizabeth. Web was engaged to Ruffin's next-oldest daughter, Abby. While courting her for the past year-and-a-half, he had gotten to know Exley quite well...much to his sorrow.

It was Exley's job to oversee the slaves and to handle the buying and selling of them. Web, who had the same job on his father's plantation, was kind and compassionate with his slaves. His observation of Exley's merciless, inhuman handling of the Ruffin slaves had led him to discuss it on one occasion with Abby's widower father, but it had done no good. John Ruffin had a blind spot when it came to his son-in-law, and because Exley had never abused the slaves before his eyes, he refused to believe it ever happened. Even when Abby and her younger sister, Lynne, told their father of seeing Exley mistreat the slaves, he would not believe it.

Daniel Hart, who was courting Lynne Ruffin, also disliked Reed Exley. When he saw Exley and Mandrake ride up, he noticed that Exley was wearing a sidearm.

"Better get your head down, Reed!" called Jonas. "We've got a couple of slaves with their noses out of joint, and they've been doing some shooting."

Exley and Mandrake ran in and hunkered down. "Yeah, I heard it," said Reed. "I decided to come and see if I could help." As he spoke, he drew his gun, then looked at Jonas's bleeding shoulder. "You shot bad?"

"No. Mabel can fix me up once this is over."

"So what's going on?" queried Exley.

Jonas gave Exley a brief explanation, naming the two black men who were holding his daughter and son hostage.

Looking around at the others, Exley saw that the only weapon in the bunch was the revolver in Jonas's hand. "Well, why don't we get some more guns and rush 'em?"

"Web's about to try talking them out," said Jonas.

Exley gave Web a cold stare. *"Talk?"* he spat incredulously. "These beasts don't understand talk!" Then to Jonas, "They both have guns?"

"Yes."

"Where'd they get 'em?"

"I have no idea."

"Well, I say let's lay our hands on some more guns and rush 'em."

"That's a good way to get Darrel and Melissa killed," Web said. "Dexter and Orman are desperate. Put your gun away, Reed, and let me handle this."

Suddenly a shot was heard inside the shed. Melissa Hart

screamed. A harsh voice blared, "Nobody's hurt, Massa Jonas! I jus' shot through the roof! But Orman and I are tired of waitin' for you to let us go. We want those horses now! If'n we don't get 'em, somebody in dis shed is goin' to get hurt...an' it ain't me or Orman!"

"Jonas, you gonna do somethin'?" asked Reed Exley. "Or you just gonna sit here and let them animals kill your kids?"

Jonas licked his lips. "I've got to let Web see if he can talk them out. They like Web. Maybe he can do something with them."

"I doubt it," snarled Exley, "but so he talks 'em into lettin' your kids loose and throwin' their guns out. What you gonna do then?"

"I don't know," said Jonas. "Let's just cross one bridge at a time here. Most important thing is to get Melissa and Darrel out of there."

"Well, they oughtta be hanged or shot through the head in front of the rest of your slaves," grunted Exley. "If you don't make an example of 'em, the next time you whip one, you'll go through this kind of nonsense again."

"Dexter!" called Steele, unwilling to stretch the ordeal out any longer. "Can we talk?"

"We's listenin'."

Web Steele left his crouch and stood to his full height, exposing his empty hands. As Web was about to speak, Mabel Hart's high-pitched voice could be heard from the back porch of the mansion. "Jonas! Do something! They'll kill our children!"

"We are!" Jonas shouted back. "Just stay calm!"

"Dexter!" called Steele.

"Yassuh?"

"There is nothing to gain by doing harm to Melissa and Darrel. Let them come out, and we'll talk."

"Cain't do that, Massa Web! If'n we let the kids go, Massa Jonas will beat us again! 'Specially now that we done shot 'im. We ain't gonna have no mo' of those beatin's! We ain't lazy like he say. We works hard. But we cain't keep up the kind o' workin' he's puttin' on us."

"Dat's right, Massa Web!" came Orman's voice. "We knows about yo' slaves. Ain't none o' them gets treated like us."

"Well, I'm sure if you'll let Mr. Hart's children loose, he'll not beat you. His wound is not serious. I'm sure he'll not punish you for it, and will be more tolerant from now on."

"We wants to hear *him* say dat!" shouted Orman.

Steele looked down at Jonas Hart. "Well?"

Jonas's face flushed and his eyes had fire in them. "Web, I can't tell those two I'll be more tolerant! You can't expect me to just overlook this and tell them all is forgiven!"

"I think you're going to have to if you don't want to get those kids hurt...or killed," replied Steele.

"What's the matter with tellin' 'em everything's all right so they'll let the kids go...then blast 'em when they show their faces?" suggested Exley.

Web scowled at him. "You fool, Reed! There are more than thirty men in that crowd of slaves standing out there watching us. If we shoot Dexter and Orman, they just might decide to swarm in here and tear us apart."

"We got two guns," parried Exley.

"And how many bullets will you have after blasting Dexter and Orman?" clipped Steele. "Even if you could cut a few of them down, what about the rest? There'd still be enough of them to tear us limb from limb. You're not using your head, Reed."

Reed's temper flared. "They ain't gonna do no such thing! Even if they started for us, when they saw some of their black pals drop, they'd back off."

Turning to the slave beside Exley, Steele asked, "What about it, Mandrake? Would they back off?"

Mandrake cleared his throat nervously. "Well, Massa Web, I cain't say fo' sure. If they's thinkin' straight, they'd prob'ly not come rushin' into a couple of blazin' guns. But seein' two of their own shot down after they had been tol' they was forgiven just might make 'em crazy-blind mad. If'n that was to happen, wouldn't be a white person left alive on this place."

Exley was livid. "Mandrake, you keep outta this! I don't want to hear another word outta you! You got that?"

Mandrake flicked a fearful glance at Steele, who glared at Exley and snapped, "I asked for his opinion, Reed! You had no right to jump him. Why do you have to be such an idiot?"

Reed's teeth clamped together as he hissed, "I resent bein' called an idiot!"

"Then quit acting like one."

Steele looked down at Jonas and said, "Are you going to tell Dexter and Orman they're forgiven, and that you'll be more tolerant from now on?"

"Better do it, Pa," put in David. "Something's going to happen in that shed pretty soon if you don't."

Jonas pulled the bloody hand away from his wound and saw that the bleeding had stopped. Taking off his hat and throwing it angrily on the ground, he said in a hoarse half-whisper, "I can't let those two get away with this! If I do, others will be encouraged to rebel. I'll do anything to get Darrel and Melissa out of there safely, but after that, there has to be severe punishment."

"More beatings?" asked Steele.

"Yes! More beatings! They're not going to get away with this!"

"Pa," said David, "if you hadn't beaten them in the first place, we wouldn't be having this problem now. If you make it sound like everything is forgiven just to free Darrel and Melissa, then whip Dexter and Orman, that will really incite a rebellion. The best thing is for you to stand up right now and talk to them. Admit that you've been working them too hard, and that you were wrong to belt-whip them. You take any other course, and there'll be disaster."

Mabel's high-pitched voice pierced the air. "Jonas! What are you doing? Why are you taking so long?"

"I'm working on it!" Jonas shouted toward the house.

"I say we rush 'em," interjected Reed. "Those black dogs deserve to die."

"You're talking like an idiot again, Reed!" growled Steele. "You couldn't rush them fast enough to save those kids' lives."

"We'll do it *my* way," said Jonas. "I'll tell them they're forgiven. When Darrel and Melissa are safe and those beasts have thrown down their guns, we'll tie them to a tree and put the fear of God into them."

"Then I want no part in this," said Web, turning to walk away. He froze when another gunshot came from the shed.

Melissa's scream curdled the air and Mabel darted off the porch toward the shed, emitting a wordless wail. Darrel's voice was heard above his sister's scream, calling for his father to help them. Web intercepted Mabel and guided her toward her husband and older sons hunkered behind the wagon.

Dexter's desperate voice rang out from inside the shed, "Time's up! We want those horses right now!"

Jonas's ragged emotions flooded to the surface. "Dexter," he bawled, "I want my children out of there this instant!"

"No!" came the defiant reply. "You give us the horses, and like we already tol' you, we'll let Darrel and Melissa go when we think we're far enough away!"

"You'd never get far enough away!" boomed Hart. "You can't pull this kind of stuff on me and get away with it! You're not getting any horses! Now give it up! Let those kids out of there!"

"No! They're gonna get hurt if you don' do as we say!"

David looked his father in the eye and said heatedly, "Pa, your pride is going to get Darrel and Melissa killed! Dexter and Orman trust Web. Why don't you just tell them you'll set them free right now, and let them ride out of here in Web's buggy with him? After this episode, they'll never be worth their salt around here any more. Let them go. We can get along without them."

"I paid good money for those two, David!" snapped Jonas. "They're not getting out of here! They're going to get what's coming to them!"

"I still say we rush 'em!" blurted Reed.

Ignoring Exley, Jonas looked toward the open window of the shed and bellowed, "Dexter! Orman! If you harm a hair of either one of my kids, you'll die! I'll kill you myself...*personally!*"

"We'd rather die than have to live like we've been livin'!" came Dexter's reply. "We've talked it over, Massa Jonas. If'n you don't let us ride out of here with Darrel and Melissa like we tol' you, den yo' gonna have to come in after us. We'll die, but so will yo' chillun'!"

Mandrake glanced cautiously toward Reed, then said to Hart, "Massa Jonas, they means what they's sayin'. B'lieve me. They is desperate, and they's gonna do what they's sayin' if'n yo' don't let 'em go."

Reed Exley cursed and slapped Mandrake's face. "You shut up!" he blared. "I said I didn't want to hear another word outta you!"

Mandrake's head whipped sideways from the blow. He took a step back, placing a hand to his smarting cheek.

Web wanted to knock Exley rolling, but the situation at the shed was about to explode. He could tell by the stubborn set to Jonas's jaw that the man was not going to give in. Mabel was whimpering, trembling with fear, and appeared on the verge of collapse. Glancing at the slaves gathered by the cabins, Web saw them watching intently and talking among themselves. Something had to be done, and it had to be done quickly.

Turning to Hart, he said, "Jonas, will you sell Dexter and Orman to me? Right now?"

"*What?* Why would you want to buy black devils like them?"

"David's right. After what's happened here today, neither of them will be worth their salt around this place any more. I know Dexter's not married, and I assume Orman isn't either."

"Right."

"I'll give you a thousand apiece. "

"A thousand?" Jonas gasped. "Web, you know those two will bring a good eighteen hundred apiece at an auction."

"This isn't an auction, and you've got the lives of a son and daughter at stake. Time's running out. Just agree and I'll take them off your hands this minute. I'll be back with a check to cover payment within an hour."

Jonas rubbed his chin, pondering the offer.

David spoke up. "Pa, what are you waiting for? Tell the man he's got a deal!"

Jonas threw a scornful look at his oldest son, then said to Steele, "All right, Web. They're yours for a thousand apiece. Take them and get them out of my sight."

Mabel sobbed a sigh of relief.

"Dexter! Orman!" called Steele.

"Yassuh?"

"Do you trust me?"

"We does," said Dexter.

"Then you'll believe me when I tell you I've just made a deal with Jonas. He's going to sell both of you to me right here and now."

"He is? You mean we can ride outta here with you and be yo' slaves from now on?"

"That's right. I can't give him a check to pay for you until I get back home. He'll have to draw up the papers while I'm gone, and we'll close the deal later this afternoon. But you will have to conduct yourselves from this moment on as if you are my slaves. Do you understand?"

"Yassuh!" replied Dexter.

"Suits me jus' fine!" came Orman's lilting voice.

"All right. Now, how many guns do you have in there?"

"Two, Massa Web."

"You wouldn't lie to me?"

"No, suh!"

"All right, throw them both out the window."

There was a brief pause, then the two revolvers sailed out the open window.

"Oh, God bless you, Web!" Mabel said with a quaking voice.

Steele gave her a compassionate smile, then called toward the shed, "Fine! Now, open the door and let Darrel and Melissa come out."

The shed door swung open, and neither slave could be seen as first Melissa then her younger brother emerged. Sobbing, Mabel ran toward them and Jonas followed. Daniel was next, with David and Chloe behind him. Mary Ann had left the porch and was close by. She quickly joined the group.

Exley breathed a curse and mumbled something under his breath. Mandrake looked on with interest.

The faces of the two slaves were barely visible at the window as they observed the family embracing Darrel and Melissa. When Jonas was sure they were unhurt, he returned to Web's side. Web waited until the tight-knit group had passed the overturned wagon on its way to the mansion, then said, "All right, boys, I want you to come out now."

"Massa Web?"

"Yes, Dexter?"

"If'n we belongs to you now, then Massa Jonas cain't hurt us, right?"

"Right. Tell them, Jonas."

Hart shuddered and clenched his jaw, looking hard at Steele.

"You backing out now?" Steele half-whispered.

"I'd like to," came the heated reply, also in a half-whisper.

"You're a man of your word, Jonas. Answer Dexter's question."

Looking toward the dark faces at the window of the shed, Jonas said with sand in his voice, "Web and I have each other's word on the sale. I'm not going to harm his slaves."

"Come on," said Steele. "I'll take you to my father's plantation."

With fear evident in their faces, Dexter and Orman emerged slowly from the shed and walked cautiously toward the overturned wagon.

Jonas gripped his wounded shoulder once more and set burning eyes on the slaves. "You two better thank your lucky stars Web Steele happened along. Otherwise, you'd have gotten a beating like you've never seen in your worst nightmares. And if you had harmed my children, you'd have died at the end of a rope!"

"They still oughtta be strung up, Jonas!" thundered Reed Exley. "These two have more than over-stepped their bounds, and the way I see it, they deserve to die! When word gets out that they pulled this on you, there'll be more incidents just like it all over this county! Letting them get by with it isn't right. They need to pay for what they've done!" Even as he spoke, Exley whipped out his revolver, swung it on the slaves, and fired twice.

You'll find out what happens to Dexter and Orman, Web Steele and Abby Ruffin, Mandrake and his beautiful wife Orchid, and the wicked Reed Exley in **A Promise Unbroken** *by Al Lacy, the exciting first volume of "The Battles of Destiny" Civil War series. Available at your local Christian bookstore.*